Vinny the Vampire & Me

MAFIA, MURDER, AND MAYHEM SERIES (AS A ROM COM)

BY ELM JED

Vinny the Vampire & Me
A novel by Elm Jed
© 2022 Elm Jed

Cover Art by: S.Wolf.Art LLC
Senior Editor: Rae Bardom

ISBN: 9798774900121

To Mariah,
for the stories that were my light in the darkness

(the letter still hangs by my desk)

Content Warning

Contains darker themes, police brutality and assault,
forced hospitalization, torture and slight gore, and gun violence.

CHAPTER ONE
FUCKING VINNY

Why did my room smell like dark spices with a twinge of blood lust?

I shift my face to the window with a grumble. No warmth touches my skin; damn sun isn't even up yet. Noise drifts below from taxis, hateful people, and the occasional ambulance siren. Through the ambiance, I hear a rustle from the corner of the room.

Without thought, I react.

The Glock under my pillow snaps into my hand and aims at the disturbance. The safety clicks off, followed by some shuffling and a familiar chuckle.

"Why are you here?" I groan into my pillow.

A velvety voice speaks through the darkness of my eyelids. "Good morning to you too, *sweet cheeks*."

Switching the safety on, I keep the gun pointed at what I know is his chest. "Sun isn't even up yet, bloodsucker."

"I hate sunburns just as much as any other vampire. And you used to *love* mornings. Whatever happened to that bright disposition—"

"I'm actually going to shoot you this time," I warn.

"Aim for the heart that you always reject."

"How about the groin?" I tilt the gun ever so slightly down.

"You reject that, too. Put me out of my misery."

"Crybaby." The gun is put away under the pillow once again. My eyes remain shut, no point opening them.

The vampire shifts where he sits, and I just know he's sitting in my favorite leather chair. I just know it.

I pull the pillow from underneath my head and place it over my ears. Why did he have to do this so early? The damn vamp could stand in the sun for at least three hours before the rashes would start. Sure, after that he'd have some crispy edges, but it wouldn't *really* damage him. He'd just complain to Ma that he needed more aloe.

"You going to get up, sweet cheeks?" He asks.

"Stop calling me that; you know how I feel about it," I growl lazily. "Least let me have coffee first."

Suddenly, the aroma of my favorite dark roast drifts by my nose. Hazelnut swirl and sugary substances float past the bedcovers over my head. Peeling them back and pushing the pillow off, I open my eyes slowly. Swirls of red, violet, and blues tangle with each other in my forever weird blindness. Blips of harsh oranges flicker from outside of my window, the lamplight, an emerald with a twinge stark crimson. Contacts are going to be itchy today.

I fumble to gesture for the mug I know is waiting for me. He obliges and places the warm ceramic into my hand. Hazily, I sit up and bring the delicious drink to my lips.

"Eyesight shit this morning?" He asks.

"Everything looks like a terrible superhero film, and the director thought 'the darker, the better' to give that slight edge," I reply between sips. He chuckles at my response.

Careful not to spill my mug of "anti-murdery juicy-juice," my wretched eyes come upon the darkened figure of my unexpected houseguest.

Vincent Dracultelli, a.k.a. Vinny the Vampire, sits in my favorite leather chair. Legs crossed and mug in hands, he's a blurred vision of messed-up colors. If I had contacts in, I'd be able to see his greased-back black hair, accentuating his olive undertone skin, slightly pointed ears, and fangs. The only features that ever come through clearly are his crimson eyes. They shimmer against the plethora of disjointed colors across my vision. Just over 200 years old, but he looks barely thirty by human standards. I don't need my contacts to know he's also wearing his signature leather jacket, white V-neck shirt, and slacks. He's predictable like that. A slight squint toward his shoes, and I can see dried splatter across the dark soles.

"Those shoes better not be covered in blood."

"Old news, sweet cheeks. Issue with a member a few nights ago."

"Tell me they at least got a kick in before you kicked theirs in," I say as I take another sip. He makes the best coffee, one of the few reasons I don't put a silver bullet into his heart. Also, being my best friend helps him a bit.

"I thought you'd want me home safe and sound."

"Does this look like your home?" I rebuke. Vinny scoffs at the remark. He hates my apartment.

It was small, just how I wanted it when I moved to Topside. A studio with the bedroom practically within the kitchen, no living room apart from my leather chair. The kitchen has just enough room for a table and a few chairs. I own no electronics like a television, but my walls are lined with shelves of books, journals, and papers. With corrected vision, the apartment is painted light blue and white, chipped from its long years. My small bathroom next to my "bedroom" only has a shower, no tub. Vinny, like my family, despises the small space since I moved out over three years ago.

"I'd like it more if it wasn't Topside," he muses.

I wave him off as I lean back against the wall, otherwise known as my headboard. "Why you here, Vinny?"

"Pops sent me."

"Bullshit, he would have called and *not* have you wake me up at like 5 am," I counter.

"Group of ghouls came into Topside and the Underground. More will be moving in the next week, told him I'd give you the heads up. Since I was out..." he thinks of an alibi as I raise my brow, "...dancing?"

"Nice try. Why move to the city? They rarely ever come here."

Vinny's voice is relaxed as he explains briefly. "Got contact through Rodney from out West and South. Something happened with the two major societies, no other info than that."

"That doesn't make sense...."

"Hurricane season?"

I scowl at him. "You're off by a few months; it's May."

"I'm not the smart librarian."

"Nope, you're the dumb antique vampire. Why does this concern me? They come into Manhattan?" I ask as he leans further back into my chair. The desire to shoot him skitters across my veins....or kiss him. Damn hormones.

"They moved into one of the Bronx neutral zones. And the old-fashioned pricks hate half-breeds," he mumbles the last part.

I eye him a bit. Without my glasses, he looks like a weird lava lamp, which I keep to my own amusement. Speaking of bad eyesight, I place the mug on the nightstand with slight spillage. I can feel Vinny's gaze as I scramble through the top drawer. They come up empty of any glasses.

"Looking for these?" Turning my head, I can just barely see the glint of my glasses in his hands. Another reason to shoot him. "You were supposed to replace these weeks ago, *sweetheart*. Your eyesight will get worse."

"Ma isn't here to berate me. You taking her place?" I roll off the bed and practically fall off. Vinny starts to move but settles back into the chair as I stumble into my bathroom.

I know my apartment well enough; I could make my way to the cabinet without my contacts. Finally, I feel the container beneath my fingers. Like a pro, I open it and pop both contacts in. They itch like hell. Hues of the correct color swamp my vision as I blink furiously. A sigh leaves me as the last of everything goes to normal.

By human standards, I was blind. Paranormal standards? Still blind.

Since I could remember, my sight has always been like this. No idea if I was born with it. Colors contort into wrong hues and variations. Depth perception was like looking through a funhouse of mirrors. It mostly resembled looking through a galaxy filter, then a dark forest, and then fog, all rolled into one. Around age eight, Pops worked with our doctor to create special glasses for me to see. A few years later came the contacts. The glasses still have most of the wrong coloration, but the depth perception was mainly fixed. And Ma, like any good mother, thought it was a wonderful gift to have.

Staring at my reflection, I see the blues of the contacts. My irises are naturally a deep violet matching the dark hair that falls around my shoulders. The thick locks cover the shaved undercut of my head, but not the scars over my face and neck. Two long ugly scars run from the middle of my forehead down past my eyes to my cheekbones. Over the years, they've softened, melting into my slightly tanned skin. They were the prettiest I have compared to what riddled the rest of my body.

"You good?" Vinny calls out.

Rubbing my head, I walk out and crawl into bed, then grab my mug. His laughter makes me frown and look at the clock. "It's not even dawn, yet. Don't laugh at me, bloodsucker."

"Touchy in the mornings, aren't we?"

"You're the one who sleeps during the day, vamp tramp."

"Perhaps, you could come down to the Underground and wake me up, tit for tat." Vinny's eyes glow in amusement. Coffee or not, why did he have to show up the way that he did? Oh, right. Best friend privileges.

"I'm not the perverted vampire," I say. "You really come here just for some ghouls? On the side of town that *you* and my family say steer clear of?" He shrugs.

I roll my eyes as I step off the bed and make my way past him to the kitchen. My free hand goes to smack his head, but he catches my wrist with ease. In an instant, he brings my wrist to his nose and takes a deep breath in. "Feisty, even in your blood."

His voice makes my stomach clench. "You know what? Instead of shooting you, I'll stab you."

"Only if you lick my wounds." His eyes sparkle.

I rip my arm away and move. "Fuck you."

"When and where?"

I slam my mug on the kitchen counter. "Seriously, why have I not killed you yet?"

He chuckles. "Because I'm your best friend."

"Dick."

"Yes."

Damn him and the muscles beneath his shirt. I can see them ripple as he shifts in his seat. If his arms weren't covered in leather, I'd see his massive biceps and triceps. He stands over six feet tall and is easily ripped from his pureblood vampire genes. If he wasn't my best friend and didn't piss me off ten ways to Sunday, I'd take the offers seriously. My body certainly wanted to.

8

"My eyes are up here....*sweetheart*." I didn't notice my gaze had moved downward.

Ripping my sight upward, I see Vinny's tilted smile, and I growl at him. "You gave your message and ruined my morning; you can leave. And clean your mug before you go, or I'm telling Ma."

Vinny finishes his coffee as he stands up, toward me. "They also wanted me to remind you that it's Wednesday."

"I rarely miss the days I agreed to come visit, *especially* Wednesdays. Ma's omelets are the best." I sink into the kitchen chair and glance outside. Could the sun hurry up and scare the vampire away already?

The faucet turns on as Vinny washes his mug. Turning it off, I feel him move past me again. "Don't shoot the messenger."

"Two more minutes, and I might," I mumble.

I have no idea why he's put up with me for the past two decades. I'd been ruthless with him and pushed boundaries that no half-breed should with a vampire. He had the patience of a mother of twelve children with me. We both liked the word-sparring, and neither of us scared the other. Although, the weird sexual innuendos were only something he began when I was in college. I found more names to call him, and he found more ways to irk me. My family, on the other hand, saw it as a potential match.

Doubt it.

Vinny's a pureblood vampire. His family is one of the few pureblood lineages left in the U.S. He followed his bloodline into the family business, becoming the Blood Mafia Boss almost three years ago. Another twenty years, he'd have a Mate that his family would approve of. A half-breed human raised by incubi and succubi is not on that list.

"I could pick you up," he suggests, leaning on the counter.

"You really that concerned, or being that annoying? I can't tell this early." I sigh. "It's rare for ghouls, but—"

"They don't get along with your family."

"They don't with anyone."

"Still, Pops' business makes them angrier."

"Good thing I don't look like them." I gesture toward my scarred-up face.

Vinny's expression darkens, and his voice is stark. "Brenda."

"I said I didn't *look* like them, not that I was ugly." I lean back in my chair and huff. He and my family have spent my entire life telling me I was beautiful. Hell, Ma and Ricky would color in my scars whenever we got bored at the club. Ricky liked my facial ones with neon colors. Admittedly, so did I.

9

In the silence, I feel the first sunray peek through my window. Vinny gives a slight hiss at the stream of light. Doesn't hurt him, but his fangs still unsheathe themselves. I chuckle to myself at his reaction.

"Just stay away from the Bronx Entrances," he says as he moves further away from the light to walk out.

"Always do. Listened to you, Pops, and Joey since college. Plus, too many cops." I pause, remembering a bit of info I learned two days ago. "I was going to call you; stings are being set up near Carnegie Hall, Bedford Heights, and the zoo again."

He pauses, tilting his head at me. "How do you know that?"

A smug smile pulls at my lips. "You have your contacts; I have mine."

Crimson eyes light up with interest. Unless he wants an aloe bath later, he needs to get to the Underground quickly. Otherwise, he'd stay to probe for more answers. He opens the door and waves as he disappears into the hallway. The door locks behind him.

I look out the window and watch the slow rise of the sun over the horizon. Rays of light bounce from skyscraper to skyscraper as I pour more of the delicious coffee into my mug. My alarm goes off, and I quickly turn it off as I slump into my leather chair. Quietly, I sit by the window and watch as Topside New York City begins its day. After spending my entire life below the city, my human side needed this. It's perhaps one of the main reasons I moved to Topside. Well, another reason just walked out my door. There were many things I loved, but there's nothing like drinking coffee as the sun rises over the skyline of New York City.

Books shift in my hands as I place them on the shelf. Why do people put books on the wrong shelf? Especially when that book belongs across the aisle from where they put it. After classics such as Shakespeare, Browning, and Faust are reshelved, I ease myself down the aisle and double-check titles. Three years later, and most of the sections of the New York Public Library I knew like the back of my hand. Bookbindings are a part of my personal braille system. Although, braille itself was easier to learn.

Making it to the back of the library, I see the damage. The *Noctis Immortalis* sign has fangs and wings drawn on it. Damn teenagers.

I pass dark shelves of books as I reshelve the section. Three aisles made up the *Noctis Immortalis* section of the library. Professors and I are usually the only ones who check out the books. After centuries of living with Paranormals, you'd think humans were used to living with them. Nope, still bigots.

Noctis Immortalis is the proper term for the Paranormal Species on Earth. These days, people just use Paranormal, Creatures of the Dark, beasts, monsters…well, the last two were slander used by humans. Paranormals lived among humans for over two millennia, intersecting with them more and more. Yet, progress felt futile some days. There were no laws that you couldn't be with them, work with them, or live with them; it was just a social thing. I never understood why, but then again, I grew up with them below the city.

There were six main Noctis Immortalis: vampires, succubi and incubi, werewolves, shifters, ghouls, and daemons. A few other monsters, but rarely seen or heard of. In Topside New York City, you could find any of them on the streets if you looked hard enough or knew where to look. Except for daemons, you never see them. Daemons hated humans more than the other way around. Secluding themselves from society, even the other Paranormals didn't see them. They suffered the worst from human wrath. The others, like vampires and werewolves, learned to assimilate. Mostly.

Larger cities are sectioned out for the two main societies: Topside and the Underground. Topside was for the humans, with sunlight and all that jazz. The Underground was for the Paranormals, with tunnels and landscape below and its own starlight. Rome, Los Angeles, and London are among many with this setup. New York is the most well-known for its function.

The library remains quiet as I move to another section. My long black skirt shuffles around my legs. Rubbing my hand over my neck, I feel where my black turtleneck bunches underneath. Hair down and my soft boots hide any noise from me. I probably look like a proper Gothic Victorian ghost.

Making it back to my desk, I sit down and feel the Desert Eagle hidden beneath my skirts as it digs into my hip. I shift my weight and go to work as the minutes begin to tick by until Janice's voice comes up in front of me.

"Detective Drauper is back, I just saw him," her light voice carries in a small whisper. I shift my gaze past the petite blonde. Toward the stairs, sure enough, Detective Louis Drauper is coming up the stairs.

Dark sunglasses cover the brown eyes underneath. He has short tight curly hair buzzed on the sides. His deep copper skin stands out against his cream-colored long-sleeved shirt. The brown leather jacket he always wore is missing, but his badge and dark jeans complete his "don't screw with me" vibe. Actually, the lean muscles that make him move fluidly did enough for that.

A slight heat down in my nether region raises a bit, which causes me to rub my legs together underneath my desk.

"You should ask him out," Janice whispers.

"*You* should go back to work," I retort as I place some papers into a pile.

She giggles, wiggling her eyebrows at me. I force a smile for her before she leaves. My smile switches to friendly as Drauper comes up to me. It's not hard to do. The past year working with him on and off, my entire body would heat up at the sight of him, especially when he brings forth his award-winning smile, which he has as he approaches.

"Brenda, you look wonderful today," his deep voice vibrates through my skin. He takes his glasses off to reveal bright mahogany eyes, large and inviting. I shake my feelings off and concentrate on what he wants.

"Thanks. What can I help with today?"

"Straight to work, I see."

"Well, you do always come in for advice on Paranormals," I answer. "*And* every time I oblige."

Drauper walks around my desk and sits on the edge of it. His tight jeans set directly in my line of sight. Along with something else. This is going to be distracting.

I lean further back into my chair and cross my arms. My eyes shift upward in question and meet his intense shining look. My legs want to squirm under my skirt. Between the vampire and hot detective, I wasn't sure who's worse to have these reactions toward.

He moves back a little and lets up on his intense gaze. "What do you know about ghouls?"

Aw shit.

NYPD must have caught wind of the newbies in town. Suddenly, I'm glad Vinny had come by this morning. Not that I'm ever going to admit that to him. I'd never be able to sleep in again.

"Enough," I answer. He nods for me to continue. "They really don't teach any of you about Paranormals? Seriously, add it into the budget."

"Knowing about those beasts is NIIA and PSB's job, not NYPD," he says flatly. Keeping my expression calm, I nod in acknowledgment. Today is not the day to start a fight with him. His tone is enough warning for me.

NIIA is the Noctis Immortalis International Agency, which oversees everything with the Paranormals across the globe and determines the laws that protect them. PSB is the U.S. version, Paranormal Security Bureau. Wanting to keep all of society safe, just, and fair, they were developed to take care of anything Paranormal. It also kept racist humans from throwing every Paranormal into prison or giving the death penalty. Last line of defense.

I shuffle some papers and sigh. "They're classist." I receive a confused stare. "They have tiers within their communities. Revived into this or that, you stay there, like a caste system. They kind of apply this to other Paranormals, too, but of course, they think they're above them all."

"I thought all those monsters had a class system?"

"*Paranormals...*" I say harshly. "...kind of do, but there's no real repercussions if someone goes outside that ranking system. Some families encourage it. Most Paranormals believe interspecies Mating is for better health. Then again, *some* want to keep their bloodlines untarnished. Depends on the family and community. It's become more accepted in the past century for *most* Paranormals to intermingle bloodlines."

Drauper crosses his arms as he listens. "Ghouls are more particular?"

"Yeah, they think they're above *everyone*. Since they're disliked, they live amongst themselves. Usually, in damp or humid environments. Not uncommon to find them in swamps. Most live down south in the U.S. The wetter, the better."

"Ghouls and humidity?" His brows scrunch together. I laugh at his reaction, which makes him look more perturbed. The first time you learn that something considered undead likes humid places takes you for a loop.

"Their skin dries easily. Comes from being, well, bloodless." A shiver goes over Drauper.

Ghouls aren't the prettiest or friendliest of the Noctis Immortalis. Their skin varies from olive green, dark teal, and faded grey. They have large black eyes and ginger hair that hangs matted and long. It always looked wet to me, no matter how dry they were. Yet, no uglier than the drunks I've passed walking home late.

"Explains why they're rarely in the city. Plus, summer is starting," he mumbles heard as he scratches his non-existent beard.

"Yeah, that's odd...." More than odd, if a new group came in, it would have been in April or March. My stomach clenches for a moment as I realize Vinny may have been right on caution. Again, not admitting that to him.

"What else?" Drauper asks. I shove my fingers through my thick hair, careful not to show the undercut.

Not many within Topside know about my past, where I come from, or what I was. Half-breeds aren't exactly welcome where the sun shines. The library was open on who they hired, but I didn't want to risk it. Besides, people always act weird when they realize I am one. The worst experience was in college when I came up to Topside for school. A professor found out and tried to have me kicked out of the literature program due to "inability to understand the fundamentals of human psychology." Vinny took care of the professor, and most of my records were erased after. The scars kept people away, scaring them to keep their distance. Carefully over the last few years on Topside, I cultivated a persona that was almost the opposite of who I was Underground.

"They don't like being around humans or half-breeds," I start. "They love rotten food; moldier, the better. Honestly, they may be good for some parts of the city for food control."

Drauper laughs slightly at my comment. "So, these are undead beings with a sense of privilege over others?" This time I laugh.

He isn't wrong. "They get finicky with traditions. Sometimes they come off cruel because of it and what they protect. Not much different from humans protecting their families. They'll just screw with you before trying to kill you since they can bring you back from the dead."

"Speaking from experience?" His question throws me. My eyes widen as I look up at him. His careful gaze slides over my facial scars.

The scars simultaneously keep people away and invite questions. Humans always seem to think they're the work of Paranormals. I have no idea. My body is covered in them, and I don't know where or who they came from. Due to this, I had a hard time in college the first few years. Most of that time, I commuted from the Underground until I went back to get my masters. Even then, I lived on Rodney's property: The Wolf Mob Boss and my other best friend.

The humans I know up here only understood a few things about me.

One: I was partially blind with scars.

Two: I was a loner and demure.

Three: I had no family.

Four: I preferred books over people. Kind of true.

"The scars aren't from them," I respond with a steady voice.

A long breath of air leaves him, which sounds like relief for some reason. After almost a year working with the detective, he still tries to find out what happened to my face. Thank goodness for turtlenecks, long sweaters, and leggings. Otherwise, the barrage of questions about the rest would make me throw back a barrel of whiskey.

"I've encountered ghouls in the past, but nothing bad. Mainly just passing by or when I first started school," I fib a little. "What about you?"

"Here and there. Small demeanors, but only for questioning or when PSB needs to hold them in one of our cells. Most of my work encounters are with vampires, incubi, and the occasional werewolf."

NYPD could only arrest Paranormals if one: a PSB agent is present, two: they issue a special warrant, or three: they break a major law outside the neutral zones. Mob business fell under breaking a major law, so it's mostly conducted inside neutral zones.

"That's what you get for being on this side of town, then," I say and give him a small grin. He grins back. "Why all the ghoul questions? This is a first."

Drauper stands up, brushing down his shirt. His large hands move over his torso and shuffle something in his back pockets. "Nothing for you to worry about."

I narrow my eyes at him. "That's *reassuring*, detective."

His award-winning smile comes back, and he places his sunglasses on. Patting my desk, he turns to exit from the library. He pauses and looks back. "You remember what I told you last week? To stay away from Bedford Heights, Carnegie Hall, and the zoo?"

I tap my head. "Didn't forget. Besides, I never venture that way much. Doubt you'll catch me in any of your...*operations*," I tease with a wink.

His wide smile sparkles. A quick wave, and he turns for the stairs. My body slumps back into the chair as my eyes don't tear away from his ass. In *those jeans*.

Raking my fingers through my hair again, I let out a long sigh. Why did I have to be attracted to the detective? Bad news all around.

I try to concentrate on academic journals on werewolves and their significance with agriculture and farming, but my mind keeps drifting. Drauper *never* asks about anything besides the vampires, incubi, and werewolves because of the precinct he's a part of. It's how we were introduced.

NYPD had been looking for info about communities in the Underground, and a coworker recommended me as a resource. That week I had at least ten meetings with cops about vampires, incubi, and werewolves. My Masters of Paranormal History, Literature, and Anthropology intrigued many humans for my wide berth of knowledge. Even the police chief came to see me. Seriously, NYPD needed classes for its members about these other beings. The only one who frequently met with me was Detective Drauper. He always had a reason to come by and ask more questions. Or just to check in on me in his free time.

It's probably what I deserved for acting like the naïve, nice librarian with the facial scars. Other than people steering clear of me, staring at my face, or asking rude-ass questions, the scars made people pity me. I was used to it, a reality that came with the territory. The Underground was more accepting than Topside, where humans admire perfection. Scars do not equal that.

I moved to Topside to find the answer to the age-old question of "Where do I belong?" And maybe, just maybe, I'd educate a few humans with some empathy toward Paranormals before my next step. What that next step was, I had no fucking clue. So far, I've only gotten through to the detective…kind of. Even worse, I had the hots for him, and that made things difficult most days.

Except, it did make me smile whenever I thought about my relationship with the NYPD and the detective. My knowledge of Paranormals came not only from books but experience. They had no idea they were speaking to the only daughter of Alanzo Cuorebella, Incubi Mafia Boss of the Underground.

Stupid skirt got caught up, ripping from the damn grate. The metal sticks out from the somewhat smooth sidewalk. Quickly looking down at the hem, I notice the hole.

Great. Ma is gonna want to fix that. Usually, I change before visiting home, but I got off work late. The talk with Drauper hadn't eased my nerves either. It took all my strength not to call and check in with Pops or Vinny. Anytime Drauper brought up NYPD movement, my stomach rolled. I've lived my entire life steering clear of them. Now I speak to a detective frequently and have the hots for him.

Slightly disgruntled, I make my way to the Underground Entrance. The Manhattan Entrance looms above me, its black onyx archway built between two streets. The Paranormals' language, Noctora, is carved into its length. A couple of lamplights illuminate either side of the 40-foot-wide entrance that resembles an alleyway. Technically, it was.

A few shifters walk out of the entrance and give me a quick look. They recognize me and flash their pointed teeth in glee before they disappear down the sidewalk. Just before the shadows conceal them, I see them shift into human form. Apart from most half-breeds blending in with humans, shifters were next in the ability to camouflage. Shifters have reptilian aspects when in their natural form, with skin tones ranging from light teal to pale violet. They have white ivory hair and pointed, serrated teeth. Their bodies were lean, tall, and fluid-like which resembling serpents. And glowing snake eyes of gold or silver. Back in my teens, I had a slight obsession with their unearthly movements.

I pass through the entrance and climb into the elevator. The spiral staircase is for last resort only, and when my skirt isn't ripped. Punching the down button, I go below. The last of twilight disappears through the skylight of the elevator walls. The world shifts as I pass the subway system and tunnels. Within minutes, I'm below Topside and in the Underground. Buildings are formed into the ceiling, serving a dual purpose: hold up the city and create corridors. The corridors weren't much of streets, as they were brick pathways. Most Paranormals walked, ran, or flew when down here. The sky–or *ceiling*–was wired with lights to emulate stars and sunlight. During their own day–human's *night*–they turn on.

The elevator lands, and I walk out onto the Underground paths. Most buildings were brick and stone, with blacks, greys, and reds sparkling against the dim lighting. Lamplights of soft yellows and oranges flicker. Without my contacts, the Underground reminded me of a Van Gogh painting. A soft ambiance of cool colors and deep earthy tones. Home.

My heels click against the stone as I pass shops and the restaurants. Signs flicker on, and the neighborhood begins to wake up. A quick look up, I see apartments above the establishments wake up with their lights inside. Coming upon the walkway toward my home, I turn down the path. Jazz music drifts alongside soft pop as bars shut down for their day. Near the end of the path stands my childhood home, *Unbound,* a strip club and bar my parents have owned for over two centuries.

Amber lights flash the club's name with a pink tint around its sides. One of the bouncers, Darius, stands outside next to the crimson suede front entrance. Darius' shitkicker boots make him look even taller. He doesn't need it with the amount of muscle he has. A larger Incubi than most, his deep maroon skin shifts in the light as he turns and meets me with cerulean eyes and a white smile.

"Look who's home," he speaks in his deep velvet tone. Others would have creamed their pants at the sound of it. Me? Not so much. My range of immunities includes incubi seduction tactics.

Incubi and succubi could manipulate hormones and emotions. The effect happens when they release a secretion into the air or just their voices. The stronger ones, like Pops, could influence terror, anger, and other emotions. They're mostly known for their sexual tendencies, but they also help keep moods elevated. Instant serotonin boosters, if you will. Made them great therapists and social workers.

Darius flutters out his bat-like wings, pushing the door open for me. The lights inside glint off the two small horns on his forehead. I smile back and say, "Can't miss Ma's omelets."

The club is in change-over mode. It's mostly a 24/7 club, running open during night and day hours for different clientele. Bartenders wipe down the long bar and tables that scatter across the venue. The last of the strippers gather money off the dancing stages throughout the club. Others are cleaning off tables, chairs, poles, and couches. I tiptoe my way past them, trying not to cause more trouble for cleanup. The lights switch from deep scarlet over to a light amber as I make my way toward the back. My hip slams into a table as my brother calls out.

"Sis! You're almost late." Ricky's light and airy voice carries through the soft ambiance.

He's near the door to the apartment. His long black hair pulled into a braid, horns sticking out through the mesh of strands. His sangria complexion glows a deeper shade from the amber lights. As I come up, his large blue eyes flash with amusement. My brother is more of a slender build with soft facial features like Ma. He wears his favorite black mesh shirt and slacks, always well-dressed with a hint of personal style.

"I'm not late. Never am," I counter.

He sniffs the air with an exaggerated gesture. The grin he plasters on worries me. "Still a virgin? Damn, Ma is gonna be disappointed."

Rolling my eyes at him, I ask, "Who told you? Or was it the get-up?" I point at my skirt.

"You may be immune, but your hormones aren't. And *you* were worked up today." He takes a breath in. "Twice." I glare at him. More amusement dances over his eyes. "Any beings I know? That I'm *willing* to know?"

"Don't even, Ricky…."

He takes another long breath in, and I watch his gaze shimmer in glee. Damn it.

"I hate you and your incubi senses," I say as he brings me into a close embrace. "I'm in trouble the day it happens."

"Oh, Ma is gonna get a hold of your panties and pin them up over the main stage for *weeks*." Ricky turns me around and points toward the center of the main stage. My body shudders at the thought of it. With some luck, I could switch out the panties with a pair of clean ones beforehand.

Succubi and incubi traditions were specific, celebrating all stages of sensuality, sexuality, and body acceptance. And sometimes, they just sucked. Amazingly this isn't one of the reasons why I was still a 27-year-old virgin, but it didn't speed things up.

I twist from his grasp as he chuckles. Crossing my arms, I threaten. "Help her steal them and I'll rip up your favorite shirts."

"To finally see them up, I'd let you go after my whole closet."

"Bullshit, you'll cry."

"Maybe, but Ma will at least buy me new clothes if I help her."

"By the fucking starlight…" I groan loudly. "You're supposed to be on my side."

"What happened to you being excited about this tradition? It's all you talked about in your late teens." He tilts his head with furrowed brows.

"Nothing. People just change and have different priorities," I deflect. He tries to press for more, but I shove his shoulder, which does nothing. He barely moves. Stupid Paranormals and their super strength.

Ricky sighs, ruffling my hair as he walks past. I walk through the doorway and leave my shoes lined up against the wall with the others. Dim bulbs light the way up the stairs toward the apartment entrance. I enter the warm home with a deep breath. The smell of cooked eggs, toast, bacon, and spices fill my nose. Coffee and Pops' special creamer adds to the joy of the aromas that enthrall my senses. I look upon the yellow walls and dark mahogany trim throughout the foyer as I quietly make my way through. Pictures of my brothers and me line a good portion of the hallway.

My family home is a four-bedroom apartment with a large living room, dining room, and kitchen. Pops had it custom-built when the club was done. The living room comes into view with its dark green couch, coffee table, bookshelves, and television. Pops sits in the middle of the sofa with a newspaper in hand. A quick glimpse and I see Ma's figure move past the kitchen window. She shuffles about as she prepares the upcoming meal. My feet scuff the carpet as I lean in to watch her work. A smile pulls at my lips at the scene, but the slight noise alerts my father.

Pops looks up and grins, quickly putting the newspaper away as he stands to greet me. Bright violet eyes meet mine, contrasting against his dark maroon skin. His thick onyx hair already greased back for the day, his horns protruding through the mass.

"My baby girl." His soft voice lulls my bones to ease, exactly what I need after my long day.

"Hardly that anymore, Pops," I speak softly, not to alert Ma yet.

"Vinny come see you?" His brows furrow, and his arms cross over his broad chest.

"Yeah…you actually sent him?"

"You listen to him." Most of the time, I did. "Ghouls are no joke, baby girl."

"I know, Pops. I know." He nods with brows still furrowed. I can tell something else is on his mind. Instead, he switches his tone to something less stern.

His eyes shine as he searches over me like he always does whenever I come home to visit. Ever since college, Pops always made sure I was safe and sound. I understood why, so I let him scan over my features like he's surveying for more scars to appear.

Being a half-breed, his only daughter, and the child of a mafia boss, Pops had every right to feel protective of me. His own business isn't as dangerous as Vinny's or Rodney's, but it took some finagling for him to allow me to move to Topside without escorts everywhere. There's a reason I always have more than one weapon on me.

"Is that a two-piece?" He finally breaks the silence. I lift the turtleneck a little. "Didn't have those back in the day. Is that hem ripped?"

"Grate from Topside. I'll have Ma look at it. Otherwise, I'll stitch it up in the next day or so," I respond with a glance at the hem. The hole seems bigger.

"You've got clothes to change into in your old room. Ma will take care of it; we both know it." He grins and moves forward to hug me. My face becomes buried in his shoulder, and I take a deep breath. Pops always smells of Havana cigars, cinnamon, and whiskey. Deep and suave like he was through and through. An incubus made to soothe anyone's nerves, even without the hormone powers. For a slight moment, I find myself holding onto him a bit longer than usual. Pops feels it.

His strong arms keep me against him as I breathe in again. One of his hands runs down my back softly. "You okay, baby girl?"

Either the discussions earlier today rattled me more than I'd admit, or it was Ricky's question. Both made my mind wonder about what I was doing with my life. I didn't have the strength to tell Pops about it now, though. "Yeah, just a long day. Glad to be home."

I pull away and give a reassuring smile. His thumb comes up and rubs against my cheek, gently tracing over one of my scars. The warm smile doesn't falter from his expression even as the front door opens behind me.

"Are we being haunted?" I narrow my eyes at Joey as he comes up beside us.

Joey, my eldest brother, is the spitting image of Pops. Slightly more built, but he has the same violet eyes and black hair. His eyes shimmer with a taunting smile, and I want to punch him. Did I ever win a fistfight with him? Not really, but it doesn't hurt to try.

"You finally took the librarian role seriously," he says and the frown on my face only makes him tease me more. "Won't hide the fact you used to be a stripper, sis."

"You know what, Joey, *fu*—"

Pops' hand moves over my mouth as he warns. "Don't even think it. Ma is in the other room, and she'll wash that mouth out with soap."

I sloppily mumble "sorry" against his palm. Pops pulls it away and wipes my saliva against his dark slacks. His black shirt and button-up need to stay clean for business hours today. A crooked smile rises across my lips like the only favorite daughter I was. I receive a kiss on the forehead for it.

"Suck up," Joey mutters as he walks past to set the dining table.

Pops turns to follow as I head for my old bedroom when the smell of dark spices slams into my nose. His stupid voice reaches from behind, "I remember that time period, but I think you need a corset."

Instinctively, I reach for the Glock inside my bag. I don't turn to look as I point the weapon at Vinny's chest. Tense muscles push me to click the safety off, but I don't. Slowly, I look behind me to see my barrel is aimed exactly where I want it to be. Vinny's smile is small but satisfied.

"What are you doing here?" I ask.

"Waiting for you to shoot me and put me out of my heartbreak misery." He reveals his fangs slightly.

Not only do my eyes roll at that line, but my entire head does.

I put the gun away harshly and head down the hall. Vinny chuckles deeply as I disappear into my room and shut the door. My back leans against it as I take a deep breath. I could feel the heat rise deep in my gut at the thought of that smile on his face. A certain joy and calmness wash over me as well.

Shaking off the latent feelings, I change out of my clothes. My old room is a replica of my apartment. Bookshelves line the walls, a few knives here and there, binders filled with papers, and random stuffed animals that don't make the cut to be on the bed, which Ma has already laid clothes on. Looking at the rumpled mess in my bag, I agree with her pick.

Swiftly taking off my work clothes, I change into black slacks and remove my turtleneck, revealing the small lace bra underneath. I pull my hair up into a messy bun, showing off my undercut. Reaching for the green button-up shirt, I see my reflection in the mirror. Scars cover my upper body with marks that resemble burns, frostbite, slashes, and bites that scatter up past my collarbone onto my neck. The rest travel down my arms like a fucked-up tribal tattoo. Most of the deeper scars are across my chest, stomach, and back. They're visibly whiter against my tanned skin.

Dropping the green button-up, I take the black tank-top instead. Honestly, I feel safest showing the carnage of my body among my family, including Vinny.

There's a knock at the door, and before I can answer, Ma enters with a bright smile. Carmen Cuorebella, my Ma, has a lighter cherry complexion with longer horns than the rest of the family. Her hair shimmers with blue hues against ebony strands, pulled up into a messy bun revealing her undercut. Her bright blue eyes, where Ricky got his, sparkle toward me and then my skirt.

"Grate caught the bottom," I say and gesture to the hole.

"Oh, baby, I can fix that right up." Ma comes into the room and snatches the garment from my hands. I know better than to argue. She only needs five minutes to fix it when I'd need an hour. Home Ec wasn't my forte.

"Heard you had a long day, baby." Ma's voice is sultry. It rocks you and can make any Paranormal become her servant in a moment. Her delicate hands match the voice along with her well-endowed chest. She strokes back a stray hair behind my ear.

"Already talk to Pops?" I ask.

"No, but you confirmed my suspicions." A curse almost escapes me. Damn, I walked right into that one.

"I'm fine, Ma," I say, quickly turning to place the turtleneck into my bag.

"Baby, talk to me. You're usually sparring with your brothers by now. You and Ricky would be halfway through a wrestling match."

"You missed a quick one downstairs. So, not far off." Usually, I'd tell Ma whatever was wrong. I didn't have the energy today.

She narrows her eyes at me. "What about then?"

"You hanging my panties up downstairs—"

Ma's hands cup my face with delighted eyes. "Did you—?"

"No Ma!" I silence her with a shout. Hopefully, it doesn't carry outside of my room. This conversation doesn't need to be heard by other members of the family or Vinny the Vampire. "We were just talking about traditions or whatever."

She folds her arms over her chest. "Is there any prospect of when this may occur?"

"No, Ma."

"What about—?"

"Can we not talk about this now?" I plead.

"I just want to be prepared for this sacred tradition for you, baby."

"Sacred?" I force a smile. Her brow goes up slightly as my head slightly rolls with my eyes again. "It is a little weird, Ma…"

"Not to succubi and incubi it isn't. And you used to be excited about it when you were younger. It marks an important date into the next stage of life."

"I'm not a succubus, though." The swift change of Ma's expression clenches my heart. Oh, shit, that did it. Water instantly wells up in her eyes. My stupid mouth went and did it. "Ma, that's not what I meant…."

Quickly, I put my arms around the only mother I had in my life. She places her arms around me as I rest my head on her chest. Fingers clutch my back as scents of roses, cherries, and perfume fill my nostrils. Her soft skin presses against my jagged marks.

Like Pops, Ma is the safe space I need. Biologically, they weren't my parents, but they were in every other sense of the definition. Most of my heart and soul were filled with love for them, even when I spoke like a dumbass. My entire being loves them so much, and they know it, but after I moved out, Ma still worries. The changes I made since then haven't helped ease that.

"You are part of this family, no matter what," she whispers in my ear. "You are my daughter."

"I know, Ma. I wouldn't have it any other way."

"That includes family traditions, ceremonies, family business…"

"I know, Ma, I know."

"… even the panties. I want to show the world how proud I'll be when that day happens. Showcase your own discovery and happiness," her voice quivers the last few words.

Damn, if Pops finds out I made Ma cry, I'll be grounded for weeks. Even not living at home, he'll still make it happen.

After a few moments, my head nods into her chest in agreement. She holds me a moment longer, then releases me. As I step back, delicate fingers brush back stray hairs again. Just like Pops, she gazes over the scars on my face. Only for a moment before she scrunches her brows together.

23

"You need new contacts."
Mother knows best.

Most days, I love my brothers. Today I hate them.

The last part of dinner had been hell. My brothers were on their usual antics of reminding everyone about my childhood. Should be good, but not when most of the stories revolve around stripper's glitter and lube. Vinny being part of the jocularity made it worse. Mainly because he was there for most of the "adventures."

"She ran naked for like five blocks," Joey laughs.

"Better than the time she discovered lube and wanted to use it in her hair," Ricky adds.

If I break my fork, I'd find a way to pay back Ma. The slight growl in the back of my throat doesn't deter them.

"Oh yeah? What about when she tried the pole for the first time?" Joey smiles slyly at me. "Your legs were so uncoordinated."

"Shut up, Joey," I say, I'd kick him, but he's just out of reach from me.

"Didn't Gina teach her first?" Vinny asks.

"Nah, it was another dancer," Ricky answers. "She left a few years back when she was fully rehabilitated."

"Glenda," I mutter.

"Right!" Ricky points his fork in amusement. "It was *Gina* who taught her the other moves."

"Make it stop," I groan.

"Now, now," Pops speaks in his low voice. I really hope he's coming to my rescue. "She mastered the pole by the time she was fourteen. Almost as good as any succubi." Nope, betrayal by Pops.

"You know... " Vinny's smile is taunting as he looks over at me, "...I do miss your shows. You did get rather good."

"All in the past."

"Are you sure about that, *Brenda*?" The slow draw of my name makes my legs shiver. His dark eyes catch mine. I rub my legs together under the table and keep my face passive. *Best friend, nothing else, best friend.*

"*Mio cavaliere,*" Ma chastises Pops with a smile. "Enough, you've been poking at your poor sister for almost an hour." Ma shoos away their conversation. At least she has my back.

"Thanks, Ma."

I wasn't ashamed of my past with the strip club below, but it was something I was trying to leave behind. My brothers made it hard some days when they brought it back up. Even harder when you're the only child in the family for like fifty years.

Ricky and Joey were already past the age of fifty by the time I came along. Paranormals come into maturity by twenty. They were adults as I went through childhood, so embarrassing anecdotes to swing back at them. Not only that, after turning seven, I was quite the wild child. Childhood stories span from running naked through the streets to playing in a puddle of lubricant. A story I will never live down due to my curious self. It's what I deserve for growing up with incubi brothers and a strip club downstairs.

The perks? Good sex education, consent, self-love, and body image acceptance. But nothing on Topside could scar me like seeing a stripper do the spread eagle with a pearl thong for the first time. Lessons were learned.

The rest of the meal goes quietly. I gather the plates for Ma, then Ricky washes the dishes as Joey dries. Partial punishment for not leaving me alone with their teasing. Kissing Ma on the cheek, I fling a dish towel at my brothers. All three of us stick our tongues out, and they laugh as I leave the kitchen.

My ears perk up as I hear hushed voices from the foyer. Vinny and Pops stand near the front door. Carefully, I keep to the dining room but can't help listening.

"You sure about this?" Vinny asks.

"I need to do what I must for my family and business," Pops answers shortly.

"Does that include a curb war?"

"This has been *my domain* for over two hundred years, ghouls or not. Doddard will be taken care of."

"Come on, Alanzo, you know he was doing what he thought was best." Vinny eases his hushed tone.

"He's spineless, and I'm a fool for putting him in that position."

"Some people change, for better or worse," Vinny argues. "Let me talk to my father, see if he knows more. Perhaps he'll—"

Pops grunts in disapproval. "When has Bruno done anything for us? The neighborhood? Or anyone outside *your* family?"

My spine stiffens at the thought of Vinny's father. A shiver runs across my arms as I push back old memories of the ex-Mafia Blood Boss. I don't fear much of anything in the Underground, but Bruno made that shortlist.

"He may have—"

"It's yours now, Vincent. You've protected this community when he didn't. Don't go back on your word. The only reason I agree to work with—"

"Brenda, baby, do you want leftovers?" Ma's voice carries through the apartment and shuts the secret conversation down.

26

The front door opens and closes as I let out a sigh. "Not today, Ma." I finish cleaning up the dining room and shake off the weird feeling.

Pops only worked with the Blood Mafia in the past because he had to. His business and the Blood Mafia flourished when Vinny took full control over three years ago. Even though the werewolves hate the vamps, they got along a shit ton better, too. Ever since Bruno stepped down, a lot of things got fucking better for the mob families down below.

I watch television with Ma and Ricky. Ma's hand rests on my knee, her thumb caressing it slowly. A small smile blooms over me as I see her serene one. My parents are overly affectionate, and both are probably the most powerful in the Underground. They thrive on physical touch like they depend on it, especially with me. They've been overprotective ever since Pops brought me home. Joey and Ricky are, too. They just show their love a little differently.

Vinny and Pops' conversation rattles in my mind as I try to concentrate on the show. Something is wrong, more than just some ghouls who came into the city. And why bring up Doddard, Pops' second in the business? Time flies by as I try to make sense of things, with no answers as I begin to leave.

Cinnamon and whiskey invade my nostrils as Pops hugs me tightly goodbye, followed by Ma. I had moved to Topside, trying to understand what I wanted, but leaving them made that difficult. They're only a phone call or an elevator ride away, but still.

I leave after reassuring Pops I'll stay away from the Bronx Entrances. Soft jazz flows over the stairs as I head down and put my shoes on. Lights shift from an erotic to an easy-going atmosphere. Mimosas, small plates, and morning pastries float around for brunch. The first patrons of shifters, vampires, and humans are already gathering. This isn't the time for the sensual succubi and incubi, not yet. The ones who are here permeate the air with relaxation. Almost wish I'd get that effect.

The music cuts off as the entrance door shuts behind me. Darius is gone, but a new incubi bouncer stands in his place along with Joey, whose heel is kicked up against the brick wall.

"Thought I'd walk you home," he says, and his dimples show a little with a smile.

"You mean to the Entrance, you better after all that teasing." I offer my arm to him. He obliges and hooks his arm with mine.

"Hey, those were good times," he says in a soft voice. "Things were simpler back then. You as a kid and here at home."

A deafening silence comes between us as the lights twinkle above with each passing step and shops open. Paranormals bustle about with their business, and the occasional human walks the paths. Anyone else would love this calm atmosphere, but it drives me up a fucking wall.

"Alright," I say. "Spill it. What's going on?"

"I don't know—"

"Don't try that big brother bullshit on me."

"Look, sis, business is business. You know how it is."

"Joey, you've kept it straight with me before."

"Yeah, I know." He pauses. "Nothin' to worry about."

"I overheard Vinny and Pops earlier."

He stops, and his eyes widen. "What did you hear?"

"Oh, so there is something?" I raise a brow as I fold my arms over my chest. He swears a little. Sometimes Ma's tactics work for me, too. "Something about the ghouls, Doddard, and keeping Bruno out of it."

"You said years ago you didn't want to be part of what goes on."

"Pops decided that for me far longer than I ever did," I counter. "Not like I don't know."

"Not the same, Brenda."

"Come on, Joey," I push on. "I may not be part of the business, but if there's something up, *especially* with ghouls, you should tell me. Bruno was even brought up. Vinny never fucking brings him up in business."

"Not around you."

"Well, yeah…Bruno wants me back in that sewer." The scowl on Joey's face contorts into pure disdain. I wave it off. "Fine, no talking of Bruno. What about Doddard?"

Joey shrugs. "He fucked up." He gestures for me to continue walking. His hand rests on the small of my back. Easing us past some Paranormals, most of them smile and look content. I know why.

"Your aroma isn't gonna help you," I mutter.

"You and your fucking immunities. I can't use any tricks on you," Joey laughs low. "Then again…" I know what he's thinking. *If you weren't immune, I'd never have a sister.* None of them would say that because the thought of me not being around tore at their hearts.

Pops found me in the sewers, closer to the Manhattan side, underneath one of the Bronx Entrances. I was barely five, covered in wounds, partially blind, shaved, and covered in sewage. Pops thought I was a boy at first, approaching me carefully in hopes his powers didn't affect me badly. It was only when he got me home to Ma, they realized it didn't affect me at all. I was immune to everything. Almost.

Incubi and succubi don't affect me with aromas or hormone control. Vampires can't turn me with a bite, neither can werewolves. Any powers from other Paranormals for mind control don't work either. Anything that's meant to have the leg up on humans or other Paranormals didn't do shit. Ghouls couldn't change me. One bite can turn a human into the undead, but I don't have that problem. My immunities were discovered through weird circumstances, testing, and nasty playdates as a kid. No one knew why, not even our doctor, Charlene. I'm an anomaly.

I was tested as a kid to prove that I'm a half-breed, but the Paranormal part is dormant. Without anyone from my bloodline, there's no way to see what species of Paranormal I am, what my lifespan could be, or when the dormant genes would awaken. If ever.

But they kept me. Ma and Pops raised me as their own daughter, and my brothers took me in with open arms. They were my family through and through. More reason to want to know what the hell was going on.

"Joey, tell your baby sis what's happening," I prod again.

He sighs. "You heard all about the ghouls? Vinny warned you?"

"Yeah," I grumble to myself. Damn vamp and his need to wake me up before dawn. Joey looks at me funny, and I wave him off. "Ghouls came into town, got it."

"More are coming in next week."

"More?"

"Yeah. And they're taking up residence in the Bronx." He pauses and shifts the hand on my upper back. "Doddard sold Pops' apartment complex to them."

I screech to a halt. My mouth drops, and my eyes widen. "What?"

There are two reasons I'm told to stay clear of the Bronx. One: It's mostly a neutral zone, which means PSB is everywhere. PSB is great for the Paranormals, but not when you're associated with the mafia. Human or not, governments and agencies don't like them. And two: mob routes are everywhere. Most of the mafia business runs through the Bronx and larger zones in NYC. The Bronx has the most routes and tunnels. Neutral zones are safer to do business in because if you do get caught, you'd be under PSB jurisdiction, not NYPD. Anything is better than being caught by human agencies. Due to all of this and being a half-breed, which neither agency ever wants to help or deal with, I stay the fuck away.

The Bronx is also riddled with safe houses for those part of or saved by the mafia. Pops' business centers around that. He gives protection to Paranormals and humans alike, especially those he pulls from sex-trafficking rings and slave auctions. Pops deals in the black market, but he does it to get others to freedom.

"Doddard didn't tell him until after he sold the safehouses," Joey runs his hand through his hair. "I already have new places lined up for when we get our next batch of survivors, but it disrupts a shit ton of stuff. Plus, selling to ghouls?"

I let out a sigh as we continue walking. "What's Pops gonna do?"

"Knock Doddard a few pegs down," he growls low.

"Is Pops gonna…?"

He gives me a side glance. "Do you really want me to tell you what he decides?" A shiver goes down my spine.

I shake my head. "Okay, *that* part of the business, I'll stay out of."

Joey is quiet for a moment, then whispers, "Can't take the buildings back, not without causing an uproar from the Ghoul Society. They're the lowest class, sis. So, when we say stay away from the Bronx Entrances, we mean it."

"I know, I know," I say and wave him off. Half-breeds aren't liked by many, but no one hates them more than ghouls. Why? Who the fuck knows. I should since I've studied every Paranormal species. The bigger issue with the lowest class, they're like rabid raccoons sometimes. Most come from criminal families and rapists and thought it'd be better to bring back full graveyards of people. When it comes to the classist high view, they are the worst.

"Vinny and Rodney, for once, I think, will work together for protections," Joey explains as we come up to the elevators. "Mainly for those still living in the area. They've already started to spread outside the zones. We gotta handle this carefully, or NYPD will try to push past their jurisdiction. Try to be like heroes to the humans still in the area."

I scoff. "Let me guess, PSB won't be part of it?"

"Ghouls haven't done anything, so why would they? And Pops isn't gonna let them. This is mafia business, not their shit. And Vinny has his own to take care of, especially with PSB and NIIA."

"They already know about that racket, definitely the *blood* part."

"Well yeah, that's how those Paranormal fuckers in PSB get their own snacks." Joey smirks.

I cross my arms and tilt my head. "Then why is Vinny so upset? Not just because of some ghouls causing issues. That's not his route."

His eyes glow for a moment. "Not for me to tell you."

"So, there is more. Always is…."

"You've always known there's more than we can tell you or that smartass of a friend of yours," Joey expression softens, and I smirk. "He likes you too much to show you all that." I roll my eyes and almost flip him off. "Come on, sis—"

"Sounds about right for him to keep secrets from me, the territorial, overprotective vamp. My perverted best friend of twenty years is a *real* treat."

Joey teases, "I thought Rodney was."

"Shh, don't tell him. The wolf will cry." A deep rumbling laugh rises from him. Joey is the seductive incubus that gives you the high that replicates a bar filled with bikers and cigar smoke. Beer would line the walls and the scent of old wood, something familiar and safe. If he could grow facial hair, Joey would look the part.

"I won't when I see him next." He ruffles my hair and grins a little. "There's shit going on, and we're handling it. Just want to keep you safe. It's harder when you're not home and at Topside. Can't get to you fast enough."

I pat my side where my guns are hidden. "You all worry too much. Been fine for the last couple of years and college. Besides, no one wants to come near a scarred, pitiful human." I stop and look up to the skylight over the elevator shaft.

"Brenda—"

"Look," I bring my gaze back to him. "No matter what you, Pops, Ma, Ricky, Vinny, Rodney…all of you say, I'm still scarred-up and mostly blind." He lets out a long breath. "My point is, Joey, I know to love myself, but that doesn't mean the rest of the world will. Definitely not up there."

"All the more reason to come back here, baby sis."

"Terrible people are Underground, too, Joey."

"Then you hand them over to me, Vinny, or Pops to take care of. Hell, Ma will place anyone in concrete if they look at you wrong."

"You just don't understand—"

"Then help me understand." His plea makes me feel a little guilty. Guilt for harboring feelings to myself for so long, but it's for their own good. My own good.

They couldn't understand, and they didn't need to. They're all full-blooded; they know where they belong, and how to make it work, and who they could love and cherish without shame and rejection. I have the best family, but it doesn't hide the cruelty from everyone else who saw me. And they wouldn't always be there to protect me from it. Bruno proved that years ago. I had to try living on Topside. For the sake of my heart and others.

My hand rubs harshly at my undercut, and I conjure up an excuse, anything to keep from saying the truth. As much as I love my brother, I wasn't ready to talk about it, if ever.

"Let's call it human wanting." The words are a whisper as I refocus on Joey.

He keeps his gaze level with mine, and his mouth tightens. "Stay away from the Bronx Entrances, all of them. Keep your guns and phone on you." His voice is distant, and he begins to turn away.

Fuck.

"Joey."

He stops a few steps away and doesn't turn to face me. "Something happened to you when you moved to Topside. Whatever it was, I wish I could fucking fix it for you, but I can't do that if you keep running away."

"Joey that's not…"

"My baby sis from five years ago would never talk about herself like you just did, even if others don't understand." With that, Joey continues down the path, disappearing into the Underground.

I stifle back some tears and get on the elevator. Punching the button, I watch LED lights sweep past me as I make it to Topside. Before I even reach the top, I hear sirens and other noises from the city. Once I walk off, I glance at the sparkling lights above me of skyscrapers and forgotten stars. A few incubi fly through the sky and shift between buildings. I head home, ignoring the stares I get from the scars on my face and body.

I throw my bag and jacket to the floor of my empty apartment and slump into my leather chair as a siren passes. The light scent of dark spices and bloodlust fills the space, and I breathe it in. Calm washes over me as I nuzzle into the cushion, trying to be lost within the leftover scent of Vinny.

I give in to the temptation and pull my phone out. The phone rings for two seconds before he picks up and asks, "Already miss me, sweet cheeks?"

"I think I fucked up."

"Ran out of whiskey?" I scoff at him. "I'll resupply you later."

"Not with your illegal shit."

"But you love my illegal shit. You steal it from behind my bar at *The Lounge* all the time."

"Because you drive me to drink."

"And you drive my heart into the ocean. Tit for tat, sweet cheeks." A smile comes over my face, and I look out the window filled with colors I can only see with contacts. Silence dwells between us as I stare until he asks, "Do you wanna talk about it?"

I open my mouth but shut it, unsure if there's a way to tell him about my conversation with Joey. At least, not giving away the one secret I hold close. "No, not really. Just…"

"Whatever you did, sweetheart, it'll be fine."

"Yeah…." My head spins for a moment, and then I shake it off. "I should go sleep with the rest of Topside."

"Want me to wake you up in the morning?"

"Only if you promise to stand in the sun for ten minutes."

"Maybe next time. Go to sleep."

"Night, bloodsucker."

"Dream of me, sweet cheeks." The phone clicks as he hangs up. For once, I'm not going to argue with him.

"Are you doing anything tomorrow night?" Janice hovers over me with that sweet smile of hers.

"Uhh, no. No, I'm not."

"Well, Richard and I are going out and thought maybe you'd like to join us. I know you don't get out much, and it's this cute place near Times Square. Richard loves going with our other married friends." I met her husband once at a Gala for the library. He was half drunk from champagne—lightweight for sure.

"I don't know…" I say as I turn to the journals regarding historical recollections of vampires in Hungary and Poland that spread across my desk. For me, it's far more interesting than anyplace near Times Square.

"We'll keep you safe." I pause and eye her. "It's near a place where there aren't many beasts. You'll have fun with people."

The tilt of her head makes my stomach clench. She wears the expression I hate most; pity. You'd think keeping my nose in books would deter human interactions of any kind. I prefer books over most people.

"Thanks," I push out. "But I think I may pass for now." I keep my voice light. Willing myself not to show her the Desert Eagle under my sweater is hard, so I force a smile.

"Oh, come on, you never go out, sweet—"

"Don't call me that," I snap. She takes a half step back in surprise. Quickly, I notice my mistake and force the smile further. "Maybe next time."

Grabbing the journals, I stand up with papers in hands and disappear to the back of the library. My dress sweeps across the floor as I travel down the corridor toward my safe space here, giving people a quick nod as I pass. They either turn away, or their faces fall when they see mine. My mind flickers back to the night before and my conversation with Joey.

It shouldn't have been a big deal, but it feels like what I said was. I'd given a terrible excuse for my behavior, and it backfired hard. I practically told him I wanted to be human, throwing it in his face that we were different. It feels like I slapped my entire family in the face for all they've done for me. They supported me through all the years, whatever decision I made for myself.

I left for college when I was 18, like many young adults. Well, human adults. My parents didn't like me being fully gone so young. They didn't feel safe with me being on Topside at Columbia, so Pops had me commute. It wasn't until I went back for my master's that he let me move out. Even then, I was safe within werewolf territory, staying in one of Rodney's apartment complexes. All through that time, I worked at the club as a dancer, the only part of the business I was involved in. I adored it all. It was my life, and I loved it, yet something was missing. I had everything I wanted, and then I felt like I lost everything.

The day Vinny became the Blood Mafia Boss, nothing should have changed, but it did. Our friendship was fundamentally the same, but some things weren't afterward. I didn't know how to deal with it, not without losing everything. So, I moved. And worst of all, I couldn't tell him why.

Coming up to the old door, I push it open to reveal the cramped space filled with steel cabinets and shelves. I close the door behind me and make my way through the mess, putting the journals on the small desk. It's the only space I'm left alone to do my work as I organize everything for the Noctis Immortalis section. The library kept most academic journals, manuals, and dissertation copies from the colleges either in NYC or somewhere else. Most aren't placed on the shelves but kept in the restricted section and this tiny back room. My haven.

Sitting at the desk, I lean back and look at where I spend most of my days. I really did suck as a human. I don't always stay inside. I venture to a few bars that I know, the zoo, museums, libraries, and coffee shops. A few years back, during my master's, I hung around the other grads, but we drifted ways. Now, I just protect this small space.

"Knock, knock." I spin in my chair and quickly stand when I see Detective Drauper. His sunglasses hang on his button-up shirt. His leather jacket contrasts with the slacks he wears. The pants may stretch more than they should, but I'm not going to complain, welcoming the distraction.

"Detective."

"I was told you were back here. Janice said you may be busy." He peers around me toward the cramped closets. "Itty bitty living space?"

"Kinda." I look around the closet office. "Need more help today?"

"No, not today," he chuckles and brings those big brown eyes to meet mine. I don't know what to do, but my hands want to squirm at my sides as I shift from one foot to the other.

"Another species?" I ask, and he shakes his head. "Well, the list is getting smaller and smaller on why you're looking for me, huh?"

There's that award-winning smile of his. Shit, I can practically feel my underwear moisten from it. Maybe he'd end my virgin streak and give Ma her celebrations. Except, I figured this was a one-sided interest for the past year.

"Came here for a personal, social reason." Or I'm completely wrong. "I finally have a Friday night off and wanted to ask you to come out with me." Very fucking wrong.

"I...I...what?"

34

He leans against the doorway, his smile bright with anticipation. "Just a friendly outing. I know you don't get out much. Thought I'd show you a favorite spot of mine."

Apparently, my brain is not on the same wavelength as my "down under," which is screaming, "YES!" My muscles tense beneath my heavy clothing as thoughts tumble. "Go out? With you?"

I'm acting like I'd never been asked out before. Sure, it's been years, but that's no excuse to act like a flustered teen. Drauper's smile fades, his body moves away from the doorframe. The ease that had surrounded him disappears. "Maybe that was too forward. I know we've only worked together, so if I overstepped—"

"No!" My hormones scream at me not to ruin this. Slightly, his eyes widen at my reaction. I settle a moment and say, "I haven't been asked…in a while. I'm out of practice."

"Really?"

I gesture toward my face and then the books and journals that surround me. "Quiet librarian with scars. I'm easy to be overlooked."

"Thought it was part of the job. The quiet part," he muses.

"Well, sometimes," I smirk. "But so is kicking out teenagers through backdoors and making sure they aren't having sex in the restricted sections."

His brows raise.

What the hell am I saying?

Drauper's lips pull up a little as he tilts his head. I realize I hadn't given a full answer yet and feel a slight panic run through me.

Come on, Brenda, go out with the hot detective.

Folding my arms over my chest, I finally reply, "Where do you want to meet?"

*   *   *

Somehow, I let the hot detective convince me to meet him in the Bronx.

Okay, so he didn't really need to convince me. Sexy detective who helps me forget about my feelings toward my best friend trumps any common sense. Especially if he might go shirtless or wear a tank top or tight jeans or a bulldog harness, I'm not picky at this point.

My arousal remains in charge as I dress for the…date. Outing. Whatever.

I wear jeans with a maroon button-up and a long black blazer. My hair is up, showing the undercut. The only thing I'll show him of my hidden self, for now.

My eyes itch slightly, reminding me to get new contacts. I take a deep breath as I round a corner and move toward the bar Drauper said to meet at.

A bright LED sign flickers out front that reads *Charlie's*. Wood paneling wraps around the entrance and windows. The door has the name etched into the glass of it. A few more bars are speckled down the dimly lit street. Cars drive by as I shimmy my way through groups of people. Some shifters, werewolves, and succubi are already half-drunk for the night.

Almost to the door of *Charlie's*, a group leaves another bar. The place smells of fresh blood and spices I'm familiar with. Lifting my gaze slightly, I see the red of the vampires' eyes as they approach, their fangs hidden behind small smiles, but one slips a tongue over their canines.

"*Evening, vamp,*" I speak in Noctora as I show the Glock hidden in my jacket. All of them avert their eyes and nod. They say nothing as I slip past and into *Charlie's*.

There's a long mahogany bar, scattered high-top tables throughout the room, and booths covered in dark green in the back. It's lit up with deep warm light bulbs and small neon signs indicating what alcohol is served. Dark rock country music hits my ears; I recognize the werewolf singer at least. A few televisions play sports and news channels. I enter quietly past the lively people and aim for a wide-open spot at the bar.

A few minutes early, I'll ease myself with a drink. Scoping out the rest of the bar, I notice two exits in the back and kitchen area on the far-left side. Family taught me well, so did Rodney.

Within moments a bartender approaches me; bald and older, his deep eyes meet mine with a lifted brow when he sees the scars. He whips a towel over his shoulder. "What can I get you?" The gravelly voice matches the demeanor.

I hold up a twenty. "Whiskey." He clears his throat and glances at the wide selection behind him. "Red label, then." I pull out another twenty.

"Is this your—?"

"I normally drink at home from the bottle, so I don't know the shot comparison pricing."

He snorts. "Fifteen."

"Double?"

"Twenty-eight. Straight or on the rocks?"

"Straight, and thanks." He turns, pouring the drink straight up. As he slides the glass to me, I give him both bills. He eyes me a moment, and I shrug as I turn away. I catch him placing both bills in his pocket with a wry smile.

I move toward the back, taking a swig of whiskey and almost moaning from the oaky taste. I come to a table in the corner and sit to watch the door for Drauper. It offers a clear view, my back against the wall away from the other humans. Old habits.

I smell that I'm the only half-breed in the room, in a neutral zone, and I'm still a loner. I watch the door and feel the minutes tick by waiting for Drauper. My nerves begin to act up as he's now five minutes late. Trying to keep anxiety at bay, I hope I haven't been stood up by the detective when I get a whiff of familiar dark spices.

Without looking, I pull my gun out and aim to my left side in the shadows. A low groan comes from behind me as the barrel presses into his dick. I sip my whiskey with my free hand, switching the safety off.

"If you tell me Pops sent you, I'm bleeding you out in front of these humans."

Vinny chuckles near my ear. "How do you know my kinks so well?"

"It's a talent," I respond. The gun remains where it is as I glance back to see a flash of crimson eyes. "Why you here, Vinny?"

"Getting my cock shot off by a powerful female." The smoothness of Vinny's voice near me sends a shiver down my spine. My nether region enflames for a moment, and I clamp it down hard. I'm waiting on the *hot detective*, whom I didn't need the vamp seeing. "Why are *you* here, sweet cheeks?"

"None of your damn business, *bestie*." I put the gun away. Vinny comes around and sits next to me. He wears a flat cap to hide his ears but still has on his signature black leather jacket.

"Told you. Stay away from here."

"Not an Entrance; that's a few blocks from here. Including routes."

"You don't know all of them."

"Close enough."

"To be in danger."

"With you, everything is," I retort. Our eyes lock as I glower at the insipid vampire. "How the fuck did you know where I was?"

A smile rises from him as his eyes roam down my chest and back up to my chin. Crimson irises flash as he stares at my lips next. "You think it's hard for me?"

"Tracking my damn phone? Perv."

"Maybe."

"Just like an older brother, always on watch for your *baby sis*." I look away, taking a swig from my glass. Bringing my gaze back up, Vinny lost his smile and the flourish in his eyes.

"Vinny, I'm obviously fine and here for a reason. You weren't invited. Get over it. I don't do everything with you." I glance toward the doorway, still no Drauper. I'm both disappointed and relieved. Finishing the whiskey, forty dollars already gone, I'm not a blooming fucking flower at the moment.

"You promised to stay away from the Bronx." He lost the teasing in his voice. Damn, he's actually worried.

I pat my now hidden gun. "You taught me well. I won't be long here."

As I say that, the televisions change to a news channel. Both of us watch with the more sober patrons as a story reviews the arrests of ghouls on Staten Island. Another newsflash covers the Bronx and the uptick of Paranormal arrests. As the reporter speaks, I hear the buzz of Vinny's phone. He grumbles, opening it to look at the message.

"It's working hours, Vinny; better go."

"You gonna answer my question about why you here?"

"Hospitals need blood, better hurry up," I respond with a cold expression.

He finally listens, straightening himself out. "If anything happens, you know what to do."

I give a salute with my hand. "Off you go, vamp tramp."

He lets out a low huff and steps back into the shadows, disappearing through the wooden wall. One of the powers of pureblood vampires that put them above the rest. He can't do that in the Underground; mostly everything is anti-vampire proof.

Taking a deep breath, I look over at the entrance. Ten to fifteen minutes late, still no Drauper. Sliding my chair back, I stand up and grab my empty glass. About to leave it on the bar, almost taking the vamp's advice, I see Detective Drauper walk in wearing a sleeveless black shirt, jacket in hand, along with a delicious smile that makes my hormones sing in relief. I immediately forget that Vinny was ever here.

How is this detective human?

Every flex of his arms, neck, and, shit, his shoulders make my body quake. I grew up in a strip club brothel filled with seductive incubi, and he's making me fall apart. To top it off, he can hold his fucking liquor.

Another round of whiskey slides down our throats, and he makes an odd sound as he finishes. The older bartender offers another, but Drauper shakes his head. Apparently, five is his limit. Mine may be in the double digits, but only the bartender needs to know that. I've been drinking since I was thirteen. Ricky wanted me to learn at a young age, plus I was sneaky.

"Never figured you'd be a..." Drauper stops and thinks for a moment. His eyes meet mine.

"Drinker?" I finish his sentence as the glasses are collected. I nod to the bartender, and he brings us water. He seems impressed with my drinking as well. "Stay home a lot with my own bottles. Tolerance builds up."

"Going to be honest, you're the first librarian that could outdrink me."

"Not your first librarian? Damn."

"Usually, they're sipping white wine, talking about Jane Austen."

"Stereotyping there?" I smirk, and he gives me one back.

"Not quite."

"I could do the same with you being a detective."

He hums, twirling his straw. "What would you say?"

"Leather jacket for one."

"What about it?"

"Does every detective own one? Is there a surplus store you go to like nurses?" I tease.

He laughs with that deep rumbling laughter of his. Oh crap, *that* is sexy. "It's not the military."

"Close enough." I wave my hand in the air. "Seriously though, what is it with you all and leather jackets?"

He moves a bit closer to me at the bar. "Do you own one?"

I laugh and nod. He's got me there.

I barely notice the time pass. People have come and gone as we talk and drink. I made him talk mostly, which he gladly took the bait. Enough years as a stripper and bartender, I know how to get people to spill their life stories. He opened up to me like a freaking children's book with colorful illustrations.

Louis Drauper grew up in New York City, an only child, and always wanted to be in law enforcement. Starting in Brooklyn, he was promoted to Detective due to a big case he helped solve and transferred to a Manhattan precinct. It's the same precinct that brought him to my desk a year ago. His father is still alive, and Louis loves romantic comedies after long days dealing with death and tragedy.

I sip my water. "I may own a leather jacket, but I'm not a cop. Disqualified."

"No, just a librarian with a fascination for those beasts and drinks whiskey straight." He pauses, then points toward my undercut. "You have a side you don't let others see."

"You didn't think I did?"

He shrugs and brings his glass to his lips. My gaze betrays me as I can only watch his Adam's apple move while he drinks. Heat rises within me, and I feel parched. My breath slows as I watch him drink.

Wrenching my eyes away before he can catch me staring, I look toward the bar surface. My finger swirls around the glass, and I think of places where I'd put those ice cubes. Maybe I needed another shot of whiskey. Thoughts fumble over the other as my brain and arousal fight with each other. With the rate I'm going staring at his throat, shoulders, hands, eyes...I am in deep trouble.

And I'm more than happy to be handcuffed for it.

"Wanna know, honestly?" I break the silence. He places his glass down. The bar bustles around us with more of the country music.

"Know what?"

"Why I have this hidden side?" I gesture toward myself.

"Why?" He leans forward and tilts his head ever so slightly, his copper skin glistening in the low light. It takes everything in me not to jump him at that moment. He's perfect in this light as he brings his full attention to me. I almost want to tell him everything from the Underground, my family, the strip club, and being a half-breed. Except I'm not that drunk yet.

"I moved to Manhattan to start a new life after college. Didn't hate my old life, but something always felt like it was missing. It was like I'd been placed into this box due to circumstance, and I wasn't sure it was for me. So, when I came here, I wanted something new. Something different than who I was before. Maybe change perspective on life...anything. Last few years I've been trying to figure out where I belong and how."

"Have you?"

I chuckle lightly, shaking my head. "No. I think I made it worse. You'd think I'd know by now."

Drauper rubs his chin a little. I can practically see his detective cognitive skills going to work. A long breath leaves him, "Do you think any of us here have figured that out?"

"Oh, come on Drauper, you're a successful detective, own an apartment in the Upper Eastside, and all that jazz. You knew what you wanted to be and did it. Sounds like you have at least."

"Those are just things, Brenda. Just because my career may be where I want it doesn't mean I have the rest of my life figured out. I doubt anyone does. It is New York City, the city that never sleeps. Probably due to the fact none of us know what to do with our lives half the time."

I snort. "Probably because we're all having a mini-existential crisis about our lot in life. Sounds like a dissertation paper to me."

He rolls his eyes at me. Damn it. Even that's hot. "Course you'd make this intellectual."

"As opposed to what?"

"Just…accepting not everything has an explanation. Some things aren't ever going to have one, including our lot in life. Learned that years ago on the force."

"I'm a librarian." I grab my glass and salute with it. "I'm always going to look for an answer. May take some time, but I will. And I thought as a detective you'd do the same."

Drauper lets out a chuckle, leaning back in his chair. "You'd think that. But you've done enough research on those beasts to know there are some things we shouldn't pry into."

An uncomfortable prick runs over my skin. If I can just get him to stop calling them that.... "They're not that much of a mystery." I look away toward the bar's liquor selection.

"Maybe not in your books, but in the real world, it's another matter."

"You don't think I know enough about them in the real world?" I counter.

"I think people should be safe and careful. It's kind of part of my job."

I bring my gaze back over to him, and I see the genuine concern on his face as he looks at me. I don't like how he views the Paranormals, but at least he comes to me to learn. His job does entail the nastier side of them, which I can't pretend they aren't at times. I've seen and been in the claws of some terrible Paranormals.

My childhood was filled with good memories and love, but my family couldn't keep me from being bullied or attacked. There's a reason why Pops didn't want me moving to Topside initially. One of the worst instances was when I was eight and attacked in an alleyway. A few vampires tried to take me while I was going home. Thankfully Vinny was nearby and saved me. I found out years later Pops had taken care of the vampires who'd done it. They were never seen again in one piece.

I think of the months just before I came to live on Topside. My fingers instinctively move up to touch my throat, where two bite marks hide amongst the rest of the scars. A reminder of how powerful vampires could be and that without my family's protection, I needed a backup plan.

Still, I trust many with my life more than most humans. Something Drauper could never understand.

"You cops always have to bring it back to safety, huh?" I force a smile, ignoring the look he gives me. I move my hand away from my neck.

"Old school like that."

"Your drinking says otherwise. Pretty sure the old guys on the force would laugh at how little you drank tonight." I raise a brow, and he grins, the mood easing up a bit.

"You know you're a little feisty when you're not in that library cataloging shit about those beasts."

Another uncomfortable prick travels over me. It's better than monsters, but it still makes my skin crawl. The term haunts like a shadow from a bloody alleyway. Cop or not.

"Only when there's whiskey in front of me," I say deadpanned, raising a hand for the check. The bartender is about to hand it to me when Drauper interrupts.

"Hold up. I'm paying." He holds his card out to the bartender with a swift movement. I watch his arm muscles move, rippling with the slight stretch over the bar. And just like that, my arousal returns in its full glory.

My sexual desire is becoming a freaking yo-yo.

"Thanks," I say.

"I was the one who asked you out. By dating law, I'm supposed to pay."

"You neanderthal." I smile at him. His grin could alert every incubus in a ten-mile radius.

I don't acknowledge him saying this is a date in fear of ruining the rising heat between my legs. There's no way my head could wrap around the fact the hot detective would want me in any capacity like how my body wants him. Perhaps, Topside *had* ruined my outlook on myself.

Now, if my nether region could stop going hot and cold every few minutes, that'd be great.

He pays the bill, and suddenly I realize we're at the end of the evening. Or at least it seems like it. I have no idea what happens next. I never made it past the initial date part. Most people leave the bar, take a backroom, or hire a stripper. One of those don't seem applicable right now.

"Well, thank you again for inviting me out. I don't venture this far into the Bronx, if at all." I cough back the last few words. "I guess I'll see you next time you have a case or warn me about a street gang or something."

Drauper pulls his jacket on and raises a brow, his expression changing. Isn't this the point where you say goodbye? Or did I say something wrong? "Night doesn't have to end here if you don't want it to."

Oh, fuck me. Literally, *please.*

"What were you thinking?" I do my best not to stammer.

"You said you rarely come up here. Why don't we take a walk? See where we end up?"

"Walk through the Bronx? Like it's Central Park?" My eyes bulge slightly at what he's suggesting. Yeah, sure, let's walk through the *one place* my family said not to walk through.

"Plenty of people do, Brenda. Haven't you ever just walked through the city? Wander the streets?"

"Not really." I ease out of my chair, glancing toward the window. "You're serious, though?"

He holds his hand out. "Just a quick one, then I can take you home or…mine if you want."

It feels like my entire body is roaring and spasming. Chills travel down my arms and legs, conjoining in my lower region. Hormones are about to beat out every warning I was given about the Bronx. My throat feels parched again, and I'm afraid if I stand any longer, my legs will turn into jello. It makes my long overdue needy body extremely happy at the thought of finally getting to know what everyone is talking about. Dreams I didn't know I had are coming true, or some higher power finally took pity on my masochistic heart.

I grip his callused yet smooth hand as he leads me toward the doorway. We're greeted with sirens in the distance, people laughing near other bars, and the stench of alcohol mixed with colognes. A perfect NYC night, all and all.

"Where to?" I ask. He nods down the right, and I follow beside him.

A warmth overcomes me as the touch between us makes everything fuzzy. The only time I've ever experienced this sensation is around Vinny. Well, after Vinny would leave. I couldn't have him sense something was different and start teasing me for acting like a lovesick girl. It's not my fault Vinny is built like a brick house, smells like luxury and sex, and has a sultry voice that makes you melt. Plus, humor that matches mine.

The more my thoughts swirl around Vinny the Vampire, the more I squeeze Drauper's hand. Shoving thoughts away, I look over at Drauper as he meets my eyes. Just my luck to be thinking about a vampire while walking beside a handsome human. Or maybe I am being punished.

He squeezes my hand and asks, "What are you thinking about?" Yup, being punished.

I focus on Drauper and the softness of his hand around mine. My eyes zero in on his lips and facial structure to erase the other thoughts.

"That I never do this," I reply.

"Walking?" He smirks.

"I do that...."

"Then what?"

"Walking with *someone*..." Make the jump, Brenda! "...with a date." Years of living with incubi and succubi, and my flirting skills are horrendous.

"You don't date at all, do you?" He asks.

I swallow. "Like I said, it's been a while...and usually I get left wherever we meet, so..."

"You still said yes to me?"

"Obviously." Another swallow.

Drauper stops and turns me toward him. His eyes meet mine and watch me carefully. They flicker for a moment downward toward my chin, no...my lips. "Why?"

"Does there need to be a reason?" The retort comes out quicker than I can catch it.

"Guess not, but we could find out." His voice is husky and deep. Dark brown eyes stay on mine as he places his other hand on my hip and pulls me closer. The touch is amazing and wanted with fervor by the rest of me. My arousal pools in the potential panties to be hung.

I don't notice the other pedestrians who walk by in a blur as my sight remains on Drauper. I'm thankful I wore my contacts. My hips press against his, and I feel my breath catch for a moment. His hand moves up my arm to the nape of my neck. The soft warmth of him vibrates through my body. Our faces are inches apart, and I can smell the whiskey still on his breath.

"Do you want to find out, Brenda?"

My lungs are trying to remember what oxygen is. I have enough to reply, "Yeah."

Drauper draws in close, and I can feel the whisper of his lips near mine. I almost hold my breath as my eyes close. The taste of his lips just about on me...

Blaring sirens cut through as lights flash blue and red. We separate abruptly toward the street. A cop car blows past, turning a corner about a block away. Red and blue lights flash as they gather past us. A glimpse passes between us, and I see "work mode" has been flipped on for him. Without a word, I hurry alongside Drauper to the noise that's gathered nearby. His hand leaves mine, but I remain close as we approach the scene. I notice the 9-millimeter strapped under his shirt. How did I miss that?

There are two cop cars angled toward the side of the building within the deserted small street made of apartments and abandoned shops. Partially dismantled brownstones, steps, and gates spread down the street. Except, where the cops are turned in, there are no entrances. Four cops, one armed, stand outside their flashing cars in front of a long strip of brick wall.

Drauper peers at the scene, turning away after a moment. He shakes his head and gestures for us to go. "Looks like a disturbance. They'll handle it."

"With four cops? Domestic calls don't even get that kind of response. Besides, we're in the—"

"Let them do their jobs, Brenda." He begins to pull me away as I catch sight of the Paranormal.

His wings are out and torn, and his leathery scarlet color is stained with darkened blood. One horn is gone, and blood covers his face. Even from a distance, I can see the glow in his eyes against the deep-colored skin. One of his arms holds onto his side, and he sneers as a cop approaches him. My breath catches when the cop punches the incubus in the gut.

Disturbance, my ass.

Shit.

Drauper grabs my arm to lead me away. Another glance over my shoulder, I see the cop hit the incubus again, and another joins in as the armed cop keeps his gun trained. There's some yelling, and I can't make out much more than a few slurs thrown around. He isn't fighting back; the incubus is shielding himself from each hit. Why isn't their PSB Agent doing anything?

I can't tear my eyes away from the scene as Drauper tries to pull us back down the street. My chest hurts. My body rages as I watch the cops beat the incubus senseless. And then I realize.

There's no PSB Agent with them.

Drauper says something, but everything is drowned out as I focus in on the scene. I feel sick. And really *fucking angry*.

Ripping my arm from Drauper, I spin and run toward the scene. My boots hit the ground hard, and I let out a shout as I approach the cars, "Hey!"

One of the cops turns and sees me and waves me off, trying to get me to move along like a good human. Except I'm a pain in the ass half-breed.

"What are you doing to him?" I yell above the noise. My head is still ringing with each punch they gave him.

The cops stop and turn toward me, with the armed cop keeping the gun on the incubus. One of them speaks into their radio, while another is about to grab for me. Quickly, I spin out of his grasp and trip him.

The first cop says, "Not your issue. Let us take care of the nuisance."

I step out of the way again as they move to grab me. "Wanna tell me why this *nuisance* is being beaten to death by a couple of cops with piss for breath?"

"What the fuck did you—"

"By governmental and international law, you're supposed to have a PSB or NIIA Agent with you when making an arrest in a neutral zone. Unless you have a warrant given by the head of the department who oversees your precinct, you're not supposed to touch him! There are also no other Paranormals nearby to attest for handling a Paranormal witness correctly."

He sneers at me and says, "We couldn't wait for backup."

"If you're patrolling a neutral zone, you should *already* have back up in your fucking car!" I growl.

"Safety takes—"

"You're breaking at least five laws right now, not just national. I could report every one of your asses to the NIIA, PSB, and FBI for violating laws that uphold the treaties between humans and Paranormals," I seethe. They all pause as I

46

threaten their badges. Oh, sure, *that* got their attention. "Did you even ask for an I.D. or why they're here? Newsflash, neutral zone, they're allowed to walk around without your trigger-happy noses up in their business."

My body trembles in anger, but I can't let them see the slight fear or my own gun I'm ready to pull out.

"Look here," one of them tries to reason with me. "He started—"

"Fucking nothing! Not your jurisdiction!" My screech makes him take a step back.

"Alright! Let's calm down here," Drauper appears suddenly behind me, flashing his badge. "Detective Drauper. What's going on?"

"We got a call that this scum was causing issues," a cop answers.

Another cop adds, "We came in to assist since we never know how dangerous a situation can be." Oh, yeah, extremely dangerous as the incubus lays in their pool of blood.

"I've had a buddy taken out by these monsters before..." one of them murmurs.

"Yeah, and most rapes happen by white human males, but you don't see me shooting you in the groin, do you?" I snap back.

I move toward the incubus and hear Drauper yell for the cops to stand down. Lights flash against the brick walls. Slowly, I come up to the incubus, who seems barely awake and alive. His eyes bulge a little as I walk toward him.

I hold my hands up and speak in Noctora, *"It's alright. I'm going to get you out of here."*

He raises his brows and eases his hands down from his chest. I kneel beside him as he slumps against the wall. His wings are torn, and gashes spread over his bare chest. His face, shoulders, and midsection are covered in bruises.

"How well can you breathe?"

"Well...enough," he answers in a whisper. *"How do you know Noctora?"*

"Do you know Alanzo Cuorebella?" I ask.

The incubus pauses for a moment and then nods. *"All incubi do."*

"I'm his daughter," I say. He takes a sharp breath in, but relaxation eases over his expression and body. *"What's your name? I'm Brenda."*

"Michello."

"What were you doing on Topside?" He peers past me for a moment, and I subtly glimpse at the cops who stand there like vultures near their cars. The gun is finally gone. Drauper talks back and forth with them and his cellphone. I'm probably in trouble, but I don't care at this point. It depends on how they're going to approach me again in the next five minutes.

"Errand to drop off...supplies, drugs for a small non-profit...always used this street. But someone..."

47

"*They call the cops?*"

"*Disturbance of peace. They saw my wings....*" His breathing grows worse.

"*I know, I know, you don't have to explain to me. Hold on. I've got you.*" Panic begins to worm its way through my veins. Another glance, and I see Drauper is off the phone. He watches with an intensity I've never seen before. More than likely, he thinks I really am the bleeding-heart librarian for the "beasts". He has no idea.

I slip my hand to the front of my jacket to grab my phone, blinking a few times as my contacts begin to itch. Shit, I did not need to lose my eyesight in the middle of keeping cops from killing an innocent incubus. I press the button, and my phone gives a delivery confirmation as I put it away. Never, since college, did I honestly think I'd have to use it.

I check over Michello's injuries and notice his wings aren't as badly injured as the rest. His torso, though, is another story, which isn't good for incubi. Their organs are softer and more prone to injury than even humans. Wrong hit to the stomach could kill them if not treated correctly. After a moment, Michello puts his wings away. He groans as they disappear into his back and begins to fall before I catch him. I steady him, looking back to see Drauper come closer. Two of the cops disappear into their car with the lights turned off, and they drive off down the street. I scowl, not having enough time to memorize the plate number.

"Brenda." Drauper's voice pulls my attention away from the disappearing vehicle. He walks a few paces closer, his eyes strict as they shift over to me.

"He needs medical help," I say.

"No hospital up here will take—"

"Then get one from the Underground," I snap.

"Brenda…"

"*Topside* cops beat an innocent being because they were scared. He doesn't have any weapons on him, didn't use his powers, *per law*, didn't—"

"They have a right to keep the peace and safety of the neighborhood," he argues.

I growl deeply. "That's no excuse to beat the crap out of him or point a gun! There's no law saying cops can assault people without warrant or cause."

"He's not people."

My heart stops.

Ten minutes ago, I was about to kiss that man. Damn, I feel stupid.

Anger boils deep in my gut, replacing all fear. I'm about to pull my gun out to shoot Drauper in the kneecap when Michello touches my hand. I look at him and want to cry. The glow in his eyes is dimming. The dark color of his scarlet skin is becoming lighter with each passing minute.

He's dying. Michello is dying.

"They don't...care about us," Michello wheezes.

"I fucking *do."* My hands shake as I hold onto his shoulder and touch the bruised chest before me. I see it then, the darkening spot where the internal bleeding is occurring.

Fuck. FUCK. *FUCK.*

My mafia instincts kick in to force Drauper to bring *someone* here. I shift to grab my gun when a car screech echoes between the buildings. Drauper and I look to see a black elongated Mercedes SUV pull up. My breath hitches as the driver walks out, his pale skin glistening in the lights above. He opens the side door, and a sob of relief almost escapes my lips.

Anita Dracultelli.

Her long black hair is pulled back into a shining braid. Her pointed ears and ruby eyes show her vampiric bloodline. She shares the same skin tone as her brother Vinny, which compliments her black three-piece suit. Her fingers flex at her side with long pointed red fingernails skimming her slacks. Although she appears calm, I know Anita well enough. Her scent tells me she's angry. It burns my nostrils with spiced wine and perfumed musk. With a quick wave of her finger, the driver, Brock, pulls out paperwork to hand to the cops as she walks toward me. Her stern expression flickers between Drauper, me, and then to Michello. Brock comes up from behind her as I stand. I step back as he carefully helps Michello stand. My body trembles a little as I watch. Tearing my eyes away from Michello, I find Anita's gaze.

"I said I wouldn't leave him," I say.

"Always the bleeding heart." Her voice is like falling wine into a patch of thorny roses. It's smooth, gentle, but refined and threatening. *"Get in the car, baby sis."*

I begin to follow Brock when Drauper reaches for me. Anita hisses and bares her fangs at the detective. In an instant, he drops my arm and glares at her. He begins to say, "You have no jurisdiction—"

"She said she's coming with us," Anita speaks with a malicious calm. "I suggest you allow the female to do what she wishes. At least Underground, all genders make their own choices. Is it not the same up here?"

Drauper tears his eyes from her and back to me. "Brenda, don't go with them."

"Says who? You?" I answer as I move toward Anita. "See you at the library, Drauper."

"Brenda," he pleads.

"You may want to read up on what happens when you intervene with Paranormal business, especially when PSB isn't involved. Since the NYPD can't afford to teach you." He widens his eyes, and I walk away with Anita close behind me. Brock keeps the car door open for me to climb in.

Michello lays on the back seats. I carefully sit down to place his head on my lap. He easily lets me do this as Anita seats herself near me. She calls out, "Hurry, Brock. Take the Entrance closest to Charlene's, give the signal that we're coming."

The car starts up and begins to speed from the scene. I catch sight of Drauper through the windows as he watches us disappear around the corner.

"I thought you were warned to stay out of the Bronx." Anita's voice is deadly smooth.

"Vinny said—"

"I really don't want to talk about it," I say.

A cold laugh leaves her as she leans into the seat. "I have a dying incubus in my car and Cuorebella's daughter about to shoot a human detective. You were more than likely about to be arrested; more cops were on the way."

"That *detective* wouldn't let that happen." Even I don't believe those words.

"You sure about that?" Her dark ruby eyes search for answers, and her jaw ticks with agitation.

I take deep breaths to calm myself, the adrenaline about to wear off soon. "Because I was in the Bronx on a date with him. So yeah…probably."

She scoffs. "Baby sis—"

"Not now, Anita. Please…"

"Do your parents know?"

"Does it matter?" I snap back. "It was the first date. We really gonna talk about this with a dying incubus in my arms?"

She folds her arms elegantly, her nails carefully placed not to tear her jacket. I thought this week had sucked earlier; I'd been totally fucking wrong. Anita nods at Michello. "You want to talk about the blood instead? How his organs are failing because of that detective?"

"He didn't do it," I whisper.

"Let me guess; he still stood there. Like most of them do."

"Anita."

She lets out a long sigh and shakes her head. A few tears form in my eyes, and I wipe them away, focusing on Michello, who's out like a light.

Anita talks in a softer tone, the kind she'd use when I was younger. "Fine, I won't make you feel worse. We all make mistakes in dating. But a human? In the Bronx? *Really?*"

"You know, after all those warnings, I thought, 'fuck it, let's see what the action is all about,'" I grumble.

"You know, I hate your sarcasm."

"I was warned about mob shit, not…" I gesture toward Michello and back to the outside, "…not cops making arrests without PSB present in a zone they're not supposed to patrol. None of you—"

"Vinny didn't want you to know."

"Why?" I snap. She turns away from me, refusing to meet my gaze. I turn back to Michello and stroke his hair back. I hope with everything in my body he'd make it. He had to make it.

My chin quivers as I realize I may be the last one to hold him, talk to him like he was a living being. I tremble more as I stroke his head quietly, the tip of my finger going over where the other horn should be.

Realization sinks in.

It hadn't just been about mob shit. I've been blind the last few years, holed up in my library in Manhattan. I knew of arrests but didn't know the extent beyond what I had seen growing up. And even if Michello was part of the mob, those cops couldn't know that. They still attacked him.

I'd seen atrocities and the victims Pops pulled out of those situations, but that's family business. This isn't. This is everyday life, and it shouldn't be this sick and twisted and wrong. But it is, and Anita is carrying on like its business as usual. It's normalized.

Anita, like myself, grew up in the mafia. Bruno Dracultelli, her and Vinny's father, operated the Blood Mafia for centuries until he stepped down for Vinny to take over a few years back. Anita is Vinny's second in command, even though she's older. It was always meant to be Vinny's. My family, the Dracultellis, and the Wolf Mob worked together for centuries, protecting the Paranormals in the Underground and on Topside where PSB and NIIA couldn't. The Wolf Mob runs weapons and agriculture, the Blood Mafia runs blood, protection, and medicine, and Pops saves slaves and sex-trafficked victims sold in the black market. All three families rehabilitate those rescued, placing them back into society safely.

We've both been through some fucked-up shit, but this is different. This isn't part of the mafia game.

"You weren't just trying to keep me away from business, were you? The profiling has gotten worse in the area."

"When did we ever hide that from you? You've handled it better than most Paranormals." I follow her gaze out the window, watching the world switch from Topside to the Underground. "It's not good, baby sis. Cops have been getting away with…." Her voice falters for a moment. She flicks her gaze to Michello in my lap. "Beings are scared for their lives and staying below ground for their own safety. More are coming to us for protection, but there's only so much we can do."

I scoff. "Of course, the mafia has to be the ones to keep people alive."

"We've been dealing with this for centuries." Anita finally brings her eyes to mine. "It's never been right, and it's never-ending. You learn that after a few hundred years."

"You still fight." I brace myself as we take a tight spiral down to the Underground.

"We have a right to be here, and I'll be damned if they try to take that away. I haven't lived for 300 years to relinquish my space." A tight smile comes across her expression.

I concentrate on calming myself with another deep breath. All kinds of swear words run through my mind, along with anger.

"They were protecting you, baby sis," she continues. "They didn't want—"

"It was gonna happen at some point."

"Perhaps, but your family is protective of you." She pauses, adding quietly, "So does Vinny."

Lights flash past as we finish the last of the spiral down. Brock takes the car at full speed down the Underground roads. The car juts around as we drive over stone pavement. "I know. Everyone wants to protect 'baby sis.'"

Anita leans back into her seat and glances over at Michello in my arms. "Few more minutes. I think we'll make it in time."

"I may shoot those cops myself if he doesn't."

"I'll give you the gun to do it and a place to hide it afterward." Her fangs show as she smiles in pleasure. At least I'm not the only chaotic mafia daughter, but then again, it's in her nature. For all I know, mine too.

The car abruptly stops, and I hear yelling as we get out. A few shifter nurses grab Michello from my arms, and carefully place him on a gurney, and wheel him away. Dazed at this point and my eyes itching like hell, I focus around me.

Brock brought us to the main hospital in the Underground. Charlene, a succubus, owns it and is the main doctor for most of the mob families. Almost everything is privatized down here but paid for by most of the mob and given protection. The hospital gives a slight glow of mixed pink and blue hues. We head toward the cream-colored building, something that's easy on the eyes and comforting. The entrance is large, with an overhead archway for emergency arrivals. I peer around the familiar entrance and see Charlene waiting inside.

Charlene's cherry complexion appears soft in the light. Her delicate hands move over Michello as she ushers her nurses inside the hospital. She looks at me and nods, following all the nurses inside. I sag with relief, but now I really want to cry, scream, or hit something.

I slowly turn to Anita, her expression calm and calculating. "Why didn't Vinny come?"

"Business," she answers as her hand goes into her suit pocket. "I'll take you home."

"I'll walk. I need to clear my head."

"Bullshit. I'll take you. You've had a long night," she argues as she pulls her phone out and taps away.

A long-exasperated breath comes out of me, and I rub my aching eyes. "Just let me walk, Anita. I'll be fine. Already—"

Anita's voice interrupts mine, talking on the phone. "Will you tell her I'm taking her home? We're at Charlene's. And she keeps rubbing her damn eyes."

She holds the phone out to me, and I scowl. "Anita—"

"It's Vinny."

Instinctively, I snatch her phone and hold it to my ear. Vinny doesn't give me a moment to argue. "Brenda, Anita will take you home. Stay in the Underground this weekend, until we get shit cleared for you to come back to Topside."

I lean against one of the building pillars. "How badly did I fuck up?"

"You didn't shoot their kneecaps. Your restraint is getting better."

Silence comes between us; I don't know what to say. My stomach churns, my chest hurts, and my hands begin to shake. All of it halts when he speaks again.

"Sweet cheeks."

"Bloodsucker."

"Go home to Ma. I'll take care of it, sweetheart." A sob almost breaks through my chest at how calm his voice is. "And take your damn contacts out."

"Busybody."

"Only for you. Now, give me back to Anita." I give the phone back to Anita and run my fingers through my hair. She hums a few things before she hangs up.

Suddenly, I'm spinning, and my back is pressed to the wall. She hisses for me to hold still, and I'm too tired to fight back as her manicured, sharp nails come up to my eyes. She pops my contacts out, placing me into my distorted, discolored sight.

"Start the car," she calls out to Brock as she releases me.

"Bitch," I murmur.

"At least you've learned not to fight me. Besides, what are big sisters for?" I sense the amusement in her voice.

"Maybe losing an eye would be an upgrade," I mumble as I reach for the car door and practically fall into the backseat. Anita comes in behind, slamming the door. My head knocks back against the headrest, and I want Vinny back on the phone.

Brock drives us away, causing flashes of weird colors to pass over my eyes. Anita hums to herself, and I feel her staring at me. I don't look at her as I try to keep myself calm.

"Will you tell me if he makes it?" I ask.

There's silence in the darkness before she exhales and says, "Of course."

After a while, the car stops. I stumble out of the car and immediately smell her. The sweet scent hits my nostrils, and sobs build up in my chest. My eyes open to see a brilliance of distorted blues, greens, and blacks, and she's a vision of a dark violet shade against it all. Ma's arms wrap around me, and I bury my face in her shoulder.

"You're home, baby. You're home." Her voice soothes me as I take a shuddering breath and finally cry.

The whiskey I drank earlier left my body sooner than I wanted.

The toilet water and my puke make it look like a fucked-up starry night. Leaning my cheek on the toilet seat, I try to breathe in through my mouth. My nostrils burn on the inside from the whiskey that came up. Another deep breath and I flush the last of the contents into the bowl. Ma shuffles behind me.

"I'm fine, Ma," I mumble.

"Then it must be one of my other children puking their stomachs up," she says softly.

Ma had taken me upstairs to the family apartment, but a few minutes later, I was hurling up my stomach contents. I reel over the events of the entire evening. It feels like my sanity hangs by a single thread. Terror drives through me because every moment I think back to Michello in that alleyway, I see Ricky, Joey, and Pops' faces instead. I stand up carefully, then feel my way to wash my hands. Ma helps me as I try to function on my own.

Back when I lived at home, I knew where everything was. I could run around the apartment with my eyes closed. After not living at home for two years, I'd lost that.

Ma helps me into the kitchen and sits me down at the small table. A mug is placed in front of me.

"Thank you, Ma."

"Three inches in front of your left hand. No handles. You can grip with both hands." Her voice is a melody.

With her direction, I reach for the mug and find it easily without knocking it over. A few sips and the tea settles my upset stomach.

"Your father will be home later."

"Oh, no, Ma, he's working…."

"He's worried."

"How soon did you—"

"Vinny called us both the moment you pushed the emergency button. Charlene called before you arrived." Her voice is far away as she moves around the kitchen. I hear her stop and pass near the counter. She's baking, and it smells like raisin bread.

"Ma."

"Michello was delivering for your father." My breath hitches, and I almost drop the mug, spilling some tea. I grip the tabletop and my stomach twists. Ma comes around, putting her arms around me. I start to cry again. Damn.

I tremble as I hold onto her. She strokes my hair and pats me gently. Ma picks at my jacket softly as the tears dissipate. "I need to clean this for you. And the rest of your clothes. I hate scrubbing bloodstains when they're old." I give her one last squeeze before pulling away. She caresses my face. "I love you, baby."

"I love you, too." I try to stand, but she grabs my arm. "No, let me change now. That way, I can at least fall asleep at the table in a clean sweater and not smell like blood or puke."

She pats my shoulder as I leave the kitchen. It takes a few minutes longer than I care to admit getting to my room. Damn furniture is in my way. I change out of my clothes and put my guns away. Ma already has clothes set out on the bed that I clumsily put on. It's easier to just close my eyes and not deal with my fucked depth perception and dizziness. Feeling my way down the hallway, I begin clicking my tongue, finding the laundry room. I throw my clothes into the basket and rub my eyes as I walk out. They ache now from stress and lack of sleep.

I click my tongue to find my way back to the kitchen. I feel Ma's gaze on me as I stumble around for my chair like a drunk. I need to work on my echolocation again. I really am out of practice. Perhaps I need to use the contacts less and the glasses more. The glasses at least help the depth perception and sometimes the color. Hues didn't warp things together as bad.

"I need to get new glasses," I say.

"I thought you had new ones? Four inches from your right hand."

I don't even look as I reach for the mug. "Vinny took them."

"Were they old?"

"Kind of."

"Vincent only ever takes them when they're old. You keep forgetting to upgrade them with Charlene. Your father already got a few pairs. They're in your room." My head swivels toward the direction I just came from. Not worth it.

"I doubt Vinny would leave me alone if I kept up with them anyways. He'd find new ways to annoy me," I mutter.

"You and that vampire, you'd think you were old lovers."

"Aww, Ma, please not tonight," I groan.

"What? Vinny is a good vampire. He's established, well-bred, smart—"

"A mafia boss."

"So, is your father."

"A *vampire* mafia boss."

"He'd take care of you. Just like how your father and I want you to be taken care of. Financially, emotionally, physically…." She better not elaborate on the last part. The succubus wants my panties very badly for that tradition.

"Then, he shouldn't have been *necking* Chloe at my 21st birthday party. Or Natasha." I take a sip of tea as I try to shy Ma away from the conversation.

"He needs blood to survive, dear."

"Chloe, though? Blonde bombshell of the last two centuries? And Natasha? I think he just has a fetish, biting females at my parties." I slump in my chair, allowing my sweater to bunch up around me as I cuddle my mug.

The smell of fresh bread fills the air. Another sweet aroma hints itself as I take a deep breath in. Pecans. Ma made pecan pie. Every time I'm home, I wonder how stupid I was to leave in the first place. After tonight, the whole reason I moved out seems futile and dumb. I try something new, and look where it got me. Trouble. And blue balls.

Ma shuffles around in the kitchen before setting a plate of pie down in front of me. I put my mug down and search for the fork to dig in for a bite.

"Have you ever thought he was *necking* them because he knew you'd reject him?" Ma asks as she goes back to the counter.

I talk around a mouthful of pie, "Are you serious?"

"Males do that. Can't have what they want, so they go somewhere else to placate feeling rejected. They don't do emotions well, especially vampires. Even incubi don't always own up when it doesn't apply to sexual desires. Joey was like that." Ma explains.

What the hell is my day turning into?

"Ma, he's my best friend. That's it. Nothing else." I sigh and take another bite. I already wrestle with my feelings about the vamp. I didn't need Ma adding on. "I'll always be his baby sister, just like everyone else. I'll thank him for sending Anita, don't worry."

"Okay, okay…" Her voice sounds more calculated than I like. My suspicions are confirmed in a few moments. "If vampires aren't intriguing enough, I know a couple of incubi—"

I groan as I take another bite of pie.

Like the mothering succubus she is, Ma talks about a couple of different Paranormals for a potential mate and includes their gender and sexuality. I'll take anything other than humans right now. My arousal's been turned off and thrown out the fucking window.

Ma distracts me from the raging whirlwind of emotions that permeate underneath me. She talks and continues baking as she always does. It's just another Friday at home. Succubi are good at relaxing situations, even without their powers. It makes them great escorts and strippers, but even better as therapists and doctors. Or some like Ma are wonderful homemakers who revel in taking care of others. She adores it.

Ma worked downstairs as a stripper for decades with Pops. She had loved it, but it wasn't as fulfilling as the others saw it. When I came into the picture, Ma stayed home to teach me and care for me. I had been her blessing in disguise to become what she truly wanted to be. Joey and Ricky were patient with her and chores, but it's usually me in the kitchen with her most nights.

Funny, in my apartment, I don't really cook. It feels wrong to do it without her.

Pie and bread soak up the alcohol in my stomach, and tea soothes my muscle aches. My head feels heavy. Easing back into the chair, I close my eyes as I listen to Ma work around the kitchen. Gently, I'm lulled to sleep.

I'm not sure how long it is before he enters, but the aroma of cinnamon and cigar smoke drifts by, complimenting the bread baking. Blinking my eyes, I barely see anything as I can't focus on the murky shades. His steps come up behind me, and I turn to try to see a blurry face. Pops leans down, and I fall forward into his embrace. Strong arms hold me close, my head to his shoulder.

Tears run down my cheeks and onto his chest as he says, "He made it."

* * *

"It was a routine delivery," Pops says gruffly. "We'll have to reroute. Again." There were two more pies on the counter, with another placed in the oven as Pops shifts in his chair. Ma places a slice of pie and cup of coffee in front of him. I almost want the caffeine to stay awake during their daytime. At least to pay attention to Pops explain, "We'd been warned the cops were trigger-happy and patrolling without PSB."

I close my eyes to concentrate and ask, "Because of the ghouls?"

"Maybe. If anyone hates ghouls more than Paranormals, it's humans. They creep them out."

"Pretty sure they creep everyone out, Pops." I feel him look at me. "Oh, come on, the ones who used to live a few blocks down pulled pranks enough to secure that. The worst was when they pretended to hang themselves from the rafters."

Ma huffs, "Don't remind me of those fuckers."

Oops, made Ma swear. "Sorry, Ma."

Pops lets out a long sigh. "Michello will be alright because of you."

I shift in my seat. "I should have acted sooner."

"You were trying to be safe, baby girl."

"Yeah, look where it almost got him. I should have intervened the moment I didn't see a PSB Agent." I fling my hand out.

"You still acted," Ma adds in. "That's more than most can say."

I rub my hand over my hair harshly. Pops stops me from running my scalp ragged and says, "He's alive. Concentrate on that, baby girl. I'd rather you keep yourself safe."

"Why didn't you tell me what was happening, Pops? You could have told me that's why you didn't want me near the Bronx Entrances. It's not just *business* stuff."

I can't quite make out their shapes, but I see enough for Pops to nod toward Ma, who kisses both of us and leaves the kitchen. I wait a few moments before Pops finally speaks. "I didn't want you to feel guilty."

"Guilty?"

"I know why you left, Brenda." Aw, shit. Pops never uses my name. "Let me talk for a moment and explain." I nod quietly. His thumb strokes over my hand gently. "Joey told me what you said the other night." My heart drops a little. Oh, I fucked up. "I had a suspicion that things were never easy for you down here. I couldn't protect you from everything and everyone. You assimilated so well, though. Never indicated that you felt...unloved or unwanted, I hoped you never would. I'm not blind to the fact of what you are and figured one day you'd want to be closer to that side of you. I understand in some sense. There's a comfort in being around those like yourself."

A tightness grows around my chest as I hold back the quiver in my chin. He takes another breath, not moving his hand from mine as he continues. "I didn't introduce you to the business because I wanted to give you that choice. You didn't have much in the beginning, and I wanted to give you that."

"Pops..." I whisper.

"I didn't want you to feel guilty. That human side could eat you away, and you'd do something about it. I never wanted you to see the atrocities or make you choose between our worlds. You've seen the nastier side of things from the business, black market, the club, the survivors, but this...this is different, and I know you know it is. You're a smart female.

"You've always had a brilliant mind, smart mouth, and quick wit. You tried to help the first victims you met downstairs when you were seven. You became friends with those feared by others and never backed down. You'd risk your own life to help, and I don't want that for you, baby girl. Some things have changed the past few years, I've seen it in you, and change happens to people. But..." His voice cracks a little at the end. Fuck. "I don't want you to stay in this life over guilt. You have a chance to keep seeing the sunlight. It's okay. You don't need to be part of a fight where you're in the middle. It's okay."

The air feels heavy as Pops lays out everything on his heart to me. By not telling him or the others why I left, it made his own fears worsen. Damn, am I a terrible daughter?

"Pops?" I finally speak.

"Yes, baby girl?"

"I never felt unloved. Please know that. You and Ma have been the best thing to happen to me ever. Even Ricky and Joey, only when they're not spewing childhood atrocities and embarrassing me." Pops chuckles lightly.

Blinking a few times, I reach up and find his face. I hold onto the one who's been my only father, who I called "daddy" for years, who found me in the sewer and could have left me or given me away.

Some of the truth, he deserves some of the truth.

"I fucked up telling Joey that," I say. "I was just tired from a lot of things. I left to figure things out, and I'm still trying. Just know that I'm never, ever fully leaving the Underground or this family. I always felt like I belonged, even when others tried to make it difficult." I swallow hard as I push away a few frightening memories of crimson eyes. "I just needed space to figure things out, how to balance things and make it seem…fulfilling. Something was just missing."

"Did you find what it was?"

I shake my head. "Not really." Pops holds my hand against his cheek. We both take a deep breath. "Tonight has not helped with me wanting to stay up there, but I need to stay there a bit longer. I don't have answers yet, and I *definitely* don't trust my intuition right now." Or my hormones.

Pops removes my hand from his cheek. "People don't change overnight, baby girl, it takes time for that foundation to be re-laid and understood for new beginnings."

"And what if it was all for nothing? No new beginnings or whatever?"

"You need to take that chance sometimes," Pops says and lifts my chin up. "Anita told me about the detective you were with."

I do my best not to let my eyes bulge. "What exactly did she tell you?"

"Enough." Fuck me. Not tonight, but the sentiment remains. "I wouldn't worry about that, baby girl. Especially if that's what you need or want."

I pull my hands away, tossing them in the air. "I don't know if it is, though! I don't know what I want or need or how I feel about anything because it all backfires. I can't feel guilty because I'm too fucking angry at everything. Sometimes, it's just overwhelming, and then tonight…"

"Do you want to keep trying?" I shrug my shoulders, and he nods, "I'll make a deal with you."

"That's ominous."

He chuckles a bit. "I'll keep you updated on the family business, no more secrets, and let you decide what you want to be part of. Let you decide where you stand. You promise to go after what you want no matter what or *who*. And you have to open up and tell me when things feel like too much, baby girl. Let me help you."

"You sure that's realistic?" I attempt to joke.

"You'd be amazed what you can achieve with your daddy's help."

I reach for my mug but miss. Pops helps me grab it, and we both chuckle. I finally relent. "Alright, I'll keep trying and be more open, but that means don't hide *anything*, Pops. Maybe I didn't have a choice of where I ended up, but neither did my brothers."

"Just want to protect you."

I raise my brow. "I helped with runs and trafficked victims before I could drink, Pops. And you had Joey and Vinny teach me how to use a gun before I was ten. And you let *Rodney* babysit me."

"All essential needs."

"*Okay,* Pops." We both laugh a little.

He brings me into an embrace, and I wrap my arms around him, holding on tightly. I hate and love that he knows me too well. Pops pulls away, stroking my hair.

"And stop sending Vinny to me for updates," I add. "He breaks into my apartment every time."

"Your brothers would do the same."

"Yeah, but they've been breaking into my room since I was six. Mainly to handle nightmares and tickle me to death." Incubi have weird humor, but then again, it's my brothers.

"You never complained about that." Pops goes back to the pie on the table. "Not seriously, that is."

"That's because you can't talk while being tickled to death."

"Are you saying you want Vinny to tickle you?"

"Not you, too," I grumble low.

"He's a good vampire," he continues.

"And a mafia boss."

"So am I."

"Okay, *vampire* mafia boss." Didn't I just have this argument?

Pops pats my cheek lightly, the loving way he goes about to make a point. "You're a female who needs a partner soon. I don't want you to be lonely for the rest of your life."

"I'm in my twenties with dormant Paranormal genes. Pretty sure I've got time not to be alone. Doubt my brothers would let me."

"But you don't want to be a virgin that entire time. Your Ma can't wait forever to get your panties."

"Do you know how odd that sounds, especially coming from my father?"

"Do you know how sacred that tradition is to succubi and incubi for their next stage of life? Maybe you don't have succubi in your blood, but you are part of this family, and we hold those traditions dearly, especially your Ma. Your brothers did it when they lost theirs. So, no disrespecting her. You'll give your panties over when it does happen." He pauses for a moment. "And it better be with a partner who respects you."

A grin spreads on my face as I listen to him lecture me. His tone is strict as he takes another bite of pie and sip of coffee. No matter what, he's my Pops. And he'll remind me of that until the day I die, with or without his fears of me leaving permanently.

"Okay, Pops, okay." I amuse him as I hear Ma reenter the kitchen. Right on time.

"*Mio cavaliere,* father-daughter-time good?"

"Yeah, Ma." I stand up and sway a little. They both move to help me, but I wave them off. "I'm gonna lie down. Hopefully, be awake for dinner."

"I'll wake you an hour beforehand. You need food in you."

"Thanks, Ma." Somehow, I land a kiss on her cheek on the first try.

I straighten myself, clicking my tongue a few times as I make my way down the hallway. A few more clicks and I land safely to bed. I breathe in the aroma and sigh. Home.

If I can just figure out what I really want, then maybe I'd come back permanently. For now, I need to stay at Topside. If just to prove to myself that my decisions in life aren't always a wreck. Fuck tonight and everything that happened.

My arousal, on the other hand, won't decide for quite a while since it seems to get me in the most trouble. I don't need a repeat of what happened three years ago.

THE VAULT

It's the calmest dinner I've had at home in a decade. If I'd known almost being arrested would give me such a peaceful meal, I may have done it years ago with or without reason.

I stare at the bedroom ceiling as specks pass my vision. It's close to eleven-thirty am, nighttime for everyone in the Underground as my family sleeps. The soft music from the club below soothes me, but not enough to fall asleep. Apparently, the nap earlier hadn't helped the time difference.

I groan as I sit up. No way am I falling asleep anytime soon. My hand absent-mindedly goes for the glasses case Pops left me. I open it and place the rectangular tinted lenses on. My depth perception is correct, and most of the shapes are right. At least it isn't a full mash-up of impressionist galaxies.

I pull on some jeans, a tank top, and a leather jacket, and hide my gun in the back of my jeans. I leave my room and a note on the kitchen counter front and center of the coffee maker. I pull up my hair as I trod down the stairs. I'll have to let Ricky shave the undercut before I go back to Topside on Monday. I sigh at the thought of going back, even with Pops' advice and deal ringing in my ear. I *guess* he's right.

Nah, he's always right, even when he doesn't know the full situation. It was Pops.

And I did decide to go back.

Slipping through the backdoor, I saunter down the deserted path. A few lamplights remain on for the darkened alleys and pathways. The glasses make the once jumbled colors into defined greens, oranges, reds, blacks, and purples. Two decades later, and I still don't understand my vision. The depth perception is the worst, like a funhouse with mirrors wand no rules.

After walking for fifteen minutes, I see the sign hanging above an archway made of emerald and marble. It shines a bit from the lamplights nearby. I catch the words, *The Vault: Library of the Underground.*

My old stomping grounds.

A few steps lead up into the entrance. I enter through the double doors. Inside sparkles with an odd fervor from the marbling of tiger eye, obsidian, and amethyst. The receiving desk takes up most of the back left wall. Just beside it is a spiral staircase that leads to the next level. Small glass lamps with candles flicker far above me, aligning with the shelving. A deep breath in, and the aroma of old books fill my soul.

"Well, well, Little Sister, what are you doing at this un-daemonly hour?" The familiar voice brings my attention to the desk.

"Hello, Beckham," I say.

Beckham is the oldest shifter I know. Long white hair that matches his brows hangs to his hips, but it's always pulled back into a braid. His golden snake eyes stand out against his light emerald skin. His irises almost fade into his pupils, rare for a shifter, but he is old. He's taller than most, a slender body that always wears a cardigan or sweater. Only when he shifts into his human forms, do the serrated teeth disappear.

"I'd heard you were down here," he says. "Wondered how long before you'd come to your sanctuary." Like most shifters, his voice slithers like a reptile; smooth, but deep with elongated words.

"Don't let Pops or Vinny hear that. I think they want my favorite spot to be *Unbound* or *The Lounge.*"

A long finger comes to his lips. "Our little secret."

"You didn't stay up because of me, did you?" I ask as I lean on his desk.

"Rarely do I sleep. It's cumbersome. I'd rather spend my days reading and having tea." He gestures toward the small station behind me, raising a brow. I nod as he walks over to prepare my cup. "Why have you come, Little Sister?"

"Library up top doesn't have the info I'll need to look into current ghoul systems." Beckham pauses, glancing back at me. I sigh and add, "I'm also double-checking the protection laws for Paranormals, international and not."

"Would that have anything to do with Alanzo's incubus?"

"Word travels fast."

"With your family and their dealings, yes. And many of us seem to have a soft spot for you, Little Sister," he speaks slowly.

"Terrible rumor the incubi started."

"I thought it was the werewolves."

"Nah, I annoy the crap out of them, ever since I threatened to braid Rodney's and Gunther's tails together."

"They deserved it, I presume."

"Don't they always?"

"And always about fairness with you. Could make an old shifter sick." Beckham's smile widens as he places a mug of peppermint tea in front of me. His grin could make others piss their pants the way his serrated teeth glint. "You're looking into laws you said? Try the sections near *History of the Ghouls* and then *The Development of New York's Legal System.* Better to go over recent cases within the United States rather than international. Humans are particular with their laws."

The aroma of peppermint eases my senses. I take the mug and head for the spiral staircase. "Thanks. I'll bring back the mug when I'm done."

"Please, help yourself to use the station above to make more. One wouldn't want you falling asleep amongst a pile of books again, even if it is sweet for these ancient eyes." His expression shines in the odd lighting as I glimpse back. The grandfather I never knew I needed.

Beckham is the head boss of the Underground shifters, not just the mafia part. They had dealings and control of information and history. They preserve the works of humans and Paranormals alike. The mafia side of Beckham's dealings takes ownership of a few pieces worth over millions, and some are in *The Vault*. Secret services have paid a good amount for him to retrieve items or hide them. Beckham has more allies and insider information than anyone on the entire eastern seaboard, hell all the U.S. and part of Europe. He's the most cautious out of all the mafia heads and a fantastic resource for an aspiring librarian or historian. He was more than willing to mentor me growing up before I went to college, teaching me to read braille and maps, write, and navigate informational systems. That is if I stayed awake during his long lectures, which was a trial at times.

Candles flicker around as I land on the next floor. I set the mug on the table in the small reading nook in the far-left corner. Beginning to scan the rows and sections, I follow Beckham's instructions and come upon the current systems of the Noctis Immortalis. After fumbling through some books, my eyesight playing games on me, I find what I need and pile them together. I grab more than just ghoul stuff, moving back to the nook.

I flop into a seat, move my Glock around my back, and spend the next hour skimming through the books and materials, sipping tea every ten minutes. It's like studying for my master's again. Although, my master's was more fun to read about than ghouls with their…*interesting* traditions.

Dead bodies. Lots of them.

Ghouls are essentially zombies, by technical terms; undead things bitten by another undead thing. Ghouls at least have a cognitive brain function of some kind, even if it is a hive mind. The leader is usually a full ghoul, changed from the living, and their powers trickle through the grapevine. It gets more confusing when it spreads out like a spiderweb as bonds break or split. A fantastic pyramid scheme if you're into that.

Class is determined by how you're changed from the living or the dead, and its foundations are built on those who went from living to the undead. The lowest of classes is the dead changed into the *undead*. No matter what, they're on the bottom of the food chain, in Ghoul Society and for Paranormals. Their skin is hollowed out more and falls off from time to time, especially if the conversion doesn't take well. A properly changed ghoul from the living could live for decades. Many don't make the change. Some die from complications, whether they start off already dead or not.

In the U.S. it's illegal to bring the dead back to life. As if that stops anyone. You need a permit to change anyone from anything. In other countries, with the right paperwork, money, and contacts, you could pay to bring your entire ancestral line back from the dead. Weirdest black market transaction I encountered as a kid.

The clause to get out of said pyramid scheme is actual *death* death. Daemons are the only ones who can kill ghouls with their bare hands, using their iron-like claws. Everyone else needs to cut off or obliterate their head and burn the body for good measure in under thirty minutes. Or they rise again. Zombie movies got that bit right.

In the early 19th century, there was an outbreak of ghouls bringing the dead back. It spurred on fantastic stories like *Frankenstein* and zombie movies, Literature-wise, for me, it's fascinating. The epidemic lasted only five years, before daemons were brought in to level out the undead uprising.

All in all, ghouls are creepy and complicated for being undead.

I close my book and reach for literature on vampires, the more forthright society. They rely on bloodlines, good and traditional. The only way to achieve higher status is through your Mate, who must be from a pureblood or prestigious bloodline. Most families are particular on who you Mate with to keep those bloodlines untarnished; there were inbreeding issues centuries ago. Genetics don't quite work the same for humans like it does vampires when it comes to inbreeding, but siblings weren't happy about being Mated together. Some wanted to "keep it in the family," most did not.

Old traditions of Mating through families have died away in the past century or so as more vampires pressed for crossbreeding. Vampires were the last to commit to the idea of Mating outside of their species pool. Most of the Vampiric Society is still against it. Shifters, incubi, and succubi haven't cared in the last six to seven centuries. Both are a collective thinking group; the more, the merrier, the better. A good reason why Pops took me in.

I close my eyes. My mind wanders back to that black sewer filled with a stench that'd make anyone faint. Everything had hurt. My head pounded and ached while my body throbbed from fresh gashes and bruises. I was covered in blood and sewage. I remember feeling my scars on my face the first time. So much of the newer gashes burned from what I laid in.

Hours. It had felt like hours as I laid there, and people passed me with twisted faces in disgust as I cried silent tears. I wouldn't move. I wanted to die so badly, barely five years old, and I wanted to die until Pops came.

I take a deep breath in; the smell of fresh peppermint tea is close. I detect the added scent of darkened spices. I pull my Glock out and aim to the side. Safety clicking off, my hand remains steady as I open my eyes to look down the barrel of the gun.

Vinny stands there with two mugs of tea and a smirk of satisfaction. "Interrupting your wondrous nap, sweet cheeks?"

I aim a bit lower toward his groin. "Wasn't napping."

"Of course, you weren't. But just in case, I made you some tea. Beckham told me to use the station up here." His eyes remain their dark crimson even with my glasses on.

I move the gun slightly back up toward his head. "Somehow, I still want to shoot you."

"Shhhh," he hushes me. "It's a library. It's forbidden to fire one in here."

"Pretty sure that's a church."

"I'm told I'm not allowed in them."

"Says you who confiscated one of the crucifixes from the Catholic Church on Topside eight years ago."

"Anita wanted a holiday gift."

"I have a great idea for mine this year."

"Do tell."

"A silencer for my gun so I can shoot you in peace in the library." Vinny chuckles with a deep rumble and gestures with the tea. I click the safety back on and put my gun away. Tea is more important now. I take the fresh mug from Vinny as he sits down across from me with his ankles crossed. Ignoring him, I grab my previous book.

"Sounds like something Rodney would gift you. I heard you were looking for information on ghouls. I wonder *why*, sweet cheeks."

"Don't start with me."

"Only curious."

I sigh as I thumb through another book and make him wait a minute before speaking, "Issues with the cops will get worse if those ghouls came here for other reasons. They never travel in that large of a hoard or come to the city during this time. Things aren't adding up and may overlap with laws."

"Laws?"

"Societal and invisible laws within."

"Meaning?"

I put the book down and look over at him. His expression is stern, even with the slight lilt to his voice. "If the ghouls are trying something, like another undead uprising, it won't be them taking the full hit."

He hums and places his mug down, folding his hands. I'm not sure if his serious side annoys the fuck out of me or turns me on. Either way, it's unfair. The shiver down my spine isn't helpful in the slightest as Vinny leans forward slightly.

"Don't worry about that," he says.

"Then why warn me about them, at four-fucking-AM?"

"Early evening for me, not my fault you decided to switch sides and derail your timetable, sweet cheeks." He smiles, but it doesn't match his eyes.

I'm on the verge of pressing his buttons and toeing a boundary I know I shouldn't. Fuck it, I'm sleep-deprived and still pissed over the last twenty-four hours. "So, lying about the Bronx and its issues wasn't something to worry over? Lying to me for *years*? Yeah, I don't think so. You hid shit from me, Vinny. *Me.* Don't tell me not to worry when I almost watched an incubus get beaten to death. I'm gonna fucking worry."

"Brenda…"

"And PSB isn't getting involved, why the fuck not? Call Midnight if it's that bad," I say. He scowls at the mention of the name. "Fine. Don't. I know you have contacts and so do the others. Where have they been to stop shit like that from happening? And I don't care what Anita fucking says. Your protections mean shit to some."

"What the hell does that mean?" His eyes darken as I shift in my chair.

"You protect your own or whoever fucking *pays* you. Not everyone can. Humans stay away from you all automatically. Vampires and werewolves get the least of their shit, and don't even get me started on the half-breeds forgotten by both sides or worst stuck in the damn middle."

"We take care of the Underground, *all of us*, and you know that."

"What about those on Topside?" I gesture above. "If anything happens, *they* take the hit. Not the ghouls, not you, or the families, but the ones profiled every time they take a damn walk through Central-fucking-Park. Humans are terrified of you."

"Are you?"

I calm for a moment and stare at him. His eyes watch me carefully as I remain silent. In a slow, calculated movement, Vinny stands up and walks toward me. My breath catches when he puts one hand beside me on the headrest and the other on the chair's arm. He leans in close, and the scent of spices, cedar, and musk ravage my nostrils. His crimson eyes enflamed in a quiet fury, echoing with each movement. Apparently, I have a death wish to be killed by him one day; it could come true in the next minute.

Heart pounding, I dig my fingers into the armchair as my breathing becomes ragged. I'm not terrified of him, but something else makes my body scream and tremble at his close presence. Yet, I wouldn't blame the vampire if he swiped at my neck for mouthing off the entire Blood Mafia. *His* empire.

I begin to debate how I want my eulogy to go when Vinny speaks in a dark tone. "Do not tell me how humans act when you've been alive for less than a fifth of my life. I've watched them burn my people at the stake, along with the kind you call family. No matter what, we will *always* be their monsters in the night. I'll ask again…are you terrified of me?"

I keep my mouth shut even as words scramble in my brain. My chest feels heavy as I gulp. Terror is the furthest from me right now as my eyes go to his jawline and neck. I see the tip of his fangs, the warmth in my stomach coming back. I remain still, even though the heat down below rises with each passing moment.

"No," I finally say, looking into his eyes. "Never."

His head tilts, and his lips pull upward for a moment. "Then at least I have one half-human on my side."

I draw my eyes down to his neck and back up. His eyes are on my lips. And even more slowly than I had with him, they come back up to match my gaze. His scent deepens, entrancing me with the spiced aroma as he leans ever so slightly closer. His breath brushes across my skin, a tingling running through my limbs. Oh, fuck, if he does that across my entire body. His breath over my…

No! Bad Brenda! Remember arousal is a liar and gets you in trouble! This vampire is pissed off at you, not lusting!

"Sweet cheeks." My thoughts come back to the present. I see him watch me carefully. "I appreciate your fervor to protect Paranormals, but do not insult my intelligence. If you want to help, don't act like an angry child."

"Aren't I to everyone?"

His head cocks to the side, eyes flicking back down and up to my eyes. "Is that so?"

I've had thoughts of Vinny having me splayed out on bedcovers and doing things to me I'd only seen in the club, but not in the fucking *Vault*.

The last thing I need is for the vampire to know my body wants his. He pisses me off in more ways than how to cook potatoes. I hate his nicknames for me, and he's a complete pervert in language and lingering eyes. Invading my privacy is his favorite game, other than my brothers. Yet through all of this, I want to screw him so bad my legs could shake off. Or fall off. However that worked.

It's completely off the table to screw the hot, musky, coffee-making, suave, stupid, best friend vampire. Brain knows that but lower region and yo-yo desire did not.

It takes all my willpower not to touch myself or make him do it when his breath whispers over my upper lip. The hardness in his eyes does not help. Finally, I remember to speak, "Baby sister, aren't I? To *everyone*."

Vinny raises a brow and pulls back, his hands remaining on my chair. "Is that why you think I didn't tell you? Protecting our...*baby sis*?"

"Isn't it?"

He scoffs and lets go, standing to his full height. I let out a long breath of relief as he returns to his chair and crosses his ankles once more. Carefully, he picks up his mug, sipping from it like nothing happened. "You never wanted to be part of the business, mine or Pops. Why tell you anything beyond our routes?"

Insufferable. Arousal gone.

"You still lied."

"Technically—"

"*Technically,* you did by never telling me it was more than just mob shit, which goes beyond what I stayed out of. Honestly, I'm more hurt that you didn't trust me. Best friends don't do that," I whisper the last sentence.

"I get Pops' reasoning and Joey keeping his mouth shut, but like I told Pops I'm gonna find out eventually. It's the fact you hid it from me." I reach for another book and keep my eyes away from him. "You always keep it straight with me, no pretenses or shadowy stuff."

Maybe I lost more connections with them than I thought when I moved. Joey was right. Something happened to me when I moved to Topside. Not only did I feel lost in the human world, but now I was lost in the Underground. My fingers drift over the faint scars on my wrist.

"I'm sorry," Vinny says.

I look up from my book and stare at him. Vinny rarely apologized to anyone. I can tell that he's genuine with the sentiment. His crimson eyes soften.

"Thanks." I pause. "Not giving you a lollipop for it."

"Could always give you mine. I'm told it's tasty." A laugh comes out of me. A moment is all that's needed for us to make it alright. It always only took that long.

"I'll pass. You should ask Chloe or whoever you *bite* into these days." I laugh at the thought as I go back to my books. Vinny gives a long sigh, but I ignore him.

Minutes tick by as I read about the development between humans and Paranormals, which isn't a subject I'm well-versed in, especially some politics or recent events. Vinny remains in his seat without a word as I study. It's just like how he'd stay up with me when I was in college or getting my master's. I chuckle at the thought.

"What? Did you read something funny like werewolves are impotent during the full moon?" Vinny asks as he leans his head back.

I snort. "No, just thinking about how you'd do this when I was in school."

He peers at me. "You mean you writing your dissertation on my grandfather and squeezing every bit of information out of me about him?"

"Work smarter, not harder." I flip a few pages. "Do you even remember the title of my research?"

"*Dracula vs. History: A Comparative Analysis of Literature on Vampires in the 18th and 19th Centuries,*" he replies quickly and closes his eyes. "Somehow you wrote 150 pages on him."

"Aww, you do care, bloodsucker."

"Only because I lost sleep those two years."

"So, it's payback for when you wake me up at 4 AM?" Vinny says nothing, only a sly smile at the ceiling.

I shake my head and return to my books filled with dates, laws, and numbers. Most of the laws are like treaties, developed over time as each incident took place. Many of them are international, starting national, but converged as NIIA saw fit. Most of the Paranormals are ruled by the mafia and their own societies, which is why the Underground is a safe haven. It's the only place not even PSB can get to, only NIIA with warrants.

I come across something that looks like a contract from a law I know well: Paranormals can interfere with human affairs if such actions hurt another human claimed by a Paranormal. All half-breeds know this law. It's how Pops kept me in the Underground. It's also the law that scares all half-breeds because if you aren't claimed, you're fucked. There's a new addendum I haven't seen before that claims this is moot if for one of three reasons: scientific research, medical emergencies, and international arrest. Just another reason we need PSB, even if they make life hell for the families.

"Find something?" Vinny asks.

I shake my head, shutting the book. It isn't going to help me. Besides, I'm under the protection of Pops and the Paranormals if anything happens to me on Topside. My hand hovers to touch the scars on my face. There's an odd ache in the pit of my stomach, constricting my chest.

"Sweet cheeks?" Vinny's voice breaks through blank thought. My fingers remain on my face as I stare at the books.

"What makes me different from those above? Apart from immunities and scars?"

"Everything."

I turn toward him as I drop my hand. "Everything?" He nods. "I'm just about as human as they are, all of them. Half-breed or not, even by law, I'm one of them. No different—"

"You're completely different. Is that why you're doing this? Guilt?"

Did Pops send him a memo?

"No…" I'm a crappy liar sometimes.

He huffs out a long breath. "Shit sakes, Brenda, I was just trying to protect you. It wasn't because I don't trust you."

I know that. Deep down, I did, but I feel separated from them. After being on Topside and Anita seeing me with Drauper, I should have done more. Okay, maybe it is the guilt.

"You can't help what you are." I glance up past my glasses to find Vinny's gaze. His eyes glow through churned colors around him.

"You don't get it," I whisper.

Vinny recrosses his ankles and leans back. He brings his hands together and rubs them in thought, his eyes never leaving mine.

They're all purebred. They know where they belong and weren't bullied since childhood. I've always had a home at *Unbound* and other places, but it still feels incomplete. They aren't reminded every day they don't belong or could be ripped away from it by humans or Paranormals. My biggest fear, losing all of them and what I love *because* of what I am. That very fear drove me to Topside to protect them, including Vinny.

"Would you hate Pops if you found out an incubus gave you those scars and left you in the gutter?" Vinny's soft voice startles me.

Without hesitation, I say, "Of course not."

"What about if it was a vampire? Would you hate Anita or me?"

"No."

"Werewolf? Would you condemn Rodney?"

"No." I'm starting to get agitated.

72

"If you found out any of the Paranormal species had given you those scars, burned you, left you to rot in sewage, would you hate them for what happened to you?"

"No!"

"Why?" The laxness of his voice puts me over the edge.

"None of them fucking did it. Why would I hate anyone for what someone else did to me? That's absurd. You're the ones who took care of me and loved me and still fucking do. I'd never blame any of you for what happened to me, whatever it was. Don't even insinuate that I'd ever condemn you all for it. Even if it was a Paranormal who did…" I gesture toward my face. "…this. I'd shoot *them* for it."

A slow grin curls on his lips. "*That's* what makes you different. You're part of this mismatched family for life, whether you like it or not. Don't know who screwed with your head, but you don't have to prove anything to *any* of us."

He doesn't need to know who. Vinny would tear their throat out. As appealing as that'd be, it's too dangerous for others. I settle back into my seat, folding my arms over my chest. I grumble under my breath, knowing the smart-ass vampire is right. Not sure what I hate more, that he's right, or that I'll have to admit it.

"Just let me help in my own way," I say.

"What would that be?"

I shrug my shoulders. "I'm not quite sure, but I'm going the route I know best. Books, papers, and information."

"Is that why you never listen to me? Because I'm not a smart librarian like you?"

"Oh, I have more reasons than that," I smirk.

He hums a little. "You'd be a spitfire in bed or off of it, but I always knew that."

"Perverted vampire."

"Prideful half-breed."

"Addicted bloodsucker."

"Tantalizing *minx*."

"Disgruntled *old male*."

"Terrible shot," he muses. I whip my gun out, pointing the barrel at his head. The safety stays off, keeping it steady on him. He doesn't flinch even a little. "Hmm, little lower. Aim for the bleeding heart, would you?"

"You don't have one, Vinny."

"Ah, so cruel your words are." I pull back and put the gun away as he grabs his phone. "Your aim does get better each time."

"Just how you taught me," I say as I grab another book.

He taps away at his phone for a moment before putting it in his pocket and standing to stretch. Like the good vampire he is, he takes our mugs to the station to be cleaned by staff. "You're here until Sunday evening, correct?" I glance up at him as he adjusts his jacket and flashes me a fanged smile. "I'll see you before you leave for Topside."

"That sounds like a promise, bloodsucker."

"So does shooting me, but I think only one of us can actually keep a promise. You haven't for almost ten years, sweet cheeks."

A small smile rises on my face. "You want me to shoot you that badly, Vinny?"

Smoothing his jacket down and then running his fingers through his greased hair, he smiles broadly. "How about a deal then?"

"Which would be…?"

Keeping his eyes on mine, he proposes, "When you finally shoot me, I'll get something I've been wanting for a long time." His eyes flick to my throat.

A chuckle escapes me. "Want my blood again that much, bloodsucker?"

His eyes shift downward and then back up to my gaze. "To a certain degree."

I laugh as I settle back into the chair. Vinny remains where he is as he waits for my answer. The smile on my face grows. "Sure thing. Maybe just to see what Pops and Ma will do to you when you take my blood." His expression almost becomes sinister, but it is Vinny. He looks that way thinking about coffee-flavored chocolate.

"Very well, *sweetheart*," he says and disappears through hues of reds, pinks, and lavenders. Some days that vampire surprises me; today is one of them.

It isn't until a few moments later I realize my skin is hot and tight. Yup, I feel flushed and overstimulated from that lasting stare of his. My entire nether region rages for a few moments longer at the thought of his eyes sweeping over my body. For some reason, the idea of his fangs piercing into my skin is a turn-on—new kink. My family will be elated to hear such news.

"So, of course, I had to screw him upside down," Ricky says as he shaves my head. "He forgot I had wings ready to go. Plus, I always have toys." He twirls my chair away from the mirror, and I see Lola's reflection as she changes into her next outfit. Ricky always shaves my head in the changing rooms of *Unbound*. It's easier to clean up, and there's more towels and plug-ins for clippers. I need the buffer from Ricky some days, and the strippers help with that.

"You ever thought of just doing more incubi since they remember you have wings?" I ask.

"Much as I love them, they always try to outdo my secretions." I don't need more info than that.

"If you love me, you won't elaborate on that."

"No judgment from the virgin." Ricky lightly smacks my head.

"Just saying because this is like the fifth one this month."

"Pretty sure it's seven," Lola teases. Her light blue eyes sparkle as she winks.

Ricky shoos us both and eyes me. "I'm trying to prepare you for when you take the leap. You seeing anyone enough to cast your judgment?"

"Why the sudden interest?" I ask. "Ma paying you? Or does she have friends she wants me to get with? My love life is none of your concern."

"Not love life, sis, it's your *sex life*. You think I love all those partners?" He pauses with the razor. "Well, not in that way, just love what they do to me."

"Ah, don't we all?" Lola hums as she shimmies into her sequin thong and rhinestone tube top. Her curly hair unfurls around her shoulders, dark against her light pink skin. She disappears through the doorway as the music changes and people cheer. It's Sunday night, their day just starting, and they'll be rotating strippers soon.

I spent most of the weekend in *The Vault* rifling through books and journals. I couldn't find anything to help the situation on Topside. I even searched for something that could require NYPD to teach about Paranormals. Nothing. I'm stuck teaching Drauper if he decides to come back to the library. Something I once looked forward to. Now, not so much. To top it off, I'm running on little to no sleep and have to go to work in ten hours. How long can I last with only caffeine?

"You're quiet." Ricky breaks through my thoughts. "You're usually yelling at me over my adventures or telling me to stop begging you to come back to dance."

"We calling them adventures now?"

"I could record them and call them your future lessons instead?" He leans toward my face and grins. I want to punch him, except I love my beautiful brother too much.

Ricky's considered a perfect incubus: a horny pansexual who aims to seduce males more nights than not. He kind of needs his good looks.

His face falls for a moment, and he frowns. "Are you still upset about this weekend?"

"Wouldn't you be?"

He sighs, finishing shaving. "Another day, another hit…" He pats my head lightly and takes the towel off, brushing the last of the hair away. I'm left in booty shorts and a lace bralette, which is the only way the strippers let me back here for a shave; no sports bra. A condition I can live with. "Baby sis…"

"Let's not talk about it, Ricky. I'm too tired—"

Ricky pulls me in for a tight hug. He presses my face into his pecs and holds on. I wrap my arms around him. I already made up with Joey, which resulted in a similar hug like this. Physical touch with my family was needed of late. Both brothers are a pain, but damn, if I didn't love them with everything I have, even when I want to punch them.

"Okay, but you don't get to complain about my stories," he says. "You'll have your own someday, and then you'll be in my shoes. Can't wait to find out how you handle poles outside of the club."

I stifle a laugh. "If you weren't my brother, I'd punch your lights out for that."

"Good, cause if anyone else said such nasty, seedy things, I'd gut them for your honor," he says in a comically serious tone.

"Oh, now you wanna talk honorable?" I pull back with a grin.

He shrugs against me. "As the elder brother, it's my duty to make sure you practice safe sex and explore your kinks and fetishes in a positive manner." Open conversations about consensual sexual endeavors are *always* a must in a family of incubi and succubi.

I try to pull out of his hold, but he doesn't budge. "Go back to being seedy. I don't like this side of you."

"What? We can talk about condoms instead. Proper usage of bondage! If you place ropes wrong on the wrists—"

"It can cut circulation, I know!" A giggle squeezes out of me as I try to escape again.

"Different condoms with lube? You need to—"

"Make it stop!" I struggle in laughter against his grasp and lectures. I'm thankful Ricky taught me sex education instead of Pops. I still have my limits.

"*And* edible underwear!" He is definitely taunting me now.

"Just tie me up to a pole already!" I screech as I try to tug free.

"Oh, please," Gina's sultry voice disrupts my struggle with Ricky as she walks in. "I've been waiting for you to come back and be part of the act again."

"Act all done?" He asks her.

"Very much so." Gina's large dark eyes flash down to me.

The succubus has deep scarlet skin and dark obsidian hair. She's the beauty of the club who's well-endowed, along with being a talented dancer. She's worked for Pops longer than I've been alive and taught me to dance and strip. She's the big sister I never had and, at this moment, don't want.

"What was that about being tied up? Back to your old act?" She asks and snaps off her jeweled bikini top. Her breasts bounce free and perk a little. A view I'm quite used to.

"Trying to give her lessons, but she's being wily today," Ricky answers as I try to break free again. No avail. Damn him and his vice-grip strength.

"Always good to have refreshers. Perhaps, handcuffs or plain chains instead? Though we all know you love leather most, baby sis." Her expression sparkles as she puts on her next top. A cream halter top, ending just under the curve of her breast.

"Not now, Gina," I groan.

"You were the one who always asked to be part of the suspension act—"

"*Not now, Gina.* Ricky, let me go." He shakes his head and grins. "What do you want, you trickster?"

He hums for a moment and whispers in my ear, "Say I'm the favorite child."

"You're *childish.*"

"And this isn't?" Gina waves a finger at us.

I look down at Ricky's arms wrapped around me with only my underwear on. Okay, she has a point, but at least we're consistent in sibling squabbles.

"Fine!" I relent. "You're the favorite."

He still doesn't release me. "Tell me *why* I am," he teases.

I kind of want him to tickle me like I'm a kid again. I felt more in control back then and my screaming was louder.

"Oh, you are *really* milking this, huh?" I glare at him. Gina's silky laugh carries as she switches bottoms.

Ricky hums to himself and whines, "I need something to hold me over until next time. Plus, I gotta deal with Joey all week with routes. Give me this, sis."

I grumble and struggle a few more times before hanging my head in defeat. "You're the favorite because of your wonderful personality, beautiful smile, perfect body, and charismatic demeanor. You're the perfect child." And he lets me go instantly.

I straighten my bralette and glare at him. I remove the clip and toss it onto the long counter. Ricky gives a smug grin as he cleans up. I turn toward Gina, who smiles, gesturing toward the chairs near the long mirror. The reflective surface covers the entire wall, enough room for at least six dancers to do makeup and hair. I walk over and slump into Gina's chair. She taps my shoulder, cuing me to sit up straight. I remain quiet as she combs through my hair. A few more minutes pass, Ricky pauses near me and kisses my cheek. I return the gesture as he chuckles, leaving the room. Pain in the ass brothers.

"You needed that," Gina whispers, pulling a few strands into some braids.

"Being handled like a play toy with my brother?"

"Normalcy is good for aftershock," she states as her delicate hands move over my hair and skin, braiding my hair while the music from the main floor vibrates the walls. If she's late for her next set, someone else will take it, an unspoken rule amongst the dancers. It's how they assimilated the new ones, especially if they come from the black market. Some need more time than others.

My eyes close as her soft movement lulls me. Gina is quite powerful as a succubus, but even without her powers, she could caress someone into ease. She learned a lot from Ma. Her hand pats my head, signaling we're done. I open my eyes, her gaze meeting mine through the mirror.

"What?" I ask.

"Why haven't you moved back? You've been miserable since you left." She settles against the counter.

"Something everyone seems concerned with lately." Standing up, I stretch my arms overhead. My shoulders hurt from being held captive.

"The girl who danced here years ago would never have talked about leaving. You swore you'd work here and *The Vault* and have your own apartment five minutes away, not fifty with an elevator ride. What happened, baby sis?" Gina asks as she sits down.

"It's been years. Why's everybody asking now?"

"I beg you almost every three months to come back and be my partner again. The stage is lonely without you. So, tell me." She pokes one of my breasts, and I scowl.

"Life happened," I reply.

She sighs longingly. "I miss the younger you."

"Doesn't everyone?" We exchange small smiles.

Paranormals, even ghouls, cherish children since they don't come along as often as humans have them. The mafia families hadn't had a child for decades until I came around and became everyone's little sister on the block, the mafia, and the club. Besides my family, half the Underground dotes on me, referring to me as their own. Most settle on the nicknames "baby sis" or "lil sis", titles I've grown to love and understand their reverence.

"Come back to work here," she pleads.

"Those days are past me, Gina," I say.

"You miss it, admit it."

I shrug as I go to my bag to grab some clothes. "Only if you don't tell Ricky that I do."

"And tell me why you haven't given Ma your panties yet," she scolds. I glare at her, and she smiles mischievously. "You *swore* to me you were ready *years* ago and that you had someone who you wanted to pop that cherry."

"Things change, like people." I was smart enough back then not to tell her who.

Gina pouts, "How about a compromise and you wear pasties and tassels for my birthday? Pretty please?"

"How about *my* birthday?" A familiar voice asks.

In a millisecond, I pull out my gun and aim behind me without looking. I turn my head to see I aimed dead center at Vinny's chest. Not bad.

He's wearing a dark pinstripe suit and his family's ring with his hair greased back. Oh goody, he's fresh from a work event.

"Remember our deal, sweet cheeks?" His smile shines as I stand up entirely, holding my aim steady.

"Have I shot you?" I ask.

"Not yet."

"That's the point." I put my gun away, and Gina laughs. "Don't encourage the vampire, Gina. Can't believe he's allowed back here."

"He's a favorite. For more than one reason," Gina purrs as she scans him.

I turn toward them and place my hands on my hips. "You know, I used to like you, Gina. Lately, it feels like you're against me."

She smiles at me and winks. I roll my eyes and glare at Vinny, who looks…starstruck?

The black of his pupils are large as they remain not on my face but my chest. Heat washes over my body as his wide crimson eyes bear into my skin. My muscles tighten and my heart races as my lower region begins to pulse and tingle. I want to walk over to Vinny and press him against the mirror. I want my chest to move against his chiseled—

Okay, WHAT. Stop.

I blink a few times and look down. I'm still in a bralette and booty shorts, bearing out all scars and deformities. It's not the first time I've been practically naked in front of Vinny. Hell, he's been to my shows in the past. It's been years, though. Maybe he forgot how badly jagged the scars were, since hardly any part of my body is smooth.

Trying to shake the feeling off, I grab a tank top, pulling it over my head. "Can you hold back those hormones, Gina? Otherwise, Vinny may turn into a puddle when he sees your top off or the next girl walk in."

"Nothing to do with that," Gina purrs.

She stands up, waves a little with a knowing smile, then saunters through the door, brushing her fingers across Vinny's chest and shoulders. The touch makes him tear his eyes away from me to her. She whispers something in his ear and disappears. Looking away from him, I grab my jeans and pull them on.

I need a nap.

"What do you want, bloodsucker?" I ask.

"I said I'd see you before you left. Although seeing more of you than usual was *quite* the gift." Vinny talks smoothly, even though his eyes are hard on me again.

Placing a hand on my hip, I tilt my head at him. "Seriously, do you have the goal to say *every* perverted thing that comes to mind?"

"Only for you, sweet cheeks." He smiles and sits in the chair closest to me. "Besides, we have business."

"Oh, *do we*?" My sarcasm makes him chuckle.

"Yes, it seems I gained a visitor at *The Lounge*, a *human* visitor." His voice switches to a dark tone. I don't like where this is going. "He inquired about a *human* female who disappeared with a vampire Friday night. Seemed distraught and didn't trust me."

I fall into the chair near him and snort. "Who *actually* trusts you, Vinny?"

"Everyone, except you," he pouts.

"Bullshit, yeah, I do."

"Prove it."

"I don't check my coffee if you've poisoned it."

"Good enough." His expression changes from leisure to pleasure.

"Who was it? Please don't say police."

He sighs, "It was the police."

"Shit."

"But it was a detective."

"Double shit."

"Oh, language is colorful today. You know the man?" Vinny focuses on my face.

I rub my hand over my face and let out a huff. I should've known Drauper was going to look for me, but I figured it would be on Monday at the Library, not the Underground. Maybe a wiretap or two at work.

"You know that detective I told you about? The one I give info about on different Paranormals? That's the one." Don't mention the date, Brenda. Don't give Vinny that ammo.

"Yeah, the one you had the date with." Too late. I'm gonna kill whoever told him.

Keeping my hand over my face, I grumble, "Yeah, that's the one. He's looking for me?"

"Worried about you. Probably thought a vampire hulled your virgin ass down here forever. He hadn't seen you all weekend."

I smack at him. "I don't work weekends. He knows that."

"He went to your apartment."

"What?" I almost screech. His expression is stern but not as stark as the tone in his voice. Nothing is worse than when Vinny gets territorial.

"He said he checked everywhere. Last person he saw you with was my sister. So, of course, he comes down to *my* lounge to see if you've been kidnapped."

"Just waltzed into *The Lounge*?" I ask.

"Charged in more like it. Warrant from NIIA."

"Fuck."

"Not today." Vinny pauses as I glare at him. "Anita took care of it. You're clear at least."

Clear or not, I gotta go back to Topside. I still have a job and life to return to, kind of. If Drauper and the NIIA didn't get past the Blood Mafia, I should be good. I dodged a bullet.

"Still gonna go to Topside, aren't you?" Vampire reads my mind. Yesterday I may have said I'm staying here, but now I want to run circles around Drauper out of spite.

"I have a job."

"Quit."

"Not that easy."

"It's not the mob," he muses.

"I need to go back, Vinny." Everyone is gonna give me a headache or an aneurysm.

"Just stay down here."

"Join the party with everyone else who wants me to stay. You can get a room at the Underground Carnegie and have a wonderful gala discussing what I'll be wearing next." I give an eye roll at the entire thing. Vinny remains silent for a moment with a concentrated expression. My eyes close as I lean my head back. "I know you're thinking of some way to make me stay."

"I don't share well."

"Don't I know it."

"Brenda."

"Vinny."

He mumbles something under his breath and stands up, adjusting his suit and refixing his ring. I prefer leather-jacket-Vinny. This looks too much like his damn father. I hate it.

"Promise me one thing at least," he says.

"If you say don't go near the Bronx Entrances, I'm shooting you in the foot."

"Keep your guard up around that detective. If you go on another date, take the smaller Glock and keep the Desert Eagle at home." Vinny keeps a serious expression as he heads for the door.

I cock my head. "You pissed off at me now?"

He pauses at the door frame and turns with a forced smile. "Only when you don't talk dirty to me, sweet cheeks." With that, he disappears. I blink quickly, a little confused.

Damn, is he actually jealous?

I should have slept.

Even wearing my glasses, eyes throbbing underneath, I can barely concentrate on the papers before me. It's quiet in the library, even for a Monday. A relief as my entire head pounds. I left my contacts in too long Sunday, and I'm paying for it now. Along with lack of sleep, my head wages war. Thank goodness there's a coffee shop near the library. At least I have peace and quiet with my coffee this morning.

"Good morning, Brenda." I stand corrected.

Turning my head slowly, I force a smile toward Janice. She wears a wide, gleeful grin as she strolls into my closet office. She scrunches her nose at the papers littered around me that I spent most of my morning rummaging through. I have until Wednesday to reshelve most of the records and journals in the restricted sections.

"Morning," I say as I take another drink of coffee.

"So..." she says apprehensively. Placing my cup down, I look at her to continue. "I was approached by Detective Drauper this weekend."

"You worked?"

"Saturday, I did. They needed help with one of the kids' reading groups. It was *so* much fun, by the way. You should come by next time. The kids are—"

"The detective, Janice."

She giggles. "Oh, right. He was wondering where you were, and I told him you'd be home since it was your day off, which I *thought* he knew. Do you know why he came by?"

"Don't worry about it. Thanks." I wave her off, going back to the papers in front of me.

"Did something happen?"

"No," I say softly, not wanting to snap at her again. My headaches don't need to get worse. Except it seems like she isn't taking no for an answer.

"I just thought—"

"Janice."

"He only ever comes by on weekdays. It seemed like something happened, and I heard you went out with him Friday.

"It's nothing, Janice."

"It's just that—"

"Please, just drop it!" I hiss under my breath. She jumps, surprised at my reaction with wide eyes. I take a deep breath. Even with the migraine, I speak calmly, "I don't want to talk about it." The air becomes heavy. Her eyes widen in shock. If I just blew things out of the water over the detective, I'm going to *really* lose my shit this time. "Thank you for trying to help, Janice. But please, don't worry about it. I'll talk to him the next time he comes by."

She doesn't move, her hands working into a nervous stupor. I push down the last of my defensive aura. Finishing my coffee, I take another deep breath. "I have a headache, Janice, and lots of paperwork. Sorry I snapped. It's just been a very, *very* long weekend. So, I'm just tired." I need a nap without being interrupted by a certain vampire.

Her mood switches instantly. "Aww, I'm sorry. You should have told me; I have some aspirin in my office. I can get them." Sometimes "pity me" acts work.

"Just took some," I lie so she'll leave. "Waiting for them to kick in."

"If you need anything else, please just say so."

"I'll be fine as long as I stay back here where it's quiet."

"Alright, can I bring you some tea later? Or dried fruit to help with the headache?" Is she serious? Is that a thing?

"Thanks, I'll let you know." No, I won't.

She nods, leaving me in the small, cramped space. I sigh and slump in my chair, rubbing my temples. I want to scream or throw something. Maybe tomorrow I'll call in sick and hide under the covers. That sounds like the best idea I've had all week.

I spend the next hour alone researching laws, but there's less to use up here, a downside being at Topside. I debate what to do next when a knock comes from the door. I stay silent, hoping they'll go away, but they keep knocking.

"I'm busy," I call out.

"You sure?" My body freezes as Drauper's voice responds.

Shit. Fuck. Damn. WHY.

I look at the books on ghouls, classes, and laws strewn about my hiding space. Given the circumstances of the past weekend, it doesn't look good. My mind blanks for a response as I scramble to put books away. "Still busy."

"Even for a...friend?" I don't like the sound of his pitiful voice.

I grab more journals, stacking them over the books and shoving them in a corner. "Are you still that? A friend?"

"I don't know." There's some remorse in his words.

I double-check the gun under my skirt and the .22 under my sweater. Both are secure. No other escape. After a moment, I say, "Come in."

Drauper creaks the door open. He wears a dark shirt under his jacket, and his sunglasses are off, which brings my distorted vision to his darkened solemn eyes. "I looked for you."

"Did you?"

"You weren't at your apartment."

"No reason to be."

"Where were you?" He asks.

"None of your business." My voice remains leveled as I cross my arms. Not going to let him into my head. Hopefully.

He lets out a long, exasperated sound. I wonder how many times he tried calling my phone or knocking at my door. At Vinny and Pops' discretion, my phone was changed and updated to family-only per protocol. Drauper wasn't on that list.

"You disappeared in the middle of the night with a vampire," he says. I keep my mouth shut. I wait to see if he knows more, but he doesn't let on that he does. He sighs, crossing his arms over his chest. "I'm not going to arrest you if that's what you're worried about."

"Why should I worry? *I* did nothing wrong," I state.

"You threatened officers."

"They almost beat an incubus to death and *actually* broke laws. I don't see a warrant for *their* arrests."

"They were doing their job."

"Bullshit." I keep my ground but try not to rile myself up.

He lets out a long breath, shaking his head. "*That* incubus was a *dealer*."

"What proof you got?"

His eyes widen. "We have records, including where he may have been that night."

"Where?"

"I can't tell you that."

"*Won't*. Got it." He opens his mouth to argue. "Don't. I know *exactly* what he was doing. And he didn't have anything on him, so I doubt that's why the cops stopped him. You can try to justify the cruelty all you want, but you won't change my mind. Stop trying, *detective*."

He drops his arms as the air thickens, and his glare softens for a moment, then hardens again. "How do you know that?"

"You have your sources, I have mine."

"And yours are correct?"

"Mine don't beat other Paranormals for no reason." Usually. Silence reigns again, and I think I pinned him this time. "Unless you're here to arrest me, you can leave." I turn away and go back to work.

I feel him come closer, and my body flinches as he stops next to my desk. The smell of leather, gunpowder, and shampoo invade my nose. Huh, he smells different.

"I was worried about you," he says. "You disappeared, Brenda. There was no trace of you, and your coworkers didn't know—"

"They don't need to know what I do on my off-time, neither do you. I'm getting sick and tired of people saying where the hell I should be," I grumble.

"What does that mean?" His eyes tear into mine, waiting for an answer of any kind.

I let out an exasperated breath and rub my temples. Damn, the headache is coming back. "Look, thanks for worrying, but I'm a big girl and can take care of myself."

"Not going to say there'll be a next time with those beasts, but for my own peace of mind, I needed to check in with you."

I nod to keep him off my back, or he'll keep hounding me. Last thing I need is him finding my connection to the mafia. Turning away, I wait for him to leave, but he doesn't.

"Do you want anything else?" I ask.

He shifts, adjusting his jacket. He clears his throat, "Werewolf movements?"

"Not unusual this time of year."

"It is if they're believed to be part of a certain family."

"Don't worry about that," I answer flippantly. "Probably because of the…ghouls you mentioned." I remember he had told me that, at least.

"Werewolves are pack-minded, right?"

"Yeah, think like a wolf, and you'll get their mentality. Why do you think so many live outdoors?" At this point, I'm only answering to see what he knows.

"Animal instincts?"

"Not that basic."

"Then why the city?"

"Technically, they live below it," I smirk.

"Semantics."

"Why are you asking?" I turn, eyeing him through my rose-colored glasses. He adjusts his stance and glances at the maps I have out.

"Movements with ghouls, vampires, and now werewolves. PSB isn't telling us anything. Officers are getting worried. More movement than any of us want right now. The Underground Mafia is forcing our hand to react." Why the hell does NYPD care, especially outside their jurisdiction?

"Ghouls came into town; do you blame them?" It also happens when the mafia is covering its tracks, which is what it sounds like. Damn it, Rodney.

"I'm asking for help here. Dangerous beasts are trying to claim a part of this city, and we're trying not to let that happen. I'm trying to make this city safer." I quirk a brow. "Those arrests *need* to happen because PSB isn't doing anything."

"Uh huh."

"How much do you know about—?"

"Second floor, farthest on the right, a few shelves down." His brows scrunch together. I add, "Books for you to read on your own. I have work to do." My limit has been reached and I don't have enough "anti-murdery juicy-juice" to level up in the "give-a-fuck" department. It feels like everything I've told him the past year hasn't stuck. I gave him info on how packs move five months ago when Rodney was causing a scare during some gun-running. "You can find all the info there about werewolves. I'm sure Janice can help you."

"Brenda—"

"Have a good day, detective." I pick up a few journals and walk out, leaving him in the small space.

I drop the journals on my other desk and use a side door. Smokers pass me as I go to the alley. Taking my glasses off, I rub my eyes as swirls of reds, oranges, and greens invade my vision. It's chilly out, even for May. I lean against the wall and look up at the sky. Something deep in the pit of my stomach tells me shit is just starting. This past week has been chaotic.

I sigh and beat my fist against the brick beside me. The past year, I thought Drauper was different from the other humans I met. I hoped he wanted to learn, to understand. Nope.

Beasts. I hate that word.

I put my glasses back on and pull my phone out. I dial, and it starts to ring. I wonder if I should start smoking. Nicotine may help the headaches and caffeine addiction.

The phone clicks. "Hello?" He answers.

"Will you be on Topside this evening?" I ask.

A pause. "Lil sis, you *did* change your number. Was it my fault?"

"Why would it have anything to do with you? It's been three weeks since I've seen you, Rodney."

"At least you didn't try braiding my scruff last time. Or my back hair."

"Not my fault you don't trim regularly. Pretty sure your father taught you better than that," I laugh.

"Why you asking if I'll be on Topside? Finally had enough with that vampire and want a *real* male around?" Rodney teases.

"Brute."

"Ouch. Always harsh."

"Topside or not, Lassie?" I ask again.

He pauses and shuffles something around. Probably his bed covers. "Yeah, I've got business up top. Gonna tell me why you asking?"

I'm loyal to the families, and I also hate Drauper at this point. Spite kicks in. "Got cops asking about pack movements and ghouls. I'm being annoyed by vampires, and I thought I'd bring you into the mix."

He grunts. "So, it's true you kept those cops from beating a Paranormal to death?"

"Uh huh."

"Pissed about it?"

"Uh huh."

"Getting back at the vamp for hiding shit?"

"Quicker than I thought you were."

"Never had a female say that before." There's silence followed by a deep chuckle. "Come to the restaurant and make sure you're packing. My guys have gotten trigger-happy, especially the new ones."

CHAPTER THIRTEEN
DONNY'S

How does an area run by werewolves smell of teakwood and pine?

Rodney practically owns the small neutral zone within Washington Heights and near Harlem. He has enough PSB agents on his payroll to keep it that way. There's the occasional slip-up with weapon-running, but such is the normality of mobsters.

Relief washes over me as street lamps flicker on in the dusk hours. I adjust my hoodie and the gun underneath. I put my contacts in earlier and dressed a little more comfortably for my lingering headache. Maybe I just need more water. I pass staring Paranormals and instinctively check my hidden gun. When Rodney says his wolves are trigger-happy, he means it.

I approach *Donny's*, Rodney's steakhouse named after his grandfather, Dominick "Donny" McLycan. He'd been one of the longest-living werewolves before he passed in the 50s—silver bullet to the heart.

A pack of wolves walk by me and grimace at my face as I make it to the entrance. Pushing the door open to *Donny's*, I'm stopped by a large werewolf. His skin is a deep grey, and his eyes are a familiar bright blue-grey. Long hair sweeps down his broad back and shoulders, canines just visible over his lips. This form isn't even the scariest.

Werewolves have three phases they can shift into. First is being a wolf that rivals in size with small horses. Their second form, a partial human form where their skin replicates whatever fur they have in their wolf form. They also don't lose the long canines, claws, and thick fur on their head down their back. In their third form, they stand upright like humans but are covered in fur, and their heads stay as a wolf. Their jaws are one of the strongest next to vampire fangs and daemon claws. I've only seen that form a few times. Usually, they only use it in fighting or keeping natural predators away. They rarely need a reason in NYC. Except, the frenemy in front of me may prove that thought wrong.

I pull back my hood and greet him, "What up, Marcus?"

He growls and looks me up and down. "You trying to get shot looking like that?"

"What?" I raise my arms in surrender as I look at my attire. "All the cool kids are wearing this."

He scoffs and looks back down. "Doubt it."

"What do you know, oh ancient one?"

A lip curls upward to show more of his canines. They're longer than most vampire fangs. "At least wear your damn leathers next time."

"Protection purposes or…?"

"You won't look like riffraff trying to get in. Then again, you usually just cause trouble." My jaw drops in fake surprise. He snorts. "What are you doing here?"

Marcus and I have a long-standing relationship of not getting along. Most find my sarcastic behavior amusing; he did not. I think it's a great game to hone my teasing skills. He's waiting for the day when Rodney tells him he can eat me. And not in the way where I'll enjoy it.

"*Technically*, you'd be up here for me." Marcus deepens his glare. "Came to talk to Rodney. He told me to meet him here. He in the back?"

"Yeah." He grunts but doesn't move. Oh, he's *not* in a fun mood tonight. Wonderful.

"Gonna let me through, or do I need to call him?" Damn werewolves and their tempers.

"Didn't tell me he'd have visitors, apart from the normal."

"You saying I'm not normal?" He raises a brow. "Don't answer that. Not like he tells *you* everything."

"You mean like Vinny?"

"Ouch." I clutch my heart dramatically. "Hitting hard tonight. Must be having a dry spell with that limp, hairy dick of yours. Forget to shave, and now you can't find it?"

He growls deep, and the snarl around his lips salivate like he's about to rip into me. Pretty sure I ruined my chances of getting past him.

"Lay off, Marcus," says my saving grace, Gunther, as he comes up behind the grey wolf. "Rodney told me she was visiting. Personal matters." Gunther claps Marcus' shoulder and looks over at me. One of the few bodyguards who doesn't hate my guts within the Wolf Mob. He's also large like my arch enemy but has reddish skin and bright hazel eyes. He wears a shirt and jeans with a dark leather jacket. "Follow me, lil sis." I carefully walk around Marcus and follow after him.

Gunther leads me through the restaurant of werewolves eating breakfast toward the main bar. The establishment is modeled after a woodsy, dark country aesthetic minus the cow skulls hanging on the walls. And plaid. Aromas of fresh eggs, toast, steak, and coffee fill my nose and cover the lingering scent of gun smoke. My stomach grumbles, and I think of siphoning food off Rodney. Gunther stops me near a barstool and gestures toward it. I watch him disappear through the back hallway as I sit down.

"Piss off Marcus?" Victoria's sweet voice comes from behind the bar. I turn to see the white wolf and her pale, azure eyes. The dark outfit contrasts against her ivory fur and skin.

"He started it," I answer.

She giggles and pulls out a glass. "The usual?"

"Double whiskey straight. And put it on Rodney's tab for making me deal with Marcus. He knows we don't get along." I grin as Victoria makes my drink.

"Probably wanted to rile you up."

"Don't need help in that department." I glance around and see the familiar faces of Rodney's crew and others who watch me carefully with their eyes pinpointed on my position. A shiver runs over my spine as a few scents deepen.

Victoria hands me my drink and starts to clean nearby. "Haven't seen you in a bit. What brings you around?"

"Easier to get a hold of Rodney on Topside."

"Challenges below?" She cocks a brow as she puts a few glasses away.

I shake my head at her. "Rodney just doesn't like me around Vinny. He's jealous Vinny is my BFF and not him," I joke.

"Males and their pride, no matter the species."

Another sip and I glance toward the back. Ten bucks Rodney's in a poker game and thinks he can win. He rarely did. He sucks at it.

I suddenly inhale gunpowder and grease, which isn't unusual for this place, but I don't recognize the scent. My hand moves to the inside of my jacket as I concentrate on Victoria before me. Her eyes move behind me and back.

"People seem high strung," I whisper to her. "PSB knocking on your doors?"

"You'd think that, but it's mostly the NYPD." Victoria grabs a new glass to clean, her gaze flashing toward the patrons around us. "They keep interrupting runs, right on the cusp of the zones. Rodney will probably tell you…"

A chair scrapes behind me, and I rest my hand on the hidden gun. Heavy footsteps approach, and now I can smell the wolf closing in. It feels quiet for a moment.

"You look new," he growls, and my hair stands on end. "And you ain't a wolf."

"Leave her alone, Travis," Victoria warns.

"What? These half-breeds think they can go anywhere. You can smell her a mile away, and she stinks of bloodsuckers." Victoria growls for him to back off, and I feel him ease closer.

I finish my whiskey and keep my gaze toward the bar counter, not daring to look up. His dirty gunpowder and cheap scotch scent burns my nostrils.

"So, what about it, *half-breed*? What are you doing in a wolf den? Death wish?"

"Your socializing skills are immaculate," I answer.

"I'll show you immaculate, you scarred-up, nothing bitch."

I hear the creak on my left and swing an arm around, hitting him square in the jaw. It barely moves him but shocks him enough that he doesn't see the gun.

The weapon goes off and hits his shin and other knee. He gives out a long howl. Swinging my free arm, I grab his scruff to throw him halfway onto the counter. The wolf's face smashes into the wood as I press my gun to his temple. The scent of blood mingles into the air. Werewolves stand up and draw their weapons, and the safeties ring off.

"Wanna try that again?" I warn.

Victoria runs toward the back, and I see Marcus smirking by the door.

Wolves growl in agitation over Travis, but the back hallway erupts as more werewolves enter among the snarling crowd. Travis remains still as I press my gun to his jaw. Silence settles as a rumbling growl shakes the place. I look over to see Rodney standing with Gunther.

Rodney is a large alpha timber wolf with muscles that rival only a few in the city. He has dark umber skin and fur that compliments his black hair and green eyes. His thick claws are out and glistening, and his jaw is tight as his lips pull back into a snarl. He passes his gaze across the scene and back to me. His head juts toward himself, cuing me to walk over.

I shove Travis' head against the counter one last time and hide my gun as I walk over to Rodney. He brings an arm around me, giving me a quick side hug with a kiss to my temple. He whispers, "He touch you?"

"Tried," I answer.

Rodney pulls out a pistol and shoots Travis in his other kneecap without blinking. The werewolf howls while others back away. Rodney puts the gun away and juts his head at Marcus. "Anyone who tries to touch her will fucking deal with me. Marcus, get these fuckers out," Rodney commands with a deep voice.

Keeping an arm around my shoulders, he walks me toward the back as the scene is cleared away. I glance back to see Travis snarl and gripe from his wounds. Two hours and he'll be good as new, except for where Rodney shot him. I don't carry silver bullets, but he does. Unlike incubi and succubi, werewolves and vampires heal quickly from most wounds. Purebloods can heal in a matter of minutes from regular bullets. It takes silver to do any real damage. So, Travis got to keep one of his kneecaps.

Rodney takes me to his office space in the back. Chips and cards are scattered on a large table surrounded by five chairs. Dark wooden panels line the room with shelves of books, booze, guns, machetes, swords, and knives. In the back of the room are his large mahogany desk and leather-bound chair with two guest seats.

"These damn wolves are gonna cost me more than a fucking game," Rodney says as he goes to the bar station.

"You weren't gonna win anyway," I scoff.

He turns and gives that feral, lively grin of his. "I was winning that time. Two cards away."

"Always two cards away," I mumble as I lean against the station. He pours us both a scotch. "You weren't kidding about trigger-happy. Brings back memories."

"Least that vampire taught you something right." He hands me my drink, knocking back his own and pouring another.

"Morning drinker now?" I ask as he walks over to his leather chair and takes a seat. He leans back, placing his cowboy boots on top of the desk. They match his dark jeans and black button-up shirt, the only nice things he'll ever wear. He hates suits, and since he's the boss, he wears whatever he wants.

"Feral, racist bastards trying to attack your family will do that to you," he says.

I shrug and take a seat across from him. "Just don't tell Pops or Vinny. Otherwise, they'll never let you babysit me again," I joke.

"*Clearly*, you need it," he teases. "Did you aim for the shin or go too low?"

"Thought I'd let him keep one kneecap."

"You still don't carry silver."

"Never will." I take out both guns and place them on his desk. His eyes flash as they rove over the hardware. "I only carry legal guns anyways."

"I believe I gave you those."

"18th and 21st." I eye him. "You told me they were legal."

"Aren't they always?" Rodney grins wildly. "You shoot Vinny yet?"

"Came close a few times."

"Make sure you use one of mine. It'll be like a…second-hand shot." Canines flash in the pale amber light. "But I doubt you called to talk about guns or getting *hit on* at my bar, even though one of those subjects is my favorite to discuss with you, lil sis."

"What about your business with guns?"

"What about it?" He tilts his head like a confused dog. Honestly, it's kind of cute, but I'll never tell him.

"Not running much as usual. Any reason why?"

"Why you sound like a P.I.? Thought Alanzo didn't want you around the business. Well, mine, anyway." He pauses and eyes me. "Only seemed fine with the Blood Mafia."

"Only cause of Vinny. Why you evading the question?"

"Not evading."

"Bullshit."

"You called *me* to talk, lil sis. And we don't really talk about my business because Alanzo would cut my dick off. I'll take on Vinny over you any day of the week, but not your Pops. I've heard what he can do, and I don't want to witness it in real life."

I grimace at the thought. I've seen what he can do. Pops and Ma scare everyone, and they have the stories to prove it. Family is something you don't cross when it comes to incubi and succubi, especially over their children.

"We've talked about your business before," I say.

"Dirty little secrets your parents will never know," he muses, then changes his tone. "You said something about cops. What were they asking?"

I raise a brow. "Now, who's questioning?" He keeps his hard stare on me, and I throw back my drink. He's the worst when it comes to big brother stare-downs. "Usually, it's just out of curiosity when NYPD comes to me with questions, but I think *they* think you have a hand in with the ghouls."

Rodney scoffs. "That'd be Doddard. And a few shifters."

"Lower-class ghouls scare the shit out of shifters; makes no sense for them to be involved." I place my drink on the desk. "Besides, Beckham—"

"Not every shifter listens to Beckham." Rodney takes a deep breath and looks at his gun shelf. "People who aren't under the families' protections have gotten restless. Some shooting before thinking."

"*No kidding.*"

"You have another gun in your pant leg, don't you?" I give him a smug smile. He chuckles as he takes his boots off the desk and leans forward. "You finally figured out what's going on up here?"

I cross my arms. "Werewolves aren't the only trigger-happy individuals lately."

"Since the cat is out of the bag, you wanna know why I've held back running and *why* it probably caught attention?" He stands up and walks over to his gun shelf.

"You actually gonna tell me or skirt around it?"

He glances back at me. "I don't lie like your Twilight reject."

"Ouch." Twice tonight.

I follow him over as he pulls a shelf, and it moves to reveal a large map of NYC. Red dots cover certain areas, with red lines connecting a few. Most of the dots are in Harlem and the Bronx. My stomach clenches. Rodney grabs a bottle near the map, taking a few swigs. He hands it to me next, in which I follow suit of drinking.

"We've always dealt with busts, even non-PSB personnel. Lately, cops been targeting certain areas and putting up sting operations. Civilians getting caught in between. PSB hasn't stopped anything, even in the neutral zones. Doesn't even help when you tip us off."

"What about those involved with our businesses?" I ask.

Rodney pauses, taking the bottle back from me. "Love how you still say 'our.'" I lightly push his shoulder, and he grins ruefully. He points toward a cluster of dots. "They keep hitting the same areas. Busts, shakedowns, doesn't matter what. People just end up missing or dead. No arrests."

"Wait, no arrests?" My eyes widen and scan the map. There are so many dots.

"See why I'm a morning drinker now?" He holds the bottle up. "Most of the Paranormals didn't have shit on them when they were taken. The runners didn't even have stashes on them. They'd make the drop and *then* got stopped. So, I've held back running and routes. Moving them further south, going through Manhattan and Staten. Less interactions."

"Imports at the harbor?"

"Shut down, for now. Blood Mafia following close behind."

I'm confused. Drauper said they *had* to make those arrests, but they weren't happening, and the cops were moving *because* of the mob movements, but Rodney was making waves *because* of them. Unless Drauper lied to get me to help him.

"It's not just the cops, Brenda." Rodney's voice softens, his eyes meeting mine. "PSB are joining in on the beat-ups and shakedowns."

My heart pounds in my chest. That's why none of them told me what was going on. PSB's turning on the Paranormals and NYPD's running rampant in zones they don't know or care about. Our worst nightmare collectively. This goes beyond the mafia. "How much trouble are we in, Rodney?"

He leans against his desk. "Not the first time this has happened. NIIA will probably step in before it…gets worse."

I trace my finger over the dots and lines, shivering over the amount of red. I even see a few dots where I was with Michello. I peer over everything and attempt to look for patterns.

"Something I've noticed while moving shit," Rodney says. "I've gotten less trouble moving south, not just away from the Bronx, but certain areas. The Main Entrances, for one, including areas that used to be Paranormal neighborhoods. The busier areas for shops and pedestrian traffic."

"That's where most of the dots are; populated areas of humans," I conclude, and he nods.

"It's not *just* the Bronx, only a section of it. They're being specific." Rodney gestures toward the map and wears a strict expression as he concentrates.

"You have a theory. What is it, Lassie?" An old nickname that makes him chuckle.

"PSB and NYPD are hiding something. Maybe a private institution. Someone doesn't want *us* near there."

I eye him. "You think the cops started this?"

He snorts. "Sure as hell wasn't us. Things were going smoothly. Quiet."

I sit next to him on the desk, leaning into his shoulder. Both of us look at the map perplexed. Something isn't connecting with the direct hits, what NYPD knows, and what the mafia is doing. The cops *think* they're clearing out the mob, but it's an after-effect of their actions. I believe Rodney when he says things were running smoothly. Paranormals are being forced to move. Drauper said Paranormal movements were making NYPD uneasy, but they're causing the movement. They must know that. Unless one of the agencies is setting a trap to take down all the families using the NYPD. Some fucker *is* clearing out sections of the neutral zones–specifically the Bronx.

I have to go back to *The Vault* to search for information and recent developments on the zones. It seems my time researching ghoul laws isn't going to help. Or it's not connected at all.

"Deeper than you thought?" He places an arm around my shoulders.

"Isn't it always?" I smirk. He grunts with some amusement. "Do the other bosses know this? Have they noticed the same patterns?"

"Not unless they've been tracking like me. Those dots and lines are only werewolves and shifters under my protection."

"Not the others?"

"Nope."

"What about half-breeds?"

He looks down at me. "Only one I track is you. I don't track the other half-breeds for reasons like what happened to you out in the bar earlier. Unless they're part wolf."

I sigh and stand up. "Guess I should have a chat with Pops and Vinny. Maybe Joey."

"If they talk to you."

"Yeah…." I groan as Rodney puts the shelving back. "Can you not tell any of them we had this talk? Until I do?"

"Long as you don't tell Vinny I want you to shoot him," he jokes.

"He already knows."

"You think the bullets I gifted you with his name etched on caught his attention? Or the late-night phone calls stealing you away from him?"

I laugh and shrug. "So, don't tell any of them it's *your* theory on someone hiding shit?"

"Probably, they listen to you, even *Vinny the Vampire*." Rodney sits and places his hands behind his head to lounge back.

"You're the Wolf Mob Boss; they listen to you." I sit opposite him.

"Nah, lil sis, Alanzo and Joey listen to you most days, even me…" his voice trails off, and he brings curious eyes back up to mine, "… especially Vinny."

I catch his glance and wave it off. The tone of his voice feels odd and pointed. I deter the conversation, "Just how he and I work as BFFs. I know you're jealous." My stomach grumbles, and I glare down at it. I should have eaten earlier, and the alcohol isn't going to help.

"You hungry?" He asks.

"Something tells me alcohol still isn't a food group."

Rodney stands up, grabbing my hand. "Come on. You can have brunch with me."

"Big bad wolf having brunch?"

"Hey now, we have great pancakes and steak. Besides, you always bring out the softer side of me, even when you're shooting bullets into my crew. And it's gonna piss off Marcus seeing you in the VIP section with me again." We laugh as he leads me out of his office with his arm around my shoulders.

I just want to fucking sleep.

I slam my hand on the alarm clock, and it falls off the dresser. At least it shuts up. I groan and pry my eyes open to swirls of violet, blues, and blacks. After fumbling out of bed, I click my way to the kitchen, where I smell the premade coffee. I feel for my mug and everything I need, just barely knocking things over. Without fully tripping over my feet, I make it to my leather chair with coffee in hand. It spills a bit over the mug's edge, but nothing too bad. I catch the first rays of sunrise as it turns everything pink and meshes into a mural of contorted pastels.

I called in sick to work last night. Janice backed me up, fearful of my migraine getting worse. I'm up early for another mission: going to *The Vault* to find answers to questions Rodney sparked. At least I spent the night before laughing my ass off with him. It's been a while since we just hung out. He's a hard-ass, but great to chill with. He took over as boss when I was ten, but we find time to spend together. He told Pops that he loved me the moment we met when I was six. Rodney used to call me "pup," a title only used for werewolf children. I would howl and run around like a pack wolf. I chuckle to myself at the thought as I enjoy my coffee.

Recounting last night's events, I remember I need to talk with a few more people to know what's going on within the neutral zones. Vinny comes to mind, and I shiver at the thought of him. I remember the hard stare while in *Unbound*. My nether region tightens and heats as I imagine dark crimson eyes searching over my body with that ever endearing, annoying smile....

No.

Vinny isn't that. He can never be more than my perverted best friend who makes the best

coffee and tells dirty jokes. Not after my 21st birthday.

I wanted to tell him I had a crush on him, but it backfired terribly. The memories of him kissing other girls and going back to Gina when I was younger haunt me. A reminder that Vinny would always be a two-hundred-year-old playboy. Something I never faulted him for until I saw him necking two gorgeous vampires at my own damn birthday party. Even then, I still wanted him. But whatever courage I had to tell him three years ago died the day he became the Blood Mafia Boss. I was the first one he told. And he was the first one I told I was moving to Topside. Three months later.

The baby sister for life. Fantastic to always have back-up, but lonely in the romance department. Vinny and I are best friends; that's all we can be. But it's better than not having him at all.

And hopefully one day…I'll shoot him. Just to get out all the pent-up sexual aggression he caused me through the years.

I finish my coffee and get things together for the long day ahead. Popping my contacts in and dressing my usual tank-top, jeans, jacket, and combat boots, I leave my apartment and head down the stairs. I stop by a crepe vendor for some breakfast as I make my way through the city and come up to the shimmering dark marbled Manhattan Entrance alongside pairs of werewolves and shifters in human form. Finishing my breakfast, I throw the paper from the crepe into the trashcan and enter the elevator with them. Once the doors shut, the shifters change into their original form, all with light cerulean skin. Pointed teeth shine as they hold hands. The two werewolves lean against the wall with crossed arms away from us. One of them quietly snarls as they look over at me, and I bare my teeth at them.

The elevator stops, and everyone disperses, the one wolf growling as they leave. I pass the usual shops, most of them setting up for dinner. I hit twilight hours; the time difference won't be that bad. Most are dressed well for their Tuesday night. Lights far up ahead in the ceiling shift as I turn toward *The Lounge*. It's only a few blocks north of *Unbound* and *The Vault.* Just like the others, *The Lounge* is a front for mob dealings but legit in its own running. It's Vinny's through and through, long before he ever became the Blood Mafia Boss.

I see the deep glowing crimson neon sign of the 24/7 establishment. Vampires always need blood or plasma, whatever their kicks are, to stay alive. I nod to both bouncers outside, and they flash their canines as they open the doors for me.

Brandy and leather crowd my senses in the dim lighting. Deep maroon leather seats line the walls in half circles with rounded tables. Smaller tables speckle the large area on plush carpet. The long bar on the left and right shimmer with glasses hanging above. Smoke drifts through the space as patrons sit and do their business, with a few necking in the booths. The smell of iron weaves its way to my nostrils.

I walk through the dark glass door of the back rooms like I own the place. The amount of times Vinny violated my apartment, he owed me that much to barge in. Three vampires sit in the small foyer to the three back rooms and turn quickly to face me and place their hands on their guns. They all wear button-up silk shirts, slacks, and jackets to match. Each with three or four weapons on them, not including their knives.

Vinny's head bodyguard, Samuel, gestures for the other two to stand down and flashes me a grin. "What brings you here, baby sis?"

"Need to see Vinny. He in? Or is he already asleep like the ancient being he is?" I ask. A guard snarls under their breath. This looks to be a trend for me lately.

Samuel chuckles and waves them off. Samuel has dark brown skin with tightly coiled locs that reach his shoulders. He has tattoos riddled across his body that glows under certain lights. The ink goes down to his knuckles. Older than Vinny, he still charms like a 30-something-year-old human.

"He was out in the main lounge earlier. Wasn't there when you passed through?" Samuel asks. I shake my head.

One of the guards, Matty, adds, "Must be feeding. He likes to use the one corner if he wants...*privacy.*"

My stomach drops as old memories flash; a new kind of shiver goes down my spine and heats agitation. Don't need to be reminded of that.

"You alright, baby sis?" Samuel asks.

I lighten my expression and smile. "Yeah, the bastard just owes me."

"Careful what you say about the boss," the newbie guard warns. I glance over and notice the long brown hair cascading over their shoulders, and their sharp, ruby-violet eyes narrow on me.

I narrow my eyes back. "Known him long enough and suffered his antics to say whatever the fuck I want." *Newbie* reaches for their gun.

"Hold on, Adrian," Samuel stops them. "Brenda here is Alanzo's baby girl. She looks human, but she's got the spunk of vampire, succubi, and werewolf combined. Special case for Vinny." He points toward the door. "Go out and find him. He'll want to hear any news she's got, given the latest circumstances. Matty, you too." Adrian sneers, leaving through the doors with Matty. Love the new ones. They're easier to piss off.

"How long has newbie been working?" I ask.

"A few weeks, honestly. They're a pretty good shot and protective. Came in from the north, used to run blood drive protection."

I sit down and cross my arms. "Vinny got a new guard, and didn't tell me? Takes the fun out of everything."

Vinny doesn't bring on new guards often. He travels on his own, much to the displeasure of every member in the Blood Mafia and his family. He never liked following rules.

Samuel chuckles and leans back in the wooden chair. "How you been, baby sis?"

I shrug and look around the room, which seems more violet and redder than usual. Vision change, *that's* comforting. "Not much."

"And I thought humans lived exciting lives."

"The most exciting thing about them is watching reality TV shows. If I hear about another one, I'm gonna lose it. What's the deal watching those and romcoms? They're boring as fuck," I scoff.

"People like mundane crap. I think *Jersey Shore: Vampiric Sandy Beaches* is pretty funny."

I narrow my gaze at the friendly bastard. "You made that up."

"Cross my heart," he gestures. "It's a real thing."

"What heart?"

Samuel laughs. "How the hell has Vinny not killed you with a spiked bullet yet?"

"I'm entertainment." I grin. "And who the fuck cares about Jersey?" Like any good New Yorker, I hate Jersey.

We laugh when I suddenly catch that familiar scent. Dark spices and bloodlust, a hint of coffee, just like every damn morning he interrupts me. I go for the Glock inside my jacket as I hear leather soles hit the carpet. Without turning around, I position the gun over my shoulder, aiming for what I know is his chest.

Five other guns click into place, pointed directly at me. My eyes move up toward the barrel end of Samuel's 9-millimeter. I look at the other two who have walked in, both with guns in each hand, pointed at my head and chest. At least they aren't afraid to play my games.

A smile creeps over my face as I look at Vinny. Unphased, he adjusts the cuffs of his dark sable coat, and pushes back his hair with a smile, and says, "Remember, *sweet cheeks*, we have a deal."

"Prepared to uphold your end?" I ask smugly. A guard shifts uneasily.

Vinny slowly licks his top lip and canines. "Only if you begin it, per agreement."

"I should shoot you for saying that damn nickname."

"You could, but they might shoot you, and I wouldn't be a happy vampire if you died."

"Afraid what my parents will do?"

"Among other reasons." He approaches me with a few steps. Adrian growls, but quiets when I click the safety in place and put the gun away as Vinny stands inches away from me.

I look over at Samuel. "Fuck you for aiming that thing. Thought we were friends."

"He's one of mine," Vinny answers for him.

"Wasn't talking to you, *bloodsucker*." The other guards shift their stances, guns still out.

"Put your weapons away," he orders the others. "One thing to know about Brenda Cuorebella, she'll never be a threat to my life. And she'll probably put a hole in you first." Vinny brings a hand up and swipes a thumb under my chin. My body relaxes at the small touch. "Her dormant side likes to come out and play sometimes."

"Only when you ask nicely," I tease.

"Is that so?" He nods toward his office door. "Maybe I'll try in private. What else will you do if I ask nicely?"

"Beat you with my bare hands."

"Promise?"

I shake my head as I follow him. Guns are disengaged. I see Samuel smirk at us.

Vinny's office is dark with leather and the musky scented aroma of sandalwood. His large oak desk and chairs take up most of the back, framed by old paintings and bookcases filled to the brim. To the left is his personal bar and coffee station, and to the right is a couch with a table. The room is illuminated with a soft, warm ambiance of yellow.

"Had to rile up the new guards again?" Vinny asks as he heads toward the coffee bar. I smell the roasted beans infused with the scent of cigars and rich brandy.

"Someone needs to break them in. Besides, they're gonna catch me pointing a gun at you at some point," I say smugly.

"Just remember to aim for the heart. Take me out before they get to you. Allow me that *heartfelt* death, will you?"

"I'll just shoot your dick off. Have one last smile before they blow me with holes."

"Except…I like you for what you already have. It'd be a shame to ruin any of that." His tongue sweeps over his top lip again.

To keep my body from quivering, I take a deep breath and cut to the chase, "I saw Rodney."

Vinny's expression falls, and his eyes darken in a territorial way. They put their beef aside years ago for me, though they still dislike each other. And he hates our friendship more than Rodney himself.

"When? Where? And why?" He questions.

"I'll tell you when the coffee finishes brewing."

"Brenda."

"Oh, for fucks sake, Vinny! Why the attitude? You know we go way back since I howled at the moon to copy him." I throw my hands in the air.

He doesn't change his attitude. "Why and where did you see him?"

"Last night. Topside at *Donny's*." Vinny brings his brows in close, confusion taking over his expression. It looks like I told him Rodney and I fucked in the bathroom. Damn territorial genes of his against werewolves.

"You saw him Topside? Within his territory? Do you know how dangerous that is right now?" The coffee finishes, and he turns away to doctor-up two cups.

"Yeah, but easier to find and talk to him." I'm not about to tell him how "trigger-happy" *barely* describes Rodney's wolves right now.

Vinny mumbles something as he brings the glass mugs over. I can see he's made them perfect as always. He hands mine over and sits his ass on the desk. "So, business or catching up?"

"Little bit of both." I slide down into a chair and blow on the hot beverage. I look up at Vinny and see ease come over him. Mood swings. Usually only happens when he needs to feed.

"Well, don't I feel like second best. Was it dissatisfactory for you?" Vinny attempts to be smug.

"Very funny. Quite certain Rodney isn't compensating from what I've been told anyways," I scoff.

"Doubt it."

"Pissing match much?"

"Are you making it one?"

"I only said I *talked* to him. *You're* the one—"

"Why are you here?" He places the mug down next to him a little harshly.

Vinny is rarely rattled. He could have bullets fly past his head and still laugh like it's a bachelor party. I scrutinize his behavior a bit as I watch his jaw tighten. Darkness has left his eyes, but they're hard, and his scent has heightened with the aroma of spices itching my nose. I lean back and hold my mug close. I don't like this side of him. It reminds me of what he is outside of our relationship. I'll forget he's the Blood Mafia Boss, in charge of half the vampires working below and on Topside. One word, and you'd disappear without a trace or worry. I've seen him do it. Not to mention his powers as a vampire, even if none affect me, apart from one. The only Paranormals who truly rival him in power are Rodney and Bruno. But it never scares me when Vinny reveals his fangs to me or demonstrates his strength.

I think my words over carefully, taking a sip of coffee. I don't want a headache over this later. Before I can open my mouth, he says, "I'm sorry."

I watch him rub his temples and grimace. Damn idiot hasn't trimmed his nails lately. Sighing, I put my mug down and go over to the bar, grabbing the crystal of brandy and pouring him a drink. Walking back, I hold the glass out to him, and he furrows his brow.

"I need caffeine, and you need fucking alcohol. Was the blood sour tonight?"

He takes the glass from me. "What blood?"

"Guards said you were getting the fair share when I walked in." I grab my mug and sit next to him on the desk.

"Going over ledgers for the month. No blood."

"When was the last time you fed?"

103

"Asking to fill in?"

"I'd have to shoot you first."

"At least you'd give wonderful foreplay." He smirks finally. "You never make it easy for me."

I playfully shove my shoulder against his. "If I started going easy on you, you'd go down in history as the first vampire to die of a heart attack." I stand up, moving around his desk. I know his damn map is somewhere.

Vinny sighs, knocks back the drink, then eyes me. "What's up, sweet cheeks?"

"Conversation I had with Rodney and a certain human has me thinking about something. Which book shows the map?"

"Third one on the second shelf, pull forward," he says, pouring himself another drink. "Something tells me it wasn't all usual business with him."

"Annoying his guards and a few other things." I cough under my breath. "We haven't talked in weeks. Needed to catch up."

Vinny sighs, "I know I can't tell who to be friends with."

"Just now figuring that out?" I find the book and pull it, making the case move and shift to reveal Vinny's large map. Its multiple layers cover a thorough section of the wall, with routes of his blood empire speckling across, showing most of the city and harbor.

"He's been on my heels for shit and pushing boundaries. So, pardon me for being protective when certain territories are getting dangerous. Damn hound needs to keep his pack in line," Vinny grumbles.

"If it makes you feel better, I told Marcus he has a limp hairy dick." Vinny barks out a laugh as he comes up behind me. "I know I'm diabolical."

"Learned from the best," he says, flicking his eyes to the map. "What are you looking for?"

"Did you change your routes?"

"Moved south after the ghouls came in. Some contacts warned me there were cops on Topside in neutral zones with some PSB. Now we're along Harlem streets and the underbelly of the Bronx, and I'm shutting my harbor sites down, too, just in case." I raise a brow at him, and he stops mid-drink. "What?"

"You're more open than Rodney with business."

"So?"

"I'm from a 'rival' family," I jest.

Vinny snorts over his glass. "You've done a few runs with me before, and I thought I promised not to keep secrets."

"Even mob secrets?"

"Who you gonna tell? Your antique books?"

My skin tingles as I watch his lips move over the glass and his Adam's apple bob as he drinks. I clutch my mug tightly and dip my head downward. My stomach flutters as I think of his lips doing that to my neck, chest, thighs...

Damn it, Brenda, knock it the fuck off.

"Besides..." Vinny breathes out and carefully moves a stray hair back from my cheek. I don't look up, but I relish in his touch. My skin burns, and it takes everything in me not to push him against the desk for more. "You should know, Joey took over after Pops removed Doddard a few days ago. I think they're gonna tell you tonight."

My eyes widen as I turn toward him. "Ruin a surprise much?"

"Act shocked, if you will. But you knew it was gonna happen soon."

"And here I thought you were terrible with birthday surprises," I mumble. Vinny quirks a brow, but I ignore him to scan over the map again.

"Why the fascination with the map?" He asks.

"Have you tracked where you've been hit the past few months?"

"Other than usual?" I nod in reply. He moves, undoing one of the layers above the map. The clear plastic folds over, revealing a shit ton of red dots, like Rodney's, throughout NYC. Same zones.

Fuck. Rodney is right, which means I have to check with Joey.

Joey. My brother is the boss for the incubi and succubi operations now. And he'll have to move headquarters after the whole Doddard situation. I hope they pick the old coffee shop a few blocks down. Cigar lounges and steakhouses are so 1950s mobster aesthetic. Ricky would at least be on my side.

Vinny points toward a cluster. "Where you were that night with Michello. It's why Anita was close by."

I tilt my head to the side. "I didn't ask before, but why didn't you come that night? We set up the emergency protocol to be you."

"Three half-breeds went missing, and two of my crew were killed. Silver stakes."

My breath hitches, and his jaw tightens. Not abnormal for this line of work, but it still hurts like a bitch to all.

"I'm sorry," I whisper.

"Someone was saved that night. That's something." He looks over at me, and a small smile pulls at his lips, making me smile a little. "Still haven't told me why the interest. I have far more intriguing things to play with."

"Not interested in playing."

"Not even toys?"

"Nah."

"Pity. We should change your attitude about that."

"Rodney has a similar map," I say, ignoring his banter. "Same clusters in the Bronx right near the Entrance."

"You see why I warned you?"

I roll my eyes at him. "Yeah, obviously. Still could have said why."

"Already apologized. Don't make me beg, unless…"

"Don't start." I hold my hand up, drinking my coffee as he chuckles. "You see what I'm getting at, bloodsucker?"

Vinny looks over the map intensely, then brings his attention back to me. "Targeting areas isn't new for PSB or NYPD. They've done it in the past, especially the cops. It's an attempt to gain control."

"This heavy?" I gesture toward the clusters.

"Did it in Brooklyn twenty years ago."

"Everyone or just the Blood Mafia?"

"Everyone. You can ask Pops. He and my father had to move operations away because of it. One of the reasons why most routes are in the Bronx now. Looks like we're moving to Staten or Brooklyn next."

I finish the coffee, grumbling at the constant frustration. Vinny chuckles and takes my mug, refilling it. I grin as he pours himself another glass of brandy. He sits on his desk and looks at me. "You've never had this much interest before. This have to do—"

"Detective came by Monday, asked about werewolf movement, piqued my interest. After the ghouls moved in and the incident with Michello and talking with Rodney, some of it seems connected…." Apart from the absurd amount of red, it's the placement that surprises me. The Blood Mafia's been hit in the same places as Rodney's business when usually, families are targeted separately, not together.

And deep in my gut, the area feels familiar to me. If Rodney is right, someone is hiding something, and they don't want the families to know.

"PSB and NIIA have always controlled the neutral zones, right?" I ask.

"They *patrol* them," Vinny answers. "Anyone can hold business there, but it's usually Paranormals. It's why we run our routes through there."

"But *anyone* can have business there? Human or not?"

"Pretty much."

So, *anyone* could be hiding there. I hum to myself as more pieces come into play. Neutral zones are great protective barriers for Paranormals, except when being used against us. Maybe I'm missing something about the zones. Another purpose….

"Gears are turning, sweet cheeks. What's clicking?" Vinny asks.

"Wondering if I should contact Bill," I mumble.

Vinny narrows his eyes at me. "Don't you fucking dare."

I smile behind my mug, "Oh, come on, you still upset about the itching powder incident?"

"I threw out most of my underwear because of Midnight," he growls under his breath and takes a drink. I laugh, remembering Vinny howling that he'd kill the young vampire.

"Bill's my only contact in PSB who I can trust." Vinny glowers at me, which makes me laugh loudly. "Fine, fine, I won't call Bill. His IOU's suck anyway."

"Mine are far more generous." He grins as I laugh at his discomfort. I shake my head at him as he lightly pushes my shoulders. Fine, no Bill Midnight, for now.

"I need to go back to *The Vault* then."

"What about the job you had to stay on Topside for?"

"Day off. Headache and shit."

"You know orgasms can help get rid of them? Good for boosting—"

"I'll pass, and I already know," I smirk as I gulp the last of the coffee down. It burns its way down my throat.

"Keep rejecting me, and you may get that historic heart attack." He smiles mischievously.

I roll my eyes and place my mug down. "You've lived long enough without me; you'll probably find another half-breed, scarred-up pain-in-the-ass to call you out on your shit. There has to be at least one every three hundred years."

His expression darkens with a frown and heavy lids. What the fuck is wrong with him tonight? Not the first time I've made these jokes. I feel a certain animosity from him as he says with roughness, "There's no one like you, and you know it."

"Relax, bloodsucker. You're only saying that cause you're my bestie and have known me forever." I wave my hand, and he catches it, gripping my wrist. He holds on tight and slowly brings it to his face, inhaling deeply. I feel chills run over me, tingling over my muscles. A heat brews below, and my toes even curl for a moment as he takes in my scent. "I think you need to feed soon, Vinny. You're acting funny again." My voice is soft and doesn't have the jocular tone that I intend.

"Careful how you talk about yourself around me. You already make my blood churn, don't make it boil and rage. Even if it does turn you on, *sweet cheeks*." Vinny speaks in a low tone like honey whiskey itself. Smooth, but kicks you right in the pants.

I tear my wrist from his grasp and stare at him, holding back the slight tremble down my spine. My entire body feels like it's on fire as I breathe in his scent once more, the familiar aroma that either aggravates me or makes my world make sense.

107

Furiously blinking the feelings away, I take a deep breath and turn away from him. I say nothing more as I walk out, my body ablaze and my face flushed. After I walk a few blocks, I don't feel his touch on my wrist anymore.

After hours spent with my nose in research at *The Vault,* I slump into my chair, exhausted with nothing to connect what the hell is happening on Topside. The phrase "new place, different pattern" keeps repeating in my head. I can't accept it's only that, but nothing that explains why anyone would want to clear out the neutral zones. It won't help businesses, legit or not, and it doesn't help protect humans or Paranormals. No one seems to gain anything. The mafia will have to spend resources moving routes and their safe houses. People will lose their businesses of all kinds with no one coming through. Rent will go up, and shops will close. NYPD doesn't benefit either, losing resources putting cops in jurisdictions they aren't supposed to be in. No arrests, no money. Crime rates go up without cops in other areas, their sections. Looks bad on them. So why push into these zones? No one gains from an empty neutral zone.

Unless Drauper is lying about the arrests and knows something.

The wild card is the ghouls; they may be the connection. Empty neutral zones help no one unless the ghouls want to clear the others out. They'll all be what's left, but then why keep a neutral zone to themselves? Especially if the mafia could use them as a scapegoat. Hell, NYPD could. No one ever sides with ghouls. They'd gain a neutral zone, but for what purpose?

I push my hair back and sigh, glancing over at the clock. Most of my afternoon is still unspent. I look at the books on my table and see nothing that seems to help me. "Damn it."

"Ahh, the sound of frustration." Beckham's chilling, soothing voice fills the void as he climbs up the stairs. He's ethereal in his movement, but his eyes shine with deadly wit.
It's one of the many reasons why I love him, besides letting me read materials from the private section. "Research fruitful?"

"Your library never disappoints, better than Topside." I cringe, thinking of the mess I left behind in my office.

Beckham takes a seat next to me and gestures toward the books. "Humans do not regard history and its lessons as they should, especially what is considered mundane information."

"Can't argue there. Sometimes I miss working here. I have a harder time keeping records for them than Paranormals."

"You see why my business ventures are important, then. Plentiful subjects." He smiles widely, his pointed teeth shining in the small light. His long fingers move over the various books stacked on the coffee table. "Decided to try your hand in your own business? Or joining another's finally?" His eyes glint. I glance toward the materials which pertain to business laws, jurisdictions, and mob records.

"Not quite. I'd never start my own or…." The bite marks on my neck pulsate, and I keep my hand away from touching it. Clearing my throat, I shake my head. "Everything is already established down here. Don't need me adding to the chaos."

Beckham hums, gesturing toward the empty mug in front of me. I nod and the old shifter takes my mug to the drink station as he talks, brewing the peppermint tea, "It does please me that even after your time above, you still see yourself amongst us. Even if you *mingle* with police."

"I don't *mingle*," I counter. "I grew up with you all, I don't think I'd ever be able to turn my back on everyone."

"Why leave us to live in Topside, then?"

"I wanted to add more books to my collection."

Beckham chuckles and hands over my fresh mug of tea. "Maybe. Or you wanted a chance to live in the sunlight forever and abandon the shadows?"

"Sunlight at least hides the shadows that haunt us."

Beckham's snake-like eyes watch me intently. "What haunts you, Little Sister?"

I lean back into the couch, my gaze watching the tea swirl in my mug. A lot haunts me, some I remember and some I don't. All of it seems to have ruby eyes; some kind and distant, and others are bloodthirsty and boil with rage. "Some things can't be changed, like DNA or what we're meant to be. We can't change what we are."

Beckham pats my knee, brushing it softly, then brings a single finger over my scars and stops a long nail at my eyes. His features soften as his gaze comes to mine. "Do you remember the first time you came here? You desired to read and learn stories but thought you couldn't due to your blindness. A few short weeks with me, you were reading braille better than myself. And then, you taught yourself how to read when Charlene made you those glasses. Would your younger self believe you are a librarian now? Your days reading and writing multiple languages?" I scrunch my brows, and he smiles, "You overcame an obstacle that was set against you. You can achieve other things with the same tenacity, without needing to abide by anyone or anything."

The conversations of late with family are sounding like a broken record. Except, all I can think about is Vinny and that impossible road.

"And do you have any advice to *achieve* these things?" I ask.

"That would be too easy," he grins.

I scoff and say, "Keep your secrets, oh great wise one."

He chuckles at me. "I must have my own tricks up my sleeve. Business requires such things; never show your full hand. Always have something to bargain with."

Wish he had told me that years ago. It would've saved some heartache. That's what I get for taking poker lessons from Rodney.

"I think I bargained everything a few years back," I say, restacking some of the books and sitting back down beside him. "I appreciate the encouragement, but I don't think your advice is the solution I'm looking for."

"Sometimes our solutions to problems become a festering virus instead."

Beckham's eyes find mine and glint with some knowing. I don't think he understands my solution to stay on Topside *has* to work. I can't move down to the Underground, not when it endangers people that I love. Festering virus or not, I won't let the threat I was given years ago to become true.

I remain quiet, sipping my tea as Beckham stands and looks over the books I've gathered. "You have looked into a *specific* area, have you not? Where the attacks took place?"

"Finally caught on?".

He smiles and says, "Not all my cards at once."

"I've looked and looked. Nothing abnormal, no connections."

"Not everywhere, it seems." He walks over to the stairs and pauses with his hand on the rail to look at me, his expression grim as he asks, "Perhaps, near where Alanzo found you?"

He disappears down the stairs, and I gasp. The cluster I'd seen on the maps, that's why it felt familiar. I know that area. Even if it has been years since I dared go near. Shit.

I scramble from my spot and go toward the map section. I fumble through everything as I find a recent map of the Underground. I lay it open across the floor and trace my fingers over paths, blocks, and sewer systems. And then there it is. Plain as day.

I should've noticed at Vinny's. I should've noticed at Rodney's.

Two of the red clusters on both maps were directly above where the ghouls moved in. It can't be a coincidence that it's where I was found. Most likely another reason why my family didn't tell me what was happening. I bang my head against the shelf. I'm a librarian, not a private investigator. I can barely keep track of all this information. As I put away the map and other items strewn about, I hope my family isn't keeping more secrets from me to be safe.

I want to go back to life where I was telling Ma not to take my panties.

*   *   *

111

Somehow, I got stripper's glitter on my hands.

I grab a towel from my desk and wipe away the atrocity of pink glitter off my skin. Damn it, Gina. After the show, I'd tried to slip through unnoticed, but she was working and pulled me into a shimmery hug. At least I made it into my parents' apartment without much noise.

It's only 3 pm, which means my stomach won't make it to breakfast. I sneak a few muffins to my room, nibbling on them as I flop onto my bed, my head still spinning from information and emotions after visiting Vinny and Beckham. I bring my hand up and look over the smaller scars, following them up my forearm and toward my bicep. Long gashes have healed jaggedly, worse over the rest of my body. I drop my arm beside me. I just need someone to pull a lever and allow myself to fall into hell. At this point, it's easier than figuring out anything. I doubt I'll ever learn why I was left in sewage. Or get explanations for the scars and shadows that haunt me. And I'll never fully have Vinny.

Reality is cruel, and Paranormal Societies suck. I should know; I've studied them.

I sigh and drift into sleep, hoping the nap will help. Random stars litter my vision in the darkness, a milky way of streams and streaks of sky. The darkness I revel in until it all vanishes.

Everything is bright.

Blaring white lights invade my vision, scorching out the darkness. My dark abyss replaced with churning white. Fluorescent. Artificial light that makes my eyes hurt and throb inside my head. It sears into my eyes. The light blinds me, and I feel myself scream without sound. My head hurts. My chest hurts.

Everything hurts.

A clinking sound vibrates next to me like gnats smacking into a bulb. Tink. Tink. Tink. Over and over again.

Am I still screaming? The light hurts. I ache as it envelops me into a bright hell. My eyes burn as I try to look away, but something keeps them open. I try to peer through the brightness. Nothing. Tink. Tink.

I want out. I want to go back to the shadows. Back to galaxies that form before my eyes. Violet. Blue. Crimson.

Please let me see his eyes again.

Anything but this. Another soundless scream rips from my throat.

Make it stop.

Make it STOP.

MAKE IT FUCKING STOP.

"Hey, hey, sis…it's okay."

My eyes pop open to see Joey's wide violet eyes peer down at me. One of his hands holds onto my shoulder, the other caressing my head. I curse under my breath as cold sweat drips from my trembling body. Joey gets on the bed and wraps his arms around me, repeating, "It's okay, sis…it's okay." I hold onto him, burying my face into his shoulder. Damn, it's been weeks since I last had a nightmare. Not as bad as being blinded by fake light, though. I shudder and breathe in his warm scent of cinnamon and clove. He lays us back down, and I rest my head on his bicep.

"Almost didn't catch you in time," he whispers.

"Maybe you're losing your touch," I joke.

He's wearing a loose tank and silk pajamas. I must've woken him up before Pops, who used to come in after me most nights. I had nightmares frequently when I was a kid until my teens. Pops was out working most nights, and Ma held things over down below, so Joey and Ricky would watch over me. Usually, I don't make much noise, but they know somehow. He'd come in and lay down next to me like this, and we'd lay in bed and talk into the early hours. The nightmares mostly stopped, but Joey hadn't. Best big brother a female can ask for.

I shudder again, and Joey holds me closer, looking at my dresser. "Is that stripper glitter?"

"Gina," I answer.

"You should know better than going through the front door by now," he chuckles.

"Some lessons never learned. Or maybe I have a fascination to see how many times I'll get lube, glitter, or whatever on me."

"Used to be covered on stage."

"Only cause of Ricky." Joey pokes my arm, and I swat at him as he pulls me in tightly. I'm thankful he doesn't ask about the nightmare. He rarely ever does.

"Staying for breakfast?" He asks.

"Yeah, skipped work today. I had shit to do and then saw Rodney, then Vinny, and well…" I look at him as he watches me, and he lets out a long sigh.

"He told you, didn't he?" He asks, and I nod. "Damn vamp can't keep his mouth shut."

"Makes it easier to track gossip."

"I wanted to surprise you. He never lets me have anything," he mumbles.

I snuggle into him and poke his nose. "Aw, come on, knew it was coming. Matter of fucking time. *You* just needed to tell Pops you were ready."

"Pops actually asked me." He shifts his gaze back to me.

My eyes widen in surprise. "Fucking hell, really?"

"Yeah. Either I did well with the Doddard situation or—"

"He wanted to keep the business tight."

"Maybe. Glad it's official. Ma's over the *moon*."

"Oh, I *believe* it," I giggle. "Guess I'll just have to get used to you being the big-time mafia boss now." I look up and watch shadows move across the ceiling. Joey absent-mindedly caresses my shoulders.

"You should give me a cool new title like Diablo of the Underground," he says.

"Are you fucking serious?"

"What?"

I snort, "Leave the nicknames to me, you suck at it."

"Here I thought you were gonna beg me to move headquarters to a coffee shop or something," Joey teases, but my eyes light up as I look over at him. He brings his hand to his face. "Damn it, you are."

"Please, please, please," I beg. "If you have any love for me as your baby sister, you'll do it."

"Wow, pulling the big guns, aren't we?"

I grip his arm and smile broadly. "Ricky would decorate it. He won't annoy you for like thirty years."

Joey grumbles, but there's a twinkle in his eye. He gives a few dramatic moans. "A coffeehouse?"

"Do you know how many fucking steakhouses, lounges, and clubs there are? Seriously, what is it with mobs using those as fronts? The stereotyping is ridiculous. Change the game."

"Not because you want free coffee?"

"Added bonus." I smile smugly. "Maybe I'll come down more often."

"Knew you loved coffee more than me." Joey pushes me a little. I push back, and we laugh quietly before laying in silence for a moment, with him tracing over particular scars and me patting his arm, relishing in his touch.

"Sis," he says. "I know we talked about what's happening in the Bronx, but there's something else." The conflict in his voice worries me as I nod my head for him to continue. We keep our gaze toward the ceiling. "A lot of shit's been happening. Pops is reconfiguring tunnels and using sewers to get people out….where Pops found you. The last time you were there you puked your brains out. I didn't want you to go searching and then realize…"

"Hey, hold on, Joey," I shift and turn to look him over. He meets me with leveled violet eyes glowing a little in the dim light and I tilt my head. "That's why you didn't tell me?"

"Apart from Pops not wanting you in the middle, the area doesn't exactly hold fond memories," he says carefully as my gaze drifts toward the other wall. Joey brings me into an embrace again, and I hug him back. "Look, we're overprotective because we love you. You're a blessing that came out of nowhere, the best damn thing to happen. Ma got the daughter she always wanted, and you changed Pops for the better. That shitty place is just a reminder of what we can't heal."

"I know, Joey...I know," I whisper into his chest.

He pulls back and stares at me. "You'll always be my baby sister, and I gotta do what I can to protect you. I'll kill anyone who makes you feel or act the way you were those first few months. My new title may help do that. With your consent, of course."

I relax and smile gently. Those first few months were the best and worst. I may have been found, but some scars don't heal quickly enough. "Which makes you the best big brother ever."

A smile spreads over his face. "Don't tell Ricky that."

I fall back from his arms, flopping into the bed. "How did you *ever* survive before me?"

He laughs. "Whiskey and letting him dance."

"I think your plan backfired."

"Says the librarian who still finds stripper glitter on her." I push him off the bed. He lands with a thud and small groan. "Playing dirty, you been with those werewolves lately, too, huh?"

"At least you don't wrestle me half-naked." I crawl to the side of the bed and peer down at him.

He rubs his neck and squints at me. "Ricky made you swear he's the favorite again, huh?"

"What do you think?"

There's a gasp from the doorway. I look over and see Ricky's mouth wide open in shock. "Slumber party without me?" He's wearing the same pajama bottoms as Joey, but no top. He skipped the lingerie tonight.

"Small chat, that's all," I say and settle back onto the bed. Ricky takes it as an invitation and hops in with me, curling up next to me and snuggling into my back, making me laugh.

"Hate it when you two have sleepovers without me," he mutters.

"I'm literally two doors down." I push him off my back, and he puts his head on my stomach instead. "How are your arms like vice-grips?"

"Pole dancing," Joey answers as he climbs back onto my bed. When did my bed become Grand Central Station?

They squish against my sides, placing me in a cuddle sandwich. Incubi and their cuddle puddles, I swear. There's some small talk, and Ricky agrees to the coffeehouse idea. Joey tries to tickle me, but Ricky stops him before we get too loud. The snuggle battle with my two older brothers isn't anything new, adults or not.

"You staying the day or just for breakfast?" Ricky asks.

"She has work," Joey answers.

"Damn, I wanted to color your scars. I got new neon blue paint. It would look great with your hair." Ricky flits a finger over my facial scars. He pauses over the bite mark on my neck and squints. "Sis, where did—"

"The last *new* paint you used stained my skin for a week," I avoid his question.

"But you looked fantastic," Ricky says. "It complimented the black you always wear."

Joey grins at the banter and tucks my head into his chest, failing to protect me from our flamboyant brother. "Don't traumatize her."

"Yeah, how about that?" I chime in.

"I do *not*. You *loved* it years ago. Best part of your routines," Ricky counters and looks at me flabbergasted. "I enhance your being into the wondrous creature you are. I am here to elevate you."

Joey nods and shrugs. "He's got a point."

I glare at him next. "Don't you dare betray me."

"Keep complaining, and I'll make Joey shave your head," Ricky threatens, and Joey drops his mouth in shock. I grimace. He sucks at shaving my head.

"Rude," I grumble.

"Prude," Ricky teases.

"Don't you *dare* start."

"Joey, tell our baby sister she needs to get laid already. She's obviously pent up with sexual aggression." My eyes narrow at him. No way am I admitting he's right.

Joey sighs, some amusement emerges from his voice, "Unless you're ace or demi, sis, I honestly don't know why you haven't yet."

"See?" Ricky pokes at me. "Well needed and good for your health. It boosts serotonin, gets rid of headaches, strengthens muscles—"

"Can we *not* talk about this while you two are wrapped around me like snakes?" I argue.

Ricky looks at me with disgust, his blue eyes shining. Joey taps my nose. "Incubi, sis, it's first, second, and third nature."

"I hate you both," I mumble.

"No, you don't," they simultaneously say, hugging me closer as I slowly smile.

"By the way," Ricky interrupts the silence. "You smell like dark spices and coffee. Have you been—"

"*Not now,*" I growl. I already had enough conversations with my parents about him. Not going to add brothers to the mix.

"*Fine,*" Ricky drags out and pouts. "What about an incubi I know?"

"She doesn't want your seconds," Joey grumbles.

"What not? I could—"

"Ew, ew, and *double* ew," I cringe. "Where's Ma and Pops when I need them?"

"About to head slap your brothers if they don't get to work soon." All three of us freeze when Pops' voice answers. We all turn to see him standing in the doorway with his arms crossed, trying not to grin. The battle for him is amusing.

"Morning Pops," we say in unison.

"Ricky, double-check the changeover downstairs. Joey, you've got payroll to handle. Biweekly is coming up. I want it all done before breakfast. Guests are coming, so get moving." Pops moves to the side, nodding toward the door.

Ricky hugs and kisses me quickly on the head. "We'll talk more."

"Yeah, right," I mumble.

Joey laughs and hugs me. Pops kisses them on the cheek before they both leave my room. I lean my head back and glance at the clock. Holy shit, it's almost 6 AM. No wonder Pops is up.

"Snuck in again?" He asks.

"It was early, didn't want to wake anyone up." Even though I did. "Ma want help with breakfast?" He nods. I get out of bed and stretch a moment. My eyes begin to itch as spots and orange-ish colors flutter over my vision. I rub them harshly as I walk over to Pops.

"Sleep in your contacts again?" He asks.

"Yeah, but I think they're itchy from wearing them all day. I may switch to glasses later."

"How old are the contacts?"

"Um, a week? Only the second time I've worn them. May need to go back in to see Charlene. Colors are changing again."

"I'll get you an appointment in the next few weeks." He brings a hand up to stroke my cheek as concern riddles his face. "You had a nightmare."

Of course, he heard. "Joey took care of me."

He brings me into an embrace, his body tensing a moment. I can sense he's stressed, and I doubt me living on Topside helps. I wrap my arms around him tighter and breathe in deeply. Anything left from the nightmare and earlier dissipates in his arms. His dark scent calms me as my body relaxes into the hug. He kisses my head, rubbing my back lightly.

"Love you, Pops," I murmur.

"Love you, too, baby girl. Go help your Ma. Coffee is brewing." His voice is less rough.

"Alright, sorry if we woke you," I say as I let go and we walk down the hall.

"Can't be mad if what wakes me up are your brothers caring for you. There's nothing better to rather wake up to."

"Maybe don't tell Ma that. Pretty sure she'd want to be the best thing." We both laugh, and he pats my shoulder as he disappears toward the foyer. I continue into the kitchen and smell fresh bread baking.

Ma moves around the kitchen, putting ingredients into a bowl. Bacon is laid up, eggs set to be cracked, and flour coats the counter. She hums to herself as she fixes the stove temperature. My mug sits near the coffee maker, and I smile as I pour coffee into it.

"Want help, Ma?" I ask.

She beams as she turns toward me, wiping her hands on her apron and approaching me with open arms. Putting my mug aside, Ma embraces me fully with a cheery voice, "Good morning, baby. Drink your coffee first."

"Good morning, Ma." I kiss her cheek and let her go back to her prepping. I sit at the kitchen table. Ma takes help when she needs it and rarely ever does, but I was taught to always offer.

"You sleep at all?"

"Not really…." My voice trails off, thinking back to the bright lights in my nightmare.

"How were the muffins?" Her brow quirks.

"Always the best."

"Course they are," Joey states as he comes in. He grabs a mug and pours himself some coffee. He kisses Ma on the cheek and walks past me. "Why you not helping Ma?"

"She doesn't want it, Joey. Not yet." I narrow my eyes on him for the accusation.

"You should—"

"Should nothing," Ma intervenes. "Get to your business and then get back to wash up for mealtime, son. Grab a muffin to hold you over."

Joey shuts his mouth and does what he's told. He glances over at me, and we stick our tongues out at each other. A small grin pulls at his lips as he walks out as Ricky comes in, grabs a coffee and muffin, then kisses Ma before leaving. Pops walks in and grabs Ma's ass front and center of me. I avert my eyes and stare at the scars near my wrists. He kisses my head and leaves with the others.

"Joey tell you the news?" Ma asks once the door shuts. I make an affirmative sound. "Pops is proud. Always wanted him to take over but never felt right. It never does, though," Ma adds quietly.

"He'll be fine and do great."

She pauses and looks at me. "Everything has just been hard and confusing lately. Nothing new, but…."

I walk over and place a hand on her shoulder, and she rests her hand on mine. Damn, the last few days have sucked for all of us. Ma never liked to admit she's worried. The times she does aren't the easiest for her.

"Joey knows what he's doing," I reassure her. "Just another title for him to hang over my head and bribe me to come home more often."

"Would it work?" She looks back at me.

"If he used Pops and you, maybe." I grin.

Her expression softens. "As much as I prefer you home, I'd never make you do something you don't want. Even if I don't like it. I raised you to be your own female of worth."

I look around the kitchen. "Speaking of being a female of worth, let me help you?"

She pats my hand. "Grab your apron and take care of the batter. We may have enough time to make another batch of muffins."

"Pops said something about guests, is that why?" I ask grabbing my apron. Ma just starts to hum as she goes back to her baking. I quirk a brow, but follow her instructions.

As we work in silence, it really hits me how things have changed so much. Joey's spent the last ten years on the financial side of the family business since he's good with numbers. They wanted him to take over years ago, but it was dangerous due to the business, interacting with other families, and the black market. Tracks need to be covered, people paid off, connections created, and power maintained in the community. All mafia business is dangerous, but pulling Paranormals and humans from trafficking is difficult, mob or not. Pops' business saves a lot of victims from the black market. They'd have nowhere to go or a future if he hadn't…I don't want to think about it.

Pops started the business in Europe. He started the mission to get people back from being bought centuries ago. It carried over to the U.S. when he moved along with the black market. Most governments are too overwhelmed, lost in the slave trade game. Pops gets them out. Some stay in *Unbound,* weird as it sounds, but for incubi and succubi, it's their saving grace. In the market, they'd be used for their hormones, forced to do unspeakable things in the trade.

Vampires are sold for fangs and blood and were sent to rehabilitation centers Pops created years ago until Vinny became the Blood Mafia Boss. Now, Vinny sends them to his own people for protection and rehabilitation. Beckham finds homes for the shifters, whose hair, teeth, and organs are sold for a shit ton, alive or not. Werewolves are kept in cages, shaved repeatedly until their dying breath, and sold for their canines and claws. Rodney gives them sanctuary out West on rural farmland. He and his father, Frederick, have contracted ranches that rehabilitate all Paranormals before going back into the real world. No one wants to be near ghouls, so they're rarely found. It's even rarer to see daemons. Back in the day, they were used for experiments and clipped for their feathered wings, at which point, they couldn't survive long after. I don't blame them for disappearing into mountains or non-human areas. Paranormals are strong and powerful, but some weapons are specialized for them. Silver bullets are the least of their problems. And it isn't just Paranormals either.

Humans are relocated to shelters in the city, care centers, and safe houses. Some, if injured badly, are moved to hospitals that can keep them. Those places are on our bankrolls. Later, some are moved north to Connecticut or Vermont. Human victims are rarely kept Underground, most too traumatized being somewhere similar to where they were trafficked.

Most mafia families within the east, Midwest, and north are their only lifelines. Their businesses keep Paranormals alive and out of chains. It's the dirty work that government agencies, human or not, won't touch. The market is "too big" for them to handle, not wrong, but no excuse to look away. Some PSB and NIIA Agents are easy to pay off knowing what the actual work involves, like my prankster friend, Bill Midnight.

I look at the full meal of pancakes, casserole, bacon, muffins, fruit, coffee, and juice we prepared when I notice his scent of dark spices the moment he's in the foyer. I reach for my gun, then realize I hadn't put it on being at home. Damn. Thinking quickly, I grab the rolling pin and swing the tip at Vinny's chest. He grins and says, "I prefer your other method."

"Dying to get that *contract* settled?" I cock my head with a small smile. His eyes flash a moment, and his stare deepens. "Maybe I'll just beat you over the head instead."

"Not in my kitchen," Ma warns as she pushes the rolling pin down and kisses Vinny on the cheek. Traitor.

"Good morning, Carmen. You look absolutely radiant," Vinny coos after her. She swats at his shoulder and smiles. My eyes roll back with my head following along. "Do you need a compliment this fine morning, sweet cheeks?" Vinny smiles broadly, leaning against the counter.

"Will it include me bashing your head in?" I propose.

"Only if it's foreplay."

"I knew you were a masochist."

"Only for you, which you've trained me with each wounding word." He dramatically places his hand over his heart. I scream internally.

"Hold still. Maybe I'll slice your throat instead."

"*Now* we're talking." Vinny's eyes flash with glee, and his fangs elongate. Aw shit, I did myself a fowl. Never invite blood play with a vampire. Damn, I'm losing my touch.

"Enough flirting," Ma interrupts. I snort, and she smacks me with a towel, smiling. "Vinny, unless you're here to help, I suggest waiting in the living room."

Vinny turns his attention to Ma and says, "Actually, I need Brenda. I have someone for her to see. I wanted your permission before letting them in." She nods with a tight smile, and I take my apron off and follow him out to the dining room.

I glance back and see sympathy on Ma's face. "Who did you bring?" I ask Vinny.

"He wanted to see you, and your family thought it would be good, too." His voice is a whisper.

"What the hell are y—" I stop when I see him standing next to Anita.

The hue of his skin is back to normal. His wings are bandaged close to his body in his loose shirt and jeans. His face isn't as grim as the last time I saw him. He isn't in pain.

"Michello," I whisper.

He smiles a little and bows his head, speaking in Noctora, "*I wanted to thank you for what you did. For saving my life.*"

"*You're well, then?*" I ask, moving slowly toward him. He's alive.

"*Well enough and ordered to not work for a while. Charlene was strict about that.*"

"*I don't disagree. My father can—*"

He stops me with his hand. "He's already taken care of everything. So has your brother."

My throat constricts, and my eyes begin to form tears. A sudden urge to cry overwhelms me with relief, and Vinny places a hand on my back. I walk forward and carefully put my arms around Michello. He delicately embraces me, and I begin to cry.

"Michello, did we ever tell you baby sis knows how to work a pole proficiently? Besides the one drop." Anita's fangs glint with her smile. Fucking traitor.

Joey scowls at her. "She perfected every routine five years ago, especially after Ricky threatened her with lube."

"Lube?" Vinny quirks a brow. My boot connects with his calf under the table, but the bastard doesn't flinch.

"Gina is notorious for her stripper's glitter; she learned it from her." Joey coughs out a laugh as I glare at him.

Ricky nods and says, "I *did* get her to use lube for—" He stops as I grip his balls under the table. His eyes bulge at me. It's the only tactic I know growing up to keep Ricky's mouth shut. I don't give a shit where or who notices. He's *not* telling them what happened.

"You swore to never talk about that," I growl low.

"Let Ricky go, baby girl," Pops says without looking up from his plate.

Ricky gasps softly, letting everyone know he's let loose. I wipe my hand over my napkin and settle my expression, glancing at Michello. He holds back shock and amusement mixed with a grin. I've learned over breakfast he's worked for Pops for years, done runs with Ricky and Joey, worked in the club before I arrived, and moved to the clinics on Topside years ago.

Anita flashes me a grin before she and Vinny turn toward Joey and Pops to talk. I turn to Michello and whisper in Noctora, "*Sorry you had to see that.*"

He chuckles and responds in English, "Must be hard being the only child in the neighborhood for decades."

I scoff. "Yeah, great growing up for protection and stuff, not for embarrassing stories with no ammo to fling back."

"Children are rare and precious," he says softly with a tilted smile.

"I may never see any in my life," I say, reaching for my water. Michello creases his brows, and I can practically feel Ma's gaze on me. I know I shouldn't broach the subject, but I do anyways. "Not all half-breeds live a Paranormal lifespan. Those who are tested can know, but you need a bloodline from the Paranormal side to see. Mine is a dormant mystery."

"Must be scary, not knowing."

"I'll take the time I have now and hope for the best." I glance at Ma, who's now speaking with Ricky. I look over at Vinny, who's talking with Joey. His fangs glisten as he grins that annoyingly handsome smile of his.

"Let's hope you'll be with us a long time. I'd hate to lose a new friend so quickly," Michello says.

"Yeah, me too." I smile and put my water down as I sit quietly while Michello joins others in conversation. I look at them, the weight of time ticking away in my chest. Then again, there's probably nothing to fear. Based on my immunities, I more than likely have a life span that matches them. No way could I be *that* cursed.

Standing up from the table, I take my plate and Michello's to the kitchen while the others talk about the Underground and business. I need alcohol. I open the cabinet for some scotch. Pouring a glass, I take a few sips and begin to clean up.

A new musky scent drifts into the kitchen as Michello's voice rises from the doorway, "Perhaps I can help?"

"Ma would cut me into ribbons if I let you. You're the guest, no working, per doctors' orders." With glass in hand, I gesture for him to sit.

"I doubt dishes are dangerous."

"You have no idea in this household." I chuckle as I take another drink. I point again at the table. He finally complies. "Want a drink?"

"Still early for us, perhaps not," he muses. Damn, his voice is smooth like syrup. Incubi are like that, but each one has their own flair. Michello has more softness and elegance than most, like a renaissance painting made of watercolors. Completely different from what I grew up with, besides Ma.

I clear my throat. "So, this your first and last time to come over? I wouldn't blame you."

"I'd just call it lively."

"Aw, sweet of you to say." I chuckle as I wash some dishes. "You may be stuck with them the rest of the morning. You'll survive better than me."

"Are you leaving?" Michello stands, joining me near the sink.

"If I want to make it up to Topside before it's too late, yeah. Last thing I need is Ricky babysitting me after gripping his balls."

I knock back the rest of the scotch and look over at him. He's watching me with amusement in his eyes. A quick flash, and I remember the pain I saw there again. I remember the smell of blood on pavement and brick. My heart clenches at the thought of him being dead. Pushing out a smile, I turn to clean my glass.

"Brenda," Michello says. I keep my attention on the glass. His hand comes up to touch my shoulder, and his expression is solemn. "I'm alright and alive."

The forced smile I had falls. His soft eyes peer into mine, and my hands tremble as the terrible memory drifts back. Michello brings a hand up to cup my cheek, caressing his thumb over my scar. A tear falls from my eye and Michello embraces me.

123

His arms hold me close as I nod into his chest and say, "I don't know how you do it. Move on from the pain."

"In this business, I've seen worse."

"I thought I had, too. Maybe I'm more soft-skinned than I thought."

"I believe you mean soft-hearted, which is not a bad thing," he says.

"You sure?"

He chuckles and pulls away slightly, bringing my hands up to his chest. I smile at him genuinely. "Thank you for helping me," he says as he leans forward to place a kiss on my cheek.

The way he moves and watches me, my chest aches for such sweetness. Gripping onto him, I sense the drifting of dark spices nearby and look past Michello's shoulder to the doorway but see no one. We let go of each other, and I lean against the kitchen sink.

"It's been a while since I've seen the nastier side of the business, but at least I got a friend out of it," I say. His expression softens and becomes forlorn. I know that look, and I get the hint. "I'm not the only one leaving, am I?"

"Being stationed up north for operations, per Alanzo's request. Safer for my injuries." He answers as he leans against the sink next to me, his shoulder brushing against mine.

I tentatively bring my hand up and touch where his broken horn is. "You know, I regret some things in life, but not for being there that night. I'm very happy you're alive."

I drop my hand and he grabs it to give it a quick kiss. "The fact you turned around at all, says a lot about who you are. You were raised by wonderful people, who love you."

My throat constricts. "Don't...don't disappear, okay? A lot end up leaving and never coming back, you know?"

"I promise to come back," he smiles. "If just to see one of those famous routines of yours. Are you sure your dormant side isn't succubus?" We laugh as he let's go of my hand. It's quieter out in the other room, as they quietly clean up. I know they linger outside the door. Nosy family.

"You know, knowing them, they're probably hoping this would be...a *thing*," I whisper to him with a bemused smile and gesture.

Michello grins at me. "I think we'd both prefer to be friends, don't you think?"

"Don't like the savior complex?"

"I prefer males." A bark of laughter erupts from both of us.

We hug one more time, and I walk past the others as they whisper over their mugs. Ricky swats at me, but I easily divert him. I strap my guns and jacket back on, then take my contacts out as they've out-welcomed their stay. I put my glasses on, and gather the last of my things, and go out to say goodbye. Ma is cleaning up along with Ricky, and Anita and Pops are talking with Joey as I walk out. No sign of Vinny.

Anita waves her fingers at me in amusement, and her sultry grin worries me as I leave the apartment. Shimmering lights pass my face as I walk down into the club and put my shoes on. If I wasn't pressed to get home and sleep, I'd join a few of my old coworkers at the bar. I wave at them as I pass and nod toward Darius. I look and see Vinny waiting for me, hands in his pockets.

"Miss the line for lap dances?" I ask.

Vinny smiles. "You offering?"

"Nah, I need more caffeine or booze for that. Or at least some good tips."

"That could be arranged."

"Says you."

"I do. Tell me what brand, which coffee, and amount of money, sweet cheeks. You know I've been your best tipper." I let out a loud laugh and walk past him. He follows after me.

"Those candy bars were my favorite. You never skimped out on them." Vinny gets quiet as he continues to walk beside me. "Why you following me?"

"Getting dark."

"It's the Underground. It's always dark."

"So is Topside."

"And?" I stop us in our tracks.

"*So*, I'm walking you home."

A long-frustrated groan comes out of me. "I don't need a bodyguard. *You* do. You taught me well enough to be on my own. You should be proud."

A grin pulls at Vinny's lip which makes my toes curl. Shivers run down my spine, and I catch my breath. His hand comes up and traces my earlobe. "Oh, *I am.* You proved that last night at Rodney's, didn't you?"

Shit, he heard about Travis. "It was settled," I say and straighten my spine. "Didn't even break a sweat."

His eyes rove toward my throat and down my chest, where my guns are stashed. He drags his gaze back up to me and says, "Still it's better to be safe than sorry."

I roll my eyes and continue walking home, Vinny close behind. We walk in silence, his leather jacket swishing against mine every once in a while. We pass Paranormals on the way to the Entrance; some move completely out of the way when they recognize it's Vinny.

"You find what you needed at Beckham's?" He suddenly asks.

What was that with Beckham on not showing all your cards? "Well enough, but like the good researcher I am, not content yet."

Vinny hums deep in his throat, and I glance over my glasses to him. "You're hiding something, sweet cheeks. I love good foreplay and the dark, but not where you're concerned and after almost being shot twice in a week."

"*Technically*, the wolf never reached his gun, so…"

"*Sweet cheeks*."

"You're the one who taught me how to aim. Don't you trust your own lessons?"

"How long you going to use that against me?"

"Probably until I shoot you," I snort.

"Please do already. We have a deal, and I'd like to keep up my end. It'll be far more *enjoyable* than my other hobbies." The grin he wears is diabolical.

"Even more than this *wonderful* banter between us?" I jest.

"Oh, nothing could be better than this. You're still hiding what you found at Beckham's, *bestie*."

I snort and shake my head, passing familiar shops and people. He remains close, almost driving me up the wall with just his movement. I know I won't be able to hide what I found for long. Except, I want to find more information to back-up any theories I may think of.

"Let me find more info first, then we can talk," I strategically say.

He raises his brows. "Sweet cheeks, you actually thinking before acting for once?"

"Ouch, dick."

"Ask nicely, and you shall receive."

"Probably never." That hurt to say.

"How about roughly?" Vinny's eyes gleam, even against all the other colors. Crimson eyes.

My mind flashes back to the bright light in my nightmare. No colors. No darkness. No misconstrued hues melding into disfigured shapes. The feeling I had of never seeing that again, never seeing Vinny's ruby eyes, the only constant through my blindness. My heart clenches, and my stomach drops at the thought. My head throbs as fear begins to wrap itself around my senses, blocking everything out.

"Brenda?" Vinny asks, cupping my shoulder and cheek. I shake my head and look up to see the eyes I'd lamented over. We've stopped, huh, that usually doesn't happen. "Brenda? What's wrong?" He asks again, stroking my chin with his thumb. The sensation almost entices me to moan. Sweet and gentle. I push his hand away before I do something I'll regret, shaking my head.

"Just a nightmare from earlier. Still lingering. I'm fine." I start walking again, pushing the horrible nothingness away.

"The usual nightmare or different?" Vinny comes up close as we approach the elevator doors with a. concerned look on his face. He's the only one I ever talk about it with.

"Bright light," I answer. "I've had the dream before, but this felt sterile. Like blinding white artificial light. No jokes about my blindness either—"

"Wasn't going to." He pauses as the elevator comes down and the doors ding open. "Did it seem familiar? Like a place?"

"Nowhere I'd venture to," I respond as I get on. I'm not surprised that Vinny follows me in. He leans against the wall and watches me with hands in his pockets while he hums at my answer. The sensation of his touch on my cheek hasn't left me. It feels heated now, the lingering presence of his skin against mine. It gets worse as Vinny's gaze deepens with hunger.

Has he not fed?

"Vinny, you've been acting odd lately," I observe. "What's up?"

"Coming from the one with a nightmare about light."

"Yeah, should be you, but with sunlight and discovering no aloe vera." My response is soft spoken as Vinny shifts, looking away. Buildings, tunnels, and lights pass us, and I can smell the change of the Underground as we climb up to Topside. We stay silent for a moment, the only noise being the moving elevator.

"A lot on my mind, you calm it," he finally says.

I take off my glasses and rub my eyes a bit. "Given what's been going on, I guess I can't blame you. Maybe it's getting to all of us.".

I close my eyes and inhale his scent. Maybe I did calm him. He always calms me. I attribute it to our close friendship. The last few years, I realized I wanted more, but I'm not going to lose this. Not going to risk the calm and safety I feel in his presence. Our friendship is a reminder of the good in my life. I can't screw this up because of sexual frustration.

"Did you know you have silver flecks?" His voice breaks through my thoughts, making me open my eyes. My brows scrunch, and I shake my head. Slowly, Vinny pushes off the wall and walks to me, stopping a few inches away. He holds a finger up and traces it down my larger facial scar, pausing beneath my eye. "You only see them when the contacts are out."

"You have two black freckles," I say. His eyes never change for me. Always the deep crimson, two black freckles in his irises, top corner of his right eye. Only up close could one see them or dare to look at him long enough.

"Do I?" He asks, and I nod. "Do you see them now?" His hand leaves my face, my skin yearning for the touch again. I hope for him to stroke down my other scar, but he doesn't. A fluttering moves through my stomach deep inside.

Vinny's eyes peer into me, and I feel heat grow down below. I glance at his lips; how soft they seem compared to his quick mouth. An unobtainable treasure directly before me, filled with aromas that arouse my being. It feels like the elevator is going to combust. On the verge of risking everything, my lungs contract as the elevator door dings and the fresh air whooshes in, clearing some of my senses.

"My stop." I dodge past Vinny for the exit and inhale the city night air, in the early evening on Topside. The sound of people shouting and cars drown out most conversations passing. The smell of smoke, cars, and alcohol flush out the last of his scent. Too close, far too close. I stop and see Vinny is still following me. I narrow my eyes on him. No escape yet.

"Dangerous for you to be out," he states as he continues to walk toward my apartment. The vampire is causing havoc in more ways than one.

"I can handle myself." I catch up, flashing my guns.

"Never said you couldn't."

"You're implying it, *sweet cheeks*." I grind out the words, my body still in chaos from the elevator. Now I'm *definitely* getting frustrated.

"I prefer 'bloodsucker,'" he says as some dumbass teens shout across the street. "Besides, you're not just the daughter of an ex-boss, but the sister of a new one. You'll be a target."

"Been a target a lot longer than now. Not much has changed," I scoff.

"Alanzo had rules in place."

"Didn't stop some," I mutter. Vinny opens his mouth to ask, but I interrupt him. "I have our little emergency system on my phone, which proved to work. I'll be safe. Plus, I have friends who know me, too."

"Who, like Michello?" My body freezes, and I stare at him in disbelief. He *was* outside the kitchen. I knew it. Vinny stops, staring at me with such calm it angers me more. His voice is strict, "Don't act like—"

"Nothing happened, dimwit."

"You have better names than that."

"Fine, *Elvira*." I cross my arms and glare at him. "Who I talk to is *my* business, not yours. You seem *really* interested in that these days. What the fuck is wrong with you? First Rodney, now Michello? I watched him almost die, Vinny!"

"Brenda—"

"Don't! You half-brained soon-to-be pile of ash! Stupid vampires and werewolves and incubus! You're all too territorial! Let me be already! You bloodsucking, two-hundred-year-old playboy mafia boss...*you don't get to act like this*." I start to walk away, but Vinny grabs my wrist and holds me to look back at him. I seethe, anger rolling over me with frustration. How can I move on from him if every turn I take brings me back? Then again, I can't live without that touch. Catch-fucking-22.

I can barely make out the hardness in his stare, muscles working in his jaw. His scent is worse, burning through my nostrils. His grip isn't hard around my wrist, but enough to hold me. He knows he doesn't need brute force. I sense emotions roll through him before he finally lets me go. We stand in the middle of the sidewalk staring at the other.

"I worry about you." His words are gruff.

"No shit," I bite back. He takes a step forward, but I stop him. I can't do this. Not right after that elevator ride. Heat still pulses through me. A lingering need screams from the depths of my soul for him to touch me again. Another part shouts in warning. I'm just so *frustrated*. "You're my best friend, Vinny. I know I'll always be your baby sister, just like Rodney, Anita, and the others. But like them, even my family, you *don't* get to control me. With *anything*."

"You think *that's* why I'm here?"

"What else is there? Or do you *really* have a craving for half-breed blood? Need me to shoot you?"

"Not what this is about," Vinny scoffs, his body tense as he keeps his gaze away, watching the city move around us. He speaks without looking at me, "There's things you don't know. Within the city, Underground, business…"

I cross my arms. "More than you fucking know."

"…and what's inside my own heart."

I speak before I can stop myself, too upset to care when I should. "Oh, you have a heart? What does it want? Unfiltered, bimbo blood that you've craved the last hundred years? *Whoring* around for fresh blood like a deranged Feral vampire? Newsflash; everyone *fucking* knows."

Vinny's head snaps to me as his scent diminishes and a laxness swallows him up in defeat. "I've always loved your smart mouth, but sometimes it's crueler than a stake through the heart. Then again, I'd need one for that, wouldn't I?"

On that, he turns and leaves me alone on the sidewalk. I don't go after him. I don't yell. I don't apologize. And he vanishes through the Entrance and into the night.

CHAPTER EIGHTEEN
SMELLS LIKE TEEN BULLSHIT

Yup, I've officially pissed off Vinny the Vampire, Blood Mafia Boss. Somehow, I can live another day without swimming with the fishes.

Three days and nothing, even when I went home like always to my family, no appearance. I feel angry with myself for taking out my frustrations on him, my best friend who I wanted to fuck in the elevator. Even if I'm still mad with him being so territorial, I went too far. My emotions took over common fucking decency. Never have I thrown his escapades at him. Maybe we both need a timeout. And alcohol. And me getting laid to move on. I may bite the bullet and let Ricky set me up.

The last three days, I worked overtime as a distraction and to find more clues to what's happening. I'm on the verge of calling up my old professor, who always seemed to have answers regarding ghouls. Or I could really dig myself into a hole and call Midnight.

I lean back in my leather chair and sigh. The apartment smells like whiskey, as I've been drinking more than usual. Between Joey taking over, my fight with Vinny, and finding nothing helpful about what's happening in the Bronx, I feel drained. At least things have calmed down on the mafia side. Most of the routes were pulled from the Bronx and the cluster problem areas. It means less issues with the police, yet something isn't right.

I swirl my whiskey and ponder over the pieces; busts, PSB, ghouls, police, neutral zones, and mafia. The connection should be obvious. It's fucking mob shit. Something still itches at the back of my mind. Why was this different? It feels like a hundred-year-old bourbon finishing like a long island iced tea.

The last of the whiskey goes down my throat as it becomes night. I put my glass on the table, and the familiar New York City sounds lull me into an easy sleep. Or so I thought.

Bright fucking light.
Everywhere. Tink. Sounds vibrate near my head. Tink. The brightness of the harsh light scorches my retinas. I can't move. I'm strapped down, leather cuffs holding me in place. I can't see them. Nothing. Harsh white light burns into my skull.
I pull against the leather holding me. Nothing. Tink.
I yank again. Tink.
Let me out. Tink.
The light gets brighter, and a scream is caught in my throat. Soundless. Blood fills my nostrils, but something's wrong with it. It smells tainted. Wrong. I

pull again, hoping for anything. More blood covers my senses as white light pierces through me.

I feel it slipping, trickling down my skin, across my eyes and head. Still, the excruciating light doesn't relent. Tink.

I pull again. Tink. Cuffs rip into my skin. Tink. Blood drips to the ground. Metal scrapes with leather. Tink.

Get me out.

Tink.

Get me out. Please.

Tink.

Please.

Tink.

PLEASE. Tink. FUCKING GET ME OUT.

"Daddy!"

My body is drenched in sweat as I jerk awake and breathe erratically, clutching to the armchair. Darkness engulfs me as shadows across my eyes merge shapes and colors together. My breathing eases as I lay my head back and take in the dark hues.

No white. No false light.

Taking deep breaths, I feel my wrists. No blood. "Fucking daylights."

This nightmare was worse, so much worse. I fumble, reaching for my phone but stop as I'm about to make the call. Fuck. We aren't talking. A shiver goes down my spine, and I feel tears well up in my eyes. "Stupid nightmares."

I pick up my phone and dial. It takes two rings before he picks up. His familiar sound instantly eases me, and I want to sob like a child. "What's wrong, baby girl?"

*   *   *

Eight in the morning at the library, and I need more whiskey. I spent a good hour on the phone with Pops last night. It took some convincing for him not to come to Topside. And now I kind of wish he had.

The books throughout the *Noctis Immortalis* section are piled on the ground like trash with papers and covers torn out, while the sign hangs by a single bolt. My section. My haven has been destroyed. Great.

"Roger in security thinks it was some teenagers, but they couldn't tell through the videos," Janice explains softly, and I scoff. Of course, they didn't catch anything, and of course, this is the only section ripped apart.

She looks over at me with pity. I sigh heavily as I rub the top of my head and under my glasses. I should've worn contacts. Fucking hell. "Janice, I have some work piled up for the sections concerning agriculture and history for the colleges. Can you take care of it today? This month?" I mumble the last part.

"Oh, sure!" Her cheeriness rubs me the wrong way.

I begin to clean what's left of the section. The good news is I know how to organize this section by heart. The bad news is finding all the pieces to put it back together again. My skirt sweeps across the floor as I gather pages. I'll give myself today to clean it all up but know that's next to impossible. The library wouldn't care. They could give me the week and still wouldn't shed a tear.

Janice sighs behind me. "I can bring you the trash can and liners." Case in fucking point.

"Why? They're important books, Janice." I stand up, holding papers close to my chest. She tilts her head to the side and smiles pitifully. She's about to argue, but I speak first. "I'm not throwing away any of this."

"They're damaged, Brenda. Unusable."

"They were barely used in the first place. I doubt anyone would notice, except me, and I obviously wouldn't care if they were stapled together like a first grader's project." I hold back the seething anger in my voice the best I can. Could the library order new books? Yes. Will they, remembering the number of times I've pleaded for certain titles to be ordered only to be declined? No.

"Let's be reasonable here—"

"There are books in worse condition in the restricted areas, including the history, records, and literature sections. Most of the folios are held together by a thread."

Janice begins to wring her hands. She looks around. "They won't let us keep it, Brenda."

Right.

The people who own the library are in charge, whether or not it's a public service. I may be head of this section, but I don't have the power to protect it.

I stack more papers on the shelves and say, "I'll take the unsalvageable ones. The rest I'll get glued together downstairs or rethreaded."

She nods, pursing her lips. "You're quite the dedicated librarian," she says and walks away.

"Yeah, it's that," I murmur.

The energy to research leaves as this new mess presents itself, and I can't find anything anyway. Perhaps redoing the whole section would be good for me. Or drive me insane. It's a thin line.

I spend the next hour piling books and papers, what's left of them all. The whole books are put off to the side to reshelve later. Barely a third of the way into the mess, I debate pausing to find some coffee when steps echo nearby. I recognize the heavy stride and catch the familiar shampoo scent. Looking up, I see Drauper approach me with two books in hand. From where I kneel, I recognize the covers enough. He listened?

"Seems I checked these out in the nick of time," he comments, looking over the mess.

I clear my throat, standing up with some disheveled books. "You took my advice."

He shrugs and says, "Everyone should read."

"Or use books as papier-mâché," I say. He hands me the books, and I add them to the stack of intact ones. "If you need more…give me a week."

"Know who did it?" I shake my head, going back to collect the mess. "Has this happened before?"

"Not to this extent. Usually, it's a few missing books or just spray painting the sign."

"Do they know—"

"No. Nobody cares about books about Paranormals they fear and don't understand. Even if it can help them." He remains silent, uncomfortably shifting his stance. I let out another sigh as I shuffle some papers and put them on a shelf. "Reality sucks, Drauper. Thought we figured that out together." Drauper remains quiet and moves behind me. I expect him to leave me to my mess, but he crouches next to me and begins to gather some pages. "What are you—"

"Helping. May take you four or five hours to reach the end of the aisle."

"It's my job, though."

He looks over at me. "Cleaning up ruined books and ripped pages? When in the interview process did they prepare you for that? The same time when they taught you to shoot a handgun?"

I freeze. The hidden Glock in my shirt pushes against my leg as I turn toward him. A teasing smile rises on his face. A joke. He's making a joke.

Rodney better not have lied about these guns being legal.

I shake off the scare and ask, "Find anything useful when you were reading?"

He nods. "You're right about their class systems. It's a little insane how intricate it can be. The dead are more interesting than I thought."

"Just in general?" I muse.

"More than I'd like to admit," he smirks, and I smile back. "Didn't help much, though. Even if work has calmed down."

Looks like it isn't just the mafia who's eased back. Maybe Vinny and Anita were right. Just a passing normality. Arrests will uptick and then go back down, like a fucked-up roller coaster ride.

It's quiet as we shuffle through the mess of books. The air doesn't feel as tense as last time, but I'm not certain. He did listen and read finally. Maybe, just maybe, we could…

"Can we go back to how it was before?" Drauper finishes my thought.

I blink back my surprise that he even asked and say, "Look, Drauper—"

"We don't agree on things, fine, but can we talk? Try again?" His deep voice is a whisper.

"Technically, we're talking now. Although, I'm usually teaching you. I *may* be a little impressed you read something I suggested." I feel myself begin to ramble, unsure how to move forward. "I mean, you should read anyways. I shouldn't have to tell you."

"Brenda."

"Unfortunately, I need to rebind all these books first. The colleges could lend you some things if you say it's for work, but then again, it already is. I could just answer for you, like before—"

"Brenda." Grabbing both my hands, he stops me. I peer through my glasses to find his face. "Hold on; you may scare someone here from the amount of talking you're doing."

"Very funny."

He chuckles and grins slightly. The old chill he caused weeks ago returns, slowly but surely. It's different than before, skeptical and unsure. Yet, still warm.

"Brenda, I want to know if we're still at least…friends."

I sit hard on the ground and stifle my grimace from the pinch of my gun. He sits with me amongst the shredded mess, not letting go of my hand. The forlorn feelings I had all week come back. I'm tired of being lonely. Tired of being frustrated. All I want is something safe and familiar. "Yeah, we are."

He quirks a brow. "Didn't sound that convincing. I should know."

"Long couple of days." I nod toward the mess. "And no drinking on the job, something about being irresponsible."

"Huh, same with mine." We both chuckle as he lets go. "Speaking of drinks, can we try that again?"

"Who's trying? I've been succeeding all week," I snort.

"Together, I mean. You can choose where."

"You buying?"

"Sure."

"There's a bar near one of the Entrances of Central Park I used to go to. Tonight. I'll write down the address."

"You're serious?" Between the nightmares, angry best friend, shredded books, I'll agree to anything at this point. I'm also out of alcohol at home. Priorities.

"I mean, I could decline you."

"No," he laughs, picking up some books to hand over. "Just thought I'd have to convince you more." I shrug, gesturing toward the mess. "Maybe tonight will be good for both of us." A small grin pulls at my lips. Maybe the detective could redeem himself.

I move some of the books further down the aisle. When I come back, Drauper seems perturbed. "What?" I ask.

"I thought they stopped doing these kinds of things," he says, handing me a few ripped pages from a journal I'm not familiar with. A quick glance toward the shelves, I see we're in the *Anatomy and Biology* section. Looking back to the pages, I notice the headline: *Experimentations*. The title alone informs me it should be in the restricted section.

"It's just an academic journal. Probably, not from recent studies."

"Brenda, this is dated like twenty years ago." He points at the date where my sight can barely register the colors, but he's right. "And it looks like it was in conjunction with Columbia University."

I skim through the paragraphs, focusing past the discolored hues of the page. Why didn't I wear my contacts today? I focus on the sentences that describe the unsettling testing, and my stomach begins to twist into knots. "This doesn't seem right. I know about every book in my section, but I'm not as familiar with the science materials. If it's from Columbia, I can ask about it. I work with my old professor from time to time to get new copies of medical journals and other resources."

"Maybe it's for drug testing and just a typo in the date." The twist in my stomach doesn't leave.

"Testing on Paranormals without the overseeing of the NIIA was banned decades ago. Especially on half-breeds since they share DNA between Paranormals and humans. If there is any drug testing, it has to be approved by the FDA, PSB, NIIA, and quite a few other agencies due to malpractice and nonconsensual experimentation on people."

"How do you know about that?"

"Librarian," I smirk, and he scoffs. "The professor I mentioned was part of medical teams developing new drugs about ten years ago. I still work with her from time to time. Dr. Rhonda Quincy." Except she never called them experiments. None of the medical personnel I've worked with have.

"So, like how they developed anti-venom?" Drauper asks, and I nod.

I put the paper in a separate spot and change the subject to get rid of this weird feeling, "Thanks for helping, by the way."

"It's what friends do." I see a glimpse of his signature smile.

"Yeah, and as such, let me know if you have any questions for me."

"Well…" His voice trails off as he scratches his head. I grin, nodding for him to continue. He laughs a little embarrassedly. "It's a little sensitive in information, but some buddies on the force thought you may know something."

"Go on," I coax as I sift through some bindings.

"What do you know about the Underground mafia?"

I barely hide the falter in my hands, hoping he doesn't see the stumble. This day is getting better and better. If anyone says "TGIF" to me, I'll stuff their mouths with breadsticks and flip them into the Hudson River. How did *any* of his buddies think of me for that? Pops should have taken care of any tracks I left. Was it past cases I helped with?

I plaster a smile on my face as I take a calming breath, "Apart from some good gangster movies? Al Capone worked with shifters, and John Dillinger was a vampire."

"You serious?"

"No, not the vampire part." He chuckles, easing my nerves. Crisis averted. I think.

"Just thought I'd ask since you specialize in Paranormal Studies, you may know something. Shot in the dark." And, technically, he didn't miss.

"Well, get me drunk enough tonight, and maybe I'll tell you more secrets. Like Bugsy Siegel was a defective incubus and Pretty Boy Floyd is out West living his best life as a rancher." Drauper laughs. He doesn't need to know the part about Floyd, whom I've met once and seemed nice enough for a gangster anyways.

"I'll let you get back to your cleanup. Give me the address, and I'll see you whenever you're off," he says.

"Postpone until next year? Got it," I tease as I write down the address on some scrap paper and hand it to him, somehow avoiding any slip-ups about my life or the mafia.

He looks at the paper then says, "It's a date." He remains where he is for a moment, and I scrunch my brows at him. Drauper then smiles and leaves, and I catch myself watching him, his scent lingering in the aisle.

Once he's gone, I move to the back of the section and pull my phone out. Checking my surroundings, I push the speed dial and wait for him to pick up. The phone clicks, and Rodney yawns into my ear. "This better be good, lil sis."

"Heads up, a detective is asking about the Underground families again," I say.

Rodney shuffles something against the phone. "PSB?"

"No, just a curious human detective. There's a reason I've been talking to him for over a year." Well, and his infectious smile and leg muscles. "But his questions have been a little pointed lately."

"Aw, you worrying about me, lil sis?"

"Someone needs to." He chuckles. "I know things settled, but I thought I'd clue you in."

"Already double-checking a few things, but new intel doesn't hurt." Rodney gives another yawn. "I'll check in with my contacts. Thanks."

"Anytime." I pause, unsure telling him, but I do anyway. "Let Vinny know, too?"

There's silence on the other end and fabrics rustle before he finally speaks, "Still not talking?" I keep quiet and look down the aisle. "Four days and no response? That's long for you two."

"Rodney, just tell him." I think for a moment. "And Joey. Not like the bloodsucker is special or something."

"Alright, lil sis. Be safe. I don't feel like chowing down on humans this weekend."

The line clicks, and I look at my phone. My chest feels heavy as my fingers flex, almost wanting to call him next, knowing I should. Except I don't know if he'll pick up. I put my phone away, shaking away the feelings and concentrating on tonight. A distraction, a really fucking good one, and maybe I'll have fun. Maybe.

Or I'll say fuck it, get drunk, and fuck the detective. That'll distract me for sure.

I'm just lonely and sexually frustrated enough to do it. And maybe it's about time to give up Vinny. Accept that he'll never be the one. Our fight may have been an omen. A reminder I played all my cards a few years back. Beckham is wrong. Some obstacles can't be overcome. And at this point in life, beggars can't be choosers.

I look at the mess around me. Yeah, most definitely.

Chapter Nineteen
BALTO

I leave the library with the aisle at least clean. Some of the books are back on the shelves, not really arranged. Another librarian will organize them this weekend. The rest of the destroyed materials are stacked in my closet office or the basement. My workload for the week. Yay. I need to replenish the alcohol at my apartment. Or have a good screw. Both possibilities for the evening.

I walk through Central Park toward the bar. I've been there a few times before, one of the few public venues on Topside I visit. It's a hole-in-the-wall bar, the perfect place to sit in a corner and drink…or do something else. My skin tightens as I check my ponytail. Hormones are coming back full force, though loneliness will do that to someone. I feel like drowning in a sea of dying emotions that should be locked up forever. The more I think about not having a certain vampire, the more I want someone else to do the job. Or maybe I'm being spiteful.

I skim past some joggers around a fountain, trying to clear my head. Suddenly, I see Gunther and my frenemy Marcus. Gunther notices me first. I put my hands on my hips and greet them, "Well, hello, have you two found the three little pigs? Or did the straw trip you up?" Marcus growls under his breath, scaring off a few people nearby and attracting a few shifters' attention. "It was the sticks, wasn't it?" The taunt makes him snarl again.

"Spunky tonight, huh?" Gunther gestures for Marcus to back off. "What you doing here, lil sis?"

"You're on *my* turf, wolfie. Isn't *hoss* on the other side?" I ask.

"Careful how you speak about the boss," Marcus warns. His deep voice would have sent anyone else running. But I'm spunky tonight—no good verbal poking in days will do that.

"I know things about Rodney that would make you blush, *Balto*." The darkened growl I receive makes me smile. Gunther places a hand on Marcus' shoulder, shaking his head.

"Careful, I may actually let him take a bite," Gunther teases.

"And survive telling Rodney that in one piece?" I scoff. "You'd have Pops to deal with too. So, good luck. Although, some primal play might be what I need. Balto, you up for it?" Marcus snarls. "Take that as a no."

"No vampires to bother?" Gunther holds back laughter.

"Been busy with shit. Haven't seen them." I cross my arms. No way am I telling Gunther Vinny wasn't talking to me. For all I knew, Vinny is just fucking his favorite females. He'll come back. He always did, smelling like someone else's perfume. Though I wish he'd hurry up, I don't want to keep staring at my phone like I'm in a rom-com. Besides, Vinny and I will go back to taunting and teasing like normal. Right? Right.

I change the subject and ask, "Why you two here?"

"Route check-ins," Gunther replies, waving off Marcus as he growls. "She already knows; boss told her. Plus, Joey took over this week."

I almost stick my tongue out at the grey wolf. "I'm annoying, but *all-knowing*, Balto."

"Quit calling me that," Marcus snarls.

"Get Rodney to ship whiskey to my place, and I'll consider changing it." The growl I receive tells me I'll have to get my own. Damn. Maybe next time.

"Alright, enough," Gunther says and turns to Marcus, whispering something in his ear. Marcus loosens one last snarl before walking down the path. Guess playtime is over. "Lay off, lil sis. He may actually snap your neck, given his patience is running thin."

I snort and cross my arms. "That's the way I figured I'd go out, starting a *mob war*. Werewolf snapping my neck, it'll be great for the history books." And a plot twist for the vampires.

Gunther grumbles, stepping closer to me. "Must have been a shit week since I last saw you. What's up? Shooting Travis wasn't enough?"

"I run into you on the way for a drink, and you think I'm gonna spill my guts? Not that easy, Gunther."

"*So*, something *is* up. You and Vinny fighting?"

"Why would you think that?"

"Every time you two ain't talking, you both act like someone shoved spears up your ass without kissing it first."

"We do not," I argue.

"You do, and everyone knows to steer clear, hoping you two don't kill each other until you make up. Been thick as thieves since you were fourteen. He say something stupid again?"

I ignore his comment and become snippy. "Miss the part where I was meeting a friend?"

"Is it Vinny?"

"Topside for a drink?"

"Yeah, you'd sooner drink at his place. Better booze." Gunther sighs, leaning in close. "You *never* meet people up here, always below unless it's *Donny's*. So, come on, what's up?"

A short exasperated breath leaves me as I drop my arms, showing some surrender. "Look, I already called Rodney today for something. He knows what's going on." Kind of. Not really. "Don't worry, okay?"

Some people pass by and avert their gaze, trying not to run into some succubi. "Kind of hard not to, due the last 24 hours," he says.

I turn back to him. "Okay, what does *that* mean?"

"Thought you talked to the boss?"

"Didn't get that far, come on, speak."

"Oh, *I'm* supposed to open up now?"

"You just said something ominous, so you might as well tell me. And if it's why you're on Topside so early, I gotta know."

Gunther glances over at Marcus leaning against a tree growling at a passerby. He keeps his gaze on the grey wolf and speaks softly, "Something happened last night."

My stomach drops. "I thought things were going smooth." Gunther shakes his head and looks at me. "What is it?"

"I don't think Rodney or your brother would want—"

"Don't fucking do that to me." I point my finger at his chest. "Fucking tell me if something went sideways."

His gaze flits back over to Marcus again, whose ears prick, trying to listen in. Gunther's scent changes slightly. I can sense more unease. Gunther doesn't want him to know what he's telling me, not unusual, but not good. His voice is extremely low as he explains, "Two half-breed wolves disappeared. They were under Rodney's protection. Found out some half-breed shifters went missing over a week ago, too. All from the Bronx, even though we're mostly cleared out. Rodney's getting *everyone* out now. There are some still refusing to leave, Paranormal and human alike." He pauses with a deep breath. "Suggestion? I'd stay away from that area if I were you."

I quirk a brow. "If it's half-breeds under Paranormal supervision, then PSB should be stepping in."

He scoffs and shakes his head. Right, they aren't stepping in. Along with the ghouls moving in, Paranormals being targeted by cops, and NYPD having no idea what was going on, people are now going missing. Fucking fantastic. Explains why Rodney doesn't want to eat humans this weekend.

"Seriously, Brenda," Gunther whispers. "Stay away from all the old routes. You'll have more problems than werewolves growling at you."

"Long as you're careful, too. Hate to lose you, only because I'd be left with *Balto* to draw and quarter me at sunrise."

"You and your damn nicknames."

"Do you want one other than wolfie?" I ask mischievously.

Gunther stifles a chuckle. "You know, life would be boring without you twisting tails and shit."

"Whatever did you all do before I came around?" I ask as he gives me a quick hug.

"Tell ghost stories around campfires while we drank hot chocolate."

"Don't lie. We all know it was lemongrass tea with crumpets."

"It's good for your digestive system!"

I wave at him as I walk onward and attempt to settle the unease that riddles my mind. Darkness begins to settle in the twilight hours as streetlights flick on for the evening. I let the noise of the city comfort me as I cross the street to the sports bar and pass by some Paranormals, more coming out as night descends.

The bar is filled with diverse groups of people and Paranormals, smelling like beer and nachos. I look around and see that I'm first to arrive again—must be typical for Drauper. I choose a small table in the back, wave down a waitress, and order a drink.

Rock music and sports television play in the background. Pretty sure it's soccer and baseball; sports aren't my thing. The waitress comes back with my drink, and I wait for Drauper. Ten minutes past the agreed time. I'm beginning to realize his timing sucks, which must be terrible for a detective.

He finally walks in wearing what he had on earlier but looking a bit more disheveled. My body heats, and my stomach flutters. I swallow, battling feelings as I wave at him. His smile practically glows through my glasses.

"Never work for the subway; people would riot," I tease.

"Work never stops for cops," he says as he sits down. "Never would have guessed a sports bar for you."

"It's homey."

"Do you even watch sports?" I shake my head. "You just like the ambiance?"

"Alcohol is cheaper, no one gives a shit, and it's close enough to my place. It's relaxing enough, and my coworkers don't know it exists."

He chuckles. "I get that. Sometimes we all just need space, get away from what others expect from us."

My body stills as he talks. Drauper gives the waitress his drink order, who promptly returns with it in hand. Bringing his attention back to me, we begin to talk. It's easy like before, something that doesn't seem forced. I feel like I can breathe again. The night moves on as the conversation does. I find myself laughing with him as we order nachos and fried pickles. A distraction I need. Except, a tightened feeling warps its way over my skin. Somehow, with the distraction of Drauper and the bar, I miss Vinny more. And I want more than anything for him to show up.

Drauper's musky scent makes my sexual aggression want to come off hiatus and embark on new journeys. At least I wouldn't miss Vinny anymore.

"You never played sports?" Drauper asks.

Pole dancer and gunslinger don't seem like an appropriate answer. "Nope. Always been a big reader, maybe because I started later in life learning to."

"If I didn't know you, I never would have guessed that." He points towards my undercut and leather jacket.

"Where I grew up, a lot of people dress like this."

"Why not wear it at work?".

"A leather jacket? Drauper, you may get away with it at your job, but not mine," I say, and he laughs in agreement. I watch him bring his drink to his lips, and I shiver as a heat brews below. The scent of his shampoo and musk stirs more of it in my core. My body cannot wait to get laid.

"Where did you grow up?" He asks.

I wave my hand to the windows, lying through my teeth. "Just outside of Yonkers."

"Didn't like it?"

"Trying to find something new."

"Ah, right, the whole finding yourself." I nod, pursing my lips. "Has the move been worth it?"

I shrug and look away. Pops told me I needed to go after what I wanted. Joey wants me to be myself again. And Vinny...fucking Vinny. The person that only shows up in my fantasies lately, a reminder I haven't moved on in the last few years. I'm supposed to "figure things out", but after every step I take to find the missing piece, I feel less like myself.

"I hope so," I whisper.

I bring my eyes up to him, and the chatter around us disappears. His warm eyes watch me intently, and my heart aches. I want to be held, have hands stroke back my hair, lips pressed against my cheek or neck, and whisper secrets in the dark. All done with a familiar smile.

But not from Drauper.

I haven't moved on at all, and tonight won't help either. Raging hormones aside, my heart still yearns for those crimson eyes. And I can't do that to Drauper, to use him. *That* isn't worth it. Even if my nether region protests.

I finish off my drink and say, "I should go. It's getting late." Drauper pays like he promised. I attempt to leave in a hurry, but he remains close behind me as we exit. I inhale deeply the fresh, city air as colors merge in the darkness with lamps that cover the street and the piercing pink lights of passing cars.

I may have just finished a few drinks, but I wanted to go home and do it alone.

"Brenda, what's wrong?" He asks, trying to keep up with me.

I shake my head, trying to smile at him. "Tired, and I need to think over some things. I'll see you soon, Drauper. This was nice. Bring bookmarks next time you visit the library."

"Wait a minute—"

"Station is down the other way," I say as I move down the sidewalk. He grabs my arm suddenly, pulling me back to face him.

Drauper clears his throat. "We were having a good time, at least I thought we were; what happened?"

"Nothing."

He scoffs, loosening his grip. "You're scared."

"No, I'm not."

"Bullshit."

I scowl. "Bullshit back."

He lets go, throwing his hands out. "What the hell? You *wanted* to go out. We talked, had fun, now you're leaving me on the sidewalk?"

"Yeah, that's how these outings end. You go your way, and I'll go mine. Pretty sure you're down that way. Though I have—"

"You really think that? *Friendly* outing?" He touches my arm and comes closer. We drift to the side, closer to the buildings. I keep my mouth shut; uncertain latent emotions will betray me. "You're afraid that this could be something more."

"No, I'm not," I argue. "I just need to *go*, Drauper."

"Brenda."

"Louis."

He heaves a sigh and shifts his stance. "You're nothing like I thought you were, but I don't care. You've been faking for who knows how long, and you're afraid I'll see the real you. Look, you can't pretend forever around others, real or *not*."

"I do not—!"

"Whoever you are, I don't care, and I'm not scared. I know shit went down last time, and we don't always meet eye to eye, but...fuck...don't run. *Stop* running." My eyes widen. "Stop fucking running, Brenda."

My heart clenches, and I try to breathe through my emotions. "I'm not...I'm *trying* not to, but everyone keeps making it harder and—"

"Do I?"

"I don't...maybe....yes? No! I don't *fucking* know!" This is too much, all too much. I don't know what I want. I feel like a pathetic teenager whining to have *something* of hers, but what I do want, I can't have.

Drauper's voice carves its way through my thoughts. "Then just stand still."

He grabs the nape of my neck, pulling me forward, and his soft, luscious lips crash into mine. My back presses against the wall of a building as he kisses me like his life depends on it. I flounder with my hands, keeping them at my sides. I've dreamt of this. Wanted it. And it's better than I thought.

And I'm empty.

After what feels like hours, he pulls away and meets my gaze. He watches for a reaction and carefully loosens his hold on my neck. I think my brain short circuits for a moment because I'm speechless. We stand in silence as people pass, the city moving on with its business.

Finally, I rasp out, "I need to go, Louis. I'll talk to you soon."

Moving swiftly, I dodge him and walk down the sidewalk. Halfway down the block, I run. Sprinting and not looking behind me, I rush home. The heat once deep in the pit of my stomach is long gone.

What the hell is wrong with me? I've wanted that. I've wanted that for almost a year, even after everything that's happened. Earlier, I hoped to go home with him, and I just ran. I ran just like he said. Zero points to me in this round.

I felt nothing. Nothing. Weren't you supposed to feel *something*?

Coming up to my apartment building, I stop and scream silently. Pathetic. I'm fucking pathetic. My hands are shaking as I grip the iron rails leading into the building. I walk up the stairs, pushing back frustrated tears. I reach my floor, ready to get drunk, but I realize two things.

One: I'm out of alcohol. Two: My door is slightly ajar.

Pulling my gun out, I come up to the door silently. Steadying myself, I kick it open and aim the barrel at the intruder. My frown remains in place.

"I'm not fixing that," Vinny says. Gun still pointed at him; I kick the door shut behind me. He drinks from a glass and holds out another, sitting in my damn chair. "Need a drink?"

"Showing up for kicks?"

"You were awake this time. I should get points for that."

"Oh, look, the bloodsucker has manners. Next time, don't sit in my favorite chair." Safety back in place, I toss the gun on the bed and sit on the edge. I gesture for the drink, and he puts it in my hand. "Did you get me more alcohol?"

"You were busy. A.A. didn't work out?"

"Terrible donuts. Not worth sobriety."

"Noted," he says, sipping his scotch. I focus on the noise outside and think of my neighbors, who seem unphased I kicked my door down. "You weren't home or at *Unbound*. Thought you went back to being a stripper somewhere else."

"You'd be the first to know."

"My second thought was that you went to Beckham and swore to never leave his library." I *should've* thought of that. "And my final thought was that you ran away with that damn detective and started a new life as a housewife. Burning every omelet in your wake." He downs his drink, and I almost spit up mine.

I stare at the liquid and the want to scream comes rushing back. I toss my glasses to the side, colors and shapes melding together.

"No retort?" He asks.

"I'd suck as a housewife."

"You were never meant for it," Vinny speaks softly as I look up through my hazy vision, his figure a disarray of colors. I can't find his ruby eyes. "So, you were with—"

"I'm fucking sorry for being an ass," I blurt. "I know I'm a bitch sometimes and don't keep my mouth shut when I should. And you have a heart of silver."

"That'd fucking kill me."

"Well, gold would clash with your color scheme, and bronze isn't your color."

"Clash with the jacket, hair, or eyes?"

"I was going to say teeth, but maybe bleaching them would help."

"Blood diet will do that. You should try it sometime. It may be the missing fetish you've been looking for." I finally see his ruby eyes and grin a little.

I clear my throat, swirling the liquid in my glass. "I missed you."

"I've been gone longer."

"Yeah, but you usually harass me with prank calls, texts, or deliveries at the library."

"I hear you need new security." I sigh, fumbling to put the glass on the table and slump back on the bed with a groan. "Ruffians have infiltrated your castle, sweet cheeks. Is the library doing anything about it?"

"Not a thing. I was able to salvage most. I'll need more bookshelf space soon. Can shelves be built into ceilings?" Vinny makes a noise that tells me no. I take another deep breath and smell it. The aroma drifts by and I perk up. "Did you make coffee?"

"It seemed a bit late for you." My hand shoots outward, palm up. Screw getting drunk, Vinny made coffee. He snorts with laugher, and I listen to him move to the kitchen, coming back to place a mug in my hand. The warmth comforts me, and I hum as he whispers, "I missed you, too."

"Friends?"

"Friends."

I smile and sit up as Vinny settles back into my leather chair. He grumbles, "Do you know how boring it is being around only Anita and my father?"

"You should run away, start a pyramid scheme." I sip the perfect cup of coffee.

"Too much paperwork." We both chuckle at the thought. "I can take some of those damaged books. I have space in my personal library. You keep the werewolf books, though."

"You'd really do that?" I ask.

"Of course, those books are precious to you. They deserve either a burial, new resting home, or freedom from human hands." My heart warms at his statement. "Besides, it'll be harder to sneak in here with stacks of books in my way."

Ruined it. "Pervert."

"Drunk."

"Pot calls kettle black. At least it's nighttime for me."

He chuckles, and I notice he's drinking coffee now, too. Well, never mind. At least he needs to stay awake. Sleep is overrated for me lately anyway. Maybe I'll get lucky, and he'll stay most of the night. Pretend nothing exists outside. We can go back to the times when things weren't complicated and feelings didn't get in the way and jokes flew out of our mouths freely. And I really did miss him.

"You alright, sweet cheeks?" Vinny asks.

I rub my head, clearing my throat. "Haven't slept lately, might need a new hobby besides cleaning up after gremlin humans." I take another swig of coffee. Maybe that's why I'm grumpy this week, no signature 'Vinny Coffee.'

He shifts in his seat. "Going back tomorrow?"

I shake my head. The mess will still be there Monday. No point wasting a weekend. I'm also curious if anyone *would* reshelve what's left, like the odd find of Drauper's.

"Hey, Vinny."

"Hey, sweet cheeks."

"First, let's not fight again. It sucks."

"Deal." He chuckles.

"Second, do you know anything about recent experiments on Paranormals?" I ask, and I hear him inhale sharply. "I came across a journal about it, pieces of it that is, but it was marked from twenty or thirty years ago."

"One thing PSB is good at, stopping shit like that," he answers. "Black market is the only concern when it comes to that bullshit. No one keeps paperwork for those to trace. Everything else is monitored. *Officially,* they stopped years ago."

"And half-breeds?"

"Not sure. Depends on who they fall under. Why the—"

"Figured you'd give it to me straight. Whatever I found was probably just drug testing. Maybe labels were misplaced. It happens with those papers from time to time. Especially if they use ghostwriters or underpaid grad-students." Maybe I should reach out to my old professor. I was due a visit with her soon anyway.

Vinny scoffs, "Sure."

"Don't give me that."

"Come on, sweet cheeks, they can't take us seriously enough to get information, correct? Might as well short-hand it and just burn the books."

"Ouch."

"I didn't mean that," he says as his mug clinks on the table. "Did you at least see *where* it came from? Any other context?"

"I may be overthinking; seem to be doing that lately. I'll find where it belongs to when I clean up at work. Maybe, nothing." I knew exactly where to look, and it wasn't at the library.

I set my coffee aside without spilling it. Fully laying down in my bed, I stare up at the ceiling. The thought to throw myself over the Washington Bridge seems enticing. I take a deep breath in, letting the aromas in my apartment calm my nerves. I hope I'll sleep tonight, and no nightmares will come.

Vinny rustles up beside me and then pokes my side. I scooch over, and my bed dips as he lays down next to me with one arm behind his head. We say nothing, staring into, well, nothing. The slight warmth of his body invades mine as our breathing syncs up, and I smell the dark spices and bloodlust of Vinny. My stomach flutters as my body feels light yet taut.

"Don't you have a mafia to run?" I ask.

"They can survive for one night without me." His voice soft next to me. "Didn't lie about the calming thing, and the last few days have sucked. Everyone gives me heart palpitations."

"Your silver heart, don't forget."

"May stop stakes from going through. Good job, you found a cure against piercing damage." We laugh as I watch stars dance across the ceiling.

Vinny adjusts a little and says softly, "Rodney called me."

"Yeah?"

"I actually had to talk to him," he says. "I'd say you owe me, but the intel was actually helpful."

"You two had a conversation, and I wasn't present? I change my mind for a future birthday present." I joke. He chuckles, and we become quiet.

In the peace I've not had for days, I begin to decipher connections and patterns. It may seem like a crazy notion, but what Vinny said about the experiments did give me an idea. I know people who may have answers, and I'll take crazy theories at this point. I also haven't investigated the medical or testing side that PSB overlooked. Half-breeds are disappearing, and it sends a shiver down my spine.

Vinny turns to rub the side of my shoulder and arm. My skin heats from his touch, and I hold back a moan at the back of my throat. I swallow my emotions, keeping my body still. I ache for his arms around me, holding me.

"If I told anyone you did this, you'd lose your status as the bloodthirsty mob boss," I say.

"Have you actually seen me like that?"

"Twice. Not my favorite side of you, but you almost tearing out Rodney's throat over coffee? *That* was entertainment."

"Noted for the future. 'Tear out windpipe of werewolf.'"

"You ever hear of Balto?"

"The dog from Alaska?"

"You know what, never mind." I laugh to myself and snuggle further into the bed as he lays next to me. A few minutes pass, and I finally ask, "Don't you have virgins to scare into the night?"

"Yet, my charms don't work on you." His suave voice sweeps over me.

"Never have." My heart aches as I pretend to stifle a yawn. Vinny pulls the covers up over me. "Seriously, Vinny don't you need—"

"I'll stay a bit longer," he whispers as he settles fully next to me, just out of reach.

I drink in the scent of him, succumbing to the body that's next to me. I'd stay content like this because at least he's still in my life. I *needed* him. I needed Vinny in whatever capacity I could take. This *had* to be enough.

Carefully, my hand moves between our bodies and finds his hand, holding it gently as we lay in silence. I concentrate on that touch, hiding the tears that run down my cheek. This is all I'd ever receive. Deep down I know, I'm only destined for heartbreak.

CHAPTER TWENTY-ONE
LITTLE DERANGED EINSTEIN

Memories of my college days overwhelm me as I enter campus and walk through hordes of students. I'm taking a long shot, but I'll never forgive myself if I don't try. Neither would my old professor if she found out I didn't thoroughly research.

I approach the *Paranormal Science* building of Columbia University, where I spent a good portion of my undergraduate and master's despite my focus being in literature and history, but it was for one person. Most professors who teach in the *Paranormal Studies* departments are Paranormal or half-breeds, but Dr. Rhonda Quincy is one of the few human professors. A few other grad students and I have the privilege of calling her "Dr. Rhonda." She's a specialist in the biology of Paranormals, my contact to get academic journals for the library, and now my resource for this mysterious medical experiment journal.

At the end of the hallway, I find the familiar door with her name on it, and I knock. I hear her muffled "come in" from the other side, and I open the office door to see the usual mess of books and papers that fill her office. Pretty sure I learned my upkeep from her. She looks up and smiles. Her dark brown skin stands out against her pale blue top and lab coat. She pushes back a few black curls of hair as she stands, her golden eyes lively. Only she would be so vitalized on a Saturday morning before finals.

"You weren't kidding about coming in early," she says, walking around her desk to greet me with a hug.

"Early bird gets the worm. I think you taught me that."

"Nothing like a good sunrise to start the day." She pauses, looking at my dark sweater and long skirt, the very prude librarian look. The only professor who knows of my past as a stripper and approves. She was never a fan of my career change.

"It's comfy."

She sighs and settles behind her desk. "What can I help you with?"

I sit in one of her office chairs and say, "I've had some issues at the library, and I need a favor."

"Issues?"

"Well, some kids, kind of, destroyed most of the *Noctis Immortalis* section," I explain, and her mouth drops. "The Inquisition could have taken tips, honestly. I spent most of yesterday cleaning and salvaging what I could, but half the materials don't meet the library's standards to keep."

"I can ask the college to help with the restoration."

"Already covered to save those pieces, but I need—"

149

"Copies of any dissertations and journals that you may have lost or can't keep?" Yup, one of the many reasons she's my favorite human.

"Yeah, a lot of biology, anatomy, and medical resources were torn to shreds. It's not our usual time of the year to get stuff, but I thought I'd ask to start working on getting copies."

"Absolutely, but I may need some time. My grad students are busy this week with finals. I'm sure I can call the heads of the other Paranormal Departments if you need other subjects."

"You have no idea."

"That bad?"

"Wasn't really exaggerating with the Inquisition joke."

"Uneducated people will be the end of us all," she grumbles as she stands, grabbing some paperwork and a set of keys, and then motions me to follow her down the hall. "Do you know what titles you need to replace?"

I pat my small satchel. "Yeah. I can come by Monday to pick up copies that can be handed over quickly."

Dr. Rhonda nods as we leave one building into another. The archives are kept away in a separate location for safety reasons. The NIIA made it mandatory to station certain resources in several places. Libraries worldwide keep academic works, literature, medical journals, and dissertations that colleges approve as official within Paranormal Studies. The universities keep the originals and hand over copies to the public to help educate people of the different beings and bridge the gap. Lot of good that's done so far.

We come to the archives, and she opens the door to a room filled with metal shelves and drawers and the smell of fresh paper, cleaning supplies, and ink.

"We've had some material borrowed over to Harvard and Cambridge last week, so if you don't find a particular title, let me know," she says, adjusting her hold on her paperwork.

"I should be done around lunchtime." I pause, wondering if I should ask her specifically what I'm looking for, but halt. Drauper could be right about it being a typo, and I'd cause unnecessary worry. I need to find where the paper belongs first. "I'll check for any new sources, too. Always good to update the library's catalog."

"Very well, I'll be back for lunch, and we can catch up. Perhaps, discuss your wardrobe choices." Her brows lift as she closes the door behind her.

Before I became the Head Librarian for the *Noctis Immortalis* section, the library would request new items from nearby colleges. I took a more hands-on approach, searching for materials that range in a wide variety, which the library didn't have when I arrived. It also gave me a chance to see what Columbia received from other universities before anyone else.

I venture toward the back section, marked from a few decades ago. Do I need new source material for the library? Yes. Do I feel comfortable telling her I'm also using this time to look up something fishy? No. At least, not until I know it's simply a typo.

I go through drawer after drawer of drug listings, testings, and medical procedures and come across medical findings on ghoul skin grafts, shifter blood against cancer, vampire venom for broken bones, werewolf saliva for curing baldness...okay, I didn't know that. Then, I find something about anti-venom, antidotes, and vaccines against Paranormal powers, but nothing matches what Drauper found. All of them are labeled correctly, nothing saying "experiments". I'm about to shut the drawer when I see the last journal in the back and pull it out. Dated twenty-four years ago, *Antidote Testing: Noctis Immortalis*.

The only one labeled with a rejection stamp.

Flipping through the pages, I see the last half of the journal is blacked-out. The parts I'm able to read sound like demented torture procedures under the premise of medical testing. Near the back of the journal, I find the page that Drauper came across.

Bingo.

Glancing across the archives, I write down the rejected title, placing it back.

I notice it's been logged in with others under the singular medical center head: *Traloski*. The name seems familiar, but I can't put my finger on it.

I move on to double-check they still have the titles I need copies of. Some were gone with notations left saying Harvard and a few other universities have them loaned out. There are a few new titles I don't recognize, one of them discussing white blood cells in ghouls and developing a new anti-venom. I'm writing down the title and authors mentioned when Dr. Rhonda comes back to grab lunch.

"Find something new?" She asks.

"A few journals. I still wish I had a filing system like this," I say as I put away the journal. I follow her out of the room as she locks up.

I think of the Traloski journal. My curiosity grows, knowing now it wasn't a typo but rejected medical findings, something the library would never have in the first place. We turn down the hall, and I say, "I noticed a destroyed journal in the library and found it here, something about a testing center I never heard of in New York. It's the only rejected file I found the library has. Would you know anything about that?"

She scoffs, "Do you know how many 'medical testings' or 'centers' get disbanded or rejected by PSB each year? Most are drug centers for the black market. People try to pass them off as medical centers when they're just doing horrendous things with untested drugs. Worse if the FDA or CDC has no idea if those drugs even exist, since prescription drugs for humans aren't the same for Paranormals. *Both* sides need to be monitored. Even if they are rejected, we have to be aware of them and learn from them. At least with NIIA overseeing most studies, it's easier to track medical findings that are helpful."

I have a déjà vu moment and ask, "What about half-breeds? Most are included in studies and testing."

"Correct. Most can withstand the drugs used by humans and Paranormals. Usually, they're fine with both, their DNA allowing better reactions and monitoring. The hard part is getting them to agree to those studies and deciding who takes over jurisdiction, but it's usually NIIA."

My curiosity keeps climbing. "And ghouls? Since you know, the whole undead thing?"

"Long ago, they were used in the past practically as lab rats; if they died, they could be revived."

"Until the Treaty of 1946 declaring the ghouls their own rights, under the Paranormals."

"Yes, but the testing problem with having them part of studies, any symptoms they'd show won't be the same unless they're born from a ghoul and human mating, which is rare." I shiver at the thought. Not the imagery I needed today. "After the treaty was invoked, the ghouls rarely agree to be part of these studies, not worth going through the pain of coming back to the living."

"Was Traloski doing those tests then?" I ask, and she stops in the hallway, scrunching her brows. "I noticed some of his findings."

Pursing her lips, she begins walking again. "Don't worry about gathering anything from his *studies*. No one needs them."

"Is that why I don't recognize the name?"

"He was 'researching' antidotes, another attempt at vaccines, and testing went wrong. I was only beginning my undergraduate studies when NIIA shut his centers down." Her voice is tight, odd for my old professor.

"What kind of testing?"

"The kind that was outlawed decades ago. He was obsessed." She adjusts her jacket harshly as we walk around a corner. "He tried again and again to start his research but was stopped every time for using dangerous techniques that ultimately black-listed his findings and deemed them obsolete. Rumor has it the NIIA took care of him, except the aftermath."

I can tell I'm pushing the subject as we near the lunchroom. "I'm probably done for the day, but I'll be back Monday to pick up the other journals. If I missed anything, I'll let you know. Thank you again."

"Of course. I have finals to contend with this week, so I'll have my grad students who are free to work on it." She presses a small smile on her face.

"Sorry for bringing up Traloski," I say as we stop by one of the food stations. "Unauthorized experimentation is not a fun subject. I can see why you never brought up his research in class."

"You didn't know. Not something a literature enthusiast needs to know when you have Dr. Frankenstein," she smirks, and I laugh. "Most of us in the medical field look at him in disdain. What he did could have had catastrophic results. His antics may be why there's more government control in testing and a larger rift between Paranormals and humans on Topside. It's hard enough to make those relationships, even with those willing, like you, to share vital information that can help bridge the gap. It must be worse being a half-breed, caught in the middle all the time."

My stomach tightens as she grabs a tray. Clearing my throat lightly, I ask, "Where was he doing his research?"

"South Bronx, I believe."

Well, fuck.

CHAPTER TWENTY-TWO
PARANORMAL GANGSTER

This café has shitty coffee, and the glare I give it isn't going to help me in the slightest.

I put the atrocity down and look across the café. A werewolf sits near me reading the newspaper, a few ghouls whisper in the corner, and some humans are most intrigued with their computers. After I left Dr. Rhonda, I spent the rest of my afternoon at an off-beaten-path café to further research Traloski. I hoped the atmosphere would help, but alas, all I got was crappy coffee and a stomachache.

The only things I found on the internet were pop-ups saying I didn't have access to look at the information and more blacked-out sections of journals. The items I could gleam were testing procedures against the Geneva Convention, NIIA, and the Armed Forces. Reviews of Traloski's work were brief but effective in scaring anyone away from the medical field. The scientist had suggested draining all blood from a vampire and transfusing it with a ghoul to obtain new forms of regeneration. The coffee in my stomach feels like lead as I remember what I read. I close my laptop and sigh as my phone dings with an image of an empty bookshelf from Vinny that says, *there you go nerd.*

I chuckle and write back, *Thanks. I'll even be nice and let you choose what to take.*

He replies, *Mostly erotica. I'll give demos on what I read.*

I roll my eyes and put my phone away. Late afternoon hits as I leave the crappy coffee behind and walk down the street toward the closest Underground Entrance. I pass a few shifters changing into their human form as I pick up another coffee from a street vendor. An incubus passes me, and I can practically taste his heightened scent. I pay for the coffee and cheekily wave at the incubus with a smile. He stutters, making me laugh as I enter the elevator and lean against the wall.

"Nice try, pinkie," I say to myself.

A few succubi enter the elevator. One of them looks at me and asks, "You Cuorebella's kid?"

My brow rises. "How'd you guess?"

"Ricky said be weary of the prudish librarian with scars. I know of better things to wear."

"I'm good with being the prude of the family. Balances things out with Ricky."

"Interesting. Heard you were the quite the dancer." Her smile glows against her mauve skin, trying to affect my hormones.

I focus on the passing images outside the elevator, cold trickles over my skin from the temperature change. "Not everyone is meant to stay a dancer."

She takes a deep breath in and muses, "Hung up the heels, but not the panties? Fascinating life choice."

I slide my gaze back to them and the other one hums, "I could change that." Her eyes match the other like they both want to claim a prize. Typical succubi.

"You'll have to get in line."

"Oh, I can wait. Anymore scars?" She points toward the jagged lines across my face.

"Weird fetish," I muse.

"Slave trade does things to you," she says as the elevator stops. "Thanks to Cuorebella, all we have left are fetishes. See you around, *librarian*." They both leave with grins on their faces. I officially prefer being called "baby sis."

I make my way toward *The Vault*, and the late staff let me in to wander the aisles. I follow the weird lighting of greenish lamps and amber candles as I move toward sections I barely know and venture across the medical and science sections. It takes longer than I care to admit, but I find what I'm looking for. At least, I hope I did.

I pry open book after book, only finding histories of experiments, nothing recent enough about Traloski. I don't even find his name in noted doctoral or scientific works. Dead fucking end. I slam my hand against the shelf and huff. Damn librarian curiosity and stubborn streak, the more walls, I hit the more curious I become. I leave the aisle and walk past other familiar sections, pausing near where I almost had a mental breakdown. Maps. And that curiosity takes me forward.

Quickly, I start looking through the archives and pull out map after map of the Bronx in the last few decades. Placing them on top of the other, I finally find his stupid name, and it's labeled over a facility, but in small print. It *had* been in the Bronx thirty years ago outside the neutral zone. It isn't far from the Entrance near the stadium. Looking at the more recent maps, I notice it's now gone, an open lot. Well, Dr. Rhonda did say the authorities sacked the place. I had a lead on a mad scientist from over two decades ago, and the building is gone. If it's him or someone trying to replicate his studies, I have nowhere to look except the *entire* Bronx. That's *if* any of this has anything to do with the disappearances or ghouls.

Maybe someone paid the ghouls to hide whatever is happening there. Or a mad scientist is trying to recreate his medical findings. Or ghouls and said mad scientist are working together to make their own undead army. Or it's another mob family trying to rise through the ranks, causing chaos to obtain their own borders. Or someone is starting a summer program to teach cops *Shooting Paranormals is Good for the Economy.*

Or…I'm slowly losing my mind. All viable possibilities at this point.

I need to find more on Traloski himself. In the back of my mind, the thought beckons but kicks at the idea, and it doesn't feel right. Even more reason to go back to Columbia on Monday and scavenge for something that isn't black-listed.

I leave *The Vault* and wander the streets of the Underground in the twilight hours, making my way toward the club to surprise Ma and Pops. Wheels screech behind me, and I turn to see a black car as it stops beside me. The door opens, and Anita smiles as she gestures for me to get in, her long black hair loose around her shoulders.

"Finally kidnapping me?" I ask as I take the seat next to her.

"Long as I get to gag you." She shuts the door, signals the driver to get moving, then scans me. "Your attire may be an interesting kink. Never knew you were into the Gothic era. Good times, even with the corsets."

"Memories?" I tap the wall between Brock and us. "*Unbound,* Brock."

Anita leans back and smiles with fangs shining, holding a glass of blood. The violet color in her long velvet dress brings out the paleness of her skin. "You're never here Saturday mornings."

"And you're up rather early."

"Never slept." She sips her drink, coating her lips in crimson. "I see you and Vinny finally made up. He stopped acting mopey. Don't take as long next time."

"We're not that predictable."

Anita scoffs and gestures toward my head. "Ever since he made you cry about dying your hair blonde, your quarrels are predictable."

"He said I looked like Barbie."

"Most females take that as a compliment," Anita argues.

"Being compared to a plastic doll that humans play with to dress up? Hell no. Nope."

Anita laughs, and it could chill someone's blood. I wouldn't be surprised if it happens to the glass in her hand.

I shrug and lean further back into the seat, waiting for her to taunt me more, but the vampire has other ideas. "Vinny has always been protective of what he thinks is his. Although it comes with the territory, he's quite distinct in his choices to obsess over. He cares about you. More than anything else in this world."

"We're best friends; of course he cares. Sees me as a little sister and been attached to me since I was seven. And I care about him, too." I stare at her, unsure where this is coming from.

"How dense are you, baby sis?" Anita's scolding voice burns into me while she puts her glass down, clinking as she nails me with crimson eyes.

After last night, I don't need a reminder of worthless wants. A manicured nail comes up, carefully tracing down one of my scars. I try to avoid her piercing gaze. "Don't know what you're talking about."

She clutches my chin, frowning as she tugs me to look at her. "If you don't feel that way about him, fine. But don't break his heart along the way. Let him go, at least."

I swallow as her fingers leave my face. Not the first time a vampire threatened me over Vinny. "Don't know—"

"Things fucking changed. And you know it." I freeze, not looking at her. "He stopped being himself and you turned into this...prude, angry *human*. You left and he hasn't been the same."

"Pinning this on me then?"

"You *belong* down here with us. With my bro—"

"I *had* to leave," I growl.

"No, you didn't."

"Anita."

"What do you think was going to happen when you left? You almost break him and act like a damn child." Her words prod and peel at old wounds.

The bite marks on my neck pulsate, causing me to see more red. "Shut up."

"All you care about—"

"None of you understand!" My voice rises. "Stop pretending you know what I need or want. *I had to leave!* Don't make it worse by *guilting* me over Vinny! *You don't get to do that!*"

I pound the emergency button, and the car screeches to a halt as I jump out. I turn to slam the door and glare at Anita's passive face. There's enough guilt and self-hatred within me that I don't need from her. "No matter how hard I try, I will *never* fully be a part of this world. You want to tell me how I'd fit into Vinny's? With the purebred vampires? *Your* world? Your *father's* world?" The scars on my neck burn like fire as I remember Bruno's teeth on my neck, the blood he took, and his final threat to leave Vinny and the Vampiric Society alone.

Anita says nothing as her eyes widen slightly and her scent dampens. "I'm not stupid, Anita. I'm a realist. One day, your brother will settle down with another bloodsucker. I'll *always* be baby sis. Vinny knows that. *Let me live with that.*"

I slam the door and sprint down the path through a small alley toward *Unbound*. A block away, I slow down and attempt to ease my aching lungs. I can feel the tears in my eyes as I pass the bouncer and walk through the club doors. Fuck, I'm not going to cry. I ignore the bartenders, strippers, and Gina as I move through the club and come to the door of the apartment. I freeze as reality hits once more, my fingers moving up to brush against the bite marks Bruno left as a warning and his cold lesson.

Reality hurt.

I don't need to be reminded I'm barking up the wrong tree. Vinny and I are best friends, that's it. I'm left to fantasies, fucked-up humor, coffee, and long whiskey nights. I know where we stand due to circumstances. If Vinny ever chose me, he could lose his business, family, status…and cause a rift in the mafia that could lead to destruction.

If he ever chose me…

But I could never ask that of him. I can't compete with two hundred years of his work and time. Or his own species.

As I fumble for my keys, the scent of cigars and cinnamon drift into my nostrils, and tears come to my eyes. I turn to face my father, who stands with his arms crossed and brow creased in confusion as he asks, "What's wrong, baby girl?"

"Just you and Ma tonight?" I wipe my nose and hold back tears. Pops nods and drops his arms. I don't get another word out before he yanks me into an embrace.

"No need to explain yourself. Always grateful to have you home." I wrap my arms around him as my tears fall onto his shirt and he caresses my back softly. "It'll be alright. Do you want to talk about it?" I shake my head. He gently pulls away and kisses me on the forehead. "You can go upstairs to Ma. I need to finish some things. Unless you want to stay down here."

My eyes dart toward the bar, and Pops smooths back my hair. He nods, leading me over to the bar, where he watches me take a seat before leaving to check in with the strippers. Thankfully, Bobby is bartending and places some coffee in front of me. I grin weakly and take the mug in my hands.

Waitresses and bouncers move quickly as the changeover commences and the lighting of the night changes to hues of violet and blue. I raise my coffee at Gina across the room, and she gives a vulgar gesture with her smile. Pops swats at her to get to the back and winks at me before disappearing through one of the tunnel doors.

As a child, I didn't like being away from Pops for long. I'd cry, worrying that he wouldn't return home. I spent most days curled up in his arms or a sling on his back. When I got older, I'd stay at the bar and listen to him work as I do now for what seemed like hours. Familiarity eases me as I listen to Pops and breathe in his scent. I'm swirling my finger in the cooled coffee when he pats me on the shoulder and brushes my hair, gesturing for a hair tie. I pull one out of my satchel and hand it to him as he detangles the strands from my little run.

"Why the tears?" He asks.

"Stupid girly things," I answer as he starts French braiding my hair.

"No such thing, baby girl. Now, you gonna tell me what's wrong, or will I have to bring Ma into it?"

"Please don't. It'll turn into a discussion over my panties again."

"Didn't bother you before," he murmurs.

"I just...I don't know."

"So, it's about a male then?" I frown at the mirror behind the bar and see his smug expression. Damn, I really walked into that. "You think I won't see them worthy? Approve of them?"

"Pops, you don't think anyone on this earth is worthy. Be honest here."

"Price for being my daughter." He gently ties my hair into the braid. "I'll bend some rules if you like them well enough. You'll end up shooting them before I can anyways."

"Just how you raised me."

"Exactly," he says, sitting beside me and holding my hands in one while turning my chin to look at him with the other. His deep violet eyes stare at me, and I sigh in defeat, too tired to fight or argue at this point. Besides, I want Pops to know *something* at this point.

"Let's say I do...like someone," I whisper, my words caught in my throat. "What if it's not...possible to be together? Or they don't want it? Cause I'm not...that? Not good enough...to even...this sounds childish."

He sits back and rubs his thumb over my hand. "Not that childish. I didn't think Ma ever liked me before I courted her. Next thing I knew, she's throwing me into *her* bed. Sometimes we hide emotions to protect ourselves from heartbreak."

"Still feel dumb."

"Aren't we all when it comes to love and lust? What makes you think you and this *person* can't be together?" I look away as worry trickles through my spine, my chin quivering as he wipes away tears on my cheek. He places a hand under my chin, making me look up at him. He's blurry through the tears. "You need to tell him."

"Come on, Pops, he doesn't want me," I say. "We all know what he's like, who he...takes to bed or—"

"We both know that's not why."

"He clearly made his decision at those parties." My voice trembles and falls to a whisper.

Pops lets out a long sigh. "Quit lying and hiding behind old anger, baby girl," he says as I shake my head.

"I need to, Pops."

"Baby girl..."

"There's an entire bloodline, mafia, society, and his *father* to remain loyal to. And a life that hasn't changed for the past two hundred years, I don't need to mess it up because I'm...I'm... fucking lonely."

Pops grips the side of my face, "Then just come home, baby girl."

I scoff. "What happened to you telling me to figure things out and determine what I want or—"

"Fuck what I said." I snort with laughter. "If you're unhappy and feeling alone, come home then. No point dragging out sadness when there's no one there to uplift you on the hard days."

"Pops..."

"I can't make you come home," he says, wiping away another tear. "But I just want my baby girl to be happy with who she is. Because you're perfect as you are. Damn those societies and their old ways. That's what got you thinking he may want that, too. You won't know unless you talk to him."

I sniffle a little and Pops reaches over, handing me a napkin. I take it with a shuddering breath, fear in my heart bubbling to the surface. "I don't want to lose my best friend, daddy. Cracking jokes. Practicing my aim. The nicknames. It...it *has* to be enough. I can't chance ruining it. I just can't. I don't want to lose him because of bullshit mafia politics and societies."

"They're exactly that. Bullshit."

My thoughts go back to the night before of Vinny lying beside me, just out of reach, and the peace I felt. Never would I risk losing that. Maybe someday I'll find someone to replace the ache. I thought I would on Topside, but nothing. Even Drauper couldn't fill the hole that was there.

"I'll be fine. I swear, it's just..." I try to get the words out. "I'll figure it out, somehow, but right now, I'll stay on Topside. Find some way to...to make it work."

Pops nods and strokes his thumbs over my hands. "I know, baby girl, I know. It doesn't make it any easier to see you like this."

I take a deep breath, trying to calm the last of the anger and hurt. "Thanks for not pushing for me to, you know, find a good incubus to settle with or a shifter with good teeth."

Pops stands up, stretching slightly. He gestures for me to stand and takes me into his arms, rubbing my back to ease my nerves. "I don't want you to be alone, baby girl, but if you could stay single and never have your heart broken over someone, I'd be a happy father. At least, I know you'd never feel heartache."

"Isn't that against your genetic code? Being single?" I smile up at him faintly.

"Perhaps, but if it means I never need to see you like this again, I'll fight against it," he says and kisses my forehead.

"How I feel, I agree with you." He lets go and hands me my satchel. I pause while taking it from him, smiling a bit more. "Thanks, Pops."

"I love you, baby girl."

"Love you, too," I say as he leads me to the apartment, and we walk through the front door.

"Carmen, our daughter is here!" He shouts as he closes the door behind us, then looks at me. "You staying the rest of the weekend?"

I nod. No point going back to my apartment. I can't get to Columbia to investigate more until Monday. The library will still be a mess, and I'm not ready to face Drauper anytime soon. Maybe I'm a coward hiding at my parent's, but my give-a-fuck meter has run out.

Ma comes out of the kitchen and beams. "Baby, you never said you'd be here this weekend. A wonderful surprise." She hugs me tightly, and the scent of cherry blossoms calms me. I feel her gesture to Pops behind my back.

"Hey, no parental secret sign language," I mutter as she releases me.

"Shush. Staying the rest of the weekend?"

"She is," Pops answers as he kisses Ma on the cheek. "She can help fix costumes with you. Baby girl, she's doing sequins. She'll need the help."

"Will Gina be there?" I ask, and Ma nods. "Deal."

"Need the girl time?" Ma asks as she takes my arm, leading me into the kitchen instead of the dining room. I drop my satchel near the couch as I follow.

"Something like that," I murmur. Pops touches my shoulder gently as he walks past us to the coffee. "Maybe I'll put in an application to work downstairs again." Ma lets go and puts her hand to her chest. "I'm kidding, Ma."

Pops chuckles as Ma fixes our plates and says, "Don't tease me like that. I'd have to refit all your outfits again and buy new fabric."

"Sorry, Ma."

I sit down with Pops as we hide our smiles, and Ma sets down the food. It's a quiet meal with the three of us. I finally tell them about the vandalism at the library, which neither is happy about it and to want to look further into the incident. They also offer to keep the books the library won't keep, and I change the subject asking about Joey. He bought a coffee shop for his front, and a small victory shouts within as Pops tells me about the renovations that will soon occur. Business as usual. They're like they always are.

After dinner, Pops goes back downstairs, and I help Ma clean up before taking out my contacts and lying on the couch reading a fantasy novel in braille while she folds laundry nearby. She tries several times to get me to go to bed, but I refuse. I'd stay up for their whole day to be near her. Old habits from childhood rock through me. The comfort of familiarity and normalcy washes over me as she hums, pressing dress shirts.

I fall asleep at some point and wake up later with my head on Pops' lap. Ma is at the other end of the couch with my feet draped over her lap. Her slight movement tells me she's knitting. Pops watches television quietly, a mug of tea at his side as he keeps his attention to the screen. I remain where I am, deciding this is perfectly where I need to be. I feel at peace and know no matter what, I'd have this. After all that's happened recently, this is what I needed.

I'll always be their little girl—a role they wholeheartedly take with pride. I could live to two hundred years old and still have this. And wouldn't mind remaining as such.

"Needs more glitter," Gina says.

"The hell it does," I argue.

"Language, baby," Ma scolds me.

I glance down at the sequined bra I'm in. Gina pushes her breasts up as she folds her arms, disappointed at the lack of sparkle. I'm more of a leather person. Ma checks the straps over my shoulders, then moves to the attachable accessories.

"There should be more sparkle, Carmen," Gina says.

"Oh, for fu—" I grumble as Ma nods and pulls out a box of sequins. Please let her add the glitter part once I'm out of it. I agreed to being a mannequin, not the next show award. "Ma, can you add glitter after I'm out of this? I don't need it following me home."

Ma sighs in amusement, "Alright, baby."

It's Sunday, and the weekend home was worthwhile. There weren't any nightmares, which I took as a good omen. I've spent the last few hours working with Ma and Gina, the stripper from the peanut gallery, apparently.

Ma pats my shoulder, and I strip the costume off, leaving me only in my briefs. Gina pokes one of my exposed breasts. My scowl doesn't deter her from doing it again, and she comments, "They seem fuller."

"Seriously? I need a padded bra to make it look like I have half the tits you have," I mutter.

"Could arrange to have matching sets. I know someone." Her smile becomes wider.

"Gina, leave my child alone. She's perfect," Ma intervenes. "Baby, please put on the dress in the back. We'll be done after that. You need to go home soon to get some sleep before work."

I stick my tongue out at Gina, and she licks the top of her teeth as she swats one of my boobs. I push away her hand as I go to put the dress on. My breasts can hardly hold up the strapless number with rhinestones and sequins hanging from the sides, giving a fringe look.

"Was this made for Gina?" I ask, gesturing towards the top. "Because I'm feeling flat, only she has mountains to fill this."

Ma hums as she pins the dress I'm in. Gina sits down near the mirrors, clicking her tongue at me. I stick mine back out again, which she mimics. Suddenly, Gina's eyes narrow, watching me studiously. Not good.

"Alright, all done," Ma says, patting my arm. "Take that off and then come upstairs to take some food home. Gina, Alanzo wants to see you later about adding more males since Angelo and Jesse left." Gina gives an affirmative sound as Ma gathers her materials and heads toward the door. "No mingling with other strippers."

Gina pouts at the reminder, then perks up when Ma leaves. "Who did you kiss and when, baby sis?"

"What?" I ask as I strip out of the dress carefully.

"I can practically *smell* him on you. I'm surprised Carmen didn't say anything, although she is your Ma. She'll wait until you admit it first." Gina lounges in her chair and takes another sniff. "Don't recognize the lingering scent. Someone new? Human?"

I undress, beginning to dread being around this succubus lately. "Don't wanna talk about it."

I've avoided the subject and the detective while I've been here like the plague. And I would've have gotten away with it, too, if it wasn't for beings who can sense hormone shifts and lingering scents that not even a bloodhound could detect.

"Oh, come on, give me something, baby sis. You kissing someone is groundbreaking. Talk to Auntie Gina."

I glower at her. "Not comforting coming from you."

"Hey, I helped with your first French kiss." My glower doesn't falter. "How much have you learned from me?" She doesn't wait for me to answer. "Everything. Including dancing and stripping."

"Okay, not telling you shit," I say as I pull on my bra and finish getting dressed. "There's nothing to talk about, Gina, because nothing's gonna happen."

I almost fall over putting my jeans on as she pulls me into a chair. I look up in annoyance, her smile sparkling in mischief. She tries to work her magic on me to no avail. "Come on, talk to me. We both know you won't tell your brothers or parents even though you tell Pops everything. This is a sister thing, though."

"I don't tell him—"

"You're his baby girl, yeah you do. Now, why can't you tell me about it? Was it bad?"

Her last question throws me. I realize I hadn't thought about it. Not that fully. "No, it was…good."

"Wow, convincing."

"No, really it was." I think back to everything that's happened, the fight with Vinny, kissing Drauper, the ache in my heart. "I'm just a mess, Gina."

"When are you not?" She giggles and waves off my glare. "Why the mess? They with someone else? They moving to another country? Was it a werewolf and their breath stunk?"

"That's stereotyping."

"Throw me a bone," she smirks. She nudges my knee, and I smile. "Tell me or I'll get Ricky."

I give in and sigh. "He's a detective. *Human.* Topside."

She raises her brows in surprise. "And?"

Is she serious?

I gape at her. "And? What happens when he finds out about my family? He doesn't even know I'm a half-breed or that I grew up here with the *mafia.* The moment I tell him, he'll throw me in jail or exile me back down here forever or to a different state."

"Don't tell him then. Just go have fun and hook up. You finally got kissed after how many years? Don't tell him shit."

"What?"

"You don't need to date the man to have sex. Nor do you need a heart to heart or be together *forever.* It can just be a fling if you're worried."

"Maybe I want my first time to be with someone I'm a bit more honest with," I scowl, crossing my arms.

"Then don't do anything."

"So helpful."

Gina laughs at my deadpan tone. "Do you like him?"

"I don't know."

"Are you friends? Acquaintances?"

"Friends? Maybe…"

"Wow, convincing," she says again.

"Quit it."

"Look, darling, figure out what you want with him first. Friends, something more, or knowing if he'll exile you to the Underground. These things take time, especially interspecies dating. Or just say fuck it and fuck him. Truths don't need to be part of sex. Terrible threesome at times." The succubus is either wise or has terrible advice.

"Have you lied to someone you've—" Her laugher cuts me off. "Alright, alright. I should've just slept with one of the strippers years ago."

"Against policy and Pops would've grounded you. Ma would've been satisfied with your panties, but Ricky would hound you for a better Mate." She thinks for a moment and adds, "Joey would've beat them up and thrown a party."

I hang my head back, closing my eyes in frustration. "I'm just gonna ignore this and hope any feelings disappear. If there actually are any."

"He made the move?"

"Yup."

"Why do you care then?"

"I didn't, not until you started prying," I grumble.

"Bullshit, baby sis. You're trying to run again because you're overthinking. Explains why you've been down here all weekend. So, either you got feelings for the guy, or you're feeling guilty for playing with his heart." She eyes me. "Or you're wrestling with something else."

I want to throw Gina from a roof today. Mainly because the horned she-devil is right.

I give her the middle finger, getting out of my chair. She smirks, "So, I'm right. Should've just stayed a stripper where there's no detectives, especially humans."

I yank on my jacket and take a deep breath. I'm beginning to rethink my life choices, and my old job seems better each day. Those days seemed simple enough. The grin on her face makes me want to rip her favorite bra to pieces. "I'm staying single forever."

"Where's the fun in that? Don't diss sex, foreplay, or fetishes until you've tried it."

"What if I'm—"

"Not ace or demi, baby sis. Seen the way you look at certain males *and* females. Not it, so don't go disrespecting my friends cause you're being a chicken." I love Gina, but right now, I really hate her.

I head for the exit. "Well, those all sound like better options than this."

"It's hard to open your heart when someone else holds the key."

I stop with my hand braced against the doorway. Gina's chair scrapes on the floor as she walks over and puts her hand on my shoulder. I say in a low voice, "That key is long gone. And it's gonna stay that way, for a lot of people's own good."

"Even if it means turning you into something you hate?" I scoff. Gina's words hit me to my core. "He stopped coming to me years ago, Brenda."

I leave before I start to cry. Taking deep breaths, I ease the tenseness in my muscles as I head upstairs. I walk into the apartment and give longer hugs to Ma and Pops than usual before leaving with leftovers for Topside. Pops narrows his gaze at me as I leave, but I force a smile before disappearing downstairs. I push away the conversation with Gina as I walk toward the Entrance. A longing to stay overwhelms me as I lean against the elevator and watch the lights flicker and change below. My phone buzzes and my stomach drops as I glance at the screen and decline the call. I bang my head back against the side and swear under my breath and plead for a nap and whiskey. My phone buzzes again and again. I decline it, cursing under my breath. Ready to down a new bottle of whiskey, the elevator doors open and reveal Vinny standing in the way.

"No fair, I can't reach my gun," I groan and show my armful of food containers.

"Not nice to ignore phone calls, sweet cheeks," he says as he puts his phone away. "Unless, of course, cell service went down."

"Maybe I don't wanna talk." Not exactly a lie. Vinny is the main proponent for my turmoil, but he also makes me feel better. A troubling catch-22.

"You didn't even tell me you were below. Why would you wound me so?" The hand over his heart is a little overdramatic.

"You're a noob," I say, walking past him.

He follows after me and scoffs. "No bloodsucker? No pervert? I'm hurt."

"How about bastard? Demented blood prick?"

"That's better. Here I thought you skipped caffeine today. Still doesn't explain some things. What's up, sweet cheeks?"

He swerves with me down the sidewalk in the muggy summer evening. My jacket sticks to my skin as I look over at him. "Don't call me that."

"Not until you call me bloodsucker again."

"Fine, *bloodsucker.*"

"Doesn't have the same ring to it."

"Oh, for fuck's sake!"

"*There* she is! I was worried a weekend with your parents domesticated you."

"You can fuck off now. Don't you have a coffin to wax? Fluff the silken pillows you keep between your legs?" I practically growl at him.

He takes a couple of the containers from my hands, quirking a brow. "You're avoiding me. You never avoid me."

"Says you who disappeared for like four days. Pot calls the kettle black, grandpa."

"Because I was frustrated and angry. For the last fifty years, people have told me to watch my wrath; otherwise I'd make my grandfather proud."

I snort at the very idea of Vinny even doing half of what Dracula did. "Yeah, stakes through heads and bodies just aren't popular anymore."

"What's wrong, sweet cheeks?"

"You calling me that damn name. Maybe I just wanted a few days alone with my parents. Not everything is about you." The last sentence is heavy in my mouth. I continue walking, hoping he won't push more.

He stops as I walk on. "I know Anita saw you."

Damn it.

I pause as he rejoins me and says, "She and our father had a few meetings without me these past few days. Then she's fucking livid and goes to you for some reason. The morning she does, *you* hole up at *Unbound,* and Alanzo tells me to stay away."

I spin toward him. "You talked to Pops?"

"He talked to me." Vinny makes it clear with piercing crimson eyes, his scent heightening. "Said to keep my distance and to tread lightly. Apparently, our little spat was enough to worry everyone and stick their noses in my business. We both know how much I hate that shit. So, what did Anita tell you?"

I steel myself and remain passive. "Nothing."

"Calling fuckery there, *sweetheart.*" He brings his face a bit closer, and his harsh scent invades my senses. A chill goes down my spine, but I keep myself still. "What happened?"

I notice beings passing us and keeping their heads down. Having a confrontation with Vinny the Vampire, Blood Mafia Boss in the open isn't a good idea. "What does it matter?"

"It matters if others stick their noses in *my business* and *life.*"

"Wasn't me."

"Never said that, sweet cheeks," he says, running his hand through his hair. The movement makes my core tighten. I focus on the hurt this past weekend and ignore the need to touch the vampire in front of me. Stop it, hormones. *"You* are a part of my life, whether anyone likes it or not. You're my best friend, and I don't like others screwing with my things."

"Territorial again, pervert. And I'm not a thing. Maybe I should hang out with Rodney more…."

"He can go howl at the moon and hope the moonlight turns him into a dachshund." We both grin, and the tension in the air eases. Smoothing his hair back again, he speaks in a softer tone, "What did she say?"

I wave him off. "Don't worry about it."

"Brenda."

"Seriously, Vinny." I harden my tone. "Don't worry about it. Just let me go home to sleep before I have a long-ass day replacing journals and books."

He gives back the containers. "Do you want help?"

"It'll be daytime, bloodsucker. Much as I'd like to see you as burnt bacon, I'll decline. The moaning alone from your crispy skin will hold me over the next year for laughs, but I can always rent a movie."

He narrows his eyes on me. "What about *other* moaning?"

"Slid right into that one, huh?"

"There are other things you can slide on. Far more enjoyable." He smirks, and I shake my head, smiling faintly. This. *This* is why I can't tell him; I'll lose the banter and quick fixes to arguments. The pit of my stomach falls deeper as I ache and push away destructive feelings.

"I'm going home to sleep, nothing more. Your bodyguards are probably losing their minds not knowing where you are. The new ones may have already started getting drunk."

"Part of the position."

"Give them a raise. Oh! Let them shoot you in the leg."

"Only you get that privilege."

"This is why you're my BFF."

"Only for you, *sweet cheeks*."

We both smile, and I wave a little at him. Vinny doesn't follow me, but I feel him watching as I head home. No running or sprinting on my part.

I'm a fucking coward.

Dr. Rhonda sent me a message Monday morning that she and her students are too busy with finals for me to go back to the archives. The list I gave her would be sent to the library, with no reason for me to visit. I'll have to find another excuse to go searching through the archives again.

It's Thursday, and I'm still holed up replacing and cataloging everything while I wait for new copies and continue to hide from Drauper. Coward. Whenever I think I'm being pathetic, I amaze myself with something new. Thankfully, the restricted section is off-limits to outsiders. And my routes to the Underground are not public knowledge. So, my cowardly lion ass hides while gluing books together.

As I'm organizing pages, the phone rings with Dr. Rhonda's number popping up, and I answer, "Afternoon, Professor. The shipment hasn't arrived yet if you're checking."

"Yes, I know. I'm calling to see if you need time again to look at the archives."

"Well, you said you'd send the rest of—"

"Yes, I know Brenda," she says quickly. "You seemed troubled about something last time with your findings, much like how you'd get during most of your projects. Anything on your mind that you need answers to?"

Once again, I appreciate how perceptive my old professor is.

"Yeah. You'll let me look through the files?" I look around and whisper quieter. "Even if it may not be for the library?"

"As long as you don't turn *my* archives section into a similar disaster on your hands, I'll let you browse." I know she's partially joking, but it's hard to tell. "You were respectful in your college days; I believe it carried over. Otherwise, I'd never allow you to be alone in those archives in the first place."

I peer at the mess surrounding me. Anything is better than staying down here another day. "How does tomorrow sound? I could use a break from the hurricane aftermath."

"I have exams all day, but I have a grad student who can check you in."

"Alright."

"Good. Her name is Lindsey, and her office is two doors down from mine. Meet her around 9 AM. She has red hair with freckles. Young and bubbly. She'll annoy you."

"Was this your plan all along?" I muse a little.

"Pranking my favorite student? Never." The line clicks off, and I chuckle, thanking whatever lucky stars I have.

I inform Janice I won't be in the next day, saying I'll be at Columbia. As always, she doesn't question me, leaving me to my business the rest of the day. It's nearly six in the evening when my phone rings again. I look at the number and sigh as I answer, "You should be napping."

"I need a favor, sweet cheeks."

"Straight to business. Worries me even more." I frown when I hear him sigh; he actually sounds tired. "Vinny?"

"I need to stay on Topside tomorrow night for some of the evening. Thought I could just stop by your apartment, but the last time I did, you about destroyed your own door and almost shot me."

"Because *you* were in my apartment unannounced. Probably one of the sanest things I ever did." He doesn't bite back. "Vinny, why can't you stay at one of—"

"Business reasons," he replies shortly. A few clinks tell me he's already drinking.

Great signs, all and all.

"You sound grumpy."

"If you knew what I had to deal with in the past 24 hours, you'd...well, probably burn down *The Lounge*."

"Oh, I'd do that for a quarter."

His snort of laughter is a relief. He isn't completely out of it. "Just for a few hours that night, sweet cheeks. I'll even bring the quarter and some whiskey."

"Deal. You drive a hard bargain, bloodsucker," I say as I place some books on the carts. "Are you staying at *The Lounge* tonight?"

"Office is better than..." His words trail off, and it worries me more. He only ever stays at the office for one reason, and his name is Bruno. Although Vinny's apartment is above *The Lounge*, he doesn't stay there if there's been an argument. Usually, in fear of ripping it apart, which he has in the past.

"I have three stacks of books to finish up. Just go to my apartment now, don't make a mess. Take a nap, and then go deal with whatever dipshit made you sound like a depressed emo werewolf. I'll be home later, so you can sleep in my leather chair this one time. When you come back tomorrow night, you better have that whiskey."

"I'm a depressed punk bloodsucker; get it right."

"The way you're grumbling tells me differently."

"Thanks, sweet cheeks."

"Go defile my leather chair." I hang up on him and work until 10 PM.

Vinny is knocked out in my favorite leather chair as I enter my apartment quietly, take my contacts out, and go to bed with most of my clothes still on. I awake to my alarm going off with coffee sitting on my nightstand. The bloodsucker is gone, but he left a note.

After getting my contacts in and drinking some of the "anti-murdery juicy-juice," moaning in delight, I read the note. *See you tonight, sweet cheeks. There's whiskey already in the cupboard.*

I decide the alcohol can wait until tonight as I dress with my Glock inside my leather jacket and go into the muggy, gray Friday morning. It looks like rain, and the university is busy with students and professors heading to exams. As I approach the building, my phone buzzes. Half expecting it to be Vinny, I look to see it's Drauper and decline the call. I decide the archives are a great place to hide. I'll stop being pathetic when my backbone grows in, which doesn't seem anytime soon.

I pass Dr. Rhonda's office and find the door she directed me to. After one knock, I'm greeted by a bright overcompensating smile on a round face filled with freckles. Bright green eyes meet mine, and I notice the flowery blouse she's wearing. Yup, my ex-professor is screwing with me.

Miss. Congeniality takes a quick breath before rambling, "You must be Brenda! I'm Lindsey. So nice to meet you! Dr. Quincy said wonderful things about you. You're the Head Librarian for the *Noctis Immortalis* at the public library, right? That's so amazing!" No amount of perfect "Vinny Coffee" could prepare me for this.

"Technically, that's my title, but not that big of a deal. Glad Dr. Rhonda gave me such high marks." She shakes my hand and she gasps looking down at the small scars that riddle my wrist, keeping her hold on me.

"Those are some nasty scars. What happened?" Where did she find this kid?

I yank my hand away and divert the conversation. "Can you take me to the archives?"

"Oh! Right, follow me." She closes her door, almost bouncing down the hallway as I follow at a normal pace behind her. It's a 9 AM on a Friday during finals week. How does she exist? "I also have access to other record rooms. Dr. Quincy said something about you maybe needing materials in other areas."

"Other areas?"

"Something about replacing journals for different subjects and findings? I was thinking this morning you may want to investigate the other archives to see if any of that is what you need. Or add new journals to the public library. That may be good. It's not like the information here is secret—"

"Lindsey," I interrupt, and she stops to smile at me. "What are these archives for?"

She flips her hand in the air. "All kinds of subjects, like sociology, anthropology, chemistry—they've probably been updated since you were a student—medical studies, biology—"

"Okay! Okay," I say, attempting to stop her again before she lists off Columbia's majors and minors. "I thought the archives I've always been to is all Columbia had. At least within the medical field. They couldn't have updated it more since last I was here to retrieve items for the library."

"Oh! That's because this one's for the specific studies cleared by the NIIA, PSB, FDA, and CDC to become public information." She explains as we walk around a corner.

"Wait, those rejected are still kept here? I thought they were moved to Boston?" She shakes her head. It explains why I hadn't seen anything unless it's stamped with approval by all the boards for the public. Maybe that's why Dr. Rhonda was upset when we talked about Traloski. His findings weren't supposed to be in there. "Can I look at that archive this afternoon? The ones not granted public access yet? I know I'm asking a lot here, but it'd be good to know for the future—"

"Oh sure! One of the reasons why I brought it up. Dr. Quincy always talks about sharing knowledge..." She babbles on as she leads me to the archives and opens the door, leaving me to work until she returns at lunchtime. I sigh as she leaves me in wonderful silence.

Hours later, all I find are more blacked-out documents. More dead ends. Yay. Thank goodness Vinny brought whiskey. Just in time for lunch and hopefully coffee, I hear Lindsey just outside the door, but she's with someone else. Fear wrecks through me as the deep familiar voice answers her.

Why is Drauper here?

I spin in place trying to find a place to hide, but the door opens. I scramble to stand normally as they enter the room. My gaze meets Drauper's, and his brow rises.

Shit.

"I was on my way over when I ran into the detective," Lindsey says. "He was looking for some information on institutions that may have been in the Bronx, and I thought, well, I'm already going that way, come along then! Did you find everything you needed?"

"Yeah, mostly," I say in a tight voice. "Morning, Detective."

"Morning, Brenda," he says.

"You two know each other? Wow! Coincidence! I was even thinking of referring him to, well, you! Since the public library—"

"Thank you, Lindsey," Drauper says, holding a hand up and giving me a wide-eyed expression.

"Well, you won't find much here," I say. "After what I looked through, you may want to go to city hall instead for building permits and facilities." Would've gone there myself, but I had Beckham's treasure trove below. His are more accurate in measurements between Topside and the Underground.

"Darn! I'm sorry, Detective," Lindsey says with a pout as I walk past them. I can feel Drauper's eyes staring into the back of my skull.

"It was a long shot. Thanks. Heading to lunch?" He asks me as Lindsey locks the door. I try to avert his gaze.

"Yeah, I've been coming here to see what the university can replace for the section destroyed, and I have another room Lindsey will show me later," I explain before the young girl could. "I'll meet you in the lunchroom, Lindsey. I know where it is. The detective and I have something to discuss." Time to pour Miracle-Gro on my spine.

"Alright! See you there!" She practically sings and leaves.

I have no idea why I'm doing this to myself, but anything is better than Lindsey spilling everything. I meet Drauper's eyes as he stands with arms crossed over his chest, partially hiding the badge hanging around his neck. He's on duty. The stare becomes heavier and heavier with each passing moment.

"So…" I awkwardly begin with no idea what I'm doing.

"You've been avoiding me," he cuts right to the chase. Also, didn't I recently have this similar conversation? Why is this the go to presumption? They're kind of right, but still. "I've been trying to contact you."

"Busy. Exploded books. How did you find me?"

"Wasn't here for you. Just coincidence. But I would have known you'd be here if you picked up your phone this morning."

I gesture toward the closed archive room. "I was preoccupied. Obviously."

Drauper sighs and drops his arms, rubbing his chin where there's a slight shadow of a beard. The movement would've set my lower region on fire weeks ago, except it doesn't. "Why are you avoiding me, Brenda?"

"Busy," I say again, and he glowers at me. "My entire section was destroyed, and I had to replace and reglue all week. You think I want to spend all my time in the basement doing that?" Mostly telling the truth.

He eyes me a moment and says, "I guess not." He's easier to lie to than Vinny. "Fate just brought us together today."

Yep, the cruel monster.

"Yeah," I say and begin to walk down the hall with him close behind me. "Are you going to city hall next?"

"Probably."

"Anything on Paranormals I could help with? Save you a trip or two?" I extend the olive branch. Mainly to clear my conscience and hope my backbone grows with it.

He scoffs and looks over at me. "Not gonna complain that I need to read more?"

"Still have to stitch the books up."

Drauper looks around as we exit outside. "What do you know about the beasts being sold on black markets?"

Well, hello, old twist in my stomach. "What about it?"

"There may be a new ringleader in the Bronx." I clench my jaw. If the others have been hiding this from me, I'm gonna shoot more than just Vinny. "We've had reports of people going missing. The surrounding area near those ghouls that moved in."

"Humans?"

"Half-breeds." So, they finally caught wind of it.

"Ghouls don't like half-breeds, but not enough to kidnap them," I say, my throat feeling dry.

"I've been looking into places that could hold dead bodies. Nothing so far where they could stash them. Even PSB isn't looking into it."

I stop us both just inside the next building, veering him toward a quiet corner of the hallway. "You're breaking jurisdiction investigating ghouls without a PSB Agent."

"People are disappearing, and PSB isn't doing anything," he explains in a low voice. "And even half-breeds that *could* fall under my jurisdiction, I've been blackballed by higher-ups."

I clutch my head, scratching the shit out of my undercut. "They should fall under your jurisdiction automatically, if not claimed by a Paranormal family or Mate. You could check PSB records, maybe they found—"

"No bodies. They may be stashed away or given to the black market. The mob is doing this, and no one is doing anything."

"That's why you asked about them."

"Who else but the mob can make people just disappear?" Drauper flashes a smile at a few passing students.

My heart clatters hard inside my chest. No way the mafia is part of this. They're trying to stop it. *Our* people are going missing too. "Why do you think that?" I ask.

"Why not the mobs?" Keep your mouth shut, Brenda. "They'll sell whoever and whatever for a dime. Evidence is disappearing. It always points to them."

Students start to swarm the hallway, and I pull Drauper further into the corner. "Do you have anything that could actually confirm that?"

175

His gaze flicks behind me toward the students ignoring us as they head to lunch. "I have a contact, and they confirmed that all their minions have pulled out, now the mob is almost gone. Nothing."

"Who's your contact?"

"I can't tell you," he says, and my gut twists a bit more. "But most of the South Bronx is a ghost town, not just the Paranormals. The mob is planning something."

"Stealing people?"

"You have a better theory?" He crosses his arms, deep brown eyes watching me earnestly.

"Okay, Detective, which mob family? There are dozens—that I've researched," I add quickly.

"You seem defensive."

"Cautious. If you think ghouls can be territorial, wait until you piss off the others. And they've held grudges longer than your existence. Others and I have spent a long-ass time trying to get people to trust more Paranormals, and this will ruin that. Mafia or not, they run the Underground. Not to mention, you'll lose your badge if you go any further without proper authority."

"We're working in conjunction *with* PSB, who's telling us not to move. *They're* worried it's the Blood Mafia. Their boss has been on the move lately, and he's not good news. We're keeping a low profile, and I figured I'd find more info before looking around."

The more Drauper talks, the more I want to call Vinny and tell him to never leave my apartment. Then again, this is a Tuesday for the bloodsucker. I remain passive the best I can and ask, "No snooping yet?"

He shrugs. "It's a neutral zone, but I need a warrant or a PSB Agent to agree to go with me."

I scoff, "That's why the building zones. You're trying to see where they could stash bodies, but you can't go forward unless PSB, or your chain of command, permits you first. Those schematics could be your ticket to a warrant to go searching."

"Basically."

"More ballsy than I thought." He also has a death wish if he tries to bring Vinny in. I know the vampire has done some terrible things and gotten away with it in the past, but his record is ironclad solid from persecution. All the mob bosses are. Even so, I've learned how to be territorial from Vinny and my father. And I'm gonna help protect them from the curious detective. "Drauper? When you find whatever you're looking for and have a warrant, before you go 'mystery gang' on your own, call me. I'll go with you. I know the area."

Drauper's brows move inward, his forehead wrinkling as he crosses his arms, bringing his face a bit closer to mine. "You gonna pick up the phone when I call this time?"

I swallow harshly and say, "Yeah, yeah, I will."

He looks at me and softens his expression. "We good then? You and I?"

"Yeah…" My voice falters, but I take a deep breath and say, "Just give me some time, okay?"

He nods, pausing before he moves his gaze away from me. I watch him disappear down the hall as he puts his sunglasses back on. A shuddering breath leaves my body as I prepare myself to deal with Lindsey again.

*   *   *

Metal cabinets, shelves, and stacks of books line my vision. It's worse than at the library. I peer down the labyrinth of discarded and unreviewed journals and paperwork that Lindsey brought me to. I follow her and ask, "Is there a section on medical testing at all?"

She taps her chin and looks around. "Definitely have a medical area. Which subject? Drugs, antidotes, anatomy, disease control…?"

I hadn't thought that far ahead and decide to take a chance. "Know anything about Traloski and his studies?"

She tilts her head at me. "The mad scientist?"

No argument there. "I know his studies weren't fully reviewed; this may be the best place to find something. Thought it would be good to have some of his…um, findings. To compare with successful doctors and works, that is. Good to have those kinds of sources." I bullshit my way to hopefully find what I need.

And it fucking works.

"Oh, that's smart. His stuff is probably down here. He's kind of taboo to speak of, and his ethics were, like, not *nice*." That's a way to put it.

"I've heard," I mumble, following her as we pass a section on growth hormones. "What was he even testing for?" I ask as we reach the anatomy and drugs sections. "Something on antidotes? I haven't heard of him until recently and can't find much about him. How do you know about him?"

"Only grad students in certain departments like biology learn about him and what *not* to do. He told CDC and PSB he was using his experiments to find cures for cancers by using Paranormal blood types infused with chemotherapy. He told something entirely different to NIIA about testing for AIDS to get funding."

"Really?"

"Yup, and all kinds of people went to him because they thought he had antidotes, for like a lot of things. It wasn't until, like, ten years into him owning his facilities that NIIA and PSB busted him for experimenting wrongfully on humans and Paranormals." She stops at a cabinet and gestures toward three drawers. I open the top one and see they're filled to the brim with manilla folders stamped with sigils from four different government and international branches. Dr. Jekyll was busy.

Flipping through some of them, I mutter, "He didn't have other hobbies, huh?"

"PSB and NIIA collected most of what he did. Columbia and two other universities have copies. The originals are kept by PSB for safe keeping. The professors, other than Dr. Quincy, treat him like an urban myth, like, warning us what happens when you cross the NIIA, CDC, or PSB."

"Uh huh," I say as I flip through more folders.

"There was this serial killer who imitated his testing in Florida. And there was this other guy in France who tried to replicate his medical trials. I'm surprised the public library doesn't at least have something on any of them."

"Scary monsters in the dark. Hard to keep those materials. Hence why I've gotta hand collect more copies." I thumb through some pages of names. "Who are these people?"

She shrugs, twirling her keys. "Test subjects. I wasn't kidding about *everyone* going to him for help. People really believed he had cures for AIDS and cancer. Even the CDC believed in his theories of using shifter bone marrow to eradicate affected CD4 cells. All of it was lies."

I'm not sure whether Dr. Rhonda purposefully gave me the smartest gossip girl in her grad program but I'm grateful she did. "Apart from his unethical advances in testing, is that what he's most known for?"

She opens another cabinet of folders, her hair falling over her shoulders as she picks through them. "He's, like, renowned for testing immunities from Paranormals in human blood."

My fingers freeze, and I drop a file. It feels like I've been drained of blood.

"Oops!" Lindsey picks up the file and hands it back to me. "He wrote this study on how the infusion of certain Paranormal blood types, coupled with human blood, *could* create immunities against most Paranormal powers. His theory focused on massive cell deconstruction in young ages, infusing the blood and nerves with T-cells that only Paranormals carry. But it was just a theory. No way to prove it without his extensive research and whatever. He did try, though, without the consent of numerous agencies who had no idea what he was *actually* testing for. All universities cut funding when they found out he was doing it on nonconsenting beings, brutally, and that's when PSB and NIIA, along with the CDC and FBI, shut him down."

My heart rate is going a little too fast, and it takes everything for me not to shake. I try to keep my head straight and process everything as my throat dries out. I clutch the cabinet and say, "Thanks Lindsey. I'll come back to the office when I finish."

"Oh, sure! I'll be out of here around five for study groups."

"And if I take longer?"

"It locks when you close it, no worries. Call me if you need me!" She waves and leaves, unaware she left me in a puddle of woe. The moment the door shuts, I throw the folders across the floor and start sifting through them, looking for anything about his subjects.

I peer past black blocks and names, nearing the end of the third drawer. Piles of his folders are next to me as I reach in the far back of the drawer and see five folders labeled: *Immunity Testing*. The CDC and PSB sigils of disapproval cover the list of techniques, types, and species.

And then I find it.

I pick up the small folder labeled: *Immunity testing: Children*. I open it with shaking hands and read through the paragraphs detailing the failures and successes of the children mentioned and tested on. Born into the program he created, none of them have names. I almost drop the file as I come across the last five children.

Some immunities didn't work, killing two of them. One survived with full immunity but lost their legs to tests. The fourth died from organ failure. The last one was scarred, blinded, and didn't pass a final test. I run my fingers over a photo of the children next to each other—all of them under the age of five. The little girl in the far-left corner looks into the distance, her eyes a deep violet with silver flecks in her irises.

And two large scars down her face.

"Fuck…fuck…*fuck*."

I scramble to shove folders back in the cabinet and throw the files with my past into my bag. My stomach twists, and my lungs hurt as I struggle to breathe. I don't give a shit that I'm stealing. Right now, this belongs to me—the last living being from an insane man's science project.

I rush out the door, knowing no one will care if it's gone anyways. The lock clicks behind me as it shuts, just as Lindsey said. My chest aches more and more with each step down the hall. I make it outside, where students hurry past as the sky rumbles and darkens. I have no idea what time it is. It doesn't matter. I need to get home. Now. My head spins, and it feels like the roar of a hundred waterfalls fills it.

A science experiment. A fucking science experiment.

A lab rat for someone's plan for immunity. And for fucking what? I was the only one who survived and *still* got dumped down a sewer. Nothing that riddles across my body is hereditary; that small chance is gone. Everything came from *him*—the madman.

I don't even know what I am.

Rain pelts down just as I make it to my complex out of breath, running up the stairs and slamming the door behind me. Thunder echoes outside as raindrops land against the windows. I throw the folders on the kitchen table and rip my jacket and boots off. I find the whiskey in the cabinet and down a few gulps after I pop it open. I find the papers with my face on them.

#37.

My name is a number.

I was born into the program, like the others, called hybrids. My fingers shake as I read the long list of "treatments" including blood transfusions, electric therapy, water therapy, fire, knives, I.V.s…

Horrors of what my childhood was before the Underground unfurl before my eyes. I remember none of it. Even when Pops found me, I had no memory, only fear of water, being touched, light…it all makes sense.

I have no idea how long I spend combing through the papers when I come across the last file, a letter from the NIIA, the dissolution of the program. No record of the remains of the bodies, even after I was dumped, only marked "deceased." There may have been others like me, left to nothing.

Rain pounds on the window and thunder rolls as darkness consumes the outside and inside of my apartment. Only the kitchen light stays on while I stare at the papers before me, whiskey bottle in hand, occasionally making its way to my lips. A certain numbness overcomes me. I've wanted an answer to my past. Now I wish I hadn't looked. And there's nothing I can do. The program is gone. *He* is gone. A stain that's forgotten in the back of a steel cabinet. *Urban myth.*

A flash of lightning catches my attention, and I rub my eyes and groan. A stifled scream comes out of me as I get up, throwing the bottle into the sink. Glass shatters, and the liquor I could have drunk disappears down the drain. I scream again under my breath in aggravation as I start to look for more alcohol. Nothing. I go back to the table to shove some of the papers back into the bag, unsure what to do with them now.

"Damn it! Fuck!" I slam my hand on the table. Tears gather in my eyes. "What the fuck am I supposed to do?"

Soft footsteps sound outside my front door. The lock clicks, echoing through the apartment. I pull out the gun from my jacket and aim for the intruder, wiping any tears away as the door opens. A snarl comes out as another flash of lightning illuminates Vinny. He turns the lights on and drops his sopping wet leather jacket to the ground.

"Get out," I sneer. I don't want him to see me. Not like this.

He pauses at the corner of the kitchen, looking at my gun. My hand trembles slightly. His gaze comes up to mine. "Brenda."

"Get out."

His eyes narrow. "You agreed I could—"

"*Get out.*"

"It's me…Vinny. What's wrong?" His voice is too calm, like he's approaching a wounded animal.

"I know it's you." I try to keep the gun still. "Get out."

"I brought more whiskey. Just like I said I would. You can have dibs…" He approaches me slowly.

"Not now, Vincent," I growl.

Shock rises over his expression. "Full first name? You sound like Anita calling me that."

I take a step closer to him, the gun pointed at his chest. "*Vinny, get out of my apartment.*"

He pauses and places the new bottle on the kitchen counter. I watch him survey his surroundings briefly. His attention comes back to me. "What's wrong? Talk to me."

The ease of his voice shakes me to my core. I know he'll get through to me, make the dam break. I don't want to say any of it out loud. My lungs hurt, trying to keep steady as the weapon eases down from its mark. Everything hurts. My heart aches, my body is wracked with fear and anger, and screams claw at my throat. I want to forget what I found. I want to be held. All of it needs to be a damn nightmare.

I'd been a science experiment. And right now, I fucking feel like it.

I stalk around him, kicking his jacket to the side. I walk toward the front door and say, "I don't want to talk." My jaw works overtime to keep from sobbing or screaming. He watches me and takes another step toward me, but my gun goes back up. "I will fucking shoot you this time, Vinny."

"Rather than talk?"

"*Yes.*"

"You tell me everything, sweet cheeks. Always have." He takes another tentative step.

"Don't call me that." I click back the safety.

"You always tell me your secrets…fears…whatever is wrong. And the fact that you won't tell me, means that you need to." His voice slowly lulls my muscles into ease. It helps stop the trembling of the gun.

"Not this," my voice shakes. "Nothing can undo this."

His voice darkens a moment. "Was it the detective?"

A broken sob comes from my throat. Vinny pauses, his expression growing cold. Murderous even. "Nothing to do with him. Just grab your stupid leather jacket and leave. You *can't* fix this, Vinny. None of this. What's done is done…just *go*." I slam a fist into the door behind me, searching for the doorknob.

"What the hell does that mean?"

"Leave, Vinny."

"Did someone hurt you? Threaten you?" His tone becomes harsher, but the care in his voice makes me want to shriek even more.

"No! Please…Vinny, leave, just…." I want Pops. I want Ma. I want to be back on the living room couch where everything is fine. I want…I want….

"Brenda." The last of the shaking stops, and I bring my gaze to his. He's five feet away. An easy shot.

"Don't make me shoot you."

"You won't."

"Bet."

"We already have."

"Fucking *hells!*"

"Brenda…"

"*Vincent.*"

"Sweet cheeks—"

"*I told you not to call me that!*" My scream rings out just before the ricochet of the gun echoes through the small apartment.

CHAPTER TWENTY-SIX
FUCKING VINNY

Holy shit, I shot Vinny.

Dark red blood seeps out of Vinny, and he doesn't move as he slowly takes his gaze down to the bullet hole in his leg and the blood streaming through his pants. My mind roars into nothing, dismissing the thunderstorm outside and void of any thoughts from before.

Vinny slowly and carefully brings his gaze back to mine. I'm met with dark hooded eyes as he takes slow steps toward me. "It's not silver," he comments.

"I never carry silver," I whisper as the gun clatters to the ground next to my feet. My back presses up to the door as he approaches me. I'm not scared of him, but I did just shoot the Blood Mafia Boss of the entire eastern seaboard.

Crimson eyes track every movement I make as my breathing becomes shaky. "The guns were never meant for *us*." The husk in his voice causes my spine to tingle. My mouth keeps shut.

The anger, fear, distress, and confusion leave me. It evaporates into nothing as I watch him, and the scent of his blood collides with the dark spices. The aroma pierces through me, filling my nostrils. He stops a few inches before me and leans forward, placing one hand near my head while the other clicks the lock in place. Heat pools down into my stomach and into my core as I begin to tremble. His scent engulfs me as everything becomes fuzzy. I can barely think or breathe as my heart pounds. I glance down, and the blood has stopped running. Normal bullets can't do shit to vampires, especially purebloods. He didn't even flinch when it hit him, going straight through his leg. The bullet now in my apartment wall.

"We had a deal, sweet cheeks," he says with a gleam in his eyes as I meet his gaze.

I gulp and nod slowly. "Blood for blood."

"Didn't think you'd ever do it." He brings up his other hand, trapping me fully against the door.

"Neither did I."

"Are we upholding or backing out?" He asks in a deep rasp. No smile. No taunting. His eyes roam over my skin and down my neck. His fangs lengthen, and my breath hitches.

My stomach tightens, and a tingling sensation encompasses my nether region. I barely contain the shiver that runs through me. My toes curl at the sound of the roughness so close, and my body begins to rage, forgetting why I was angry before. Instead, I want to cry for different reasons. So close, he's so close, but so far away from me.

I give in, and I nod. "Promise is a promise. Blood for blood, Vinny."

His hand comes up, tipping my head to the side as he pushes my hair back. Relief flashes over me, grateful he chose that side. I don't want to explain the fang marks on the other side of my neck.

My skin tightens as his breath comes dangerously close over my skin. The heat from his breath drifts over me, sending another shiver down my spine. I know bites hurt, but this is going to *hurt*. It could be like ecstasy, though, and with him, it would be. A thrill runs through my veins as his tongue moves up the side of my neck, and my legs wobble beneath me.

Fuck me. I'm not going to last.

"Do it already." My words are barely a whisper. "Take the *damn* blood."

I brace myself as his mouth comes closer, but his lips press against my neck. Vinny carefully kisses my neck, moving toward my jaw. Another kiss goes behind my ear. His breath is like heaven as soft lips kiss against my skin and racing pulse. He's being so gentle. I can't take it as my heart pounds and my fists tighten at my sides.

Tears stream down my face with each soft kiss pressed to my skin. I don't deserve this. I fucking *shot* him. Words tumble out of my mouth, "Fucking bite me, Vinny." I spit out. "I shot you like the bitch I am. Just take the blood I owe you."

Vinny pulls back, bringing his gaze to mine. His eyes are warm with no look of mischief or winning a bet. He brings his thumb over my cheeks, wiping away the stray tears. "You misunderstand me, sweetheart. That's not the *blood* I want."

Confusion washes over me. What is he talking about?

His hand moves down my body while his fingers trail down the side to my hips. He stops at the top of them and squeezes my side slightly as his thumb caresses over the top of my jeans. The tip of his finger carefully grazing my stomach. My eyes widen as I begin to understand. The ache around my heart begins to cease, the tightening of my core becoming stronger, and the trembling changes into anticipation. The heat below becomes worse, consuming most of my thoughts. Vinny keeps his calm demeanor as his thumb moves over my jaw, trailing under my lip.

"Vinny…"

"Tell me to stop, and I will," he says. "You've been taught well, full consent, sweetheart." He doesn't sound like Vinny, my best friend of so many years with his husky tone and growl that cause more havoc inside me. "If we're doing this, I'm going all the way and not holding back. Do you understand?"

My eyes widen as I nod slowly.

"Say it, sweetheart," he commands softly.

"Yes."

He brings his lips closer to mine, just barely over them. I can almost taste him. "Do you want me to stop?" He asks.

I shake my head, and he raises a brow. "No."

His eyes flick down and back up to me. "Do you want me to kiss you...sweet cheeks?"

I stare into the familiar crimson eyes. Eyes I longed for and dreamed of. My throat tightens, and my tongue lightly moves over my lip in anticipation. "Yes."

Without hesitation, his lips come to mine—my heart almost bursts. My hands, once frozen at my sides, reach up and grip his shoulders. His hand moves to the nape of my neck, holding me in place. I taste the sweetness and spices that have tantalized my senses for so long. His tongue moves over my lips, prompting me to open mine. As he dives in, I finally taste him; dark whiskey aged in barrels filled with spices from across the world. He's *exactly* how his scent was to me.

I relish in his kiss, and tether myself to him with my hand holding onto his hair. I pull at the soft strands, trying to bring him closer. Vinny's chest presses against mine. The heat deep inside me enflames into an inferno as I cling to him.

He pulls away from the kiss, and I whimper at the lack of contact. My hand doesn't leave his hair, trying to hold on. He doesn't laugh at the sounds I make but cups my face and meets my gaze as seriousness settles over him. "Do you want this?" He asks softly. "Us together? Because I'm not going forward unless you say it."

"Yes." I don't think. I don't need to. Everything burns for his touch.

"Yes, what?"

"Vinny, I want you to fuck me."

A satisfied laugh rumbles deeply from his chest. He grips my hips and lifts me, wrapping my legs around his waist, bringing me closer to his eye level. A soft smile pulls at his lips just before he kisses me harshly. I let out a moan as he holds me closely to him, walks us over to my bed, then lays me down beneath him. Vinny pulls away from the kiss long enough to say, "Oh, I promise I will, but tonight isn't about fucking. It's about laying claim, and you're going to enjoy *every damn minute.*"

"Territorial."

"Only for you, sweetheart."

Vinny rips my shirt off and goes to work on my jeans, throwing them to the ground. I prompt him to take his shirt off, and his muscles ripple before me as I shuck it off him. Vinny stills as I reach up slowly, trailing my fingers down his chest and abdomen. This doesn't feel real, like it's all a dream as I watch his chest heave with a deep breath. Thunder rumbles and the lights flicker, causing shadows to dance across his body. My hand slightly trembles as I move it across his chest. Vinny places his hand over mine, holding it to him.

A different kind of rumble vibrates between us as I bring my eyes up. I meet his gaze and see the dastardly satisfied smile on his face as he expertly kisses and moves underneath me to take off my bra. It leaves my chest bare to him, and I take a shaky breath. The closest he's ever gotten to see me naked is when I was stripping, but I never went fully nude. Apart from my family, not many have seen *all* the scars that distort my skin. I fight an old instinct to cover them, remembering faintly where they come from.

I stop when Vinny growls darkly, "Better than I imagined."

Surprise hits me. "You imagined…?"

"Yes, more times than I can fucking count." Vinny captures my lips again as he begins to knead the breasts he's dreamed about. My hips move on their own fruition as the sensations burn through me. His hands massage over my skin, my core tightening for more. I feel my nether region heat down past my legs, causing friction. The movement is almost too good, but what almost sends me over the edge is when he flicks my nipple. I gasp as he smiles against my neck. He presses another kiss, moving down my chest and trailing his tongue over my skin.

One of his hands moves down past my stomach, over the apex of my thighs. I rub my legs together as he sweeps over the top of my underwear. A finger caresses the edge of my panties, drifting over my heightened skin.

He kisses me again fervently, speaking against my lips, "Making history here, sweetheart."

"You want them as a souvenir?" I rasp.

Vinny hums to himself and pulls away to stand at the end of the bed, raking his gaze over my body. I look up at him as I lay there, unsure what to do. His tongue moves over his upper lip and back down, and his fangs elongate again. I don't move, enraptured watching him look at me like I'm the sexiest thing he's ever seen. Vinny removes my panties painstakingly slow with a smile. Once off, he holds them in the air like a prize, flicking his eyes to me.

"Pervert," I say with no sting to my voice. Damn, why does he look good doing that?

He drops the panties to the floor, his smile not leaving him as he grips the side of my hips, pulling me toward him. I almost squeak from his grab. He's harsh but doesn't grip me too hard as his hands travel down my legs. His fingertips trace over various scars and back up again.

"Vinny…" He kneels at the end of the bed. Oh, fuck me...

"Blood for blood, sweetheart." Vinny smiles as he swings my legs up over his shoulders. A gasp comes out as I try to protest until his tongue sweeps over my folds.

My head flings back as his lips press into me. He practically drinks in the heat that seems to pour from between my legs. I stifle a scream as he licks over the nub at the top. My hands grip the side of the bed as he expertly begins to eat me out. He sucks and licks, creating sensations I've only dreamed about or tried to master on my own. Except he blows all of that out of the water. One of my hands reaches, threading through his hair. I grip him as sensations run through my body and a scream becomes stuck in my throat. My muscles and hips begin to shake and quiver with each lick. The movement of his tongue through me and into me shakes me to my core.

This is what I was missing out on? Damn.

Vinny barely pulls away from me and commands, "Scream." The moment he says it, the scream in my throat lets loose as ecstasy moves through me. The vibration of his voice against me causes spasms. I let go of him, clutching the bed. My muscles convulse as I come for him for the first time, the orgasm harsh as he continues.

He inserts his finger into me slowly as his tongue continues in licks and swirls against tender spots. Short breaths are all I can do as he slowly pumps me with one finger. He carefully places another with the first. I realize toys are nothing compared to this as I let out another shout.

Vinny pulls his face away, continuing with his fingers. They hook and scissor, moving around me like he's exploring. His thumb presses down on my clit, circling it carefully. I shout again as my muscles convulse around him. Stars ripple over my vision as my body tenses, another quick orgasm rampaging out of me.

He eases his fingers out and places my legs down from his shoulders. As I look up, I see him lick off his fingers, reveling in my taste.

He then walks around the bed, pulling off his pants as he goes into the bathroom. Confused and about to ask what he needs, he comes back with a towel. Lifting my hips, he places the towel down beneath my ass and legs. I look at him funny, and he only grins. "Protection, sweet cheeks?"

I flick my eyes to the bedside table. He raises a brow, walking over to open the drawer. "You actually have some."

"Ever since I was threatened in the first place."

"Don't tell me who. It'll ruin the mood." He grins as he opens the packet, drops his underwear, and puts the condom on. I'm too transfixed on his ass right near my head. Holy fucking gods. It's damn perfect from centuries of physical activity. Vinny grabs the lube that's in the drawer and walks back over to me. "Smart female."

"Well-taught."

"You'll keep learning." He watches me as he pours some of the lube on his fingers, then sweeps some on my tender area and onto his cock. He then climbs onto the bed over me.

I gaze up at the crimson eyes above. They shine a little as he moves down to kiss me again. I thread my fingers through his soft hair. So much I've imagined and dreamed, it's either better or exactly what I thought. I hold on with his tender kiss as he moves a hand down to my hips. Vinny spreads my legs more, opening me up to him. He pulls away from me, the taste of him making me see stars.

Staring at each other, it's like everything stills, and I have to remember to breathe. Vinny hovers above, ready and willing, but his eyes search deeply into mine. "One last time," he whispers. "Because there's no going back, I'm not giving you up if you give me this."

A sob catches in my throat. "Vinny."

"I've loved you for longer than I care to admit." My breath hitches. "It may be stupid to admit it now…" he looks down to our almost joined hips and back up, and a quick laugh comes out of me, "… but I can't unless you knew. This isn't about a bet. A score. A notch, sweetheart. I love you."

All the heartache and fury from the last few weeks—hell, the last few years—wash away. Fears are boxed away in far corners. Words I've wanted, craved are spoken out from the best friend I've struggled for, ached for.

Vinny presses his forehead to mine, his breath encasing my senses. "I know you feel it, too. At least, something…."

I struggle to breathe. A shiver goes over me, and my chin trembles for a moment. I run my fingers through his hair and down to stroke his cheek.

All that I've dreamed, hoped, wanted…so had he. I wasn't alone. We're both idiots.

I yank him down, kissing him harshly. Tears streaming down my cheeks as I open fully and speak against his lips, "I love you, Vinny. I love you."

A gasp goes through him, and he holds my head to keep our mouths together. His lips press harder as his tongue traces my lips. Our tongues entangle as we both try to taste more of the other. After feeling like forever within the kiss, he moves away enough for me to say, "Seal the deal, bloodsucker."

A growl leaves Vinny as he situates himself. His cock presses in, and all air leaves me as he slowly slides himself into me. My muscles clench around his thickness, and I quicken my breaths. Slight pain trickles through me as I attempt to concentrate away from it. Vinny pulls his lips away and begins to whisper, his hard member slowly moving in little by little. "Relax, sweetheart. There you go, breathe…I'm here with you."

I barely hear his words of encouragement as I feel him move. Slowly pumping, one of his hands massage my inner thigh and up to my abdomen. I clench my jaw a few times as pain ripples through me, pleasure from the rest of my body fights it, refusing defeat. I dig my fingers into Vinny's back. He continues at a slow pace, allowing my body to get used to the new sensations and adjust.

"Vinny…" I plead.

"You're doing good. Relax. Next part may hurt." What does he mean "*next part?*"

I understand when he seats himself fully into me, and I scream through a whimper. Vinny doesn't move for a moment, giving me time to breathe and adjust to him. I'm a virgin, I have no idea what size is average or not, but at this moment, he's *huge*. Then again, I'm pretty sure he's above average in size. It feels like my legs can't move, the sheer size of him keeping me in place. He kisses along my throat and jawline and asks, "You okay?"

I nod. "Uh huh."

"Sweet cheeks…"

"No vibrator could prepare me for this." I gulp through my sarcasm.

Vinny ducks his head into the curve of my neck and shoulder. He chuckles, and my body relaxes hearing it. He brings a hand up, caressing one of my breasts. "Well, glad I exceeded some expectations."

"Don't get…*cocky,*" I retort. Vinny moves, and I whimper from the sensation as he chuckles again. He kisses along my neck, kneading my breast more. The added sensation causes me to relax the last of my muscles. Slowly and gently, he begins to thrust.

With each passing movement, the sensations become better and better, and the pain begins to fall away as Vinny moves. His thrusts are slow but begin to speed up as he watches my reactions. I moan more as I hold him close with my arms. I wrap my legs around his waist at some point as he deepens each plunge, making me throw my head back with a shout.

Lightning flashes outside the same moment shivers travel through my body, and heat overpowers all my senses. My body shudders as I clutch to Vinny, his breathing becoming erratic. Another scream leaves me when he hits my inner walls. A lightness engulfs my head, my muscles quivering.

I don't know how long it lasts. How much time passes as Vinny moves into me, allowing me to scream his name and other profanities. A growl rips out of him, almost shaking the apartment. His fangs reach my neck, and blood trickles from my vein. All I feel is pure ecstasy and bliss, the orgasm obliterating any thought. Vinny roars out his own orgasm, clutching me like I'll evaporate. My body limps into nothing as he holds me, pulling my entire body into his.

I feel myself drifting into bliss, my hands roving down his back and his arms. We both catch our breath as the adrenaline wears off. Vinny kisses me once again, driving me deeper into that bliss. Carefully, he starts to pull out of me. I wince at the odd pain, and he kisses my cheek before he steps off the bed. I'm clouded in post-orgasm to wonder where he's gone. I presume to get rid of the condom.

A few moments later, I'm surprised by a warmth down below, but it's not from me. My eyes fling open to see Vinny use a warm, wet towel to clean me up down below. I barely glance past to see why and suddenly realize why he put the towel down before. Should've known. He winks at me as he disappears into the bathroom with both towels. He's back in bed with me soon, pulling a blanket over us both and cradling me into his arms, holding me against him.

I shiver suddenly, emotions of old beginning to trickle back. I clutch the blankets over us. This is a dream. It's not real. I feel myself start to spiral. Vinny brings me closer, his hand stroking down my arm and side. His lips drift over the shell of my ear, trying to calm me. "It's okay, sweetheart."

"Vinny..." My voice sounds hoarse and distant. He kisses me gently on the forehead, refusing to let anything come between us.

"Deep breath," he tells me. I do, and his aroma encases me in warmth. I finally relax when his words echo in my ear, "I love you..."

The rain continues into the night as I awake with my head pressed into the nook of his shoulder, feeling a warmth I've only felt from holding hands. Dark spices, bloodlust, and other scents fill the room. I hum, which seems to stir the vampire.

"You steal all the blankets," he murmurs.

"My bed, bloodsucker."

"You should be nice to your guests." He twists, placing my back against the bed as he covers over me. A smile creeps onto his face, and ruby eyes gleam with desire. I grip his neck, bringing his soft lips to mine, and faintly feel his fangs brush over my tongue. The tenderness of him makes me moan. "If I'd known I could make you react like this, I'd have done it years ago," he says against my lips.

"Why didn't you?"

"Thought you only wanted friendship." I pull back, looking up at him. His brows raise. "I'm guessing you thought the same?"

"I mean, we've always been friends. We call each other names, use perverted language, share secrets, stupid jokes, dumb come-ons…" I gasp as it hits me. I *honestly* took that all as best friend things. "Holy *shit*, I'm stupid." I smack my face with my hand. Anita's right with me being naïve. I know he liked me, but not like *that*. The damn vampire has been dropping hints. How could I have missed it? I thought he only teased me because he could get away with it. The idea that he loves me at all beyond that seemed too far away. Impossible.

"Don't call yourself that." He pulls my hand away as he lays down next to me, propping his head on his arm. "Besides, this is a two-way street. I hoped that you'd understand with what I *didn't* say. But subtlety doesn't work on you."

I stare up at the ceiling, and an itching feeling reaches my eyes. I grumble and begin to get out of bed, but Vinny reaches for me. "I need my contacts out. Unless you want me fully blind?" He falls back into the bed, mumbling about me being quick about it. I stifle a laugh as I go into the bathroom and take the contacts out and use the toilet. I wash my hands as a thought drifts forward. I stumble back, my sight finding the outline of Vinny and his ruby eyes.

"Okay, I'm not stupid," I say. "I just suck at subtle signs. But how long? The whole…*love* thing?"

"You have to answer, too. Not embarrassing myself alone."

My stomach twists as I hold back the instinct to touch the bitemarks he hasn't noticed yet. I know him well enough; he'll keep his lips sealed until I talk. Guess he's right. I hold my hand out, and we shake on it before settling back into bed, the storm raging outside.

Vinny takes a deep breath and then explains, "Honestly, I've always loved you, you know that, but it wasn't until you were twenty that I realized it was something more than 'brotherly' love. No calling me a pervert, I didn't have any of...*those* thoughts until you were an adult. I hated myself for it. Disgusted even. And afraid your Pops would kill me."

I scoff under my breath. If only he knew of recent conversations. "Well, I can't say anything about the whole age thing. I'm worse. I was probably around sixteen or seventeen when the crushing started. And not in the 'big brother' way."

"That long?"

"Thought something was wrong with me. Crushing on my best friend? I didn't feel that way with anyone else. I'd known you my entire life. For fucks sake, you babysat me when I was a toddler. Taught me math and helped with braille." Vinny lets loose a shaky breath. "I also just...*wanted* you to stay my best friend. If I told you I liked you, maybe you'd leave. You were always there, and I didn't want to think about life without you."

We sit in silence with the rain being the only noise before he pulls me closer to him and quietly asks, "What happened?"

I tremble a little as I think about those specific moments of torture, then I take a deep breath. We had a deal. "I saw you with Natalie and some others at my 19th birthday party. Seeing you with them, I figured I'd always be your 'baby sis' like everyone else. So, I left for college hoping maybe I'd meet someone and get over it. And I thought I'd try, cause I was older and smarter, but on my 21st birthday, you were with others again. I felt dumb."

Vinny's silent and doesn't move, and I become fearful of his reaction until he says, "You're not the stupid one. I am."

"Hey, two-way street punk. If I can't say it, neither can you."

"I still hurt you."

"Not like you knew. You were just living your life."

"Except I had growing feelings for you and felt ashamed. It scared me. While you were at college, I...fucked anything that wasn't you, hoping to erase it. A phase that'd pass, and I'd see you as 'baby sis' again. Then you went to get your master's and something broke inside me. Not having you around felt like torture. And then I became the boss, and you moved to Topside. You distanced yourself, and I thought you didn't—"

"I didn't want to get in the way," I speak gently, and his hand drifts over my cheek. "And I needed to move on. I felt like I couldn't below, so I moved. Trying and hoping, *again*, something would change." Among other reasons and threats, but now isn't the time.

"Did it?"

"No," I answer quickly. I realize something and say softly, "You started calling me sweet cheeks when I left for grad school."

"Felt wrong to continue calling you...*baby sis*."

After a few silent moments, I shift to hover over him and find his ruby eyes in the darkness as a smile spreads over my face. For two people who tell each other everything and know each other's tells, we suck at this. "You're telling me I could have had your dick since I was like twenty-one? Did I mess that up?"

"Technically, I offered multiple times. Lost track over the years."

"True."

"You threatened to shoot it off, which you would've missed out, then."

"Sexual aggravation at that point." My eyes narrow. "Don't think I won't if you look at another female."

I can barely make out his grin. "Territorial much? Barely been a couple of hours, and you're threatening non-existent females."

"Non-existent? You've had a harem since the 1800s."

"Haven't since you left for your master's. Meant it when something broke."

"You're fucking kidding me." Holy shit, Gina was telling the truth. I mean she usually does, but still.

"You think I'd joke about that? Blue balls since you left me to write a paper about my grandfather." I laugh as he pouts and grumbles.

"Two hundred years, and you went without it for like...five years." I kiss his forehead teasingly.

"It was terrible."

I press my forehead to his. "You were *honestly* waiting for me."

"And it felt like you were taking forever," he teases. "I was about to change tactics until you made that deal of ours."

I scoff and start to dismount, but he grabs the nape of my neck, bringing my lips to his. Warmth envelops over me, and I fall into him, tasting as much as I can. Damn, we've been idiots. I've had my own reservations and fears, but it wasn't as one-sided as I believed. All other thoughts, I keep far away as I hold onto him. His tongue explores more of my mouth, and I sigh as he caresses his hand up my back. I forget everything that's outside other than him.

A buzzing sound interrupts us. Vinny pulls back and swears, gently placing me onto the bed. He walks over to his jacket, and I hear the soaking wet thing drop to the floor as he answers his phone. I snuggle under the covers and into my pillows. It's nighttime for me but working hours for him. Vinny is still the mafia boss, and he said he'd only be able to stay part of the night.

I touch the scar on my neck and try to ignore the words his father threatened me with. My stomach clenches as I pull my hand away.

Vinny remains on call, and I hear shuffling come across the way as I peek through the galaxy of purples and blues. He finally hangs up, and I smell coffee brewing. I sit up as the aroma drifts by me, mixing with his scent.

"What time is it?" I ask.

"For you to have coffee."

"Okay, bloodsucker." I chuckle, then frown with realization. "You gotta leave, huh?"

"Not yet," he says in the kitchen. I hear shuffling and then silence. "Brenda?"

I groan as I fall back into the bed. "I thought I'd least get another hour before you'd use my name again." I get only silence from him. "Vinny?"

He gasps, and I sit up, trying to look through my stupid eyes, but all I can see is his outline near the table. Where the table the paperwork that explains my existence and pushed me to shoot Vinny lays. Sex brain leaves me in the mist, and all emotions come crashing back.

"What is this, Brenda?"

"Vinny don't—" I scramble out of bed, almost fall into the leather chair, fighting through the sea of jumbled colors and shapes as lights flicker over my sight, ruining my perception. "Don't—"

I crash into Vinny, flailing my arms to grab the folders as he holds me against his chest. "Hold on, wait a minute…you need to explain—"

"No, I fucking *don't*." Everything was damn near perfect; I don't want it fucking ruined by that monster.

"Is this what upset you?"

"Vinny, don't—"

"This is why you shot me? You didn't want me to know?" Vinny hauls me back to bed, tossing me onto it. He pins me against the mattress, grabbing my chin so I have to look at his crimson eyes. When they meet mine, my body starts to tremble, remembering what I read. Vinny isn't angry; there isn't even a hint of him being upset at me. There's a steadiness to his breathing as he holds me down. "What are those papers?"

I swallow hard. I shake my head and close my eyes, tears beginning to stream down my cheeks. I don't want to talk about it. Think about it. Not yet. Vinny hushes me and wipes away the tears. He kisses both my cheeks and then my lips, easing the tightness in my chest. The shaking in my limbs don't stop. I don't want to say it.

He softly whispers, "Sweet cheeks…"

"Just read them," I rasp.

Vinny stills before he gets to his feet and goes to the table. I sit up and hold myself close as he reads through the papers in the satchel. His breathing quickens as he continues, and his scent worsens in the air, burning my nose. An angry heat wafts through the small apartment.

His voice is gruff. "Where did you—"

"Columbia," I whisper. "Looking into the disappearances in the Bronx and…" Tears stream down my cheeks in waves.

Papers flop onto the table and Vinny is back, taking me into his arms. He lifts me onto his lap, holding me close and tucking my head under his chin. He tries to soothe me as he strokes my hair back. "I'm sorry, sweetheart. I could—"

"Told you…you can't change this."

He kisses my forehead, rubbing his hand over my back as I hold onto him. "You're still here. That counts as something. And you gained more than you ever would have in…there."

My voice cracks. "Don't tell my family."

"They've been looking—"

"Please."

"Sweetheart."

"Please. Give me time…please," I softly sob as he nods, not letting me go. The more I think about the paperwork, what happened, the more I feel broken—a freak show.

Vinny kisses my cheek, clearing away the tears. "Okay. We'll wait to tell your family. You won't do it alone. You're not alone." My heart clenches. I grip onto him tighter, nodding into his chest. He takes a deep breath. "Don't hide things. Not from me. We both realized how idiotic we can be. Let's not make it a pattern."

I almost chuckle as he lifts my chin and gently kisses me, easing my body and mind. My hand comes up to caress his cheek. He hums, running his fingers down my body. I'd gladly go for another round, just to make the last of the tears disappear, but his phone chimes again.

Vinny growls as he pulls away. "Damn werewolves."

He kisses me quickly and places me back on the bed. Picking up the phone, he grumbles down the line as he goes into the kitchen. I pull my legs in and stare off in silence until Vinny taps my leg and eases a mug into my hands, pulling the blanket over my shoulders as he continues with the conversation. A smile grows on my face as I sip the delicious drink.

Vinny finally hangs up and gets dressed. His clothes rustle, moving as he gets his things together. He wasn't kidding about the damn werewolves. He pulls on his jacket and leans over to kiss me on the head. "I don't want to leave you, but Rodney needs back-up."

"You're actually helping him?" I ask with a raised brow.

"Business transaction."

195

"There it is," I muse. Vinny remains where he is, his hand coming up to stroke my cheek. "I'm alright."

"Sweet cheeks."

"Go, I'll be fine. You helping Rodney is the crime of the century. And you just gave me fucking coffee."

He laughs and takes a sip from my mug. "Read a book, nerd."

"You're still a pain."

He kisses me harshly and walks to the door. The locks click, but there's a pause in his steps. He stammers a little and it takes me a moment to realize why. I grin at the two-hundred-year-old vampire as the tension in my chest eases as I say quietly, "Love you, bloodsucker."

He smiles through my foggy vision. "Love you, sweet cheeks."

The door shuts behind him, the locks clicking into place. I carefully wrap myself in my blanket and take my mug to my leather chair. The rain continues, and the night seems darker. I'm not sure what the hell happened in the past twenty-four hours, but not going to complain about the sex part. Ease tries to settle in my bones, but fear knocks at my heart. I *will* ignore it. Not going to address it, not yet.

I stare out through the window and fall asleep in my leather chair. After a few hours, I wake up to use the bathroom, stumbling through my messy apartment. I put my glasses on and start to clean up the mess within my home, ignoring the blood for now. The paperwork stares me down on the table. I debate whether to tell my family what I found or talk to Vinny about it first as I collect clothes next. After going through them, I notice something is missing. I rip off my bedding, searching for them in my sheets and on the floor. The happy and content feelings rush out, and a new wave of rage hits me.

I'm gonna kill him.

Vinny is a dead vampire, and this time, when I shoot him, he'll bleed more. The bastard took my *fucking panties*.

Slow-ass elevator.

After shoving my contacts in and destroying my apartment, I confirm my panties were swiped. Five phone calls and Vinny doesn't pick up. He *knows* what he did. The Blood Mafia Boss will choke by my hands.

The elevator dings, and I shove my way out to run down the path. Why did I choose a loyal son of a bitch for my first time? Why did he have to be respectful of other traditions? He could've at least taken a pair of clean ones, but *no*.

And why didn't I sleep with that dancer Ricky paired me with years ago?

It's late afternoon in the Underground as I sprint past people and Paranormals hiding from the storm on Topside. I rush toward *Unbound* and see Joey standing outside the front entrance. The lights aren't flashing, and the sign isn't lit. SHIT.

The instant Joey sees me, he opens the door with a cruel delighted smile and yells, "Incoming!"

"Where's Vinny!" I screech as I aim for my brother.

"Congratulations, sis! About time!" He holds his arms open like I'm not on the verge of slicing throats.

"Where's Vinny!"

Joey laughs and attempts to get in my way. I snarl, knowing exactly what's happening inside. He tries to grab me but fails as I give him a swift kick and punch to the stomach, and he doubles over and laughs more. I slam past my brother entering the empty club with only my family, Anita, Brock, Gina, and *fucking Vinny*.

He's near the back with Ma beside the apartment door. Pops is at the bar with Ricky and Anita with a glass in her hand. I look up and see my black briefs hanging above the main stripper's stage, fully on display to show I'm not a virgin anymore. I bring my gaze back to meet Vinny's eyes and pull my Glock out, aiming for his chest. I click back the safety, and no one moves. "You took my underwear, *bloodsucker*!"

"Sweet cheeks…" His hands go up in surrender as he eases behind Ma.

"I'm gonna shoot you Vinny, and this time it'll hurt!" I charge, and Joey swipes the gun down before I make the shot. My older brother wrestles with me, and I escape him with another hit to his gut. I rush toward Vinny, growling as I aim my weapon to his crotch.

Vinny, the centuries-old pureblood vampire, mob boss of the Blood Mafia, runs and hides.

He rushes behind Ma, shoving himself through the apartment door, and slams it shut, locking it before I can get to him. I pound my fists on the door, trying to tear myself through, and shout, "Damn it, Vinny!" as my family sighs.

"They were for your Ma!" He argues through the door.

"Come out here and face me, coward!"

"Not until *all* weapons are away from you. That includes bottles of liquor. You shot me once today already!"

"You shot Vinny?" Ricky asks.

"*Finally*, took you long enough," Anita comments as she takes a swig from her drink. I snarl at her, and she hisses back in jest.

"Get your ass out here, Vinny!" I pound at the door again.

"Promise not to hurt me for doing what your family wanted," he yells from the other side. "This was important to them, and you know it! You would have never given them over!"

"Yes! I would have!"

"You'd have given them clean ones! Admit it!" Damn him.

"He's got a point," Ricky chimes in.

"If I can't shoot Vinny, you'll be next on the list," I threaten, pointing at my brother. His mouth drops in shock, asking what he did to deserve this and backing away with his hands up. I seethe as anger fuels me. "He at least should have told me!"

"Come on, sis. You'll get them back," Joey says. "Eventually."

I growl at my brother, whose eyes sparkle at my rage. Gina giggles on the side, and I feel like I'm going to explode.

"Brenda," Pops' calls calmly, and I pause my rampage. His calm demeanor is a warning sign. I turn to see his crossed arms and stern expression. I take a step back from the door and click the safety back on the Glock. "Vincent came here as soon as he could to give them to your Ma, even though he had business beforehand. She placed them where they *should* be." I wince at his tone, and the anger starts to diminish as realization settles in. "You know how important this tradition is, especially to your Ma. He accommodated her, like the respectful male he is."

If I told Pops how Vinny broke my virginity track record, would he still call him that? Probably.

"Pops…" I whine.

"No, baby girl," he stops me. "Vampires have different rituals and traditions for life, and he's putting that aside to honor yours. He's showing respect to you and *your* family traditions."

"Yes, Pops."

"Now, stop trying to shoot the vampire and apologize to your Ma for stepping on this tradition. Wouldn't want to be disrespectful to her, *would you*?" I glare for a moment at Pops and see for a brief second a twinkle in his eyes. He hit below the belt.

I slowly turn toward Ma, who's moved a few feet away and seems torn between crying from joy or sadness. Either way, I don't want her to cry. I'm going to be grounded for weeks for this. I don't think I've been in this much trouble since I was sixteen. A quick look at Pops confirms it. He's right. I overreacted because it was *Vinny*, and I know I can get away with pointing a gun at him. Still, my damn panties? I mean, I knew it was going to happen, but come on!

I walk towards Ma and open my arms saying, "I'm sorry, Ma." She embraces me and holds me tight while sobbing into my hair. "You can complete the tradition," I mumble.

"For the full celebration?" She asks.

"How long?"

"24 hours."

I sigh. "Deal."

Ma kisses my cheeks as her sobs turn into the more joyous side and relief. She pulls away and goes on about how proud she is of me taking the next step and stages of life for succubi as I nod until she joins the others to get ready for the party. I stand there feeling like the worst succubus daughter ever.

Pops comes over, putting his hand on my shoulder. "He did the right thing. No shooting him, at least not for this. Was he at least careful and used protection?"

I don't even groan at the question; it's too normal at this point. "Yes, Pops. But can we not?"

"Did you at least enjoy it?"

"Aww, come on, Pops—" Okay *that* isn't normal.

"Baby girl," he says sternly. Damn it he's using his dad voice. No fair.

"Yes," I mumble as my brothers approach.

"Good, I didn't want to castrate him for being disrespectful. Was it a one-time thing, or is he planning to Mate you like we discussed—"

"Pops!" My eyes widen, and my jaw drops. This is not how I saw my weekend going. I figured I'd be sobbing in my bed for the next 72 hours getting drunk. Although, it could still be on the table at this point.

"Vinny finally settling down, sis? You're a miracle worker!" Ricky comments as he ruffles my hair.

"Our lessons work that well?" Joey asks as he takes the gun from my hand. Rude.

"No," I growl.

"We all know it was Gina," Ricky says.

"Now wait, what about—"

"Boys, leave your sister alone," Pops says. "This is a talk between her and me."

My head and eyes roll at once at the ridiculousness of it all and say, "Pretty sure it's not, Pops."

"Baby girl."

"Pops, not now, *please*," I whine. Great they actually got me to whine. Am I sixteen again? "Let me get through this party, get my panties back from Ma, and take a nap. Please, I beg you."

Pops backs off and smiles as he goes to help Ma with the preparations. Anita and Gina laugh from the bar, and I give them both the middle finger. I head for the apartment door, but Joey grabs my arm. I shove him off me and growl, "Not gonna hurt him."

"You sure, sis?" He asks with raised brow. "Still kind of pissed."

"How about I shoot you in the leg to hold me over." I pull out the other gun hidden in my pants. Joey's eyes widen, and he busts out laughing along with Ricky as he pulls me into a vice grip hug. "Stop being nice and happy, and let me be angry for five minutes."

"Never," Ricky says.

"I hate you both."

They reply in unison, "No, you don't."

I shove past them and pound on the door. "Is it safe?" Vinny asks from the other side.

I roll my eyes and say calmly, "Yes, open the damn door." The door barely opens an inch as ruby eyes peek through, watching me carefully. I scowl at him. "You seriously hid from me?"

"Already shot me once today. And you've stabbed me in the past."

"You scared the shit out of me with that prank!"

"Not enough for you to stab me with a letter opener."

"You barely bled."

"It was made of silver, and I needed stitches. It hurt for a week. Who knows what damage you can do now, sweet cheeks?"

He opens the door fully as the club gets busy behind me with Ma making phone calls, Pops and Anita talking, my brothers setting things up, and Gina gathering strippers and employees in the back. This is going to be a whole shebang meant to celebrate and embarrass me. I hope it won't be as eventful as Ricky's. I glance at my hanging underwear and grab Vinny.

He barely protests, "Hey, sweet cheeks…"

"I don't give a shit if you have business or other plans. Pops is asking about Mating, Ma is throwing the party of the decade with my underwear strung up, and I just found out what the hell happened to me decades ago. Indulge me for the next hour or so." I pull him behind me through the apartment, into my bedroom, and slam the door shut, whipping my jacket off and pointing to the bed. "You're gonna make me scream so loud that my family will leave me alone and never ask me about my sex life ever again."

Vinny's brows lift.

I toss my gun to the side as I yank my shirt off. A smile rises on his face as I take off my pants and say, "Protection is in the bedside table, and there's more in the living room if we need it. You promised to fuck me, so get on with it."

I stand fully for less than a moment before Vinny slams me against the bedroom door. His lips crash into mine, and I taste the bloodlust as his scent deepens. His hands rove over my skin, stroking across my stomach and pulling my hips to his. I gasp as he inserts a finger inside me, and he growls, "Deal's a deal."

In the past twelve hours, I've learned that Vinny is good at upholding deals that pertain to sex. During our fucking session, Ma comes by to check on us and knocks on the door as Vinny makes me scream with his tongue. She immediately left in a hurry, plan working wonderfully.

Sometime later, we lay on my bed out of breath, my body in a state of ecstasy. Vinny is even better when I don't need time to adjust to his size.

"I could have had that for *years*," I complain.

Vinny chuckles. "You've said that like four times now, *darling*."

"Ew, change the name."

"You've always complained about the nickname. I'm trying to accommodate you."

"Choose another, *honey*." We both shudder. "Sounded so wrong on so many levels. You're staying as 'bloodsucker.'" Vinny pulls me close, kissing me deeply and trailing his fingers through my hair. My voice is muffled against his lips, "Kissing and sex won't help you."

"Pretty sure it has, *snookums*." Vinny and I recoil from each other, wincing at his terrible word choice. "For both our sanity, you're remaining as sweet cheeks."

I grumble as I climb out of bed. He attempts to grab me, but I dodge him as I snatch my underwear. Thankfully, these won't be stolen. Deep down, I know I'm not getting the others until the week is over. Deal or not.

"Complete hit and run you are," he says, lounging on my bed and watching me dress.

"You did it first."

His tone softens. "I didn't want to."

"I know, don't worry."

"Brenda, what you found—"

"Not now, Vinny. Later." I throw his pants at him, hoping to forget the paperwork that's still stacked on my kitchen table. "Get dressed."

Vinny sighs heavily. "Alright. Throw me my underwear; you might steal it out of spite." I dip down and toss the briefs at his face. He grins as he catches them.

"Alright, bloodsucker, part of the tradition is us both being there. And you better be ready for Pops to ask about Mating, and Ma will probably ask if you did your *job* right. Leave out details, or I'm spiking your drink. Avoid Joey and Ricky at all costs because if you give them details, I *will* shoot you with silver bullets." I pause and add, "That includes Gina." I go to my closet, shoving through the hangers for a better top.

Vinny is silent, and I wonder if this is all too much. I debate tossing another joke at him to calm any unease he may have when he asks, "Do you want to be Mated?"

The shirts in my hands drop to the floor, and I turn to see him standing in just his pants with a worried expression. Is he serious? He can't be. It's one thing to say he'll never let me go, but another when it comes to Mating.

I open my mouth a few times before speaking. "It's been less than twelve hours since I shot you. Isn't that a little fast?"

"We've known each other for two decades."

"Don't make it creepy."

"Grave robber."

"Cradle snatcher."

"Perfect pair."

I try to go back to looking through my closet as I talk, "How about we don't talk about this and get drunk first? Get my underwear back? A nap? I keep asking for one, and I don't seem to be getting good ones. Maybe another round of sex will ease the tension, but that doesn't seem—"

Vinny grabs me, pressing my back into his chest. His arms wrap around my torso, holding me close, while one hand gently covers my mouth as he kisses me on the small spot underneath my ear lobe. "It's rare when you ramble. Enjoyable, but not helpful now. I'll take care of Pops. You don't need to answer now. Just think about it."

I try to speak, but my voice is muffled. He lifts his hand, and I narrow my eyes at him. "I don't ramble."

"Said it was rare."

We stare at each other for a few moments, and I sigh. "It's a lot."

"I know."

"And it started because *you* couldn't keep your nose out of *my* business." I'm losing steam and arguing points.

"Pretty sure it started when *you* shot *me*." Vinny kisses my neck. "And I'm pretty sure I told you to shoot me in the heart since you rejected it for so long and gave me blue balls. You never did like taking direction."

"Which time?"

"Not the point." Vinny turns me to place a kiss gently on my lips. He lifts my chin to look at him. "Let's get through tonight and then talk. We both know there's more to this, which means there's going to be a shitstorm to navigate, sweetheart. So..." he kisses me again, but more deeply, and my toes curl as shivers run through me, "...we'll talk after this weekend."

"Do I get more sex?"

"You're a fiend."

"Look at my family. All the signs were there."

"There's groups for that."

"How about a nap, finally? A *really* good one?"

"After the party."

"Deal."

We finish dressing and go downstairs to the club filled with succubi and incubi, with Charlene and Gina near the bar. I see Anita and Brock are the only outsiders here, but I stand corrected when I see Beckham near one of the stripper stages. The room is filled with intoxicating scents of arousal and excitement. I glance at Vinny, who looks unperturbed. The added hormones from the succubi and incubi must have been short-leashed.

I'm pulled away from Vinny over the next five hours with Gina making sure I have a drink at all times with Ricky as backup. Strip shows, dancing, and shots flow around the room. Lots of shots. At some point, Gina gets me up onto the main stage, a feat no one has been able to get me to do for three years, but I don't use the pole like I used to.

We laugh as an old routine pops into our heads, turning the dancing into something more erotic and fun. She whispers a challenge into my ear, and I accept to see what we'll make happen first.

One: Scare Anita out of the club.

Two: Make Pops blush.

Three: Make Vinny blush.

Four: Have me earn two hundred in tips on stage.

The thought to come back and strip again crosses my mind until Pops takes the four hundred dollars from my bra upstairs. Once a club manager, always a club manager.

Hours later, going deeper into the night for the Underground, I make it to bed alone, unfortunately. Anita practically dragged Vinny out to clear some business. He's still a mob boss, I guess. At least I get my nap and sleep.

I awake hours later to my phone buzzing. The screen glares at me with an orange tint as I sit up and putt my glasses on. My breath hitches as I read the message from Drauper, *Meet me in three hours at the Bronx Entrance. I found something.*

I throw my blankets off and put my pants on.

CHAPTER TWENTY-NINE
IN THE DARK OF THE NIGHT

The last time I used the Bronx Entrance was in college. A chill runs through my body as I look at the unkept elevator doors. No onyx marble, just steel with copper lining. A slight testament to what NYC thinks of the area. I get on and ride upwards to Topside. Lights begin to switch as I near the top, approaching early evening above. I know at home most would still be asleep after the celebration. My metabolism with alcohol is quick. Either good genes, or I'm an alcoholic. Probably the latter.

I pass the subways and tunnels of the Bronx, coming up to the surface. Twilight meets me as I leave the elevator and bring my jacket in close when I feel a slight chill. I turn down the street and walk toward the address he sent me. After a few blocks, I see Drauper standing under a flickering lamplight near a drugstore.

"If you had shown up in a trench coat, I'd have thrown you in the Hudson," I tease. Drauper doesn't smile, taking his sunglasses off. Well, *he's* not gonna be fun tonight, and the hard look in his eyes tells me enough. "You didn't get the warrant, did you?"

He grunts. "Nope."

"You talk to PSB?" His hardened expression stays the same. "You're worse than I am with authority, and that's saying a lot."

Drauper crosses his arms, remaining serious. "You said you'd help scope out the area. If you don't want—"

"Where are we snooping, Scooby-Doo?"

"Seriously?"

"What? Notorious werewolf detective and his human companion? Fine, I'll be Scooby, you be Shaggy."

"Brenda."

"I'm ornery tonight; deal with it. I got my nap. I'll come with you, warrant or not. Where's the place?" I gesture around us.

He lets out a long breath and nods down the block. I follow him through the busy district filled with people, businesses, and apartment complexes, most of which seem abandoned. I recognize the buildings we pass. An uneasy feeling grows as the farther we go, the more the activity around us thins out.

"Most of those ghouls who moved in stayed in this area," he says as we pass the line of the neutral zone, street signs indicating exactly where we are. This zone used to be the conglomerate of the mafia territory and covers most of the South Bronx and West. It's one of the larger zones of the city. We pass some ghouls and werewolves coming out for the evening in a small park. A shiver runs down my spine, and my hand twitches toward the gun hidden at my back.

I don't like the quiet. "They make a fuss?" I whisper.

"No, they moved right in, almost two hundred of them. The apartment complex there and the one beside it," he says, pointing out the apartments. "No paper trail. Another hundred directly below in the Underground."

I recognize the small sigils on most of the doors. They were the complexes owned by Pops for safe houses before Doddard carelessly gave them away. They were easy to access because of the tunnels running underneath our feet. Pops uses them to transport people out of the city, but Drauper doesn't know that or that the ghouls in the Underground are further north, not directly beneath us.

I keep my breathing slow as I follow him. "Wanna go snooping through their homes? Your job that boring?"

He glares at me and stops us at a corner. I look around and notice the quiet has become worse. Even those walking by are eerily silent. Vinny and Rodney weren't kidding about pulling out. Their guards are gone, and I try to ignore the twisting fear of being so far away from any backup. I brush a hand over my phone in my back pocket.

The detective catches my attention as he points toward a building a few blocks down and says, "Abandoned facility turned community center. No records of who owns it."

"PSB? NIIA? Their area and jurisdiction. They usually own what's left."

"Privately owned. No names attached."

The only privately owned properties here should belong to the mafia under a pseudonym, not blank. Drauper somehow found the only property not owned by the mafia or government agency in a mob territory.

"Anyone use it?" I ask.

"Just the homeless. The last event held there was ten years ago. Birthday party." I had to hand it to the detective, he knew how to dig.

"Must have been a *killer* apocalypse theme." I stare at the stained walls, taped-up windows, graffiti, and trash along the sidewalks. "You think that's where people are disappearing to?"

"Only place unmarked and unowned within the perimeter. Ghouls moved in right next door. Probably, trying to hide something with their stench."

"Or it's the only place for them to come to?"

"*Or* the only place to cover up where people are missing? Those apartments are tempies"

I scrunch my brows. "What the fuck are you talking about? What are tempies?"

He motions for me to follow and leads us closer to the complexes. "People who stay for a few weeks, and then they're just gone. I tried to find any records, but nothing. It's like a weird foster home without anything that says who lives there. Nothing on the Paranormal side either."

"If you don't have records, how do you know any of this?"

"I've got an inside person." Oh, fuck me, and not in a good way. There's a rat in the mafia.

The entire system in the Bronx is fucked if Drauper or others catch wind of the Underground Mafia operations. A rat can blow every single operation in NYC, Underground and Topside included. My chest constricts, and I wonder if I can discreetly text my mob boss hotline, but I need to find out who the rat is first.

"What contact?" I ask, and he gives me a side glance. "Come on, who am I gonna tell, Shaggy? My books?"

"The more I get around you outside the library, the more I'm confused about your antics and language."

"Only just started, just wait, it gets better." I grin. He doesn't respond as we walk closer to the center.

Drauper has us duck down an alley. Always a good sign. Not. He checks if anyone is nearby before saying, "A shifter. Used to work for one of the mob families."

I'm gonna kill Doddard. "Used to?"

"Yeah, for an incubus named Alanzo who's the head of his own mob for like a hundred years." Add a few more centuries. "There were other names, but I know it's him. He's like that bastard Dracultelli. Never been caught. They're good, too good, which doesn't make sense about the screwup."

My spine stiffens as he talks about my family, and I clutch my jacket to keep my hands still. Just another day for them, Brenda, just another day. "What screwup—?"

He suddenly presses me against the building and holds a finger to his lips, nodding down the alley. I peer over his shoulder and see ghouls walk into the center and disappear into the darkness near the door. Werewolves pass with their hackles raised. That's comforting. The longer I'm with Drauper, the more I want Vinny or Rodney with me.

"There you go," he says. "Ghouls are using the center."

"Great detective work. Want a Scooby snack?"

"That could be where the missing people are going."

"You honestly think the mafia is taking people off the streets into there? Using ghouls to do that? Seriously, Drauper, it'd be easier to raid a cemetery and deal with the consequences."

"Do you have a better reason for how all this adds up?"

"Another birthday party? Although, I think they need a better guest list." He scowls, and I roll my eyes. The pieces of this damn puzzle have too many sides. Nothing fucking makes sense. I push aside and say, "Stay here."

He grabs my wrist. "What the hell are you doing?"

"Checking out the building. I look like I belong here," I whisper as I point to my facial scars. "You smell like a cop, a *human cop*. You'll get us nowhere."

"I'm not letting—"

"What you gonna do, arrest me?"

He frowns deeply. "You're human, too."

I point at my face again and smile, leaving him in stunned confusion. I don't need him finding more clues and screwing things up. I leave him in the alley and stroll toward the abandoned building. Do I think he's right about the building being sketchy? Yeah. Mafia and ghouls using it to hide bodies? Not really.

Drauper did find the one building I was looking for, somewhere in the middle of the shit show that didn't belong, except the ownership doesn't make sense. If it was privately owned within the mob territory, *someone* in the Underground Mafia would know who. Except, what I found in *The Vault* told me they didn't. This part of the zone belongs to the mob, no way Drauper was getting that warrant. Beckham protects the families, and he controls the shifters, who control the courts. We're in the area where most half-breeds are disappearing, near Rodney's old routes, and where Michello was assaulted. It also happens to be next to the Main Bronx Entrance and where the ghouls are staying. Coincidence seems too fucking easy. Someone is pulling strings.

We've been careful, covering our trails, business as usual, and it's still going to bite everyone in the ass. Not just the mafia, but PSB, too, if this outlier puts more people in peril. Something smells and it's not the ghouls. I'm beginning to understand why Vinny and Rodney were grumps the past few weeks. I'm already grumpy dealing with this and the detective with a death wish.

I pass some werewolves, all of them hiding their faces and flashing their pieces at me, and I flash my own. Their mahogany and CLP scent worsens. They're Wolf Mob. Their routes are abandoned, and they aren't guards. What are they doing here?

I try a few of the center doors, but nothing budges. Fantastic. The smell of dead flesh fills the air, smothering the last of the scents from the werewolves, and I notice most Paranormals have disappeared. Lights flicker through the apartments in the quiet as Drauper waves from the alley for me to come back. I motion for him to look on the other side and continue down the block, watching briefly as he does what I suggest. The street is mostly vacant and dark, with a few lamps flickering into the night. I hear clinking from nearby and see two male ghouls huddled over something illuminated in their hands. Their skin is gray, and deep ginger hair hangs past their shoulders. They look human enough while moist clothes cling to their skin. I give them a small nod as I continue investigating the area. Windows grow dark as I pass them. Everything is shut down and void of any life as cars screech in the distance. I focus past the smell of old rotting flesh. Nothing abnormal, just quiet. A sign the cops are out.

I begin to wish I'd listened to Vinny, Gunther, Joey, Pops…everyone at this fucking point on about coming here. I reach for my phone, on the verge of calling one of them, when it buzzes, and I pick it up to hear Drauper on the other line. "Find anything?"

"Darkness, dirt, and foul stench."

"Same," he replies as I turn down an alley with old barrels, dumpsters, and cans lining the brick walls. "All the doors are locked. Can ghouls go through walls?"

"Only purebred vampires and the top ghoul of a Hive Mind can, but even then, it's rare. Otherwise, they're using keys." Something clanks behind me, and I turn to see a figure moving through the darkness. They spin away from me, and I see wings. Feathered wings. "Holy shit."

"Brenda—?" Drauper's voice disappears as I hang up, shove my phone in my pocket, and run after the figure through the darkness into an alleyway. Turning the corner, I see the grey wings on the figure wearing a black leather jacket and catch the scent of leather, patchouli, and beard oil. My feet pound against the pavement as I call after him. "Hey! Hey, stop!"

I scramble around another building corner. Nothing. I come to a dead-end alley. I gasp for air, staring at the emptiness before me with only dumpsters and nasty puddles. Groaning in frustration, I find two gray feathers near one of those disgusting brown puddles. I pick one up and examine it.

Daemon feathers.

Well, this just got better.

"You look lost," a raspy voice says behind me.

I pull out my Glock as I spin on my heel, aiming at the voice. The gun comes upon a young ghoul with long ginger hair past their hips and vacant eyes. Dirty, ragged clothes cling to them, barely hanging from their shoulders.

"Not really," I reply and fully stand with my gun trained on them.

They tilt their head. "Mama always said to help strangers."

"Your Ma sounds wise. You live in the neighborhood?" I slowly ease my gun down, keeping my sight on them. They're younger than their teens, probably changed early. "Ever been inside that center? The one down a few blocks?"

They look where I suggest, then shake their head. "Are you a half-breed?"

My spine stiffens, and I keep my expression passive. I clutch my gun a bit tighter. "Maybe, what's it to you?"

209

They giggle. I should've stayed home and continued with my nap.

"I've met others like you." They turn, beginning to walk down the street toward the center. "Careful, though sometimes not." I follow them cautiously back to the empty street, smelling nearby ghouls watching from the shadows. They stop in front of me, tilting their head and smiling. Please don't let me shoot a kid. That's not how I want my weekend to end. "Are you with the doctor?"

I feel the blood drain from my face and my stomach drop. "What?"

"The doctor. Always asks for his half-breeds, but we don't know who. We bring who we think he wants." Their vacant black eyes watch me.

"Who—" Shots fire in the distance, and the ghouls in the shadows start running toward it. I recognize the gunfire. Wolf Mob. I click the safety off my gun and run down the street, looking back to see the young ghoul wave at me. I run at full speed around the corner to the chaos of ghouls, werewolves, and humans fighting as bystanders watch the riot, either yelling at the commotion or dragging people inside. Sirens blare and lights flash in the distance as wolves fall back. I scan the area for Drauper, and I find him in a fight with some ghouls.

Shit. We're not supposed to be here.

I run into the fray, trying to pull the ghouls off him and screaming for them to back off. I'm knocked to the ground as shots ring through the air, my head slamming to the pavement. Pain travels through my back as I try to get up, but then something stabs me on the shoulder and arm. I kick at it and make contact, toppling two ghouls over who stop to stare at me. My head begins to pound, and searing pain goes through my shoulder. Their eyes widen, and I follow their gaze to the bite marks on my shoulder

My head swims as the sirens, screams, and shots echo around me. I try to stand but land back on my ass, weapon clattering to the ground as lights flash across the brick.

Drauper appears, and I can barely make out a word he's saying as he screams at me. Words jumble together, and I can't make him out. I rasp, "I'm fine. I'm—"

"Brenda…hold on…Brenda!"

I groan as the venom spreads through my veins, but it'll pass. I just need…

I'm held down suddenly and feel a prick sink into my neck. My body begins to seize. Muscles spasm, burning overtaking my limbs and insides. A scream escapes my lips as I try to fight off Drauper and the human medic over top of me, who's trying to give me another dose.

The pain will only get worse. "No!" I scream. "No anti-venom! Stop!" I struggle against their hold as I'm given another shot, my muscles convulsing and shaking. Anti-venom and antidotes wreck my body, inciting uncontrollable seizures and sickness. They're my fucking kryptonite.

They strap me onto a stretcher, and my eyes burn as I weakly wrestle against them, everyone yelling as lights flash and sirens go off. We're moving. They're taking me somewhere.

Where are they taking me?

I thrash against the restraints and see bodies on the ground. Paranormal bodies. "No!"

What have they done? What have they *done*?!

"Calm down," Drauper says. "We're getting you to the hospital. You were bit, Brenda. We have to get you out of here."

I bring my gaze to him as my breath becomes shaky. The lights within the ambulance invade my vision. They're white. Too white.

No. NO.

"Let me go! Please! Let me go!" My lungs burn as I scream, and I stop when there's a familiar howl. My head snaps to the side, and I see a grey werewolf standing along the edge of the gathered crowd, pushing their way through as the cops train their weapons on him.

"Stand down!"

"Back into the crowd!"

"Get back, beast!"

A snarl rips from the one I call Balto, and fear tears through me as safety's click off.

"*NO! Get out of here!*" I scream in Noctora, and Marcus stops. Paranormals in the crowd pause as I find his gaze. "*They'll kill you! Get Vinny! Please! Get Alanzo!*"

His eyes widen as I writhe on the stretcher, convulsions overwhelm my body, and screams tear through me. I bite down on another shriek, and blood trickles out of my mouth. Bright lights surround me, and I feel myself begin to hyperventilate. It's like my retinas are on fire as I try to fight against the restraints. I convulse from the drugs, knowing it will get worse. I toss and try to see Marcus one last time as they close the doors.

My nightmare comes to life. Panic surging through every portion of my being as I scream in horror, "*Daddy!*"

CHAPTER THIRTY
MY FUCKING NIGHTMARE

Everything hurts.

It takes three medics to hold me down as I fight and thrash. Their shouting overwhelms my senses as I try to shut out the blinding lights that sting my eyes, burning into my skull. Each convulsion through my body makes me whimper in pain.

"What's wrong with her?" Drauper asks them as sirens blare outside.

"She shouldn't be reacting like this," a medic answers. "We may have been too late."

"You got it in under five minutes! Greg, double dosage!"

I pull at the restraints, my throat burning from screaming. My bones feel like they're snapping, and there's pressure in my chest as I struggle to breathe. Fear rushes through me, I don't know where they're taking me or what they'll do. The more needles and IVs they put in my arms, the more it seems like I'm slipping from reality. Whirls of color move past, and I keep losing focus, tears streaming down my face as my contacts begin to scratch.

The ambulance abruptly stops, and they open the doors as more voices join with the rest, wheeling me away from the lights of the vehicle. I calm for only a moment as I pick up the scent of being outside until I smell the anti-septic. Bright, white light invades my vision again, and the air chills as they rush me down the cold hospital hallway. I tremble in fear as the all-consuming sounds of ticking lights, screaming people, and wheels tip me over the edge. Horror coupled with the physical pain, and I thrash and scream harder. Shouts fill my ears as hands hold me down, and no one listens to my pleas.

I can't breathe. I can't see.

I fight to escape the numbness, aches, and terror as we come to a halt. They quickly move me and place me back under leather restraints around my wrists, ankles, and mid-section. I'm chained. I panic and scream as I lose my sense of reality and drown in unlocked memories.

I'm a child. Traloski and his workers hover over me. White lights blind my damaged retinas. Needles prod and knives slice down my arms to insert venom capsules. I shout in pain and horror. Water washes over me filled with anti-venom while burning and freezing my skin. Nurses shout for the doctor. Drauper is yelling. Traloski's rubber gloves press into my chest as he inserts blood.

I'm slipping. I'm slowly losing my mind.

Through the fog of burning pain, brightness, and horror, I smell him. A homing beacon of dark spices and bloodlust trickle like a lifeline into the nightmare. Shouting ricochets, and I thrash for him. His scent burns my nose as fury blasts into the hospital room.

"*Release her!*" Vinny's voice shreds into the room.

Drauper shouts, "Who the hell are you?!"

My body convulses again, and I whimper through the pain, keeping my eyes shut as muscles spasm. I concentrate on Vinny's scent, inhaling the familiar aroma.

"You have no right to hold her here."

"Excuse me—" A nurse tries to intervene but shuts up when Vinny's growl shakes the room.

"She is under the jurisdiction of the Noctis Immortalis, not humans. She's..." My mind goes to another memory of needles, knives, matches, and a scalpel trailing down my face. Twice. I scream bloody murder and thrash as the next wave of pain overcomes me. I fight anything that comes near until his hand touches my face. His voice is soft, "Hold on...sweetheart. I got you."

"Contacts...*please*," I beg as my head moves from side to side.

People yell as Vinny carefully opens my eyelid and takes out both contacts, whispering to me. "Hey! Get him away from her!" Drauper yells as relief sends more tears down my face.

My body spasms again from the drugs, and I sob uncontrollably. There's shouting, and Vinny lets loose a thundering growl, pausing movement coming toward us. Voices collide as my restraints are ripped away and needles leave my body. I whimper as I grab for the scent of dark spices.

Doctors protest as Vinny brings me into his arms and says, "I'm getting you out. Hold on, sweetheart." His scent washes over me as I cling to his chest.

"You can't take her!" Drauper yells while others murmur in fear.

"She's not your concern," Vinny says, beginning to leave.

"The hell she isn't!" I tense at the sound; afraid I'll be ripped from him.

"Careful, Detective." I choke in relief when I hear the new voice. Vinny pauses, hovering near Joey as his own warm scent mingles with Vinny's. Joey speaks with a restrained calm tone. "I doubt you'd want to explain to your chief how you interfered in Underground business without PSB present. Odd with none in sight, isn't it? Scandal doesn't begin to describe what NYPD did tonight. Imagine NIIA getting involved. Wouldn't look good, would it?"

I keep my eyes shut and turn my head slightly toward Joey's voice. He sounds calm, far more than he should be. I know that calmness. The humans in the room may not live to tell the tale of confronting two mob bosses tonight. Joey's hand gently touches my cheek, and a broken sob comes out of me as I lean into the touch. In a hushed tone, he speaks in Noctora, "*Get her to Pops, now.*"

Vinny leaves with me in his arms. I clutch to him as my body convulses again. It ravages through me, making my head pound. He places a hand over my head, holding it to his shoulder to keep the lights from my eyes. A flash of another memory comes with freezing temperatures and needles overtakes me. I stifle a scream as Vinny holds me closer and coos, "Almost there, sweetheart."

I revert to the young girl I was years ago and plead, "I want...Daddy...please..." I'm screaming in a shower, and the anti-septic smell turns to sewage. "Daddy...please..."

I feel cool muggy air as the clamor of the hospital disappears behind us, and I blink to see the freedom of darkness and city lights. Vinny holds me tighter as I shiver, and I hear voices shouting as the familiar scent of wine, gunpowder, and cigars drift past. Samuel. Anita.

Vinny soon halts and turns his head upward when I hear the beat of familiar wings. I sob as a breeze hits us both with the scent of cinnamon. "*Give me my daughter,*" Pops demands. Vinny's arms begin to release me, but my instincts kick in to grip onto him tighter. Pops speaks in a soft tone, "Come here, baby girl." And I let go of Vinny. I'm being transferred between them when my body convulses again, twisting and bending backward, screaming as my muscles tremble. Pops grabs me fully, and wraps my legs around his waist, keeping me in place as my body spasms. His strong arms press into my back, trying to get the shaking to stop. "*What the fuck did they give her?*"

"*I'll find out.*" Vinny's voice answers in pain. "*I'll stay to help Joey. The detective is a bigger pain than we thought. PSB will be here soon. NIIA, too, unless those humans relent.*"

"Have Joey call Carmen. Take care of the rest." Pops flings his wings out.

"*With pleasure,*" Vinny growls. I hear something crack, and people scream. Horrified shrieks ring out as I hear Vinny leave us. Another pop sounds and something crashes through glass.

"Hold on, baby girl."

Pops flies off into the night, and I find calm in the evening air as I cling to him, just barely opening my eyes to look at the darkened landscape. Relief washes over me as I drink it all in. The temperature drops as Pops soars, turning downward into one of the flying tunnels of the Underground. Shaking from the cold now, Pops holds me closer as he descends into the darkness.

Scents change as we enter the Underground and land on the brick pathways. His wings disappear into his back as he carries me home. My muscles begin to convulse again, and his arms keep me in place as I let out a soft scream. I start to hyperventilate, everything becoming fuzzy as my head pounds.

"Keep breathing, baby girl. Keep breathing," Pops' voice is calm, soothing my erratic breaths as we approach *Unbound.*

New voices penetrate my ears and mash together as we enter the club. What's left of my senses feels like they're slipping away. Then I hear Ma's stifled scream, and my heart wrenches at the sound. Familiar soft hands brush back my hair, and Ma whispers to me, trying not to cry as Pops takes me upstairs to the living room. They're talking, and I hear Joey's name and Pops snarling low.

He sits down on the couch, keeping me on his lap as I refuse to leave him, and removes my jacket and shoes. Pops continues to talk to me, though I don't hear the words, keeping me calm the best he can. Tears stream down my face as the next convulsion overtakes my body. Another shriek rips out of me as Ma comes back. Pops gives me a pill and makes me swallow.

I don't know how long I stay in his arms, rocking me through each wave of agony and stroking my head like I'm a child again. He hums low, keeping me tightly against him. Ma comes back, kissing my forehead when she can. Familiar voices whisper through the apartment but leave when Ma tells them to go. A quiet washes over the space. All that's left are trembles in my bones, silent tears, and shuddering breaths, with the forgotten memories slipping back into darkness.

"Daddy?" My voice is harsh and raspy.

"It's okay. I'm here."

I give a tired breath. "Everything...hurts."

"I know. I know." He whispers, kissing my head and rubbing calming circles into my back. The smell of cinnamon and whiskey relaxes my headache.

"I remembered...before you found me...I remembered...before the sewer..." Tears trail down my cheeks, and I feel Pops pause.

He hushes me gently. "You're safe, baby girl. You're safe. Go to sleep. I'll be here."

I hold onto him, willing myself to remember this is reality and not a dream. "I love you."

"I love you, baby. You're safe. It's okay..."

I'm a child again, except I'm not a science experiment.

I dream of bouncing on my father's leg as he teaches me to read. Ma is showing me how to bake chocolate chip cookies. I'm snuggling with Joey as he reads to me in bed. Playing tag through the club with Ricky after he colors in my scars. There's laughter echoing through the dream as I pass through memories and I slowly wake up to a familiar scent of cherry blossoms and muffins.

"Ma?" My voice cracks as I speak.

"Right here, baby." Her voice is like fresh water. "How are you feeling?"

I grumble as I adjust my position with my head placed on her shoulder and half my body draped over her as she cradles me with one arm. I feel the familiar bedspread of my parents' bed. My limbs throb and there's a dull ache in my head, my throat feeling raw. "Being hit by a truck is preferable." Ma laughs softly as she strokes my head. "What happened, Ma?"

"Anti-venom and other antidotes, more than you've had in the past. More than any human or Paranormal should be given. Worst reaction we've seen with you, but your body fought it hard," she says with a sigh.

"It felt like I lost control. Like…reality split," I murmur into her shoulder.

She's silent a moment, continuing to stroke my head. Her lips press against my forehead, and she asks in a whisper, "When did you learn about Traloski?"

My body stills from the topic change. I blink rapidly and peer through my familiar darkness of violet, crimson, and blues that swim together like a Picasso painting. I can barely make out her facial features and eyes. "How did you—?"

"You told Pops you remembered. He asked if Vinny or Joey heard anything when they got you, and Vinny gave us what you found. He said it wasn't how you wanted to tell us, but we didn't know how long you'd sleep," she says gently. "Or if you'd wake up from a nightmare." My chest clenches. I try to hold back the trembling, and she holds me close. "Shh, no, baby, don't be scared. It's okay."

"I was—"

"We know," she coos. "That *damn* hospital must have triggered the memories." Holy shit, Ma swore. "Your panic must have made the reaction to the drugs worse."

I shift, tucking my head into her shoulder more. Nestling into her, I try to mumble through my words. "I found it all before Vinny and I…before we…I was going to tell you, really, but everything happened so quickly. I'm sorry."

She clucks her tongue and smooths back my hair. "Don't worry, baby. It's alright. You're here now, and that's all that matters."

Silence envelopes us as I listen to her breathe, gently beginning to rock a little with her. I think back to the hospital and remember the fear, pain, and fragments of familiar voices and scents. "Ma, where's—"

"They're taking care of business," she replies quickly. A response I've received since I was a child, except I'm not anymore.

I sit up and lean my head against hers, and she murmurs a few sounds of uncertainty. "Tell me, Ma. Please."

Her fingers drift over the scars on my forearm. "PSB and NIIA came to the hospital after Pops got you. Vinny and Joey took care of the rest. You had walked into a...a..." Her voice shudders. "Rodney and Vinny were securing routes when the Wolf Mob saw you there, and it caused an upset. They watched someone from the main families get...taken." She shakes slightly as she holds me.

"Ma, there's something else, isn't there?"

She takes a deep breath but is interrupted. "I'll tell her, Carmen," Pops says, his scent drifting slowly into the room. I look to only see swirls of colors and a distorted figure illuminated by an orange light.

"I'll bring you something to eat and drink," Ma says, kissing my forehead. "You need something in you." She leaves me in the bed, and I hear her kiss Pops as she disappears. Pops moves to the bed and sits on the edge, grabbing my hand.

"How much trouble am I in?" I ask.

"You're not."

"Pops, I fu—"

"You walked into a sting." Oh, fuck me, it's *that* kind of something. "Wolf Mob knew. Rodney went to get evidence of foul play with the NYPD."

"That's why he was calling Vinny," I say.

"He was helping Rodney on escape routes," Pops says and sighs. "I don't know why you were up there, and I won't ask. I don't care if that detective knew about it or not, you still got sucked into something and got bitten. Humans followed their own protocol, but you should've remained in the neutral zone."

"I wasn't even in the zone?" I whisper.

Pops shakes his head. "That's why the agencies came in; NYPD and the hospital broke international laws by taking you since you're my daughter."

"Who called you?"

"Most of Rodney's crew, including Marcus." Pops' voice is tight and strained. "You were screaming for them to get Vinny or me." I take a deep breath in, remembering the horror in Marcus' eyes. Pops gently caresses my hands, and the scent of cinnamon eases those flickering thoughts. "Scared the shit out of those werewolves."

"Not the first time," I joke lightly.

Pops shifts, and I know he's trying to delay the inevitable from what he's told me. For years I've been kept far enough away from mob dealings. The moment Vinny and Joey walked into that hospital to grab me outside of a neutral zone, the rules changed for me.

"Tell me, Pops," I whisper.

He puts a hand on my knee. "Baby girl, I know we talked about you staying on Topside longer, but the NYPD and other agencies now know you're not human and have ties with the Underground Mafia. That detective even tried—"

"I'll come home, Pops." His hand tenses around my knee. "It's okay, really. I tried, and it backfired. Besides, we both know I needed to come home, and I belong down here. After what happened…it's clear where I need to be. And it ain't Topside."

He talks softly. "I'm sorry, baby girl. You'll lose—"

"Nothing important as being back home, Pops." I squeeze his hand and smile. So, what if I lost my apartment, the job at the library, and my small sense of freedom? I have a home to come back to and people to annoy. "You'll have to put up with my ass 24/7 again. Sorry."

Pops chuckles and rustles my hair. "Like old times for you and me. You can help downstairs and comfort Ricky now that Joey's busy being the boss."

I laugh. "Without that library job, he's gonna paint my scars and dye my hair every color."

"Consent still needed, baby girl. Otherwise, I'm sending him to Staten Island to open his own parlor. Your Ma may like that, actually."

His small threat towards my brother makes me snort and grin fully. Pops leans forward, giving me a close hug to hold onto him. A shiver travels over my skin, and Pops tightens his grip a moment and pulls away. "I'm sorry if I scared you…I just needed…wanted…"

"To have your father there." He brushes his hand over my cheek as I nod. My chest feels heavy.

"Pops, about what Vinny told you—"

"No, baby girl. Not yet," he hushes me. "You've been through enough in the last few days. I won't put you through more turmoil. We'll look through what you found *together* when you're fully home and recovered."

"Thank you," I whisper.

"My job to look over after you. Always." Pops kisses me on the forehead then stands up from the bed. "Might be good to be back down here. For you and Vinny."

I stare at Pops through my hazy Picasso filter. "Is he here?"

"He just got in. He wanted my and your permission first before talking." Of course, even as territorial or angry he may be right now, he's still respectful. "You alright to see him?"

"Technically, I can't really see anyone right now," I laugh softly. Pops grunts, and I relent with a nod.

He leaves as I lay back in the bed filled with my parents' warm scents of cinnamon and sweet blossoms. The horror is over, and I can finally breathe. Memories once converged into the present are mostly gone into an old abyss unless I go searching for them. Hopefully, only those stupid nightmares will ever return.

I hear footsteps outside the door and point a finger gun without looking. "Bang."

"I'll take it over the rolling pin," Vinny says as he closes the door behind him. The smell of tea, bread, and pudding follows in with him as he places a tray on the bedside table.

"Ma making you do chores?" I sit up as he sits on the side of the bed.

"Offered since I did intrude on your recovery." He carefully places a mug in my hands. I hum as the warm liquid goes down my aching throat while he watches me in silence long enough that I want to start screaming again.

"Out with it, bloodsucker." He grunts stubbornly and keeps quiet. "It's that, or you're gonna end up fighting Ricky or Joey. Maybe get some glitter—"

"You scared the fuck out of me," he says harshly as I hold the mug close. "Do you know how angry and terrified I was? It sounded like you were dying. And you almost did from the amount of fucking drugs they pumped into you. It *should've* killed you." Vinny takes a deep breath and runs his hand through his hair. "I heard your screams *outside* the hospital. It was like they were burning you. I wanted to fucking kill them. I almost did, but Samuel and Anita kept me from ripping the place apart. And that *damn cop*—"

"He didn't know." My voice is gruff. I understand him being angry at Drauper, but he didn't know. He was probably more scared of me turning into a ghoul than anything to listen to my screams. His terror, like mine, overrode everything.

"That's not the point," he growls.

"It was a mistake."

"No shit. Why were you out there?"

"Vinny—"

"You left without telling anyone where you were or leaving a note. I know I can't control you or tell you what to do...but you were in the *fucking Bronx neutral zone*. The one place, Brenda. The one *fucking* place we told you to stay away from." Wow, this is the most he's ever cussed me out.

"I was...investigating," I counter, which isn't a great move.

Vinny stands up, his scent burning through my nose. "The fucking ghouls? Drug busts? All the rest of the shit you've been looking into?" My eyes widen. I haven't exactly been quiet about what I've been doing the past few weeks, but I still didn't expect him to catch on. "Of course, I fucking noticed, Brenda. You've been looking into the disappearances and PSB pulling out. You should've come to me or even fucking Rodney before you went too deep."

"I'll admit it. I got caught off guard, but—"

"You walked into an FBI and NYPD joint operation! That's why I had to leave your apartment; Rodney was getting the last of his people out. Finding something, *anything*, about why they've been after non-mafia members." I forget how to breathe and want to ask more questions, but I can't form the words. "If you told any of us where you were going, we would've been able to warn you. Instead, you just…just fucking *disappeared.*"

I clutch my mug and try to hold my ground. "And I fucking didn't. It's over and done with. I get it; I fucked up royally by not going to the *mafia bosses* about what I was doing. What more do you want, Vinny?"

I go to put the mug down but miss the table by a long shot. It crashes, and tea spills everywhere on the floor, the smell of peppermint invading my nostrils as it seeps into the rug. Vinny touches my shoulder to keep still and picks up the mug, and I hear him grab something to soak up the damp carpet.

I grip into my hair, losing the battle to keep the calm and peace I had. He's right. If I hadn't been so stubborn, I'd have gone to him or Rodney. I should've called him when Drauper first mentioned looking into the centers. Instead, I took the worst route possible and almost paid for it. Damn it. I'm smarter than this.

"I'm fucking sorry. I screwed up badly," I say shakily, and he stills on the ground. "I was tired of being told what to do like some damn pet. We both know I can handle myself. I can shoot better than most of your bodyguards while blind, but I got caught in a shitstorm that landed me in the worst possible place. I was trying to help on my own because…because…"

Vinny sighs and sits back on the bed next to me. He puts a hand on my knee while rustling through his hair again. "I was too harsh. I'm sorry. You just went through an ordeal, and I'm acting like you shot a werewolf in a game of roulette."

"No, you're right. And no one else is gonna yell at me for being a dumbass. Not even Pops."

"That's not why, sweetheart." He places a hand on my neck and lifts my head toward him. All I see clearly are his ruby eyes. "I finally admitted I loved you, truly, and I thought I lost you. I've been through some really shitty things, but nothing terrified me more than when I heard you screaming. Pops had to subdue me with his powers. I started to tear that hospital apart when I let him take you." He grabs my hand and kisses it, bringing it to hold against his cheek. "I didn't think I'd ever hear you call me bloodsucker again. Or walk into a room with your gun in my face. Never see those silver flecks in your eyes, watch you read and study, listen to you groan at your brothers, or get threatened with bashing my head in. Hold you again. I really thought I lost my…my best friend. I don't ever want to feel that again."

My voice is quiet as I reach up to touch his hand on my neck. "No guarantee in that. You've been in this business long enough. You know that."

"Doesn't mean a vampire can't worry. Or dream that you'll always be safe."

"You dream? I thought you just went into a void, like a sleep paralysis demon."

"More colorful than that."

"Oh, right. Blood pouring from the skies, never ending food. Knew you were a glutton."

Vinny barks with laughter and pulls me forward, kissing me tenderly on the lips. "There's my sweet cheeks."

"What? You thought they cured me of my bullshit?"

"Could happen."

"Too stubborn."

"And spiteful."

"Sometimes hateful," I smirk.

"Only when you don't have coffee, which I might need to get you since you tossed your tea. You may try to drain me next."

"That's your job. Mine is to shoot you," I say, and Vinny snorts. He brings me in to kiss him again. He's tender, and it lingers. His lips caress mine, bringing us into a deeper kiss. The very taste of him makes me relax and want to fall forward into his arms.

He pulls away suddenly and says, "Do you know how much shit has happened in the last 72 hours?"

"Long or short list? And did *all* of it deal with me? Be fucking honest."

"I'm always honest." I frown at him, and he chuckles as he brings me onto his lap, putting my legs around his waist. "You got caught in the middle of a shitstorm that's bigger than you know. PSB will snoop for the next few weeks, so will NIIA, but they'll keep their distance from here. All the families need a contingency plan right now, which will take a few days as things settle, but…" His voice trails away.

"What?"

He sighs. "That detective, cops, personnel, everyone saw you with—"

"Don't start. I'm already moving back home. So, calm down, vamp tramp." I reach for the food tray, but almost topple over before Vinny catches me and hands me a muffin to munch on.

221

"You're coming back down here?"

"I know it's not safe on Topside and…" I pause and stare at the muffin in my hands. Vinny taps my chin, bringing my face back up to see his ruby eyes. "I miss home. And the reason I left doesn't seem like a…good one anyways. But I miss home."

Vinny sighs in relief, and I try not to laugh at him. For being a powerful vampire, I can shake him up pretty easily. Even before the whole sex thing. "You were plotting how to get me to stay down here, weren't you?" I ask.

"Only slightly," he admits.

"What was the plan? Go old school? Throw me in a coffin? Seduce with your charms?"

"How would I do that?"

"You tell me. *You're* the vampire." He laughs, burying his face into my neck, breathing deeply. I hear a satisfied growl deep in his chest as he squeezes my hips. "Been like 48 hours, and you're already sex-depraved, huh?"

"Coming from the one who dragged me into the bedroom."

"Virgin for a while. Needed to make up for lost time. And scare away family members." A reminder to myself that my panties are most definitely still up downstairs. "Least you're good for something."

"You'll hurt a male's feelings with those kinds of words."

"Thank goodness it's you, then."

"Yeah, thank goodness it's me, sweetheart." Vinny kisses me on the neck, traveling up my jaw and across my skin before he reaches my mouth. The sweep of his tongue along my bottom lip causes a shudder. I moan a little as he kisses me fully, his fangs just touching my tongue. I almost drop my muffin as I hold him closer, my legs clenching around his waist.

Vinny pulls away, and I whimper. He chuckles and says, "You need to rest and eat. And we're in your parent's room, sweet cheeks."

Damn my parents for putting me in their bed. "Muffin will be enough sustenance."

"You need another nap."

"No I don't."

"Clearly. You're still going back to bed." My brows go up. "Alone."

"Party pooper. And here I thought you loved me."

Vinny harshly takes my lips against his. My breath hitches as I breathe him in and let him devour me. His tongue fights with mine, and he lets out a breath that makes my body shiver. I cling to his back, dropping my muffin.

He eases away and says sternly, "*Never* mistake how much I love you."

"Noted," I whisper. "You should remind me again."

He fights back laughter, looking at the closed door. "You were definitely raised by the Cuorebella's."

Two days later, and I'm still sore.

Maybe dragging Vinny to my bed wasn't helpful, but it did boost my morale. There's no way I'll complain about the sex, even if it means throbbing muscles. Apart from doing the devil's tango with Vinny, my family doted over my recovery. Pops and Joey took care of everything on Topside from quitting my job, getting me out of my lease, and discreetly moving my stuff back to the Underground. Not exactly safe going to Topside unless I have escorts.

Ricky watches television with me in the living room while Ma makes supper. I'm half-tempted to go help her with the crap Ricky is having me watch. "Bro, who gives a shit about their loveless dating life?" I groan. "The fights are even boring. I could go down the corner and see better right hooks."

Ricky gasps and clutches his chest. "Don't say that! Veronica and Emily have an *epic* showdown! And Georgie finds true love and seduction!" I roll my eyes and head at him. "Hey! We watched that action flick last night."

"It's only two hours, not five! Seriously, how are there seven seasons of this?"

"It's entertaining and funny." Ricky frowns as he sits back.

I sigh and walk to the kitchen. The apartment smells of lasagna and fresh bread, making my mouth water. Okay, being home does have wonderful perks.

Ma smiles as I enter, humming as she cooks. I take in a deep breath of garlic, butter, and tomato, and ask, "Do you want me to set the table, Ma?"

"Not for a bit longer. Your father and brother will be home late. I invited Vinny and Anita."

"Something tells me Vinny is gonna be over almost every meal," I mumble to myself as I grab a glass and pause. There's only one reason for all four to be back late for dinner. "Ma, why are they gonna be late?"

She doesn't look at me as she continues cooking. "Emergency meeting. Bruno called it."

My stomach drops. Not good. He's not supposed to do that anymore. "Bruno? Why?"

"No prying into their business, baby." Ma gives me a warning glance.

"Ma, what's going on?"

"They're taking care of it."

"Ma."

"Brenda, baby, you just came out—"

"Bruno calling meetings ain't a good thing. Vinny's boss now." She doesn't say anything as she works around the kitchen. Her silence makes my stomach twist, and my headache begins to filter back. "Tell me what's going on, Ma."

No reply.

I slam my glass down and go to the kitchen doorway. "Ricky, why was there an emergency meeting?"

Ma runs over and cries, "Brenda!"

Ricky watches his show and says, "Territories were compromised after that joint operation. Contingency plans are being put in place since most think NYPD and that detective are to blame. Well, they kind of are. Last night, NYPD released a statement that ghouls moved in to sell and use drugs, and now the families are anxious."

I scoff. "Ghouls don't sell drugs. They *literally* can't use them. Whole undead thing."

"Well, yeah, *we* know that, sis." Ricky turns on the couch to face me. "Humans up Top are dumb. So, we gotta secure our areas, and Bruno wants the Bronx territory back and the routes back in."

My chest clenches, and my mouth drops. "That'll start a war with NYPD and PSB." I rush to my bedroom, throwing on my jacket and guns. I fucking forgot about the information I learned a few days ago. The families are walking into a damn trap. Ma and Ricky are in the living room with the television turned off when I come back out to put on my boots.

"What are you doing, baby?" Ma asks.

"PSB and NYPD aren't why the routes were moved," I answer. "NYPD has been allowed to run rampant because they thought *we* were moving out before the busts. They think *we're* the ones taking half-breeds off the streets. Someone wants everyone out of that area, and they're about to succeed." Details from the sting flood back fully, and I rasp, "Doddard told Drauper about the safehouses, which means we have a rat that could take *everyone's* operation down."

Ricky's eyes widen. "What? Why didn't you—"

"Because I almost fucking died, Ricky, I fucking forgot," I snap. "Drauper said he had an informant who worked for Pops. He knows which areas are controlled by each family. Drauper hasn't said anything because PSB hasn't done shit to look into the ghouls or disappearances. If we go after NYPD, his precincts, more people will find out. The moment we step in...we're all in trouble."

I head for the door, and Ma calls out, "Ricky, go with your sister." I stop and stare at her. She speaks calmly, "I don't want you part of this, baby, but I won't risk losing everything we've worked toward. Go warn your father and brother." I smile slightly at Ma, and she nods, trying to keep a stiff upper lip. "Be home in time for dinner. I don't want it getting cold."

Ricky quickly gets his gear, and we rush down the stairs through the club. "They're at *The Lounge*," he says as we run down the paths through evening foot traffic. Of course, they are; typical meeting place for the bosses. "We won't be allowed in, so you got a plan?"

"Give me a minute," I smirk as we reach the front doors and barge in. The place is quiet, but I know there will be chaos through the next room. Yanking the doors open to the back, we're met with guns and barrels pointed our way. Ricky puts his hands up, and I glare at the group of guards: Marcus, Adrian, Samuel, Gunther, Darius, and Brock. I grin, and most of them groan seeing me.

"We need in there," I demand as they put their weapons away.

"Bosses and captains only," Samuel answers, keeping his tone level. Even though Ricky and I are from a main family, we're not allowed at the table unless invited. Technically, not even allowed this close to the meeting. Mafia rules suck, but it doesn't mean I won't try. I've already done stupider things this week.

"I really need to get in there. They may put us in war," I argue. Ricky's hand drifts over my shoulder.

"That's their business, not ours," Marcus speaks in a soft tone. I meet his eyes, and they aren't angry or annoyed. Something flashes over his gaze, and he takes a small step back. I think the wolf is warming up to me.

"It is if they get into a dumbass war with Topside. You'll all be dying and killing for it. Not them." They exchange glances with each other and keep quiet. No retorts? That sting really did them in. "Wow, I actually shocked the thirsty bitches and puppies." They all growl and tense up. "Much better."

"Brenda," Ricky warns.

"Can't do it, baby sis," Samuel says.

"Look, vamp tramp—"

"Unlike you, we *listen* to orders by our boss," Adrian snaps.

"I'm a brat by nature."

"Careful, lil sis," Gunther intervenes, crossing his arms. "The bloodsuckers are touchy this evening." Two vampires snarl at him.

"Don't start," Samuel warns.

"Blame your *ex-boss*," Gunther growls.

"Will you just let me in!" My patience growing thin.

Samuel sighs, "Baby sis—"

"Darius," I say, turning toward the incubus. "Little help here." He holds his hands up in surrender, except it's not what I need right now. "Just ask Alanzo–"

"You gonna make us say it?" Brock's deep voice cuts me off. I meet his crimson eyes, and they pierce through me. He says through gritted teeth, "You're still a half-breed, and they're not allowed in."

"Watch your fucking mouth!" Ricky growls, and Darius' wings punch out. Everyone starts shouting, and the air becomes tense as emotions rise. I can feel the incubi powers advance as the guards growl and snap at each other. Stupid, loyal *Paranormals!*

"That's it!" I scream and whip out my pocket knife, pulling my sleeve up. Ricky follows and gasps, reaching for the knife as I kick at his shins before pressing it to my skin. "Ricky, if there's one thing I know, it's Paranormals."

"You're gonna cause the vampires to flip out," he hisses.

"Exactly."

"You've lost it, haven't you?" He asks as I rip the blade across my forearm, careful not to hit major tendons or arteries, and let my arm hang. I pull my Glock from my pants, and the guards pull out their weapons and point at me. No way am I getting past these guards, so someone on the inside needs to. Loopholes are my favorite.

"Five," I whisper to myself.

Drip. The vampires sniff at the air.

"Four."

They begin to salivate, and others bring their gaze to my bleeding arm.

"Three."

Drip. Ricky curses and backs away as safeties click off.

"Two."

Gunther and Samuel snarl.

"One." The barrel of my gun comes down as the door slams open with a crack. I stare down the weapon right at Vinny's heaving chest. A smile rises on my face as I check my aim. "Perfect timing."

Vinny lets loose a reverberating snarl that commands only the vampires to step back. He lets out another thundering growl for the rest of the guards to follow suit, dropping their aim. He prowls toward me with a fanged smile as I keep the Glock trained on him.

"I literally can't with you," Ricky whimpers, slumping against the wall in relief.

"Sweet cheeks," Vinny whispers as he grabs the barrel of my gun and puts it back into its hiding spot. He grabs my bleeding arm, raising a brow. "You rang?"

"Thought you needed a snack," I tease.

"Ravenous." He strokes his tongue over the wound, licking back the blood. A quick press of his lips over the opening, pulling out some blood, he seals the wound. The one thing I'm not immune to. Vampire sealing abilities. "You interrupted my meeting."

"You were bored, admit it."

"Come to make it better?"

"Right now, in front of everyone?" I smirk.

His eyes flash. "You're learning, sweet cheeks, but not right now. Something tells me that's not why you've interrupted my boring meeting."

I breathe easier as I look up at him, taking in his scent, and I ache to hold him. Fear of what may have already been done urges me forward. "You can't go after Topside; agencies could be waiting for you. There's been a rat."

Vinny cocks his head with his fangs still elongated from feeding, and glances at Ricky, then back to me. "Sweet cheeks, what—"

"You'll start a war, actually, a bloodbath. A bad one. We'll lose our chance to figure out if PSB is hiding anything. The ghouls will be caught in the crossfire. More people will—"

He brings his lips against mine harshly to shut me up. I gasp and allow him to distract me, ignoring the murmuring throughout the room. I remember we aren't public outside the incubi/succubi community. He pulls away and grins. "I was trying to tell you, come on in, sweet cheeks." I grin back at him.

Vinny grabs my hand and leads me away from the guards. Before disappearing through the doors, I stick my tongue out at the guards. Samuel does it back. Marcus smirks, like, *actually* smirks. Ricky asks around where the alcohol is.

Vinny takes me to the back into a room I've never been in before. It's a large, darkened room with lit candles and lamps hanging around the walls. The giant space has a long table in the middle where all the bosses sit with a few guards near the back. I gaze over them and, unfortunately, see him first. Bruno.

He's the original copy of Vinny, except for a few wrinkles and a sharper chin. Dark crimson eyes follow me with malice and contempt as I hold onto Vinny's hand. Bruno sits at the far end of the table, closest to the door. Anita is next, and then Beckham. Rodney sits opposite Anita, next to his father, Frederick. Further down are Pops and Joey. A few other captains sit at the table whom I don't recognize, but most are in charge of areas outside the city.

Vinny sits at the end of the table directly opposite of Bruno, stops at his chair, and whispers to me, "Sit on my lap?"

"Misogynistic or territorial?"

"I just like—"

"Finish that thought, and I will yank your fangs out. Sit down." He smiles slyly and sits in his chair, gesturing for a guard to bring me a chair, but I shake my head at him as I stand next to him. No way am I going to be here long, especially from some of the glares I'm getting.

I've officially entered the worst lion's den of the Underground and Topside combined. Two of the lions being family only make it worse, and it means no dessert for two weeks.

"Vincent, explain the intrusion of this…*person*," Bruno says, the only being in this room who can make me feel insignificant. It takes everything for me not to touch the throbbing scars on my neck. His eyes blaze as he watches me. I haven't seen him since then.

"Careful with your words, Bruno." Pops' voice rumbles from his position. "Although this is a surprise, Vinny is allowed to invite her back here. And we are holding this meeting at *his* establishment."

Pops and Joey's wings are out. The pissing contest must have begun without me. I glance toward Anita, who remains passive in expression, twirling something shiny in her hand.

"She has concerns and a proposition that I believe we need to hear," Vinny replies coolly.

Bruno's gaze hardens as he protests. "What could she possibly—"

"I was there that night with Rodney and Marcus," I interject. "I have a right to say my piece before you begin a war that will ruin us." Eyes draw toward me as I interrupt one of the most powerful vampires on the East Coast of the Continental U.S. Apparently, I woke up today and chose violence.

The air grows cold as I keep my gaze steady on Bruno, fighting back the urge to run away screaming. He glowers at me like a predator who wants to drink their prey dry. Instinct is ravaging against my brain. I remain steady, remembering why I'm doing this as I recall the Paranormal bodies on the ground and the cops assaulting Michello.

"Detective Drauper knows who owns the safe houses," I continue. "There's been a rat. And the fucker's been giving him access to routes, movements, territories, and who knows what else." I glance at Joey, and his brows furrow before something clicks. He leans over to Pops, and I smell a strong scent of cinnamon. "You go in there to take over or reestablish routes, and it *will* be over. The detective isn't going to tell anyone, not soon at least, due to how he came about the intel."

"How do you know he hasn't gone to PSB already?" Anita asks.

"He didn't have a warrant or the jurisdiction to be in that neutral zone." I pause and look over at Vinny cautiously. "That's why I was with him. Finding out what he knew and keeping an eye on him."

"And we're supposed to believe you?" Bruno growls. "A non-member protecting on behalf of the mafia?"

"The detective was also looking into the disappearances," I counter, my voice almost shaking. Come on, Brenda. "Most of NYPD and PSB think we're the ones behind the disappearances and possibly hired the ghouls as a diversion of some kind. You go in guns ablaze, and those ghouls will suffer worse."

"You want us to protect ghouls?" Rodney asks with a slight grimace. "They'll move on. They always do."

"Only if the Head of the Hive Mind says so," I argue. Rodney's brow goes up. "We still don't know why they're here, but if we let this happen, they'll die. For good."

"But you'll get your safe houses back, won't you?" Anita questions, still twirling the shiny thing.

I see bigotry doesn't just run in humans. "They're part of this world, just like the rest of us. They're being used."

There's some grumbling around the table before Fredrick speaks with his deep voice, "Explain."

I take a deep breath and say, "Ghouls don't deal drugs. They can't use them at all."

"You're not on the streets with us, lil sis," Rodney says. "They can—"

"You use them as mules," I say, pointing at him, and his eyes flare. "They're being used to hide something, either with PSB, NIIA, a rival mafia family, or a wild card. The worst hits are around that area and above the ghouls living Underground. Not only that, but NYPD also thought you started moving *before* this. That's why they upped their operations. Someone is playing all of us, and they're using the ghouls as a diversion to fight over." Rodney remains quiet as he leans back, rubbing his chin.

"For what, Little Sister?" Beckham's calm voice drifts over those present.

I pause before admitting, "I don't know." The pieces of the puzzle I've found are still up in the air. I don't trust everyone at this table to relay everything that I know and found. Right now, I have to concentrate on keeping a war at bay. If I don't stop them, the entire police force and agencies will burn down the Underground and every Paranormal with it, mafia protection or not.

"We lost people the other night, and almost you, due to the FBI, PSB, and NYPD's fuck-up," Fredrick says. "Yet, it seems you're defending them."

"PSB doesn't get involved with anything mafia-related unless they *know* they'll make an arrest. They're not around for weeks, and then all of a sudden, they show up with more backup for ghouls '*dealing*?' That doesn't make you question if something else is going on?" I counter.

"Something is always going on," Joey adds, and my heart sinks as I look over at my brother. "And whenever that something crosses a line, they pin it on us. So, of course they'd think we're taking people off the streets. The feds go from one bullshit excuse to the next."

"This is why we don't let riff-raff in," Bruno mumbles darkly.

I scowl at him. "Retaliation isn't going to help anyone."

"Are we really going to listen to a *human* sympathizer?" Bruno sneers at me, and the others murmur. Rodney growls low.

"You'll cause unnecessary bloodshed! And the ones who will suffer the worst will be the ghouls. Just because you don't like them or understand them doesn't mean you sign their death warrants for your damn routes!"

"Not only a human sympathizer but a bleeding heart for *ghouls*, too," Bruno snarls. Oh, he's trying to hit below the belt.

My arms begin to shake as I take a step forward and lean over the table. "*Every* Paranormal will be in danger, mafia protection or not. Your people will bleed on the streets of New York, caught between the crossfire. Unclaimed half-breeds will take the fall and mixed couples—"

"We are responsible for our *own*! That is all!" Bruno roars.

Vinny's hand spreads on my lower back, warning me. He's letting me fight my battle, but he's about to pull me back. His scent grows stronger as Bruno seethes from across the room while the others watch carefully.

I growl, "You don't have a business without them."

Bruno slams his fists onto the table as he stands, causing Pops and Joey to snarl warnings and others to shift uncomfortably. The captains move their chairs back. Beckham is the only one who's still, watching me intently with a pointed smile.

"Get out!" Bruno roars. "You have no business here! You know nothing—"

"I grew up in this!"

"Do not—"

"I have watched, lived, and breathed all of your businesses since I was a kid. Including yours, you antique Dracula wannabe!" I scream back as a hush goes over the room, and all eyes are on me. "For twenty years, I've been there for every route, danger, and territory. I was there helping gun runners for Rodney and shot the bastard who got a kick at Gunther. I was there when Pops brought in the group from Cuba after military testing. I was there during the hospital breakout. I watched the aftermath and was alongside your children when they made the decision to move people out of Staten Island! I'm not sitting at this table because I rejected the chair out of respect for my father!"

I stare down the male who made me run away to Topside with my mouth shut. Fuck that. My eyes burn as I hold back tears and say the words that have boiled inside me for years. "And because it'd tarnish your perfect fucking table for a dejected, scarred-up half-breed bitch that your son used to babysit in your damn dusty, disgusting study! Well, guess what. I'm gonna make sure he ends up *fucking me* in that *damn* study of yours!"

Bruno's eyes flare, and his fangs elongate. "*You fucking insolent, conniving whore—*"

The tension snaps at those five words. Rodney shifts into his hybrid form and snarls, saliva dripping from his jowls. Pops and Joey rumble, their wings unfurled and sharp claws ripping into the table. Vinny emanates a growl with such force the table and lamps vibrate. He removes his hand from my back as his fangs punch out.

Bruno rears back slightly, sneering with a growl. Rodney and Vinny return the gesture even louder. Bruno glares at Vinny and says darkly, "How dare you! I raised you—"

"To be the Blood Mafia Boss, which I've succeeded. Nothing more from you, *father*," Vinny snarls, causing several lamps to burst and the table to creak. "*Never* speak to her in that manner again."

A hush travels over the room, all of those at the table poised to attack. Joey has his hand on Pops' shoulder, but I can sense my father's power unfurling itself. The tension grows worse as Bruno's eyes flicker to Anita, who remains silent, ever watchful. The chill in the air suddenly eases and is replaced by something far more sinister. A calm, collected, and angry Beckham.

"It seems we have more to think about than we first presumed," Beckham says as he stirs his tea. "Dear Little Sister would be correct for handling this appropriately. Routes can be regained; people cannot. The Bronx will become PSB's, and we'll move to safer locations for now. The ghouls will be left alone and out of harm. After centuries of trying to cultivate relations with humans, even us mobsters have an obligation to protect races of all kinds. I believe we should discuss how to move forward without revenge."

Beckham is without a successor, captains, or guards but sits with a poise that outmatches all the bosses. I hold back a smirk as Bruno flings his gaze to the old shifter.

Bruno sputters, "You're suggesting we give in—"

"Tsk, tsk, Dracultelli, you forget a few things in your old age," Beckham says in a malevolent tone. Bruno says nothing as his face pales, and I see Pops' eyes glow as Joey lets go of his shoulder. "First, Little Sister is quite beloved through the families. You forget she's completed multiple traditions across the families, including a pup ceremony and blood ritual for your species. Her words carry weight due to her empathy towards all Paranormals. Second, you are no longer the Blood Mafia Boss; your son holds the title. No matter how hard you bellow and crash this table, your words come, perhaps, third even to decisions. Lastly, I have *particular* favoritism with librarians, and you just insulted *my protégé.*"

Fuck the tension from before, it's nothing compared to Beckham calmly threatening Bruno in front of every Boss of the Underground Mafia and their captains. I only told him I'd screw Vinny in his study. He gives a bone-chilling smile, his serrated teeth glinting in the lamplight. "Perhaps, it'd be best for you to slink back to your precious society, where there's a lack of fundamental comprehension of the mind."

Bruno's eyes flare, and his jaw tightens. Without a word, he turns and leaves the room, slamming the door behind him. I feel Vinny quiver slightly as he puts his hand on the back of my neck. Rodney shifts back, but I see his anxious eyes and Fredrick's raised hackles while Anita is frozen next to the old shifter, clutching her glass. I flick my gaze to Joey as he reaches for his drink. I watch Beckham raise his tea with a knowing smile toward Pops, then flicks his gaze toward me.

Everyone in the room had been influenced by Beckham and Pops. Beckham controlled Bruno's responses while Pops raised the terror in their minds around Beckham. And being the one who's immune to them, only I know what they just did. I almost forgot he's one of the few shifters who can do that. He wasn't kidding about tricks up his sleeve.

"Vinny whispers near my ear, "No idea Beckham could be that—"

"Terrifying?" I ask as I watch my father, who keeps his gaze on me as he sits down. A small smile pulls at my lips, and I wink at him. He barely nods and calls over a captain. I turn and smile at Vinny, hiding their secret. "You haven't seen him when someone destroys a book or mentions the Library of Alexandria, which reminds me, don't tell him what happened on Topside."

"Deal."

CHAPTER THIRTY-THREE
VAMPIRE GA GA

Everything's packed.

All that's left of my life on Topside are some outlets and Vinny's blood in my empty apartment. It's mid-afternoon, late for Joey and Darius, but they wouldn't let me go to Topside alone to say goodbye to the place. I'm still in limbo on how safe it is to travel above the Underground. Joey had the furniture cleared out two days ago, and the last of the boxes were taken downstairs.

It's been five days since the mafia meeting.

After Bruno left, Pops gave no indication to the others what he'd done, and I wasn't going to spill the beans either. Once Pops powers diminished and influenced the air with a calmer aroma, Joey laughed, Anita drank heavily, and Vinny whisked me away after the meeting to show me a new sex position. I also start working for Beckham in the next few weeks once I settle back home. Thank goodness because I'm going to need a buffer to live in the Underground again.

A smile grows as I look at the emptiness. The small space I had these last few years was good enough, but not anymore. Sighing, I grab my bag when I hear steps from the hall.

"This is the last of it, Joey—" I stop when I see the familiar badge.

He's wearing the brown leather jacket, and his badge hangs from his neck. He's gotten a trim lately, and the beard is gone. Not a bit of fuzz on his dark complexion. The sunglasses cover his eyes as he comes into the room. "Brenda."

"Drauper," I whisper. "What are you doing here?"

"See if you're actually leaving. I'd gotten word that your lease was broken, and a new position opened at the library. Thought you'd disappear. I wanted to find you before you did." His voice is gruff.

He's not here for police matters. Good sign.

"You could always come below," I offer, and he snorts. Alright, that was a long shot. Besides our worlds being entirely different, there are mafia families now who want to skin him alive. It may be best for him to stay away. "Drauper—"

"Were you ever going to tell me?" He tears his glasses off. Dark brown eyes find mine. "Or were you going to just…leave one day?"

I furrow my brows. "What would you have done if I told you?"

He sighs. "I don't know."

"You think I didn't want to tell you? About where I came from and who I am? How scared I was if you…you knew—"

"I don't care that you're a half-breed, Brenda. You're still you. It changes nothing. It's the lying and the deceit." I cross my arms, staring at the floor. We stand in silence while Topside New York City continues its day below as taxis and cars honk and people yell in the distance. Drauper's voice almost cracks. "Was any of it real?"

I meet his dark, somber gaze, peering into me for answers. Longing. But some answers I can't give him. "Yeah, it was to me. Even if short-lived."

"Brenda, shit doesn't need to…end like this."

"No, it does, Drauper. I'm sorry I lied, but there's no getting around this," I say, and his eyes darken.

He clenches his jaw and looks across the room. "Then it's true? You're part of…of…" He can't even finish his damn sentence while he rubs his head. "Were you born into it? Coerced? Or protection, is that it? Do you even have any idea how dangerous they are, besides being Paranormal, the powers they have? The crimes they've committed. *Do you?*"

I grit my teeth. "Yes, *I do*. Don't assume you know any of it."

"It's my job to know!"

"Except, Paranormals aren't under your jurisdiction. *Remember?*"

Drauper's dashing smile I once admired is long gone. I know I'd probably never see it again. The last time I saw it was at the bar before he kissed me. A lifetime ago. My heart sinks and caves in, but even I know some things are impossible. Maybe we had a chance, but not anymore, even as friends.

"You can't change this, don't try," I whisper.

His expression softens, and he takes taking a small step toward me. Joey enters the room silently, making Drauper jump back when he walks up to him. "Detective, we meet again," he drawls. His jaw is tight, but his expression is calm.

"What are *you* doing here?" Drauper asks, looking at Joey and then at me.

I keep my mouth shut as Joey places a hand on my shoulder. My brother, the new Incubi Mafia Boss cocks his head at Drauper in a relaxed manner as he says, "You haven't heard? Baby sis, you didn't tell him, yet?" I keep my gaze on Drauper as his eyes harden. "In case it's not getting through that thick skull of yours, Brenda here is my baby sister. Those demands I made of you that night are *far* more applicable than you may have thought."

Drauper tightens his jaw, and the vein in his neck begins to pulse. I whisper in Noctora, "*Joey don't—*"

"*Go downstairs. I'll deal with this, politely, I promise. Bloodsucker's waiting for you in the limo, and he's been a pain all night.*" Joey places a kiss on my cheek.

I ease past them both to the hall but stop at the doorway to say, "I'm sorry, Drauper. And you were a friend. You really were."

I walk down the hallway, leaving him behind with Joey. I nod at the two incubi guards a few doors down. Halfway down the stairs, I stop and take a deep breath as I shove old feelings into the past and wipe away escaped tears. To lose a friend, no matter how much we didn't see eye to eye, still hurts.

The sun beats down as I leave the building, the limo sitting directly in front of my apartment. I grin and allow joy to wash over me, drowning out the rest of the emotions. I knock on the tinted window, and it clicks open as I pull on the door handle as I come face to face with the end of a 9-millimeter. Vinny smirks and cocks his head to the side, just out of the way of the small sliver of sunlight coming into the vehicle.

"It's extremely rude to point a gun in someone's face," I say.

"Pot calls kettle black."

"But it's part of my charming personality. You just look like a dick right now."

"How enticing, sweet cheeks." He doesn't move. I roll my eyes and lean on the car door. "Give me a reason not to pull the trigger."

"You really do love foreplay," I tease, and his grin grows. "You'd hate necrophilia."

"Haven't tried it."

"You'd miss my blood."

"Blood Mafia Boss, I can get new shipments."

"Boredom, then."

"You riled up my father. I won't be bored for the next decade." He clicks the safety on.

"Ma and Pops would kill you."

"My dream of dying; death by your Ma's hands."

I start counting on my fingers. "No one to yell at you, berate you, call you bloodsucker, point a gun in your face..."

"If I paid them enough, my bodyguards may do all that. And Anita would love to blast my head off."

I shrug. "Got me stumped. Guess I'll live on Topside, become a housewife with a human—"

Vinny tosses the gun aside and grabs my shadowed arm to yank me into the car, shutting the door. He places me on his lap while his free hand grabs my chin to kiss me fiercely. I hold back a moan as my fingers grip his shoulders. He growls at the back of his throat, "Vicious female, hitting right below the belt."

"Worked, didn't it?" I smugly respond. A rumble of laughter emanates from him as he gives me another bruising kiss. One of his hands searches nearby as he pushes a button, and the car moves, while something else clicks into place. "What are you doing?" I ask.

"Taking what's mine." He unbuttons my pants, stroking a finger across my hips and down below. I shudder and hold onto him as he uses one hand to gently rub at my clit while the other moves my pants down.

His finger circles around the apex of my folds and I gasp as another inserts itself, hooking upward. He slowly pumps the finger into me as his lips caress mine. His tongue glides across my mouth, and I moan against his taste. Fisting my fingers into his hair, he works me below. Slowly, Vinny places another finger with the first and scissors them slightly. His palm presses against me, creating more heat below. My back arches as I feel muscles begin to tighten. Vinny nips at my throat and downward. About to hit a high of ecstasy, Vinny pulls his fingers out completely. I groan in protest but am soon appeased as he undoes his pants and pulls out a condom. My breathing becomes erratic at the anticipation as I watch him and hold my breath when he presses his cock against my opening.

Vinny pauses and asks, "What human?"

"Completely forgotten," I rasp.

"Are you certain?" The seductive deep tone of his voice causes my legs to shake. I try to bring myself closer to him, but to no avail. Bastard.

"Yes," I answer.

"Do I need to remind you who you belong to?" His dark ruby eyes peer into me as my muscles clench, the heat rising within me and twisting as I cup my hands to his cheeks.

"You," I whisper in my softest voice. "I belong to you." Vinny hums and leans in to kiss me, but I use the opening to slam my hips down. His cock becomes buried deep inside me. Vinny barks out a growl as he hits my insides, and I shout. Plunging again, his cock is seated deeply within me, and my entire body roars in joy. A sensual growl comes from the vampire inside me. Moving my hands to the nape of his neck, I kiss him as harshly as he has with me. I slam down again, and we both growl. I say assertively, "But you belong to *me,* bloodsucker."
He shakingly answers, "No argument, sweet cheeks."

His hands grab my hips, and he pounds into me mercilessly. Screams are caught in my throat as I clutch to his shoulders. Muscles convulse and shake as Vinny plunges himself deeper and deeper. Back arching further, the height of ecstasy begins to hit as the orgasm builds itself upward. Moans escape as he holds onto my hips. The orgasm swells and finally washes over me, overwhelming all my senses. I let out a lasting whimper as Vinny comes inside me, grunting as he has his own release. He wraps his arms around me and leans back into the seat.

"Was that a coming home present?" I gasp between breaths.

"Well, *you came.* That's all that matters to me." I slap his shoulder weakly. He chuckles, kissing my throat. We stay together a few minutes with him nipping at my jaw a few times before pulling apart to redress. He sets me back on his lap, nuzzling into my shoulder. Freaking teddy bear.

"Why'd you come get me?" I ask.

"Pops asked me to."

"Officially Pops' errand vamp, huh?"

"Only for you, sweet cheeks." He kisses me again, caressing my face and tracing a finger down one of my scars. "I love you."

I blink a few times and do my best to hold back a fit of giggles. Vinny glares at me, but I can't get myself together, shaking my head at him. "Not laughing at you, I swear."

"Sounds like it."

"No, Vinny, it's just…I wanted to hear those words for so long. You saying it so casually is still surprising," I say, as I stroke his cheek. "I keep expecting it to be a nightmare and someone is just gonna take you away."

Vinny's expression softens. "I'll handle my father. Don't worry about it."

"Never have," I retort and plaster on a smile before kissing him again. I inhale his scent of dark spices and bloodlust, humming deeply. "I love you, too, bloodsucker."

I feel the rumble of the Underground pathways beneath us, and Vinny gives a sound of discomfort over the brick pathways. I climb off his lap, and he adjusts himself as the vehicle stops, smoothing out his hair. I roll my eyes at him, always the proper vampire. Before he steps out, I mess it up again. He stands up and glares at me before smoothing it out again.

I chuckle at him as I get out and stand. "Of course, I've fallen for a pretty boy."

"You like this pretty *male* and the way I care for myself."

"Want a lavender bath later?"

"That's what females do."

"Ouch, stereotype much?"

"Coming from the one who steals cologne from Ricky. And Gina, when you don't take a shower, again." He bumps me with his shoulder.

"I shower…with wet towels," I mumble. "Look, I hate water, okay?"

"Then you should invest in more perfume."

"But I hate it." I groan as we come up to the door.

"I'm sure Gina will help you find a scent you like."

I remember the last time she bought me perfume. "Never mind, I'll take the lavender bath."

"Hopefully, it calms—"

"Watch it, bloodsucker."

"I was gonna say nerves." Vinny leans down to kiss me quickly. He opens the doors to the club with a large smile.

Unbound is empty, and the lights and music aren't on. That's weird. Pops, Ma, and Ricky are near the back by the bar. Gina and a few others are there with their wings out. I peer up and see my panties still hanging—part of my punishment for interrupting a mafia boss meeting. I'm never getting them back. They're part of the scenery now, probably.

Pops turns toward me with a solemn expression. I feel Vinny tense, and his scent heightens. Everyone turns toward me, stepping away to reveal a familiar figure.

The daemon from the Bronx alley.

Grey feathers curve over his wings, matching the peppered silver hair on his head and along his jawline and brows. His skin is darker than I remembered. His eyes are a deep silver that pierce into me as I inhale the burnt patchouli scent.

"Brenda," Pops says, holding a hand up to the daemon. "This is your father."

You've got to be *fucking*—

Brenda and Vinny's story continue in

Sweet Cheeks & Her Mob Boss

MAFIA, MURDER, AND MAYHEM SERIES (AS A ROM-COM)

Coming Soon

Acknowledgments

This all started when walking down a bike path in the middle of autumn with my best friend. I had spewed out some random idea about a mafia boss called "Vinny the Vampire" and how insufferable he was, but a romantic at heart. The next thing I knew, I was freewriting the entire book, and the story of Brenda and Vinny came alive. It's been a year living with these two in my head, and even though their story isn't complete yet, I will mourn when their final chapter closes.

Many supportive people have been on this journey, including family and friends:

My sister. Thank you for being the best beta reader and cover artist one can have. I know I spent many nights spiraling in front of you, and you always knew what to say to keep me on track. You've been my biggest supporter and fan since before anyone ever knew I wrote stories to keep away the dark. You are a major reason I kept writing, even when others told me to stop, including myself. I could never thank you enough, and I love you with my entire heart.

My editor and best friend, Rae. Well…shit. We came a long way since those first few days walking the bike path, huh? When we first started talking about our books and moving forward, I never knew it would be Vinny who'd first grace people's bookshelves. If it wasn't for you pushing me, encouraging me, and stepping alongside me with every bump, I don't know how I'd have gotten this far. You've been a champion in support and fierce tough love, helping me prove to myself that I could do this. Thank you for being you, and never, ever fucking change.

My husband. I honestly don't know how you put up with me, but you do. I love you and cherish every moment you check on me during those late nights of writing. You always seem to know when I need tea, cookies, or just telling me to follow my gut and heart. I love you through all of time and space.

My mom. Thank you for putting that first empty journal in my hands when I was ten and reading the early poems and stories I wrote that even I know made no sense. You've always understood that art is not to be judged but is something that helps us heal and grow. Thank you for being there and checking that I have coffee to make it through the long days.

My Patreon members and Discord peeps. You all made the hard times better and made me smile on the long days I spent editing while you all made jokes and as I asked weird questions, such as the price of whiskey. During the worst of my depression, you all seemed to know what to say and do to help me move forward. Your support means the world to me because I would never have been able to do this full-time without you. Thank you.

To all who have been part of this journey, whether it was watching my ridiculous videos, reading snippets of chapters, listening to me ramble on new ideas, or just saying "Do it," thank you.

ABOUT THE AUTHOR

Elm Jed is obsessed with creating stories through writing, videos, or painting on random pieces of wood. When they're not telling their best friend a new story idea from reading a book they hate, they're playing DND, conjuring spells, playing dress-up, or going for a long drive.

They absolutely love their supportive partner and husband, who makes sure they eat between writing and reading the books they collect for their hoard.

You can find Elm Jed on social media platforms with the handle @elmojedi10

Made in the USA
Columbia, SC
13 May 2023

16587805R00145